DEAD IN THE DREGS

DEAD IN THE DREGS

PETER LEWIS

A BABE STERN MYSTERY

COUNTERPOINT
BERKELEY

The author would like to thank John Wiley & Sons, Inc. for permission to use a passage from *Knowing and Making Wine* by Emile Peynaud, translated from the French by Alan Spencer. Published by John Wiley & Sons, New York, 1984.

Most of this narrative takes place in the California wine country and on the Côte d'Or in France. Liberties have been taken in portraying these landscapes and their wineries, restaurants, and institutions. The world represented, while bearing some similarity to reality, is fictitious, as are its characters and events. Any resemblance to actual incidents or to actual persons living or dead is entirely coincidental.

Library of Congress Cataloging-in-Publication Data
Lewis, Peter, 1952-
Dead in the dregs : a Babe Stern mystery / by Peter Lewis.
    p. cm.
  Hardcover ISBN: 978-1-58243-610-4
  Paperback ISBN: 978-1-58243-548-0
 1. Wine writers—Crimes against—Fiction. 2. Vintners—Fiction. 3. Wine and wine making—Fiction. 4. Napa Valley (Calif.)—Fiction. 5. Burgundy (France)—Fiction. I. Title.
    PS3612.E9745D43 2010
    813'.6—dc22

                                                    2010005455

Cover design: Gopa & Ted$_2$, Inc.
Interior design: Elyse Strongin, Neuwirth & Associates, Inc.

Printed in the United States of America

COUNTERPOINT
1919 Fifth Street
Berkeley, CA 94710

www.counterpointpress.com

Distributed by Publishers Group West

10 9 8 7 6 5 4 3 2 1

To B.,

who took me there

For J.,

who brought me back

It was held, that every wine disease had its specific microbe. In reality, there is no such thing. Wine bacteria are the result of adaptation by a large number of species to this environment, which is in the first instance unfavorable to them. A few cells of each species have been able, with time, either by mutation or by adaptation, to attack the wine's substrata . . . and have changed into spoilage bacteria.

—Emile Peynaud, *Knowing and Making Wine*

in the beginning   nothing   raw matter   cold   dark   a void   there are two
latent on the surface of the sphere of all nature they split and then split again
from two four, from four eight, from eight, hundreds   they eat and eat and multiply
and multiply again   warmth there are thousands   they stuff themselves, eating
and shitting, their offspring the spontaneous combustion, spawning nebulae
of voracious appetite   there are millions   identical in their instantaneous gestation
roiling the waters of the void   devouring sugar, more sugar   whipping the dark chaos
into a froth of birth and death   heat   the stink of their exhalation, foul odors
of exhumation fill the atmosphere   oxygen, no oxygen   the frenzy of feeding
and coupling, gorging themselves   primitive violence of creation   bacchanalian orgy
of bubbling, frothing, stinking life and death   the boiling waters of life   quintessence
of spirit and their bodies rise and sink, exhausted   no air   no air   there is only spirit
and death and wine

1

They brought in the harvest early that year in Napa, and with it, Richard Wilson's body. A perfect flowering, a mild spring dotted with just the right amount of rain, and a hot, dry summer had ripened the fruit to twenty-eight Brix by late August. Wilson's selection, on the other hand, had nothing to do with how sweet he was.

The bar was always dead that time of year. The whole world, it seemed, was out picking. I dreaded going to work but dragged my ass down the mountain and opened the place. I did the books from the night before and swept up. A few customers wandered in, guys too old to stoop in a vineyard for ten hours straight in ninety-degree heat. By three o'clock, I'd done a staggering twenty bucks.

I'll never forget that day. It was the first time I'd seen Wilson in more than a decade, and it was the last day I would see him alive.

I was just settling into the lazy rhythm that creeps up on you late in the afternoon: time to slice lemons and limes, fill the condiment caddy, and contemplate your favorites on the jukebox. Al Green was serenading the few off-hour drinkers who'd straggled into Pancho's, asking his plaintive question "How can you mend a broken heart?" Apparently, none of my customers had a clue.

It was sweltering, so I'd propped the front door open to capture what little breeze there was. I had my back turned and was just emptying the last of a jar of McSweet onions into the caddy, when a voice out of my past said, "Pour me something I've never tasted." I turned around. He'd put on weight, a lot of weight—the college jock gone to seed—but he was immediately recognizable.

"Hello, Richard." I ducked under the backbar and pulled out a bottle, set a wineglass in front of him, and started to pour. "An old-vine Mataro that'll knock your socks off," I said, as if I had seen him only the day before. He held his hand up.

"Just a taste. I'm on my way to Norton."

"In the middle of harvest?"

"Filling a few gaps before the second edition of my California book goes to press."

He picked up the glass the way pros do, his thumb and forefinger pinching the base of the stem, twirled it deftly, inhaled, and set it down. Then he turned his back to me, took two steps, and stopped.

"I don't get it," he said.

"Get what?"

"This place, your life. You gave it all up . . . for this?"

"Yeah, Top of the Mark," I said. I had no intention of falling for it. "Where are you staying?"

"With a friend."

"Have you seen your father yet?" I said.

"I don't know why Janie moved him out here," Wilson said, shaking his head as he turned around.

"Do you really think it's possible to take care of someone with Alzheimer's long-distance? She'd have had to dump him in a nursing home."

"He's in a nursing home here. His whole life is in New York."

"What life?" I said. "The one he can't remember?"

He stared into the wine. "I feel badly that Janie's been strapped with this."

"Somebody's got to do it. You're not about to put your life on hold. At least this way he's close. She can keep an eye on him, make sure he gets proper medical attention."

It was an accusation, an indictment, and made for an uncomfortable silence.

"What about Janie?" I asked. "Any time for her this trip?"

"I was supposed to have dinner with her last night," Wilson said.

"Supposed?"

"Something came up. I couldn't make it, but I'll try to catch her tomorrow before I take off."

"What about tonight? You could see Danny. I know he'd love to see his uncle."

He sidestepped the suggestion. "You remember how crazy we were, way back when?" he said, lifting his gaze but refusing to look at himself in the mirror that lined the back of the bar.

"Yeah, pretty intense," I said, sniffing a glass that reeked of detergent and buffing out a water stain.

"As if our lives depended on what we could detect in a glass of wine," Wilson mused.

He took a turn into the room, walked to the pool table, and rolled the cue ball across the manicured lawn of felt.

"I'm headed for Europe in a few weeks. You should bag all of this and come with me," he said. "It would be like old times."

One of the regulars looked at me as if I were about to walk out the door. And it was tempting, tempting to walk away, to disappear, to leave the bar to my partner, Frank Mulligan, leave my son to Janie, to pretend I was twenty years younger, without a care in the world.

"I'm not going to do that to Danny," I said. "Owning this place is bad enough. I seem to have less time now than I did in Seattle."

"You *own* this dump?" When I didn't answer, he said, "It's a waste of your talents."

"It's impossible to waste yourself on your child," I said. "A kid changes everything."

He turned his gaze on me, but his eyes seemed to look straight past me, through me, to the bar-length mirror.

"Why'd you quit? What happened?" he said.

"After your sister left me, I thought I could deal with it. I used to love my work. Those early years. I picked up where you and I left off, tasting everything I could. I think I memorized whole swaths of Lichine and Broadbent."

"I sent you those books."

"Did you? I don't remember. Maybe you did. You were very generous. I'm sure your letters got me the distributor job and my first gig as a sommelier. You were already famous."

"Hardly. I'd only just started the newsletter."

"Well, people knew about it," I said, carefully peeling a lemon in a single, continuous spiral with a stripper. "Anyway, something changed after Janie split. Everything and everyone irritated me. I finally snapped one night. A customer I knew pretty well, a typical venture capital type, had his nose stuck in one of your newsletters and wanted to quibble that the bottle I'd brought to the table had failed to fetch ninety points."

Wilson smiled, pleased with himself. "What did you say?"

"I told him I knew you, that we tasted nearly every week together when we were kids, that there was a whole style of winemaking you write off."

"That's nonsense," he protested.

"I told him to get his head out of his ass and his nose out of your newsletter and trust me."

One of the old drunks who was eavesdropping couldn't suppress a laugh.

"You ever hear the maxim 'The customer's always right'?" Richard was offended by the story, but it wasn't the customer's happiness that concerned him. I had impugned his reputation. "So, what happened?" he asked.

"He was about to get up from the table to speak to the manager, but I told him to relax, beat him to it, and tendered my resignation."

Wilson shook his head, woefully disappointed in me. Digging his nails into a rut on the scarred oak of the bar, he dropped his voice and said, "Listen, there's something I need to talk to you about." He glanced around the room, aware now that the barflies were following our conversation. "In private. If you're not coming to Europe, can you at least run down to Norton with me? We could talk."

"You gonna drive?"

"I can't bring you back. I'm already late, and I have . . . an engagement tonight."

The way he said it suggested a woman might be involved. He tapped the stem of his glass impatiently with a fingernail.

"All right," I said. "But only for an hour or so. Janie's bringing Danny up tomorrow for the weekend, and I have to get the trailer ready."

"You live in a trailer?" he said incredulously.

"It's charming," I said.

"Jesus, Babe, you've really gone off the deep end."

"You go ahead. I have to wait for my partner to spell me. I'll catch up with you."

As I finished my sidework, I reflected on my history with Wilson. We'd first met in Kermit Lynch's wineshop, studying each other. Richard was thinner then but muscular, and he moved with the lumbering grace of an athlete as he wandered the store. He had a full head of dark brown hair back then and a broad forehead, but the nose was always his most prominent feature. It looked as if it were designed to be inserted into a wineglass. He took great care as he read the labels, his attention slow and methodical. Then, as we were checking out, he asked casually if I ever tasted in a group. I didn't welcome the distraction, I told him. He nodded, as if he understood implicitly, and asked if I'd like to taste with him, just the two of us.

Looking back, it had all the inevitability of a romance. We were that in synch. Richard's the only person I ever met who could remember everything he'd ever tasted, and in those days, we agreed on almost everything.

Frank Mulligan walked in with signature bravura a few minutes after Wilson left.

"You just missed my brother-in-law," I said.

"Wilson? Here?" Mulligan found it hard to believe.

"Yeah, didn't you know that Pancho's is now a fixture on the wine route?"

"Finally!" Mulligan laughed, then, glancing around our broken-down hole in the wall and, finding it in pristine condition, said, "Thank you, my friend. Perfect, as always."

Winery visits were a thing of my past. I'd never been to Norton, but I knew where it was. I took the Silverado Trail down the east side of the valley.

Why *had* I quit? What had happened to me?

Just as fruit ripens, it rots. By the time I walked that night in Seattle, I was disgusted by the pretension, the posturing, the bullshit. Fed up with sophomoric wine writing and the endless plays for power, I blamed it on the trade. But the truth was, I was symptomatic of what had befallen the industry. Worse, I'd allowed myself to become more committed to my career than to my own kid. That definitely made it time to throw in the proverbial bar towel.

Norton was a sprawling facility done up in wine country moderne, all steel and beams, weathered barn board, and rough-hewn stone. A gravel drive ascended through a stand of poplars. The parking lot was nearly empty, hardly surprising given the hour of day and time of year. I walked through the front door. A sign on the reception desk read DURING HARVEST, BY APPOINTMENT ONLY. I stood there momentarily, not sure where my former brother-in-law had gone. I was contemplating a still life on the wall behind a side table, calculating that its value exceeded my total net worth, when a young woman craned her head through a doorway.

"You're Babe, right?" she said. "I recognize you from the bar. Nice, huh?" she added, following my eyes to the painting.

"Form is never more than an extension of content," I said, but I wasn't talking about art. A grape in its skin had nothing on her. If she was Wilson's pretext for blowing me off that evening, I couldn't blame him.

"Follow me," she said, raising an eyebrow.

She led me down a hallway. It ended at an opening that gave on to the winery, and I could see the crew cleaning up after a long day of hauling and crushing fruit. All I could hear was Spanish. She stopped midway down the hall and opened a door to what doubled as a conference and tasting room. Wilson was already seated, a half dozen bottles arrayed before him, each with its own glass. Colin Norton stood at the end of the table.

"Hey, Babe," he said with jocular familiarity. He possessed boyish good looks and wore jeans, running shoes, and a peach-colored polo shirt with its collar turned up.

"Hey, Colin," I said.

"I had no idea," he said, obviously referring to my relationship with the esteemed Richard Wilson. My stock had suddenly increased exponentially.

I'd never much cared for Norton. Every bar has its resident band, and Pancho's was no exception. At certain times and in certain places, a rock and roll band is like a black hole, attracting every musical mediocrity in its gravitational pull, and the lines of Pancho's coterie of losers, never very clear to begin with, possessed a fluidity that saw all sorts come and go. Colin occasionally sat in on the drums, and he played them, or thought he did, in the same heavy-handed style with which he made wine—a steady, monotonous thumping of the bass with a sudden flourish of cymbals for effect. Why Wilson would be enamored of his wines escaped me.

They'd finished with small talk, and Norton was walking him through the lineup, describing what he wanted to achieve stylistically. I had no interest but took a seat. Colin put a set of stems in front of me as he waxed rhapsodically about his latest experiment, a Sangiovese Cab blend. I dutifully took a sip. If there were Sangiovese anywhere in the glass, I couldn't find it. Nor could I figure out how Wilson and I were going to talk about anything with Norton standing there.

A moment later we heard a knock, and a young man stuck his head in the door. He appeared tongue-tied and simply stared at Wilson as if he were some kind of exotic sea creature.

"What do you need, Jean?" Norton asked.

"I . . . nothing," he said, poofing his lips.

"You guys done back there?" Norton said.

"Francisco is cleaning up. I have to take off. *C'est bien?*" He spoke with a thick French accent.

"Yeah, get out of here. It's fine."

"I am going to my sister's," the young man said. He took a last look at Wilson, nodded, and shut the door.

Wilson didn't notice a thing. He was concentrating on the wines, moving from glass to glass, sniffing and scribbling away.

"A young French kid," Norton said to me. "Doing an internship."

"Look," I said to both of them, "I have to take off myself." Wilson came out of his trance. "I have to get ready for my son's visit," I explained to Norton.

"But I thought . . ." Wilson started.

"You're busy," I said. "Unless you want to swing by the bar in the morning. I open, so I'm there by ten. Nobody'll be around." I waited for an answer.

"Okay, I'll call you. It's important," he said.

"I'm sure it is," I said as I jotted my cell number on the sheet Norton had set out for tasting notes and handed it to Richard. *But not important enough to interrupt your tasting or cancel your date tonight,* I wanted to say.

I thanked Norton and let myself out. Silence had descended on the winery. Everyone had left, it seemed, for a few hours of sleep before heading out to the vineyards and doing it all over again.

2

The next morning I was sitting at the bar, nursing a double espresso and doing the books, awaiting Wilson's phone call. I smelled Janie before I saw her. You never forget the scent of a woman you've slept beside that many nights, made love to that many times.

All the same, every bar possesses its own bouquet, a distinctive mélange of stale beer, detergent-soaked urinals, spilled wine, dried citrus, and human sweat. The aroma of Pancho's was milder than most, but I hadn't been able to get rid of it altogether. Even so, that I could smell my ex-wife at all is saying something. Not about the pungency of her scent but about me. My sense of smell has been acute for as long as I can remember.

When she walked in with our son in tow, the perfume of her wafted across the bar, the memories cutting through the stink of the place and washing over me.

"Hi, Dad," Danny said.

"Hey, kiddo."

He walked past the bar to the pool table. Janie and I regarded each other from a distance. The luminous brown eyes were the same, but the splash of gray silvering the wave of dark hair that fell across her back had grown, it seemed, and I discerned a line, a tension shaping her upper lip, that I hadn't noticed before. Even so, her mouth possessed the old, familiar sensuality.

I got down off the barstool and gave her an awkward hug.

"Thanks for bringing him up."

"I don't have a lot of time," she said, slipping out of my arms.

"Enough for an espresso?"

"Sure."

I stepped behind the bar, turned the grinder on, filled the group, and tamped it down. As I pulled her coffee, I said, "How's your dad doing?"

"He's babbling in French now."

"I didn't know he even knew French." I set the demitasse on the bar. "I saw your brother yesterday," I said. "He swung by."

"Richard? Here?"

"Like a ghost out my past."

"He stood me up the other night," Janie said.

"He told me."

"Did he give an excuse?"

"Not really. An appointment, I guess. He said he'd try to call you tomorrow."

"Why didn't he call to tell me he couldn't make it?"

"He's very busy, Janie." Why was I making excuses for him? I didn't care what Wilson did. "Anyway, he said he was going to call me this morning." I glanced at my cell on the bar and lifted my hands in the air. "Still waiting."

"Do you know where I can reach him? Our father's getting worse. This whole thing is costing me a fortune."

"Call him on his cell," I said.

"I did. He won't pick up. And I left messages at the apartment he keeps in town. I get the feeling he's avoiding me."

"Why would he do that?"

"I have no idea." She sipped the coffee. "Delicious," she said, offering me a grudging smile.

"Dad!" Danny called out from the pool table. "Did you see that?" He held the cue stick over his head in a gesture of victory. It was nearly as long as he was tall.

"I missed it. Try it again," I said.

He set up the shot he had just made and craned his little body over the table. He was biting his tongue as he took aim; he made a pretty clean stroke but missed the shot.

"Let me try it again," he said, running to the end of the table to fetch the balls. "Keep watching."

Janie and I looked at our son from across the room—a distance of ten feet and the unbridgeable distance of our separate lives.

"Would you like me to find him for you?" I said to Janie, letting the question hang in the absence of a common vocabulary that married couples share.

"You know where he is?" she said, facing me.

"I think so." I had no interest in telling her that her brother appeared to be having an affair with the office help at a certain winery. "It shouldn't be all that hard. I followed him to Norton late yesterday afternoon. He asked me to. There was something he wanted to talk about." She examined me, waiting for me to divulge her brother's confidence. "Sorry. We never got around to it. He was too preoccupied."

"Tell me about it," she said. "Look, I have to go. I'm already late."

"That's funny. That's just what your brother said."

I called Mulligan and asked if he could spell me for an hour. He said he'd be down in time for the lunch rush, a standing joke between us during harvest. A little before ten, Tony, the resident pool shark who practically lived at Pancho's, walked through the door.

"Hey, Tony!" Danny cried. Tony had taken to giving him lessons when the place was dead, and his game had improved noticeably.

"Look after him for an hour, will you?" I said. "If you get a victim, have him suit up in the kitchen. Ernesto can put him to work."

I explained to Danny that I had to run an errand for his mom and that I'd be back soon. He didn't seem to mind a bit.

"Rack 'em up, Danny," Tony said, "and go easy on me."

I stood in the parking lot, called directory assistance, and was put through to Norton. No one answered.

Traffic was already stacked up on 29, the tourist buses crawling behind the tractors that were bringing in the first fruit of the day, so I cut across on Lodi Lane to avoid St. Helena. The Silverado Trail wasn't any better. I settled in for the drive.

Richard Wilson and I had tasted together regularly for nearly a year before he introduced me to his little sister, Janie. I guess I'd proven myself to him. God, she was gorgeous. Beautiful hair, eyes that went on forever, and a mouth—I'd never seen a mouth like that. And she was smart. She was in premed, studying molecular biology, and doing an internship on the human genome project. I never did understand how they did it, even after she explained it to me on a series of coffeehouse dates at Le Bateau Ivre and Caffe Mediteranneum in Berkeley. My childish notion of genetics dated to high school biology: DNA composed of colored ribbons twining around each other. Janie was deciphering code, letters scrambled into what we had thought were an infinite number of variations and then, to our astonishment, learned were not infinite at all.

I moved to Seattle to attend grad school in comparative literature at U Dub and lost touch with her, but my obsession with wine and my postgraduate career soon declared they had irreconcilable differences, and I dropped out. I began to do a little bit of everything in the wine trade, starting at a retail shop and then putting in a short stint as a distributor's rep, a position I secured with a single flourish of Wilson's pen. But I wanted to go deeper, like a root searching for nutrients. Problem was, I wasn't a salesman, and I've never fooled myself that I was a farmer.

Wine jobs were few and far between in the city back then, and the siren song of restaurant work beckoned. Wilson and I remained in touch, and I asked him to write a generic letter of recommendation. He wasn't that well known yet, but a food and beverage manager at a major hotel was an early subscriber to his newsletter, *The Wine Maven,* and a nod from the Great Palate got me the job. The hotel's budget afforded me the opportunity to taste extensively, and I devoured every book I could lay my hands on.

I watched in fascination as Wilson's readership grew and his influence increased, and even though I knew that his reputation rested squarely on the very real foundation of his talent, I was envious. My own impulse to excel, I admit, was fueled in part by an unconscious desire to compete with him.

Eventually, as his success began to demand more of him, and as I developed my own reputation and contacts, our stream of communication dwindled to the odd postcard or hurried phone call. He was too busy traveling, writing, basking in acclaim. He'd morphed from my onetime tasting pal into a feared critic, one perfectly capable and willing to wield his power and influence without compunction.

Janie hadn't wanted to leave the Bay Area, but after finishing her doctoral work, she was offered a job at one of the fashionable companies that had spun off the genome project as scientists chased the pot of gold that lay hidden somewhere within the coils of the double helix. The company was headquartered in Seattle, and she looked me up once she was settled. Within a few months, we were living together.

We worked like maniacs, putting in crazy hours. A beautiful, manic relationship, it worked, for a while at least. But once I started pulling five shifts a week, ten till midnight, and Janie was getting up at six each morning and in the lab by seven-thirty, the fun wore thin. The few moments we shared together were more like collisions.

If people had told us we were going to have a child, we'd have told them they were nuts. We had no plans to get married or to raise a family, but in one of those collisions she got pregnant, an accident that should have been impossible but never is. I rationalized our new reality, silently praying that our child would heal the wounds we were inflicting on each other and make everything right. Anyone could have pointed out that having a child will never make an imperiled couple whole—I'm not sure we would have listened, anyway—but it was too late for that.

They were quiet, brooding months. Janie resented her pregnancy, believing—quite justifiably—that having a baby was going to interfere with what promised to be her stellar career path. The silences between us were excruciating.

By the time Danny was in day care, the marriage was a lost cause. I was asleep when Janie got our son out the door and was gone by the time she picked him up. On Sundays—the only day we had as a family—I was too exhausted to notice.

One morning Janie announced out of the blue that she'd been

having an affair with a guy at work. In fact, it had been going on for months. What could I say? Whatever physical intimacy we'd known had long since evaporated. She moved out a month later. She'd been offered a job back in the Bay Area, a real promotion as head of her own research division, with serious money. And, of course, she took Daniel with her.

What seemed at first to be a trial separation turned out to be a divorce, and I followed them to California. I wanted to purge myself, to pare down, to do penance. I needed to be closer to my son, to prove something to myself and to Janie. I just wasn't sure what it was or when I'd get the chance.

I hitchhiked down the coast as far as Eureka and found a faded pink Ford pickup that I bought for $600 and christened Bandol because its color was a ringer for a fine rosé. On the Pacific coast north of Mendocino, I spotted a '57 Airstream marooned on the side of Highway 1 with a FOR SALE sign taped in its rear window, its aluminum skin pockmarked by the salt air, and hauled it across the Coast Range to the wine country in search of my Garden of Eden, as Woody Guthrie had sung.

An old friend from Berkeley found me moorage on a lot behind a ranch house on the eastern slope of Howell Mountain. I hooked up electrical and tied into the septic tank. I loved the trailer. It was like a space capsule hurtling through the void of my life, a monk's cell on the wind-blasted slopes of Mount Athos. My hermitage, I called it.

Life stripped down to its bare essentials: one burner, a sink, the toilet; turquoise appliances that had peeled over time; twin beds, a table, a bookshelf; a lantern on gimbals and a ship's clock. I was hiding out, letting the torrent of events break against the shore and wash over me. I adopted a stray tabby I named Chairman Meow, a sorry substitute for a child. It was a simple life, but I didn't mind. You need a good dog paddle in the back eddies every once in a while.

I needed to earn a living but wanted to avoid the trendy bars and restaurants. Miraculously, I landed at the one last place in Calistoga that possessed a modicum of grit. It was a real bar with a community of regulars who'd been beating a path there for years to escape the tourists and tasters and collectors, the second-career winery owners and real estate developers who'd descended on Napa and spoiled it since I first knew it as a Berkeley undergrad. Then Pancho, who hired me, took off one night, proclaiming that he'd had it with gringos and was returning home to spend the rest of his life with his wife and kids, his brothers and sisters, his ailing grandmother. He tossed me the keys, bellowed *¡Mucha suerte!* and disappeared into the night. A week later, when DEA agents in emblazoned vests turned up, their weapons drawn, I learned that Pancho had been dealing keys of grass across the bar and somehow managing to stay one step ahead of the law.

Suddenly I was the *patrón* of my own place.

At that point the green baize of the pool table was nearly as threadbare as my bank account. The SIERRA NEVADA PALE ALE sign, emblematic of my life, flickered as if lit by its own personal lightning storm. The solid oak bar was pitted and the linoleum torn and jagged, revealing patches of bare concrete. Like me, the place was beat to shit, and so I felt at home. Little did I realize that it would suck me in just as surely as had my previous career. If anything, I now had even less time for my kid. Though the court had granted me regular visitation, there's nothing regular when you own a bar. Weeks and months went by without a visit. I wasn't sure if or how I'd ever find a way back.

But I wanted to. I loved Danny. He was sweet and funny, sensitive and as smart as a whip. What I found tough to take were the looks he'd throw me: doubt, suspicion, and a mistrust born of endless disappointment. He stood on that odd cusp between childhood and adolescence where the consequences of our affections and disaffections first begin to take hold, and we both could see that a distance had crept up on us. There were moments when he'd look at me as if he barely knew who I was.

My guilt over my child was only exacerbated by the example of Frank Mulligan, whom I'd worked with in Seattle. We were an odd couple. His mom lived in Santa Rosa with his stepfather, who had been diagnosed with pancreatic cancer. A few months after I left Seattle, his stepfather died, and Frank called. He wanted to move down to keep an eye on his mother, and asked if I could find him work in the area. I told him he could split shifts with me at Pancho's and that we'd figure it out.

I was intent on making a go of it. I knew the game, its lingo and tired rituals, so I put my knowledge to good use, drawing on the contacts I'd made while working in Seattle to assemble an offbeat collection of odd bottles for the bar—old-vine Mataro, funky Zin, the first cracks at Viognier made in California—to roll out value for friends in the biz. Soon we had a following, Frank and I.

I'd wanted to return to a life that felt real, to hit some rock-bottom authenticity that smacked of integrity, to beat a path back to my son. But all I had really done was flee my life as a sommelier to set one up in Napa, mistaking it as an escape to reality. Had I wanted to escape—really escape—I'd have been better off moving to Detroit.

3

The parking lot at Norton was empty, save for an old Ducati leaning against a stanchion. The front door was locked, and I walked
around back. Barn doors stood open, waiting for the tractors to arrive,
and I wandered inside.

It was a mammoth structure that held the fermentation tanks,
a dozen luminous stainless steel cylinders that suggested a modern
dairy more than a winery, and two giant oaken fermenters, what the
French call *foudres*. The wine press was state of the art.

I heard something rustle and called, "Hello! Anybody home?"

The young Frenchman I'd seen the day before stepped from
behind the press. He looked startled to see me. He was tall and
lanky, his head topped by a nest of brown curls, his chin dusted with
an immature Vandyke. He had watery eyes and a nose that he might
grow into in a decade if he was lucky.

"You're Jean, right?"

"*Sí.*"

"We haven't met. My name's Babe."

"Babe. *Comme un bébé?*"

"Yeah. Funny, huh?"

He didn't respond, just looked at me and waited for me to explain
myself.

"How's it going, your *stage*?" I used the French word for *internship*, hoping to put him at ease.

"Fine, simple."

"How'd you end up here?" I asked.

"Colin did a favor for the man who imports his barrels. He knows . . ." he hesitated for a second, then said, "our family."

"Your family are *vignerons*?"

"Yes, of course." The idiocy of the question irritated him.

"Where?" I asked.

"Nuits," he said tersely. It was shorthand for Nuits-Saint-Georges.

"How long are you here for?"

"Just one harvest. To see how you do things."

"And? What do you think of American winemaking?"

I could tell he was sizing me up, trying to figure out how much to say.

"Well, you know, you Americans, you make one wine, maybe two. A white and a red. Chardonnay, Cabernet."

"That's not fair," I said.

"And you put everything into oak," he added.

"Not everything." I was feeling defensive. "Some of our wines are terrific."

"Perhaps," he offered.

"You don't like our style?"

"They taste fat to me—how do you say, clunky. The fruit is thick, like syrup. Stupid wine."

"Some of them can be a little coarse," I admitted, but it was hardly surprising that a young man from Burgundy whose family made Pinot Noir would dismiss Napa Valley Cab.

"Aggressive, *non*? Cowboy wine." He drew two phantom six-shooters. "Bang, bang," he said, blowing the invisible smoke from their barrels. "Even Davy Crockett makes wine."

"Yeah, Fess Parker. Pretty goofy, huh?"

He didn't laugh. "You are looking for Colin?" he said.

"Uh, no, actually I'm looking for a woman I met here yesterday. She was at the reception desk."

"Carla," he said.

"Is she around?"

"No, I have not seen her. I think she has the day off." He turned, anxious to get back to work.

"Anybody else around?" I said.

"They are picking. But they should be here soon. Any minute," he said, impatient to get rid of me.

"They're probably running late. Traffic's hell."

We stood there in a meaningless version of a Mexican standoff.

"I must get ready for them," Jean said.

"Sorry, I know you're busy. *Bonne chance*," I said, extending my hand. He took it reluctantly. "Hey, you wouldn't know Carla's last name, by any chance?"

"Fehr," he said and turned, disappearing behind a fermentation tank. He pronounced it *fear.*

I sat in the front seat of the truck and tried directory assistance again. I struck out in Napa and St. Helena, but she was listed in Yountville. The phone rang only once.

"Where were you last night?" she said.

"Excuse me, Carla? This is Babe Stern."

"Shit, I'm sorry. I thought it was Richard."

"You didn't see him last night?"

"He was supposed to come straight here from the winery. I waited for hours."

"And he never called, obviously."

"*Ob*viously," she said.

"Well, I'll ask him to call you when I track him down."

"That would be nice," she said and hung up.

I thought I should call Janie, but I had nothing to tell her. Wilson had probably driven back to the city, but she'd said she was taking their father for a battery of tests that morning. She'd be tied up for another hour, at least.

Where the hell had Richard gone?

I wanted to wait for Colin Norton, but they'd be busy well into the afternoon, sorting and crushing, so I took my time driving back to Pancho's. I actually didn't have a choice, given the traffic. I loathed driving around the valley this time of year.

There was something about Wilson's turning up that kept gnawing

at me, an element that felt out of place. I couldn't put my finger on
what had been wrong about his visit, and then it came to me. It was
the first time I'd ever seen him not taste a glass of wine put in front
of him.

As I entered the bar, Tony was giving Danny a tutorial on using a
bridge.

"Think of it as an extension of your arm," he said. "Make your size
work for you." He set a series of balls the length of the table and had
Danny move from one to the next, replacing the cue ball for each
shot.

"You're comin' along, kid," Tony said when he spotted me. "Stick
with it."

Mulligan just nodded and headed out the back. I didn't have to
say "thank you," and he didn't have to say "you're welcome." Debts
and favors were understood, and we never kept track.

I set Danny up in the kitchen, where he had his own apron.
Ernesto, the cook, gave him his regular station. He'd already mas-
tered assembling tacos—he considered nachos beneath contempt—
and Ernesto credited him with vastly improving Pancho's recipe for
black beans with the addition of port and orange juice. Where in
God's name had Danny come up with that idea?

I took my post behind the bar. If the afternoon had been any quieter, I'd have curled up on it and taken a nap.

Frank returned at four on the dot, and I wandered back to the kitchen.
Danny was butchering chickens.

"Another two, three months, you give him my job," Ernesto said,
smiling at his apprentice.

"Let's go, Danielo," I said, handing the diminutive chef's knife I
had given him to Ernesto. "*Gracias*, Ernesto."

"*De nada, señor.* He can come cook with me anytime."

I loved the way the old Mexican treated my son: full of patient
instruction and genuine respect. I need to try it myself sometime,
I thought.

As we got into Bandol, I thought about heading home but decided to pay one last visit to Norton. I wanted to ask Colin how their tasting had ended and where Richard had gone.

"One stop," I said to Danny. "Promise. I told your mom I'd find Uncle Rich."

"That's okay," Danny shrugged.

As we ran down Highway 29, I said, "You excited about school?"

"Not really."

"Sixth grade was one of my favorite years." My paternal enthusiasm failed to elicit any response. "Your mother worked very hard to get you there. And it's costing her a bundle, so I suggest you at least approach it with an open mind."

He wouldn't look at me. He gazed out the window and set his arm at an angle like a sail to catch the wind.

"When do you start?"

"Orientation's next Friday. School's on Monday," he said out the window.

"Wow, starts awfully early, but I guess that's the difference between private and public schools."

He couldn't have been less interested, a far cry from the interest he showed when we got to Norton. I'd never taken him to see a winery. By the time we arrived, the day's work was mostly done, but the sheer scale of the place fascinated him. One of the workers was spraying down the press and floor and raised the hose to give Danny a quick squirt. Colin himself stood off to the side, talking to a Mexican guy. When he spotted us, he waved, then excused himself from the conversation.

"Hey, Babe."

"Colin, this is my son, Danny."

Norton shook his hand and said, "What do you think?"

"Awesome," Danny said.

"You wanna see something cool, follow me." Norton led us from the winery through an arched doorway into the barrel cellar, a warren of tunnels that receded into darkness, their walls flocked with a stuccolike material.

"It's like the Bat Cave," Danny said.

"Go explore," I said. "I need to talk to Colin. But don't get lost."

"What's up?" Norton said as my son disappeared into a tunnel.

"What time did Richard leave last night?" I asked.

"I'm not sure. I had to take off. He said he wanted to make a few more notes, and I told him to make sure the front door was locked behind him."

"Was anybody else here?"

"I don't know. I don't think so. Just me. Why?"

"His sister—my ex—has been trying to find him. They were supposed to have dinner the other night, but he never showed. He hasn't returned her messages."

Colin's expression said, *so what?*

I said, "The young woman who was here yesterday—Carla Fehr? They're having an affair. She waited several hours for him last night. He never arrived."

Norton shrugged. "I don't know what to say, except that I'm not very happy to hear about it. I should probably say something to her."

Danny emerged from the cellar and came up to us.

"What do you think?" I said.

"Awesome."

"I'm sorry, but I need to get back to work," Norton said. "I've got to check temperatures."

He escorted us back the way we had come, stepping over hoses that lay tangled across the floor. Two of them rose to the rim of the giant oak casks from a small pump that suddenly kicked in. They must have stood twelve feet tall.

"We're pumping over," Norton said. "It's impossible to punch these babies down."

My nose picked up a whiff of something off: a barely discernible hint of mouse shit and dirty copper that was all but lost in the reductive stink of fermentation.

"How old are they?" I asked, indicating the *foudres.*

"Ancient," Norton said.

"When was the last time you scrubbed 'em out?" I suspected the wood had been infected with brettanomyces, a yeast that embeds itself in cooperage and spoils the wine.

He looked at me questioningly.

"I think you've got some brett going on," I said. It was hard to detect, but I was sure I was right. Norton seemed to resent the unsolicited advice and wanted to get back to his wine. "Well, listen, thanks," I said.

We shook hands. Norton walked over to one of the tanks and studied the thermometer on its gleaming flank.

"Cool this sucker down!" he cried to no one in particular.

4

We drove the length of the Silverado Trail north and took Deer Park Road toward home. The road wound back through the blasted rock and red earth, the cliffs streaked by the westering sun. It finally started to cool off, and the earth regained some of its fragrance. Stands of Douglas fir and alder, Scotch pine and banks of manzanita, and the trellised roses that branched like the deltas of hidden springs along the roadside all seemed at last to exhale.

On the back of Howell Mountain, the black tendrils of irrigation tubing looped like a tenuous wavelength across the tops of milk cartons that dotted the terraced slopes, little gravestones commemorating the slow death of ten thousand vines.

"What are those for?" Danny asked.

"They're there to protect the young vines."

"From what?"

"The glassy-winged sharpshooter—*Homalodisca coagulata*—a half-inch vector, as the bug scientists say, that consumes ten times its body weight in liquids per hour."

Danny scrunched his face. "What?" he exclaimed.

"Imagine drinking six hundred pounds of water every hour. That's like, I don't know, sixty gallons or something."

"Are you teasing me?"

"No, it's true. They basically suck the vines dry. Even worse, they transmit a bacterium called Pierce's disease that blocks the tiny tubes in a plant that carry water and nutrients. The vines die within a year or two. So they had to replant everything. They put those milk cartons there to protect the new rootstocks."

"Do vines drink milk?"

"No, silly. Kids drink milk. The cartons are empty."

Danny sat quietly, trying to imagine, no doubt, what it would be like to chug sixty gallons of milk an hour.

Our silence was pierced by the sharp cry of blackbirds. Flocks of finches flitted through the bushes, and high above, buzzards soared the thermals. We passed a vineyard of old-vine Zin, now no more than gnarled stumps.

"See those?" I said. "They're eighty, maybe ninety years old. Since before Prohibition."

"What's Prohibition?"

"That's when the federal government banned alcohol. Drinking liquor was against the law. And you couldn't make wine, either, but they made an exception for the old Italian and Spanish families living in the valley. Wine was just too important a part of their lives."

Ramshackle ranch houses littered the pockets of cleared land on the flats as we neared the turnoff to the trailer. When we arrived, Danny dropped his backpack on his bed—there were two in the back of the Airstream—and curled up with his DS.

My periodic attempts to quit smoking—a habit I'd acquired during the divorce—had become the butt of Mulligan's merciless sarcasm, but I never touched a cigarette around my son. I confined myself to cigars, as if that were somehow better. I grabbed a Juan Clemente Club Selection No. 2 and went outside. I needed to call Biddy Teukes, and I needed to call Gio, my on-again-off-again girlfriend.

It was late enough in the day that I felt I could call Biddy without pissing him off. Still, my fingers moved reluctantly as I punched in the number for Tanner Cellars. I waited a good five minutes before I heard my friend snap testily, "Teukes. Who's got the balls to call me in the middle of harvest?"

"Sorry, Biddy, it's Babe."

"Babe, what's cookin', brother?" he said, his tone softening. "No sweat, man. We're done for the day. I just say that shit for effect."

"I get it. Listen, I wonder if you can help me out. My ex, Janie Wilson, has asked me to track down her brother." I paused, knowing that the next thing I said was going to blow his mind. "Richard," I said. "He's MIA."

"Richard . . . *Wilson?*"

"Yeah."

"Richard *Wilson*'s your fucking brother-in-law?"

"Ex–brother-in-law."

"And you never thought to tell me? I thought you loved me. What are you, some kind of asshole?" I could picture his face, ticked and incredulous.

"Hey, cut me some slack," I said. "Have you seen him?"

"Why would I see him? You ever read a review of Tanner in the *Maven?*"

"Look, you know everybody in the valley. I just thought . . ."

"You just thought what?" I didn't respond. "No," he finally said, "you obviously don't think, but word's out he's in the valley. Sharpening his hatchet for the next issue."

"Could you make some inquiries? Find out if he's been spotted?" I asked, knowing I was pushing it.

"Your timing sucks."

"I realize that."

"I'll see what I can do," he said and hung up.

I knew that a lot of winemakers resented Richard, but I was unprepared for Biddy's petty ire. Tanner Cellars was just the sort of place that never found its way into the pages of *The Wine Maven.* Teukes probably felt neglected and unfairly maligned, but if anything, Wilson's was a sin of omission, not of commission. Better no review at all than a shitty score.

Next up was Gio.

Giovanna Belli was a black-haired beauty who'd first appeared at Pancho's the previous winter. After some casual conversation, engaging in the banter that always wings its way across a bar, one thing led to another. A couple of movies, a series of dinner dates, and finally, a night at the trailer. Other nights had followed. She hadn't mentioned her last name when we first started going out, and when she told me, I thought about cutting off the relationship. Her father, Anthony Belli, was the owner of one of the largest Napa wineries. The estate, preposterously luxurious, was modeled after an Italian palazzo and stuffed with his collection of modern art. But his daughter, in addition to being rich, was intelligent and beautiful and improbably sweet, and I found myself unable to end it. She was the first and only woman I'd been with after my breakup with Janie. I'd told her about Danny on our first date and wanted her to meet him, but the bar was too busy over the summer and I'd been forced to put off my visits with my son. We'd promised to make it happen when he next came, but now it was the middle of harvest. Worse still, Richard was missing, and I felt distracted. I hadn't prepared for dinner, and there was no way she would spend the night with Danny sleeping in the next bed.

"Hi," I said. "It's me."

"I know it's you. My phone tells me who's calling. How are you?" Her voice was quiet and lovely, and all I wanted was to look up and see her sitting across the picnic table from me.

"I'm okay," I said.

"Is Danny there?"

"Yeah. Sitting inside, playing with his little gizmo."

"That's what boys do," she said. "They play with their little gizmos."

I laughed. "Not that kind of gizmo. At least, not yet. Look, I don't think it's going to work tonight."

"Of course not. I knew that."

"Did you?"

"Yes, I did. Anyway, I'm exhausted." She stifled a yawn.

"How's it going?"

"Fine. The fruit is superripe. Twenty-nine degrees. A bumper crop."

"Bravo," I said, trilling my r. "It's not just Danny's being here."

She waited for an explanation, then said, "What's wrong?"

"Janie's brother is missing."

"What do you mean, 'missing'?"

"Missing. Disappeared. No one's seen him. He was supposed to have dinner with her in the city, then didn't show. And last night he was supposed to see a woman who works at Norton, but he never arrived."

"What do you care?" she said. I didn't blame her for not want-ing to hear about my ex-wife, even less that I seemed apprehensive about it.

"Richard and I . . ." I began.

"Richard," she said.

I hesitated.

"I'm waiting."

"Wilson," I supplied.

"Richard Wilson," she said.

"Yeah."

"Jesus, Babe!"

"I should have told you. I wanted to. It's just that . . ."

"It's just *what*?"

"I'm trying to put the past behind me," I said limply.

"You can never put your past behind you. It follows you, like a shadow." She stopped, then said, "I'll call you later."

The cigar was out. I left it sitting on the table and walked back inside.

"Come on," I called to Danny, "let's eat."

I pulled a pizza from the freezer and turned the oven on. While it was cooking, I walked back to the beds.

"Wanna see a secret?" I said.

He put down the DS his mother had bought him—the Game Boy I'd given him wasn't cool enough—and sat up.

"Did you know the berths of Airstreams hide storage lockers?" I asked. It was a stupid question. There was a latch beneath each of our mattresses in plain view. I pushed one and let the door of the cabinet down. Three boxes. "My hidden library," I said mysteriously. I pulled them out one by one and opened the flaps. "Books," I said, peering into the first, "magazines and newsletters," I said, opening the second, "and maps," I said, tapping the third.

"Hunh" was all my son had to say. He flopped back on his pillow, turned his back to me, and resumed playing.

I hauled the boxes one at a time and put them under the kitchen table at the front of the trailer.

"Pizza!" I cried.

After dinner, Danny got into his pajamas and snuggled in his sleeping bag. We read a couple chapters of *The Sword in the Stone.*

"Don't let the bedbugs bite," I said.

"Don't let the glassy-winged sharpshooters in," he said, "or they'll suck my blood."

We opened our eyes wide in mock horror and laughed. I bent down and kissed him and said goodnight.

Darkness had gathered. The fog was just starting to drift through the breaks and had already blanketed the valley floor. Though the days remained hot, the nights had turned chill. I could see nothing to the east but a sliver of moon hanging over the ragged line of a stand of pine trees that crested a deep purple slope. The wind hissed through an olive grove.

In one of the boxes I found my files of *The Wine Maven,* three folders of back issues. I grabbed the Juan Clemente from the picnic table and hunkered down with the newsletters over the last of a bottle of Jade Mountain La Provençale at the kitchen table. Chairman Meow jumped onto the bench and curled against my leg, a disinterested sphinx.

In my previous incarnation I'd followed Wilson's newsletters religiously. As I glanced through them now, I wasn't sure what I was looking for at first. Typically Wilson's reviews ran middling to good, and a few tended toward the ingratiating, but when I came upon the first of what turned out to be a series of nasty reviews, I realized there were winemakers out there whose reputations Wilson had destroyed. I decided, just out of curiosity, to flag them. By the time I'd finished, the newsletters sported a half dozen Post-its. Around midnight, I walked back, pulled Danny's sleeping bag up around his shoulders, then nodded off myself.

I had a dream: I was walking. The sun stood behind me, casting a long shadow. Janie appeared in front of me, leading me on. She would walk, stop, turn to face me, and then turn away. I could never catch up with her. She was a phantom. By the time I woke the next morning, I wasn't even sure if the woman in the dream had been her.

5

I **rose early** and walked outside. It was a glorious day. I called Janie.

"You're up bright and early," she said. "How's Danny?"

"Still sound asleep. I don't think he's ever up before ten out here. Must be the air. And the quiet. We don't get a lot of traffic."

The old, familiar silence descended on the line. All I could hear was the symphony of birdsong from the trees that surrounded the clearing.

"Have you heard from your brother?" I asked.

"Nothing." Then, after a moment, she said, "What did you guys do last night?"

"We had pizza, and then I read to him." Silence. "And then I spent a few hours going through some of Richard's old newsletters. There are people around here who have reason not to welcome him with open arms. I've put the word out that I'm looking for him," exaggerating the fact that I'd called only one person, Biddy Teukes, to make a few inquiries on my behalf.

"You think somebody might act on a grudge? Is that it?" When I didn't answer, she said, "Listen, Babe, I don't want people talking. Can't you just take care of this yourself?"

"How do you suggest I do *that*?" I said. "You have to ask people if they've seen him."

"No, you're right. It's just that . . ."

"Just what?"

"I mean, I worry about him. I know people hate my brother."

"They don't hate him. They're afraid of him," I corrected her. But she was right, and I knew it. Wilson could make or break a wine, make or break a fortune. There had to be at least a dozen people who would happily stuff his face in a barrel, and that was just between Napa and Sonoma. I'd heard plenty of winemakers say so at the bar, even some he'd treated fairly.

"I appreciate what you're doing," she said. "You're the only one I can ask."

"I'll do what I can," I said. "I promise. I'll call you later."

I flipped the cell shut. I was pleased Janie had turned to me. It was the first chance she'd given me to prove that I wasn't such a bad guy, after all, and I was intent on showing her that I could come through in a pinch.

Picking up where I'd left off, I pulled out a pad of paper and jotted down the name of every winery Wilson had treated harshly or scored poorly in the older issues. I was going to be methodical and demonstrate to Janie that I still knew enough about the wine scene to find her brother. I was startled when my cell phone rang, and assumed she was calling me back.

"Hi. What's up?" I said.

"Babe?" It wasn't Janie, but I thought I recognized the voice. "Richard?"

"No, it's Colin."

"Norton?"

"You need to come out here. Now. We found Wilson."

The espresso pot sputtered on the stove. I gulped the scalding sludge, ripped a sheet of paper from the pad, and jotted a note to Danny. ENJOY THE MORNING. I HAVE TO RUN DOWN TO THE BAR. BE BACK SOON. LOVE, DAD. I walked to the rear of the trailer. My son was wrapped in the warm cocoon of the sleeping bag, his mouth open, deep asleep. He looked angelic. I tucked the note by his pillow. I doubted he'd even be up before I got back.

By the time I'd driven the fifteen miles to Norton, the parking lot was awash in red, white, and blue flashing lights that pulsed like a frayed neon flag in the fog. The Chevys and Fords of the St. Helena police and Napa sheriff's departments were parked at odd angles, as if in near collision. An ambulance had pulled in closer to the entrance of the winery, its rear doors left open, expectant. The gurney had been removed. A white van was parked perpendicularly to the ambulance, its side door wide, its contents splayed on the asphalt as if it had been disemboweled. The evidence kits, cameras, print kits, tape recorders—everything had been pulled to work the crime scene over.

Inside there were already three cops from the St. Helena force. I recognized Jens Jensen, the chief, whom I knew by sight, and Russ Brenneke, a sergeant whom I knew better. With them was a younger, Asian-looking officer I hadn't seen before.

No one stopped me as I walked through the doors, but Jensen, tall, stern, and Nordic, froze me with a look the moment I stepped up to the spot where Norton and I had stood the previous afternoon.

"Brenneke!" the chief bellowed, "Get your fucking pal out of the way. Where's the goddamned tape? Would you please draw another perimeter?" It wasn't a request.

As Brenneke searched for the roll of yellow tape, I hurriedly took in the scene. The place was a mess. They had already brought in the first load of fruit, and there were stacked bins and a half-empty gondola in front of the destemmer. The floor was littered with the grapes they'd tossed at the sorting table. Someone had been hosing it down, and I could see boot prints and tire tracks from the forklift and tractor. Colin Norton spotted me but made no acknowledgment. He was arguing with a tan-uniformed Napa County sheriff's deputy while three Chicanos huddled off to the side, their wrists cuffed together with plastic bands. Two of them looked sheepish and terrified, while one just stood there stoically, looking directly at me. It was the same man Norton had been conversing with when Danny and I dropped by the winery.

"I've got a crop to bring in," Norton kept repeating.

The deputy stood impassive, arms folded, oblivious to the appeal. Disdain was all that was visible on his face. Clearly, the cops had ordered Norton to shut down, and he wasn't happy about it.

Brenneke approached me, readying the tape to set a second perimeter, and nodded for me to step back.

"Get lost, Babe. The chief's having a shit hemorrhage. You working tonight?" he added under his breath.

"No, sorry. My son's with me."

"I'll have to catch up with you later," he said, and stretched the tape across the floor.

I turned and wandered back through the official vehicles and decided to check out the office. Carla Fehr was hunkered down on a bench, her shoulders shaking, head in her hands, hair covering her face. The staccato click and static of walkie-talkies reached us all the way from the winery, scratching the air.

She raised her head, hearing me come in. "One of the pumps went out . . . The giant oak thing . . . The hose was clogged," she muttered. "Colin climbed up and found Richard floating inside. The smell coming off the tank . . . It's awful." She lowered her face into her hands again. "Awful," she repeated dully.

It hadn't been brett I'd smelled the day before coming off the *foudre.* It was the first bouquet of death emanating from the bloated corpse of Richard Wilson.

I needed to get back to Danny, a visceral, primitive urge to protect him rising up in the pit of my stomach. But first I needed to call Janie. I pulled over on the side of the road just outside St. Helena. I sat there a minute, looking out to a vista of flatland vineyard that extended as far as the eye could see to a line of hills, periwinkle blue in the distance. An immaculate morning in the wine country.

I hit speed dial. Janie picked up after a couple of rings.

"Danny? Is that you, sweetheart?"

"No, it's me. Janie . . ." I didn't know how to tell her. "The police found Richard this morning."

"Where is he, the stupid jerk? Is he in trouble?"

"Janie . . ."

"What is it? A DUI? I hope they locked him up. Richard Wilson, in the clink for drunk driving! Perfect."

"Richard's dead, Janie."

"Oh, no," she moaned. "No, no, no." She finally grew silent.

"You okay?"

"Should I . . . ?" I knew what she was asking.

"Stay put. There's nothing you can do here. They found him in a vat at Norton. A wooden fermentation tank." I heard her gasp. "The cops are in charge now. I'll call you when I learn a little more."

"This is unbelievable. Missing is one thing . . . but dead . . . in a vat. This isn't some kind of joke?"

"Janie, please. I would never . . ."

"No, of course not. I'm sorry."

I wasn't going to tell her I'd smelled him myself the day before, an unwelcome touch of macabre humor.

"What about Danny?" She paused. "Babe, I can't do this without you . . ."

That voice.

"Pull yourself together. I know it's a shock. I'll do the best I can. Trust me."

I couldn't believe I'd said it, and then it was too late to take it back.

There's a certain kind of woman a man keeps coming back to, no matter what the injury, no matter how severe the damage. And a certain kind of man who keeps going back. How many times can you have your heart broken and still take a sucker punch to the solar plexus?

The human capacity for pain is almost infinite. Almost.

Janie's mother had died the previous spring, and Janie decided to move her father, Bob, already in the grip of Alzheimer's, to San Francisco. Her cottage on Telegraph Hill was too small for the three of them, and it would have been impossible for Janie to care for him anyway. She found a nursing home in Pacific Heights and paid for it with the proceeds from the sale of her parents' apartment in Manhattan. During their mother's illness and their father's relocation, Richard had not so much rebuffed as neglected her. Janie was so competent that he assumed she could handle it. At their mother's funeral he'd apologized for getting caught up in the demands that fame imposed upon his life: tasting trips, speaking engagements, wine competitions, author appearances. She said she understood but couldn't help being bitter with resentment. Now that Richard had been found murdered, she'd be guilt stricken as well. They'd never have the chance to clear the air.

I felt guilty, too. Wilson's death was my opening, my one last, best chance to show her that I cared, that she could depend on me, that I was someone better than my own former self.

But I would need to immerse myself in the life I'd left behind if I was to understand who might have had a motive for killing Wilson. As I drove slowly through St. Helena, I decided to stop at a wineshop, where I bought every trade rag they had. Then I headed back up the mountain. Danny was sitting at the picnic table, eating a bowl of cereal and reading.

I sat across from him and flipped through the magazines, trying to avoid picturing Richard's body. I wanted to tell Danny what had happened to his uncle but didn't know what to say or how to put it. I distracted myself by skimming pages that I used to devour. If I'd thought of the wine scene as silly before, by now it was ridiculous. There were still technical pieces and travel pieces, vintage reports and buying guides, but lifestyle was the new thing: wine country décor, wine country entertaining, wine country markets, wine country bistros. I was reminded why I'd quit the game and congratulated myself, even if it had been a downwardly mobile slide.

The number of special events had exploded with the velocity and virulence of wild yeast: tastings, auctions, conferences, trade shows, a self-promoting hype factory, the wineries all vying for awards and scores handed out by individuals or panels composed of the same names whose bylines I saw over and over again in the pages of the trade press. And the ads! *Wine Watcher's World* sported big, splashy, four-color jobs that treated wine as though it were designer jewelry or the latest luxury model off the assembly lines of Detroit.

I took the phone and walked out past the truck so that Danny wouldn't hear me. I called Tanner Cellars and waited for six or seven minutes until Biddy barked into the phone, "What?"

"Sorry to break into your day, amigo, but Wilson was found floating in a tank this morning at Norton."

"No fuckin' way." He whistled. "Richard Wilson. I can't believe it."

"Who'd want to get rid of him? I mean, sure, he pisses people off, but *murder*?"

"Hey, some people take their bad press very seriously," Teukes said.

I knew he was right. Though I'd reassured Janie that people didn't hate her brother, I knew it wasn't true. They envied and resented him, too. He had become too famous, too iconic, too controversial.

"In a tank?" Biddy asked incredulously, as the news sank in. "How do you get a big guy like Wilson in a tank?"

"In the middle of harvest," I added. The whole thing seemed impossible.

"No simple thing to waltz into Norton unseen," Biddy mused. "So many people running around . . ." I could feel him trying to puzzle it together. "Gotta be someone at Norton," he concluded.

"I read a bunch of Richard's old newsletters last night. He liked Norton."

"In a tank," Biddy repeated. "Jesus, Colin's a goner. Poor sonuvabitch."

"Okay, assume for the moment that Norton's cleared; who else in the valley might be gunning for him?" I asked.

The line was silent, and then he said, "Well, sure. Wineries, mostly. But if you're looking for an individual, the only guy who comes to mind is Michael Matson. Great winemaker. Quiet, soft, a lovely cat. Very delicate style that could never stand up to the fat, tannic shit that shows so well when you're tasting a hundred wines at a crack. Wilson took him out at the knees. Anyway, he basically lost the ranch. He's a little bitter, but he holds his own. He splits his time between Chateau Hauberg and struggling to get his own thing going again. It's an old pig farm—just a barn and a couple of outbuildings on White Cottage Road. Low, brick red, under a giant weeping willow. You can't miss it."

Hauberg was virtually in my backyard on the eastern slope of Howell Mountain. I'd driven by it dozens of times but didn't know its owner or anyone there.

"Thanks, that's a start."

"No problem. Look, I've got to get back. The Cab is piling up."

"Do me one favor: The only *Wine Maven*s I have are from years ago. Bring me some recent stuff to look at after you get off work."

"*Bueno*," Teukes said.

I returned to my reading. The magazines I had just bought leaned to favorable reviews—the formulaic run-through of color, bouquet, and extraction, their high marks always falling on the side of big, overly ripe fruit. I knew such verdicts came on the heels of extensive tasting: sixty, seventy, a hundred wines in one sitting. No surprise that any juice characterized by delicacy would get lost in the shuffle. But I knew most of these wineries could stomach a low score. Their pockets were deep and their production sufficiently extensive to sustain a slam or two each season. Hell, most of the boutique wineries had been bought up by giant liquor conglomerates anyway.

I turned back to the out-of-date *Maven* issues. It took me a while to dig through what I'd marked the night before, but I finally turned up Wilson's treatment of Matson's adolescent efforts. It was scathing, more devastating than anything I had read in the glossier rags.

Maybe Biddy was right, but it was hard to imagine that Matson would feel an ancient if injurious review so acutely as to plop Wilson in a fermentation tank, if he were able to get into the winery at all. Then again, who was I to say what a person whose life Wilson had ruined might do? Revenge is funny that way.

6

I **sat down** across from my son at the picnic table.

"I need your help," I said.

Danny closed the book. "Help with what?"

"A little investigative work."

"Okay," he said, his eyes lighting up. He picked up the cereal bowl and sucked the milk noisily through his lips.

"Don't slurp it, drink it. It's not wine, you know." I paused. "This is serious. Something happened to Uncle Rich."

He put the bowl down and looked at me warily. "What happened?"

"He's dead, Danny. I'm really sorry. I thought you should know."

His face shriveled in pain. He looked at me, then his features relaxed. "What happened?" he repeated, his hands dropping to his sides.

"I'm not sure. But your mom asked me to find out. Will you help me?"

"I guess." He looked down at the empty bowl, a wrinkle of worry furrowing his brow. "What happened?" he said for the third time.

"Somebody killed him."

My son's face was opaque at first. I couldn't tell if what I'd said registered, if he really understood.

"Why?" he asked, his face knotting itself again in innocent confusion.

"Your uncle was a very powerful man. He had a lot of enemies."

"What are we going to do?"

"First things first. We need to talk to a few people. Get dressed."

It wasn't hard to locate Matson's operation. I described it to Danny and let him spot it, the weeping willow on White Cottage Road and the low buildings that stretched beneath it. A Toyota pickup was parked in the shade of the tree, and we wandered around the building to a sliding door in back that stood open. Two migrants were stacking bins of Chardonnay in the shade of the willow. A young man in muddy jeans, rubber boots, and a faded T-shirt stood wiping his forehead with a bandana, staring at the fruit. He replaced a straw hat on the back of his head.

"Michael Matson?" I said.

He nodded. "That's me." He had a young, sweet face that I found impossible to reconcile with the notion that he could have murdered anybody.

"Got a minute?" I asked.

"I do, if you'll give me a hand. My wife's getting the kids off to day care, and Jesús is late." He paused. "Do I know you?" he asked.

I introduced Danny and myself and told him I'd heard that Richard Wilson had destroyed his career. My son looked at me in astonished horror.

"Help me hoist this," Matson said, avoiding my eyes. He didn't reply to my assertion. We lifted a bin of Chard and dumped the fruit onto a sorting table. "Toss anything that's broken or looks like shit." He looked at us and gave a tentative grin. Danny giggled at the word *shit* and started in, once Matson demonstrated the technique for him.

"It's simple," he said after a moment. "Wilson doesn't like what I do. I'm a fervent traditionalist. I strive for purity of statement. The finest expression of *terroir* I can achieve. I go to crazy lengths."

"For example?" I said.

"What we're doing now. Each lot of fruit isolated in the fermenter. The tanks are insulated so I can control temperatures. Native yeast fermentation, cold maceration, manual *bâtonnage.*"

Matson's hands worked on their own, incredibly fast, dexterously feeling through the fruit, picking and pitching, cluster by cluster. Danny studied him and did his best to imitate his every move.

"Work a little faster," he said, observing my son. "You don't have to be so careful. I mean, be careful but not *too* careful."

Danny sped up.

"Good," Matson said and then turned to me. "I'm obsessive, and I'm strict. I despise inflated rhetoric, inflated reputations, and inflated wine. The problem is, people don't know what they want to make. So they end up producing wine to fit someone else's idea of what wine's supposed to taste like. Take Wilson: He thinks he's championing the artisanal, but the opposite is really the case. All he's done is fuel people's crass commercial instinct. They end up making fat wines to get high scores to fetch top dollar. It's sick. And it's a vicious circle."

"Fret no more," I said.

His hands paused between the sorting table and the destemmer into which he'd just tossed a cupped handful of fruit.

"Wilson's dead," I said. "He was found in a vat at Norton a couple hours ago."

Danny kept going. I searched Matson's eyes as he looked from me to his new helper and back to me. He seemed genuinely shocked. We heard a car pull up outside the barn, and a moment later a petite blond woman with a face as innocent as Matson's walked into the room through a side door.

"Hey," she said.

"My wife, Gretchen," Matson said.

"Babe Stern," I said. "This is my son, Danny."

"Gretch, Richard Wilson . . ." was all Matson was able to get out.

I told them what I knew. Danny stopped sorting. It was the first time he'd heard the story of what had actually happened.

"Pretty weird time to visit the valley," Matson said.

"He was probably polishing copy or something," Gretchen suggested tentatively.

"Exactly. The revised edition of his book on California was about to go to press. He wanted to retaste a few things. That's what he said, anyway. I was with him late yesterday afternoon."

"Do you know . . ." Matson started.

"All I know is that they lined up a few bottles for him and left him to his own devices. He was heading back to the city, then off to New York."

Jesús, Matson's assistant, now arrived, and the three of them got to work sorting.

"Sorry, but I've got to get the Chard done today," Matson said. "I'm back at Hauberg first thing tomorrow morning."

"One question before we take off?" I asked. Matson nodded, then looked down at his hands as they flew through bunches of glistening grapes. "Can you think of anyone who hated Wilson enough to kill him?"

"I'll be honest with you," he said. "After he wrote what he did about me, I stopped paying attention. Look at this," he gestured across the pint-size barn. "We're pretty marginal here. Hangin' on for dear life. Last year we bottled three hundred cases. If we're lucky this year, we'll get three fifty, maybe four. I don't want to take on any more than I can handle. This is about as boutique as it gets. I'm sorry Richard is dead. He was a serious person. But all I really care about is my wife, my children, and my wine."

He looked at me. Gretchen smiled wanly as she plucked two brown-tinged grapes and dropped them on the ground. I had no reason to disbelieve Matson and excused myself.

"You're a good worker," he said to Danny. "If you're around this week, feel free to come by and give us a hand."

I decided to run through St. Helena and stop by the cop shop. When we got there, I stood in the waiting room, examining the police department's patch collection while Mary, the dispatcher, buzzed Brenneke. She said he'd just arrived with some suspects or witnesses, she wasn't sure. As she waved us back, Danny pointed to a teddy bear in a cop's uniform perched on a boom box above her desk.

"His office," Mary said.

Brenneke looked up when we walked in.

"I thought I told you I'd catch up with you later," he said. "I have no time for you."

"Russ, this is my son, Danny."

Brenneke nodded.

"Who'd you just bring in?" I asked.

"None of your fucking business," he said, then realized that a child was present. "Sorry," he said to Danny, and turned to me. "A few of the Mexicans. Two of 'em fled. Probably halfway to Baja by now. All they need to see is a radio antenna, and they take off. We have another two of the seasonal guys locked up. They materialize every year to help bring in the fruit."

"There was a third. He seemed more important. I saw him talking to Norton yesterday when Danny and I were at the winery. What is he, the foreman?"

"Fornes, the vineyard manager. He's back there, too." Brenneke paused. "You were at Norton yesterday?" he said, his eyes drilling into me.

"Yes. And the day before. Wilson dropped by the bar and asked me to go out there with him."

He put the report he held in his hand on the desk, rose from his chair, and walked to the door.

"Don't go anywhere," he said.

"What's going on, Dad?" Danny asked.

Brenneke returned a moment later with Mary.

"Son, would you mind? I need to talk to your dad a minute. Mary'll take you out front."

Danny looked at me as if everything had suddenly gone terribly wrong.

"Don't worry," I said. "It's fine. I'll be right there."

He glanced at me over one shoulder while Mary placed her hand on the other and led him down the hallway.

Brenneke closed the door and took his seat, rolling it out from behind the desk to within a foot of me.

"You mind telling me what's going on?" he said.

"Janie, Wilson's sister, is my ex."

"You're just full of surprises."

"When he failed to show for dinner the other night and didn't return her calls, she asked me to poke around."

"You being a well-known wine guy and all," Brenneke smirked.

"Wilson and I were close when we were just starting out. That's how I met Janie. He got me my first few jobs in Seattle, around the time you and I met." He waited for a more detailed explanation. "He looked me up the day before yesterday. There was something he wanted to talk to me about. He asked me to follow him to Norton." Brenneke still wasn't satisfied. "But we never got around to it," I continued. "There were people around—Colin Norton, a woman who works in the office, a young French kid who's doing a sort of apprenticeship—so we couldn't talk. It was something private, and we didn't have any privacy there."

He fished a notebook from the clutter on his desk, folded one leg over the other, and jotted some notes.

"Let me get this straight: He never told you what he wanted to tell you."

"Correct."

"So, what happened?"

"I left."

"What time was that?"

"I don't know, five, five thirty, maybe."

"What was he doing when you left?"

"Tasting with Norton. In a room off the reception area."

"Anybody else around?"

"I couldn't say with any certainty. The French kid took off. Fornes was probably still there, along with the crew. Their workday runs late this time of year, needless to say. Carla Fehr, the office person, may have been there, but I don't think so."

"Oh yeah, why's that?"

"Because she and Wilson were having an affair."

Brenneke looked up from his notebook.

"You know that for a fact? I thought you said that you and Wilson didn't have a chance to speak in private."

"Call it an educated guess. I know him pretty well. And when I called Ms. Fehr to ask if she'd seen him, she said he was supposed to come over for dinner and never arrived."

"And what about you? What did you do that night? Go back to work?"

"No, Mulligan had the bar. I went home to get ready for my son's visit."

"Anybody see you?"

"No, I was alone the whole night."

"And Wilson never called?" Brenneke asked.

"Not even the next morning, when he said he might drop by the bar," I told him.

Brenneke's gaze was steady. He rubbed his cheek with the butt end of his pen.

"Jesus, Stern," he said, shaking his head. He was trying to make up his mind about what he should do next. "Look, I know your kid's sitting out there waiting for you. He's probably scared to death." He thought a moment. "I'm gonna type this up and show it to Jensen. But you should know right now, he's going to want a formal statement."

"I realize that," I said as if I had fully expected it. I hadn't.

"Okay, get the fuck outta here," Brenneke said, rolling his chair to the desk without looking at me. "Just stay behind your bar and keep your eyes and ears open. You hear anything you think I should know, you call me."

Danny was sitting in the waiting room on the edge of his seat. The teddy bear seemed to be gazing down at me. They were both waiting for an explanation.

"It's fine, pal," I said, ignoring the bear. "Don't worry about it."

Easy enough to say to your child, but a little tougher to convince yourself of. It hadn't occurred to me until Brenneke said he'd need a statement that I'd inadvertently set myself up as a suspect.

7

We stopped at The Diner in Yountville and grabbed some
lunch.

"These tacos are better than yours, Dad," Danny said.

"I'm not surprised. The food is great here. See if you can figure
out how they do 'em, and you can tell Ernesto."

While Danny deconstructed his taco, I considered my history
with Brenneke. Our paths had first crossed in Seattle. He was the
kind of cop who always made you feel he had you in his back pocket.
He took pleasure in pushing people around. A little sloppy and a
little angry, he evinced the arrogance of power but was crippled by
his own ineptitude, a quality that had led to his dismissal from the
SPD. We'd done each other a couple of favors since discovering we
were both in the valley, but I doubted our friendship would count
for much under the present circumstances. The cops had no idea
what was about to descend on them once the news of the murder
of Richard Wilson got out. They'd be under enormous pressure to
solve it.

Leaving, I stepped into the phone booth and looked up Carla
Fehr's address.

"One more stop," I said to Danny when we were in the truck.

He threw me a look that suggested I was out of my mind, then
turned his back on me.

"You're not a detective, Dad," he said out the window.

"True," I acknowledged, "but bartenders and detectives have a lot in common."

He turned his head to look at me. *Sure they do*, the look said.

Carla Fehr lived in a small white clapboard cottage on a back road on the other side of the highway. Lace curtains masked the windows.

"Wait here. I'm not sure this woman's going to talk to me," I said. "I think it's better if I go it alone." Danny appeared relieved to be let off the hook. "I'll just be a minute."

The geraniums on the front porch hadn't been deadheaded in weeks. I knocked and stood there for several minutes. The cicadas' frenzied whining made me edgy. I knocked again and saw the curtain drawn back an inch. She opened the door and turned without saying a word, retreating to the safety of the living room. She was barefoot, wearing a man's shirt and blue jeans. Her hair was carelessly tied up.

The room was pleasantly if sparsely furnished, a little frilly in its taste. She plopped onto the sofa and tucked one leg beneath her. I took a chair facing her.

"Still skulking around?" She shook her head. "Don't you believe in mourning?" she asked, her tone sarcastic.

"I'm doing this for Richard's sister. She asked me to."

"Asked you to talk to me? I doubt it."

"Oh? And why's that?"

"She doesn't know about Richard and me."

The shadows cast by the lace played across her face, and the light silhouetted her body in the enormous shirt. It was a perfect body.

"How would you describe your relationship with Richard?"

She looked at me as if I were a child. A very stupid child.

"We were friends. He confided in me," she finally said.

"I don't know if he ever mentioned me, but he and I were friends, too. And he wanted to confide in *me*. There was something bothering him, something that he wanted to get off his chest. You have any notion what it might have been?"

I could tell by the look on her face—hostile, a little sad, contemptuous—that whatever it was, he hadn't told her about it.

"Look, I don't know what you're after. Richard and I were close. I mean, he wasn't here that much. But whenever he was . . . I just can't believe somebody would do this to him."

"So, you don't have a clue? No idea?"

She didn't like the fact that I was implying there was something he hadn't told her, that their relationship was purely sexual.

"Get a life," she said. "And get your ass out of my house."

Danny was standing outside the truck, throwing rocks into a field. I came up beside him, bent down, and grabbed a few myself, and we stood there a minute, seeing who could throw farther.

"Good arm," I said.

"Thanks."

"This isn't turning out to be much fun, is it?"

"Not really," he said.

"You wanna go home?"

"I guess."

"Okay, let me call your mother."

I walked to the truck and pulled my cell phone from the glove box.

"I need you to take Danny back," I said. "If you really want me to do this."

"You told him?" She was furious.

"I had to. Anyway, he was going to find out sooner or later."

"How is he?"

"He's fine. We've been working on it together."

"Christ, Babe! He's ten years old."

"You can't protect him. He's too smart. He's going to figure it out." I could tell she was fuming in silence. "Listen, you said Richard kept an apartment in the city. You wouldn't happen to have a key, would you?" When she said yes, I asked for the address and told her to meet us there in an hour.

We drove down 29 to Highway 12, and I pointed out the smudge pots and propellers viticulturalists use to move frigid air. Now they stood frozen in the dead heat. Buzzards soared high overhead.

Traffic wasn't too bad heading into the city. As we crossed the Bay Bridge, I said, "How's Grandpa Bob?"

"He's weird," Danny said, scrunching his face.

"What do you mean?" I asked.

"I don't know. Sometimes he's okay. And then . . ."

"He's very sick, Danny. You have to help your mom. She really needs you right now."

"I know," he said defensively.

It was an awful lot to ask of a young boy, to understand and make space for an old man who was losing his memory. Now he'd have to console his mother as well.

As we pulled up I saw Janie parking her BMW convertible, neatly wedging it onto a slope in front of a sleek art deco–style building on the north edge of Russian Hill. I circled three times before risking a ticket in a space in front of a fireplug.

"I don't cover parking," Janie said as we crossed the street to her.

"I'll take my chances." All I cared about was getting into the apartment before the cops beat me there.

She gave Danny a big hug and kissed the top of his head. She refused to let go, forcing him to wriggle free.

"I've been helping Dad," he said.

"I know; he told me. You're a very brave boy." She looked at me over the top of his head, just shaking her own.

"Thanks, Mom."

Janie unlocked the outer door.

"Fourth floor," she said.

"I thought he might have given you a key," I said to take my mind off her ass, which rocked with metronomic precision as we made our way up the staircase.

"I insisted, in case there was a problem. They're on the road so much."

"They?"

"He shares the place with his assistant, Jacques Goldoni. Richard only uses it—used it—four or five times a year. But Jacques stays here at least as much. They kept it so they wouldn't have to pay for hotels. It doubles as an office. They go all over the state."

I felt an ache as I passed her and entered the apartment. *Distract yourself*, I said. *Be methodical. Play detective.*

"What are we looking for, Dad?" Danny asked.

"I'm not sure. See what you can find," I said.

Janie said nothing. All that mattered was that Danny was here, with her, safe.

The kitchen was tiny but serviceable. Two cases of empty wine bottles were crammed under the sink. Another case full of samples sat on the counter.

An easy chair commanded a sweeping view of the bay, the Golden Gate Bridge to the west and Alcatraz directly before us in the distance. A stack of wine books lay at its feet. Remington Norman, Jancis Robinson, Clive Coates. Predictable stuff. What wasn't predictable were the frogs. There were frogs everywhere: porcelain frogs, crystal frogs, carved wooden frogs with wings, even a frog chandelier.

"Why does he have all these frogs?" Danny asked.

"I think it must have been a way to express admiration for the French. Sometimes we call the French Frogs."

"It's not a nice word," Janie said. "I never want to hear you use it."

"Okay, fine, Mom," Danny said, sounding surprisingly adult in his irritation.

Instinctively I turned to the desk. On it a computer printout of a calendar, squared neatly on a blotter, was scribbled up. Appointments at Norton, Diamond Creek, Viader, and Turley were penciled in and one at Chateau Hauberg crossed out. The dinner date with Janie had been hastily noted in red ink (JANIE/7:30/DANKO), and a United flight number with departure time and confirmation number was scrawled on a Thursday, one month away. The words RIOJA, NAVARRA, and PRIORAT were printed in bold caps with a scraggly line extending through the following two weeks, growing faint and disappearing as it neared October (PIEMONTE/TUSCANY) and entered November (ME: BORDEAUX/JACQUES: BURGUNDY). *What a life*, I thought. At the very bottom of the sheet the name FELDMAN was written, carefully shaded with fine cross-hatching as if doodled in the course of a tedious phone conversation.

"Who's this?" I asked, pointing to the name.

She came up to me and looked at the calendar.

"That's strange," she said. "Eric Feldman? I didn't think they were on speaking terms."

"Really?"

"He used to work for Richard. They had a falling-out."

"What's he do now?" I said.

"He has his own newsletter."

"The competition?"

"Yes, I suppose he is." I waited for an explanation. "They parted ways five or six years ago. Basically, Richard fired him, and then Eric went into business on his own. He copied everything Richard did."

I made a mental note to find out more about Feldman.

A lone file cabinet catalogued past editions of the newsletter, and an assortment of notebooks were meticulously dated by vintage and labeled by appellation: KNIGHTS VALLEY, CARNEROS, STAGS' LEAP DISTRICT. Nothing there was dated from the current year.

I gingerly picked up the handset on the portable phone with my bandana. I didn't want Brenneke complaining that I'd trashed his evidence.

"He has messages." A Post-it taped to the phone listed the voice-mail access number and security code. "Do you mind?" I asked.

"Help yourself."

I dialed the numbers. Five messages.

The first was Janie, confirming their dinner.

The second was from Carla. "Richard, this is Carla. Hurry. I can't wait."

The third was Janie again, aggravated that he hadn't arrived for dinner and concerned at his having failed to call her.

Next was a woman. The message was cryptic, the voice faintly accented: "You have to talk to me." She sounded Italian, or Spanish, maybe. I replayed it for Janie.

"Any ideas?' I asked.

"A wine rep?" she ventured.

"Probably a waitress he was screwing," I said.

Janie wasn't amused and glanced at Danny.

"Do you mind?" she said testily under her breath, but Danny wasn't paying attention. He had unlocked the door to the balcony, had wandered outside, and was gazing at Alcatraz.

The last was another male voice. "Richard, this is Eric. We need to talk, but I'm swamped. I'll catch up with you in France. I'll be at the Novotel in Beaune. By the way, your issue on 2007 Rhônes really missed the mark."

"Who's this?" I asked her as I punched it to replay and gave her the phone.

"Not positive," she said, handing it back. "But I think it has to be Eric Feldman."

"Of course. Tell me about Goldoni," I said, wandering around the room, looking for a clue I couldn't identify.

"Nothing much to tell. Italian American father and a French mother. He speaks perfect French. Kind of an asshole."

"How so?"

"I don't know. Fat, obnoxious, ambitious."

"Would he stand to gain anything if your brother suddenly vanished?"

"I suppose he might, but it's Richard who has the reputation. Jacques basks in reflected glory. I doubt he could make it on his own."

"Still, he might assume the mantle, take over the *Maven.*"

"Richard takes very good care of him. Took, I mean," she said, her tone softening as she changed tenses.

"Speaking of which, I need . . ."

I hadn't gotten it out before she pulled an envelope from her purse.

"I know you can't afford to take time away from the bar to look into this. I think that should cover it. For starters, at least."

It's humiliating to accept money from your ex-wife. I had refused her offer to pay alimony at the time of our divorce settlement—she probably made ten times what I earned—but, as it stood, I had little choice.

"Very thoughtful of you to anticipate it," I said, stuffing it, along with my pride, in my pocket.

I opened the door to the closet. A half dozen matching blue shirts straight from the dry cleaner hung beside four pairs of chinos. A suitcase lay open on the small dresser, packed and ready to zip up, a pair of Mephistos at its feet.

I turned my attention to the kitchen. The fridge offered only a jar of Dijon mustard and a half pound of Peet's French roast. Guys like Wilson ate out every night, usually on someone else's expense account.

Nothing seemed amiss in the bathroom. A tube of toothpaste, two toothbrushes, deodorant, a hairbrush. The scent of cleanser. And then the merest whiff of something else, a trace, but unmistakable. Floral.

I called out to Janie, who was wandering aimlessly, "What about women? Do you know anyone Richard was seeing?"

She shook her head. Carla Fehr was right: Wilson hadn't told his sister about her.

Janie suddenly looked overwhelmed, frailer. The place was obviously beginning to get to her.

"Danny! Let's get outta here!" I called. "Let's forget the *cherchez la femme* part," I said to Janie. "We leave the messages. The cops are probably already on their way here."

She locked up, and we retraced our steps. On the second landing we heard a plate shatter, then something crashed against the front door. Danny turned to her questioningly, not sure how to react. She wagged her finger and, when we arrived in the foyer, explained, "Psycho. He hurls himself against the walls. Stand here a moment. He'll start shouting obscenities in a second."

Right on cue, a stream of expletives.

"Tourette's?" I asked.

"Who knows? Probably forgot to take his meds this morning. Richard says he's perfectly harmless."

As she opened the door to the lobby, I inadvertently crowded her. She turned to face me, the tip of her nipple grazing my arm through her blouse. We were both startled. The familiarity and foreignness of it. I felt as if I had trespassed on my own life.

"Let me buy us dinner," I said awkwardly, patting the check in my pocket.

"No, I should get back," she said quickly. "My father . . ."

"You're right. Me too. The path's growing cold." But I knew that the only path that was cold was the one I was trying to beat back to my ex-wife.

"How is Bob?" I asked as we descended to the sidewalk, strangers again. "Danny said he's weird."

"You just never know. One minute he's fine, and the next he's lost."

"That's just what Danny said." We both looked down at our son, who stood on the sidewalk kicking pebbles into the gutter. "Speaking of which, I'm really sorry that I need to give him up early, but this could get a little tricky. I don't think it's really appropriate . . ."

"I don't think what you've already exposed him to was particularly appropriate," she interrupted.

"Look, you asked me to do this," I said.

Janie looked at me with the expression of endless disappointment that I seemed to elicit from her with everything I did. I turned, walked down to our son, and gave him a hug.

"Thanks for your help, pal," I said. "I'll let you know how it goes."

"Be careful, Dad," he said, and I stroked his cheek.

"I promise. You too. And take good care of your mom."

Janie was still watching me as I plucked the parking ticket from my windshield wiper.

"Don't worry. That'll cover it," she called.

I opened the envelope. It was a check for two grand. I blew her a kiss.

8

By the time I reached the valley, it was dusk. Bats flitted through a grove of eucalyptus. The moon would be full in little over a week. In Provence and the Languedoc, the *biodynamique* French wackos—the organically minded winemakers who spoke fluently to insects in bug language and timed their every move to the phase of the moon and the ebb and flow of tides—would be picking once it hit full. They'd have to wait another month in the cooler climes of the Loire and Burgundy if they wanted to remain faithful to the credo. They don't call them lunatics for nothing.

Before I headed up the mountain, I thought I'd stop by St. Helena and see if Brenneke was still around. He and the corporal I'd seen at Norton were going over their notes. He was none too happy to see me, but I thought I might be able to change his opinion by providing a little information.

"Wilson kept an apartment in the city. His sister met me there this afternoon. I didn't see much, but you should listen to his answering machine. Carla left a message. Confirms what I said about their having an affair."

"You already gave us that," Brenneke said.

"I spoke with Michael Matson, a winemaker Wilson trashed in print, but I don't think he had anything to do with it."

"Brilliant detective work," he said. "What the hell are you doing,

Stern? Tampering with evidence? Screwing with witnesses? You're walking a fine line, my friend."

"You told me to find out what I could," I said.

"I told you to stand behind your bar and pay attention. We've got work to do," he said, eager to get rid of me.

Two plastic evidence bags of marijuana lay open on the table. He followed my eyes.

"I can see that," I said. "You could do one more thing for me," I added.

"And what would that be?"

"Is Fornes still here?"

"Yeah. We're going to have to transfer him to Napa in the morning. Ciofreddi and the task force want to sit him down in the Blue Room."

"Mind if I speak with him for a minute or two?"

"Absolutely not. Out of the question."

"Jesus, Russ, just for a minute. Listen in, if you want."

He walked into the hallway to make sure the chief hadn't snuck into his office unannounced, and checked the reception area.

"Okay, but two minutes. That's it. And I'm right outside the door."

He escorted me back to the tiny hallway of cells at the rear of the station. He glanced through the peephole and nodded for me to take a look. Fornes lay face up on a bare plastic mattress, his arms folded, eyes wide. Staring into the void of a doomed future. Brenneke unlocked the door.

"Mr. Fornes, you have a visitor. Two minutes. I can't believe I'm doing this," he whispered in my ear as he shut the door behind me.

Francisco Fornes swiveled on the steel bed frame and perched on its edge. There was no place to sit, so I took the toilet. I glanced around the cell. The cinder-block walls were the color of a healthy tongue.

"You my lawyer?" he asked.

"'Fraid not. I'm investigating on behalf of Richard Wilson's sister."

Maybe it was his baby face, maybe it was the dark brown pools of his eyes, or maybe it was the simple humility with which he looked at me, but if Francisco Fornes was guilty of murder, my name was Bob Mondavi. I knew tomorrow I'd be ashamed to show my face at the bar, to stand opposite his countrymen and serve them beer. I had to break the tension. His impotence was killing me.

"Did you know Wilson?"

"Know him? No. I would see him when he came to the winery."

His accent was perceptible, but his English was flawless.

"What did you think of him?"

"I am not paid to think of him, and I paid him no thought."

His smile let me know that he knew perfectly well he'd turned a clever phrase.

"What was he like?"

"Arrogant. He considered himself infallible, like the pope. Except that he treated the *campesinos* like shit. Maybe worse than shit; we didn't exist." He paused and looked up at the filthy grate that covered the fluorescent light fixture. When he returned his gaze to me, his enormous eyes were lit up like a little boy's. "But kill him?" The question defied comprehension. On its face, it was ludicrous. "For what?" he continued. "I have work to do. My job is to bring in a crop. To keep it as fresh as I can. Keep the grapes from crushing each other until we can crush them. His corpse in a tank? Are you kidding? Why spoil the wine? With a fat pig like Wilson? What do you take me for?"

An extremely intelligent professional, I told myself. Why hadn't the cops copped to the exquisite logic of this argument? Too eager for a collar, perhaps. They certainly hadn't exhausted their options.

"Maybe they think you resented his power?"

"I can't afford myself that luxury," he volunteered. "I follow the work. And I have been at Norton ten years. Let the gringos look after themselves. Anyway, why would I risk my green card? Have you ever vacationed in Sonora?"

He shot his eyebrows toward the light, a quizzical look that was more answer than question. And then broke into a grin.

"How late were you at the winery the night before last?" I asked.

"I left earlier than usual."

"Meaning?"

"Maybe six o'clock. Something like that," Fornes said.

That meant he'd left not long after I had.

"Was Wilson alone?"

"I don't know. I was in the winery. He was in the tasting room. He didn't mix with 'the help.'" Fornes smiled.

"Anyone else around?"

"The crew was cleaning up," he said.

"The crew?"

"Javier. Pablo. And Jean." He pronounced the name properly.

"Jean?"

"A French kid. He's here to learn how we Mexicans make wine," Fornes said.

The guy cracked me up.

"I thought Jean left to be with his sister. He stuck his nose into the tasting room and told Colin he was leaving," I said.

He thought a moment, then said, "Maybe. I don't remember."

"What about Norton?" I asked.

"Yes, he was there, too. *Tout le monde*," he joked. "Nothing unusual. But like I said, I left." He paused. "So, what do you think?"

"I don't know. I'm going to do what I can," I said, unable to convince even myself.

"*Gracias*," he said as I rose from the toilet. I turned and saw Brenneke's eye through the peephole. I nodded and he unlocked the door.

"Stay strong," I said at the threshold of the cell. "*Mucha suerte.*"

"Fat chance," Francisco Fornes said.

Brenneke relocked the cell. We stood facing each other in the narrow hallway.

"No fuckin' way," I told him.

"Get the hell outta here," he said and pushed me down the hall, past the booking station to the rear exit. I glanced at the wall. All the questions for incoming prisoners were printed in Spanish and English on a crib sheet for monolingual cops.

"You're goin' out the back. Anybody sees you, I'm screwed," Brenneke said.

In the parking lot, four squad cars stood in silent formation, awaiting the next dispatch. I stood under a bespangled sky. Brenneke stood in the doorway.

"Maybe you should drop this," he said, already regretting his call for a little help on the side. "We can handle it."

"Sure you can," I said and turned toward Main Street.

Just as I predicted, three television vans were already in town, setting up by Lyman Park, preparing for the morning feed.

I decided to stop by the bar on the way home. I needed a drink. It had been a long day. As I walked in, I could make out Biddy's silhouette against the backlight of the jukebox. I walked up to the bar. Mulligan pulled an Anchor Steam from the reefer, popped it, and left it in the bottle. He took one look at me, then grabbed a tumbler and poured me a double shot of Oban.

"How'd you know?" I said, and he smiled.

"You okay?" he said.

"I'm not sure yet. It's pretty rough."

He stood with his hands spread on the bar, his eyes taking in the room. A group of vineyard workers had just gotten off work and had gathered around the pool table. They were laughing and carrying on. Two pitchers of beer stood on a small round, one already three-quarters gone.

Without shifting his eyes, Mulligan said, "Gio called. She's looking for you."

"I ticked her off last night. She didn't know Wilson was my brother-in-law. You can imagine how that went over."

Jake Watson, a winemaker we knew, walked in, came up to the bar, and ordered a gin and tonic.

"Hey, Babe, Frank," he said, nodding.

"Hey, Jake. How's it goin'?" I said.

"It's a beautiful thing, man. *Vendange* bliss, baby."

Mulligan set his drink on the bar, and Jake walked to a booth and fell onto the bench, putting his feet up.

"The man at the end of the bar has been waiting for you," Mulligan said.

I glanced down the bar. I didn't recognize him.

"He say who he was?"

Mulligan shook his head. I took the scotch and the bottle of Anchor Steam, walked down the line of stools, and sat down on the one next to him.

"Babe Stern," I said.

"Daniel Hauberg," he said, extending his hand.

"My son's name is Daniel," I said, shaking it.

The pink-and-green neon ironed out the wrinkles in his face, but I put him close to seventy years old. The great gray bushes of his eyebrows cast his eyes in deep shadow. The light off the Pyramid sign caught them for a moment, and when it suddenly flickered, he looked as if he'd blinked without closing them.

"Michael Matson was at my château last night," he said, his French accent tempered by a patrician and unmistakably British overlay. Realizing that his statement might not be enough, he added, "He was there all day and spent the night. He slept on a cot in the *cuverie* and never left."

I sipped my scotch, then said, "I was at an apartment Wilson kept in San Francisco this afternoon. On his calendar an appointment he had with you was crossed out."

"You know, I sold my property in Bordeaux before Wilson gained his influence. And I'm grateful that I did. My wine would not have fared well, I'm afraid. But here, I wanted him to come. I could have used a little help," Hauberg said, smiling sardonically. "But Michael doesn't want to ever see him again. And I must take the side of my winemaker. I'm sure you understand. So I canceled the tasting. Anyway, I make wine to please myself."

"Do you think Wilson maybe wanted to patch things up with Matson, maybe felt guilty about the way he'd treated him?"

Hauberg pondered this and took a sip of wine. "This is quite nice," he said, indicating his glass. "No, I don't believe that Richard Wilson ever experienced any qualms of guilt over his judgments. He considered himself completely objective and never apologized for anything he wrote. An occasional retraction or clarification, perhaps, but never an apology." He stood, lifted his glass, and emptied it. "Well, that is what I came to tell you."

"Thank you," I said. *"Bonne chance."* Now I'd wished two people luck.

"I think, maybe, you need it more than me," Daniel Hauberg said.

9

After Hauberg walked out, I grabbed my drinks and joined Biddy in his booth. There was a bottle of wine on the table and two glasses. Teukes poured me some.

"Incoming," he said, our code word for a fruit bomb, a block-buster bottle of Zin or Syrah that threatened to break 17 percent alcohol and rip your jaw off. Teukes knew I hated these wines and took perverse pleasure in laying a bottle on me whenever he could.

"I'm fine," I said, taking a slug of beer.

"Stags' Leap Petite Syrah," he said to tempt me, pouring himself another glass. "Just gets younger every day."

"If only it were true," I said.

"Well?" he said, peering intently at me through steely blue eyes. He waited, hoping for an expansive tale, but when I didn't fall for the bait, he went on, "This is wild, man. Wilson up in smoke." He chortled fiendishly and took an enormous gulp of wine.

"He wasn't distilled, asshole. He was plopped in a cask of Caber-net." I paused. "You make any calls?" I asked.

"No time."

"You bring the stuff I asked you for?"

He hoisted a saddlebag from the bench and set it on the table.

"Pony Express, Babe. The whole fuckin' archive. A few issues may be missing. I've been haulin' this shit around for years."

"You ever hear of a guy named Eric Feldman? Used to work for Wilson?"

"Oh, yeah. What a story!"

He related that Feldman had started as an underpaid assistant, stuck in the New York office taking faxes, transcribing notes, and receiving phone calls. He did the grunt work while Wilson got the glory. Then Wilson decided to take him on the road, where Feldman played stripling scribe to Wilson's high priest of *Vitis vinifera*. This went on for some time, two or three years. Trips to California, to France, to Italy.

The story had it—and Biddy had heard it from a reliable source— that at a prestigious château in Pauillac, Feldman had literally dropped his pen, aghast at Wilson's disparaging commentary on a perfectly fine, if not spectacular, wine. Registering the mutinous disturbance, Wilson came out of his sacramental trance, incredulous that his understudy might be second-guessing him.

"I can't believe we're tasting the same wine," Feldman protested.

The French were confused at first, then amused, and finally embarrassed as the exchange grew more heated. Eventually Wilson stormed out of the cellar and insisted that the château's owner drive him back to his hotel. He refused even to get in a car with Feldman. It was a typically highhanded request, especially coming as it did after ripping the man's wine apart. But how could the *vigneron* refuse and risk antagonizing the critic further?

And that was that. Upon Feldman's return to the States, he'd set up shop for himself.

"That's it, huh?" I said.

"Oh, no, there's more. Wilson had been screwing Feldman's wife. And not only did she not loyally follow Hubby into exile, she went to work for Wilson. That's why Eric moved to D.C. The humiliation was too much."

"Maybe I should gag down my revulsion and call Jordan Meyer," I said.

"Why would you want to call Meyer? He's disgusting."

"Because he loves to gossip and knows more shit about more people than anybody in the trade. If there's dirt on Wilson, he'll know about it."

But Meyer was the last person in the world I ever wanted to see again.

"Do you actually know him?" Biddy asked.

"Not in the biblical sense. Not that he didn't try."

"I thought he had better taste," Teukes deadpanned.

I'd met Jordan Meyer years before in Seattle. Portly, bearded, and dapper, he'd carved out a specialty writing about food and wine pairings for *Wine Watcher's World* and by pairing himself with young sommeliers. He spent much of his time on the road, preferring the anonymity of hotel rooms for his seductions. I'd brushed up against him once and considered myself lucky to have escaped. In truth, I'd forgotten all about him. Until now.

"I doubt he'd even remember me, which is probably a good thing," I said. "I was a lot prettier in those days."

"Ah, those goddamn, good ole, never-come-again, fuckin' old days!" Teukes said wistfully.

"Thanks for the archive," I said.

"*De nada.* Look, I'm beat. I gotta take off and get some sleep, but keep me posted. I want to know what you dig up."

He cackled, slapped the saddlebag, took a hit off the bottle of Stags' Leap, and ambled out of the bar. I watched him go. He was a lumbering child of a man with a mop of curly red hair that touched his shoulders. He towered over me, literally and figuratively. He'd been long gone from Berkeley by the time I got there, but I'd heard several versions of his story covering those years across the bar at Pancho's. In one he'd been summarily expelled after a maintenance man discovered him mixing a batch of acid at six in the morning. Another had it that he'd blown up a chemistry lab while making explosives for a demonstration at People's Park, then fled, abandoning his thesis in microbiology. Biddy did nothing to dispel the personal mythology that clung to him and, in fact, relished his own legend. He became a journeyman winemaker, kicked around Napa and Sonoma for years, knew everybody, and apparently had worked everywhere. It'd surprised me when he sought me out. Hearing that I'd arrived in the valley and taken up residence at Pancho's, he introduced himself, claiming to know my entire CV, and, I have to confess, I felt flattered.

Other than Mulligan and Gio, he was the only person with whom I'd developed a friendship since I'd moved to California.

I sat there silently awhile, nursing my scotch and trying to process everything that had happened since Norton's phone call that morning, but I was too exhausted to think. As I was getting ready to leave, Russ Brenneke walked in. He stopped by the bar, placed an order with Frank, and kept coming. He collapsed into the booth. He looked haggard.

"Can you believe this? Can you fucking believe this?" he said.

"Not really. How's Norton?" I said.

"Freaked out that he's a suspect."

"You don't really believe that he killed Wilson, do you? Richard made their reputation."

"You have to eliminate anyone who could have done it, one by one. But with his Mexicans locked up, he's trying to figure out how to salvage what's left of his harvest."

"Hey, it's just one tank," I said.

Mulligan stopped at the table and set a rum and Coke down. It was the only cocktail I'd ever seen Brenneke order.

"Thanks, Frank," Brenneke said, then continued: "He's ticked. Claims the wine was in great shape."

"I don't think whoever did this gives a rat's ass how the wine comes out."

"He's convinced that no one's gonna buy his wine this year. Thinks the whole vintage is a write-off."

"We could buy some for the bar, sell it as house wine. We could call it Blood Red."

Brenneke rolled his eyes. "Very funny. Anyway, he says it's not as if someone could just sneak into the winery. There are people around all the time."

"A winemaker friend said the same thing," I told him. "Do you bring in the INS?"

"We'll lose our witnesses if we blow the whistle. Anyway, that's out of our jurisdiction. But we can hold them, make 'em sweat a little, think we're gonna deport 'em, and see if we can jog something loose. A week or two, at most, and they're outta here."

"Migrant workers would never risk something like this. They've got perfectly good jobs."

Brenneke shrugged.

"What do you make of Fornes?" I asked.

"He's been working there for years. Norton tells us the place would grind to a halt without him." He paused. "Don't you ever try to pull a stunt like that again," he added, referring to my impromptu interrogation.

"You talk to Carla Fehr?"

"Yablonski, my corporal, swung by her place this afternoon. She told him he just missed you." He took the straw out of his drink and emptied half the glass. Then he squared off in his seat and stretched his hands on the table. "I'm pretty aggravated with you, Stern. What the hell do you think you're doing?"

"Just trying to help Janie find her brother."

"Well, we found him," Brenneke said. "So, as far as you're concerned, it's 'case closed.'"

He drained his drink and waved Frank to bring him another.

"Do you have any idea what you're up against here?" I said. "Wilson's huge. The press is going to be all over this. They were already setting up when I left the station. You need to brace yourself."

"Tell me about it. The county homicide guys are breathing down our necks. The DA's suits took the chief out for dinner and a lecture. DOJ is sending their characters from Sacramento first thing in the morning. If I don't come up with something shortly, Jensen's going to want my badge."

"Give yourself a break, Russ," I said. "You're just getting started."

"Yeah? Well, you're all done. You're gonna make your life very complicated, you keep this up. Jensen tipped over when I showed him my notes of our little conversation. And when Yablonski informed him you'd dropped by to pay a call on Carla, he went ballistic."

Mulligan delivered the second drink, and Brenneke sucked most of it down in a single draught. I realized that I'd better cool it, or they'd start thinking that I was trying to mess with their evidence, compromise witnesses, or, worse yet, cover my tracks.

"You need to understand something," I said.

"Yeah? And what's that?" Brenneke said, sitting back in the booth with a thud.

"Richard Wilson and I were close. It was a long time ago, I admit that. But we were friends, good friends. He introduced me to Janie. There's no fucking way. I was just trying to help her find him. That's all. I know it looks a little fishy, but it's a coincidence. Norton called *me* and told me to come out there this morning."

He sat there, listening.

"You done?" he said.

"Yeah, that's it. I get it. I'm out of it. It's all yours." I held up my hands.

He took my left one by the wrist, held it to my face, and leaned across the table. He was studying me as if he were trying to make up his mind about something.

"There's one more thing, but it's not for public consumption." He paused for a moment, then said, "Never mind," letting go of me. He lifted himself out of the booth, pulled a ten-dollar bill from his pocket, and tossed it on the table. "Tell your wife Jensen's gonna call her tomorrow."

Outside the Airstream, the edges of everything had lost their definition in the darkness. Bats described a terrible geometry against the eucalyptus, which cast a deeper shadow against the sky, black on black on black. The night wind whispered and a spotted owl hooted plaintively, "Who? Who?"

"Good fucking question," I said.

I pulled out my phone and sat down at the picnic table.

Gio picked up on the second ring.

"I was hoping you'd call," she said. "I can't believe it."

"Word travels fast."

"The whole valley's talking about it. Everybody's stunned. What happened?"

I described the call from Norton, my trip to the winery, and the scene I'd walked in on. I tried to explain why I'd looked for Richard—Janie's request and my history with him. Halfway through, I realized I was trying to justify myself and stopped.

"You don't have to explain," she said, her voice soothing me. "I understand. Really, I do. I just wish you'd told me. That you felt comfortable enough to tell me. Why don't you trust me?"

"I do trust you."

"It feels like you're hiding something from me." I didn't say anything and realized that my silence was damning me. After a moment, she said, "Do you still love her, Babe? If you do, you should go back to her. I mean it. I'd understand." She paused. "I'd be angry, but I'd understand."

"That's why I love you," I said. It wasn't untrue.

"I love you, too," she said. "You must be exhausted."

"I'm dead," I said and instantly regretted it. "Sorry, that wasn't meant to be a joke."

"Will you call me tomorrow?" Gio said.

"I promise."

We clicked off and I walked to the trailer, lugging Biddy's saddlebag. Chairman Meow hopped up the steps, stalled, and threw me an inscrutable look. When I opened the door, he walked to the rear of the trailer, leapt onto the bed, and curled himself into an ouroboros of fur. I put the bag on the kitchen table, kicked off my boots, and followed him to the mattress, lifted him gently, and wrapped my body around his. He stretched and laid one paw gently on my cheek like a lover, then extended his claws.

10

woke up early the next morning but stayed in bed, thinking. I wanted to put Wilson's murder behind me, but it wasn't that easy. I thought if I could only tie up a few loose ends, I could lay it—and him—to rest.

I knew I had to catch Jordan Meyer before he headed out to lunch, if I was lucky enough to catch him in New York at all. The voice at the other end of the line at *Wine Watcher's World* sounded like a sip of '61 Lafite—if '61 Lafite could talk.

"Good morning. *Wine Watcher's World*. How may I direct your call?"

"Jordan Meyer, please."

"One moment."

While I waited I listened to a recorded voice touting the highlights of their forthcoming issue: "*. . . and look forward to Lucas Kiers, our correspondent in Burgundy, covering the recent vintage of French Pinot Noir . . .*"

The silky voice came back on the line. "I'm sorry, but Mr. Meyer is currently traveling."

"Shit," I muttered.

"May I take a message?"

"Any way I can track him down?"

"Mr. Meyer is in San Francisco. You're welcome to leave a voice mail," and without waiting for my reply, she connected me. I hung up and redialed.

"Hi. I just spoke with you a minute ago. We were disconnected. Can you tell me where Mr. Meyer is staying in San Francisco? He's expecting my call."

She was clearly annoyed, and hesitated before coughing up the information.

"I believe he's at Campton Place," she said. "Anything else?"

"You've been very helpful."

It was too early to call Meyer. I brewed a pot of espresso, put Bach's cello suites on the CD player, and lit a cigarette. I needed to calm down. Over coffee, I dumped Biddy's archive onto the table. There were several dozen copies of Wilson's newsletters and half as many of Eric Feldman's *American Wine Review.* I sorted Wilson's chronologically, then weeded out the ones I already owned and had read. Each issue, while covering a range of varietals and appellations, focused on a particular country or region. While the more recent issues of *The Wine Maven* constituted a complete collection, it appeared that two California issues published after my move to Napa were missing. Biddy had said that might be the case. He had probably loaned them to friends who wanted to see how they had fared at Wilson's hands.

I was thinking I should follow Brenneke's advice and let the cops deal with it. I left the newsletters on the table, pulled James Crumley's *The Wrong Case* from the shelf above my bed, lay down, and read a few pages, but I was restless and couldn't concentrate.

I returned to the front of the trailer, sat down again, and leafed through Feldman's newsletters. Janie was right: The whole project was patterned after the *Maven*, right down to the regional headings, the breakdown by varietal and vineyard, the scoring system, even the buff-colored stock. Wilson had written Feldman's name, elaborately, at the bottom of his calendar. But Janie thought that they weren't talking to each other. Their falling-out had to have been bitter, yet Feldman had left a message at Wilson's apartment. There was a phone number on the back page of his newsletter with the subscription information. I figured I might as well try Feldman myself to hear his version of the story. There's always a story.

A machine picked up. *"You have reached the office of American Wine Review. We regret that we are not able to answer your call. Mr. Feldman is currently traveling in Europe in order to bring you the most up-to-date information on the coming vintage. Please leave your name and telephone number after the beep, and we will return your call at the earliest possible time. For subscription information, press 1 or visit our website. Thank you for your interest. Santé."*

Europe, huh? How convenient.

I walked back to the trailer and prepared a simple omelet to cheer myself up, brewed a second pot of espresso, and let Yo-Yo Ma soothe my soul. As I carried the pan to the picnic table, my cell trilled its idiotic ditty. I set my breakfast on a plank, pointed my finger at Meow, who had followed me outside, to warn him off, and trotted back to the trailer. My phone informed me that it was the St. Helena Police Department.

"Tell me you've got a break in the case," I said.

But it wasn't Brenneke. It was Jensen.

"The only thing I want to break is your balls, but Ciofreddi's going to do that for me. He wants your ass in his office at ten o'clock. Sheriff's department in Napa. Have fun."

He slammed the phone down. I wandered back to my breakfast. The Chairman had polished off a corner of the omelet and was stretching and purring in satisfaction.

"Damn it!" I said. "I told you not to touch that!" He bent to lick his paw, the feline equivalent of giving me the finger. It even looked like he was giving me the finger.

I decided it was just late enough to try Meyer. Unlike me, he was probably ensconced in his room, enjoying an elaborate room-service breakfast.

"Jordan Meyer." His enunciation was clipped.

"Mr. Meyer, my name is Babe Stern. We met years ago. In Seattle."

"Yes, Babe." I knew the name would get him even if he couldn't put a face to it.

"I'm investigating the disappearance and murder of Richard Wilson on behalf of his sister." I heard him suck air. "I'm living in Napa these days. Is there any chance we might get together? Have dinner or a glass of wine? I'd be happy to come to the city."

"Actually, I'm doing a piece on the new crop of French bistros. I have a reservation this evening at Bouchon. I'd be delighted to have company. It gets so lonely dining alone."

I'm sure it does, I thought.

"That'll be fine," I said.

"I'll call Tom. My reservation's at six thirty. I apologize for the early hour, but I need to get back to the city."

"No problem," I said.

"*À bientôt*, then," Meyer crooned.

All I could hope was that he'd live up to his reputation as a world-class gossip and that the dinner would be quick, as he'd indicated.

In the empty and echoing foyer of the Napa sheriff's department, an unprepossessing old coot with a jaundiced complexion, strands of greasy hair combed over a sweaty forehead, leaned into the reception window and froze me between his one good eye and the other, which wandered to three o'clock.

"Yeah? Can I help you?" he said.

"I'm here to see Lieutenant Ciofreddi."

"You have an appointment?" He exhibited all the charm and hospitable bonhomie of a civil servant confronted by one of his employers, otherwise known as a member of the taxpaying public.

"As a matter of fact, I do. At the lieutenant's invitation."

"Wait here," he said.

Where did he think I was going? Down to the Napa River to do a little fly-fishing? He disappeared into the back and emerged a few moments later.

"Okay," he conceded. "Go around to the side." He met me at the door and led me through the office, handing me off to a lovely young woman whose tall and slender frame was accentuated by a pink oxford shirt and black slacks. Short brown hair framed a pretty and intelligent face. She smiled as she extended a delicate hand.

"Hi, I'm Joan, Charlie's secretary. Come on back."

Open file cabinets, their shelves crammed with color-coded folders, banked the walls. We passed into another set of offices, and she directed me to the waiting area.

"He'll be with you in a minute."

A pair of inspirational posters extolling the virtues of teamwork and momentum adorned the walls. MOMENTUM read IT IS OF NO IMPORTANCE WHERE WE STAND BUT IN WHAT DIRECTION WE ARE MOVING. Good advice, since, as far as I could tell, I was currently nowhere. Maybe I should hit the road, I thought, follow Eric Feldman to Europe. I certainly wasn't getting very far on my home turf.

I sat down to flip through a magazine but was distracted by another poster on the wall, bearing the department's mission statement in the form of a list: LOYALTY INTEGRITY COMPASSION FAIRNESS LEADERSHIP. I wondered why the Napa boys had never bothered sharing these noble dicta with their brethren in Oakland or on the LAPD. Under INTEGRITY I read WE ARE DEDICATED TO HONESTY AND TRUTHFULNESS IN OUR ACTIONS AND WILL UPHOLD OUR ETHICAL BELIEFS REGARDLESS OF THE CONSEQUENCES. I made a mental note to pass this along to Brenneke, who appeared to have lost his own somewhere between the upper Klamath and Mount Shasta.

My meditation was interrupted by the appearance of Lieutenant Charlie Ciofreddi. He was a big guy, standing six-one and weighing in at two twenty. I was surprised by the tasteful style of his olive green shirt and matching suit but was brought back down to earth by the tie selection. He sized me up, must have seen something he liked, and offered his hand.

In his office, he took off his jacket and casually tossed it over his shoulder holster, which itself had been unceremoniously plunked on a cabinet behind his desk.

"So, you're a pal of Brenneke's?"

"You could say that."

"Thought you'd pay him back, help him out on this one?"

The twinkle in his eyes blended equal parts curiosity and impatience, his nose a giant question mark of skepticism stitching them together. A cop's cocktail of a face.

"Janie Wilson is my ex-wife. She asked me to poke around after her brother disappeared. I was simply keeping Russ posted on what I dug up."

Ciofreddi riffled through a stack of papers on his desk and pulled out a sheet.

"In that case, let's go through it from the beginning. I want to hear all about it—when Wilson appeared at your bar, what he said, how he seemed to you, the whole shot. And please don't leave anything out," he added, looking up from the report Brenneke had passed along.

I replayed everything that had transpired from the moment Richard had walked into Pancho's until I had arrived at Norton the morning they discovered his body. Then I described my returning to the winery and my conversation with the French intern.

"Jean . . . Pie-tot? How do you pronounce his last name?" Ciofreddi asked, pointing to the place on the report.

"*Pea-toe*," I said, leaning forward to read it.

"And you said he left to visit his sister."

"That's what he told Norton. We were all in the tasting room, and he stopped by to say he was leaving."

"Well, the sister verified his alibi. They live in Healdsburg. Go on."

I told him about my call to Carla Fehr and her pique over Wilson's failure to show up for dinner.

"Why did you think they were having an affair?" Ciofreddi asked. "Did Wilson say anything?"

"No. But when I called her, she didn't realize it was me, at first. She thought it was Richard. It was pretty clear."

"Why did you suspect it at all? Why'd you call her in the first place?"

"Have you seen her?" I said, smiling.

"I see. And then you went back to Norton?" I nodded. "Why?" he said.

"I still didn't know where Richard was. I wanted to ask Colin if he knew anything."

"And he didn't."

"No. He said he'd left Wilson at the winery."

"Isn't that unusual?" Ciofreddi asked, setting the report down. "Seems pretty strange to me," he added, narrowing his eyes.

"I thought so, too," I said. "Norton said he had to leave and asked Wilson to lock up."

"Odd," he said, shaking his head.

"I suppose so. But I can tell you, having read the last ten years of Wilson's newsletters over the past couple of days, that he had a long, and very favorable, history with Norton. My guess is that Norton trusted him with the keys to the castle, so to speak."

"All right. We'll let that go, for the moment. Tell me about Teukes. He's a friend of yours?"

I described my relationship with Biddy, how he'd looked me up when I first arrived at Pancho's, and that we respected each other's experience in the industry, as different as they were.

"You ever read Wilson's reviews of his wines?" Ciofreddi said.

"From what I can tell, Wilson never wrote about Tanner Cellars," I said.

"I mean, before Teukes went to Tanner."

He could tell from the look on my face that I had no idea what he was talking about.

"I thought you just said you'd read all of Wilson's stuff?" he said.

"I'm missing a few issues."

He fished a manila folder from the stack of papers on his desk, pulled out two issues of *The Wine Maven*, and handed them to me.

I looked at the covers. Both issues were titled "California." I checked the dates. They were the copies missing from Biddy's archive.

"Go ahead," Ciofreddi said. "Where the paper clips are. The relevant passages are highlighted."

The first, dating back four years, was a review of Tucker Winery. Wilson opened it with an apology for printing it at all but justified its inclusion by describing the expense lavished by Andrew Tucker on the vineyards and winery and the fanfare attending the release of their wines. The descriptions of the wines themselves were some of the most scathing I had ever read, and the scores—in the low to mid-sixties—assured that no one would pay the prices Wilson had printed in parentheses.

I looked up at Ciofreddi.

"Keep going," he said.

The second issue, published two years later, had a third of a page devoted to Clos de Carneros: three bottlings of Chardonnay and another three of Pinot Noir. Ciofreddi had highlighted the whole passage in bright orange, and the words—Wilson's language was, if anything, even more incendiary than his review of Tucker—seemed to burn on the page. This time he mentioned Teukes by name. The scores were in the fifties.

I handed them back to Ciofreddi.

"You ever seen these before?" he asked.

"No."

"You say you and Wilson were out of touch for a while?"

"Ten years, probably."

"Your wife ever tell you about a death threat he received?"

"Are you serious?" I couldn't believe it. Ciofreddi leaned back in his chair.

"Teukes was the winemaker at both places when they got those reviews. I was a sergeant at the time. We thought it might be him, but we could never prove it."

I didn't know what to say. No wonder Teukes had edited the selection of old issues he'd brought over. It explained why he seemed so curious about, even obsessed with, finding out what had happened to Wilson.

"The only person Biddy said might harbor a serious grudge over a review was Michael Matson," I said.

"Whom you also visited," Ciofreddi remarked, glancing at the report. "Daniel Hauberg called Jensen this morning and told him that Matson was at his winery the whole day and night. He said he'd testify, if he has to."

"I guess Biddy was trying to deflect attention from himself. Sent me off on a wild goose chase."

We were both quiet for a while. I didn't know what Ciofreddi was thinking, but I was trying to formulate what I was going to say to Biddy the next time I saw him.

"So, who's your money riding on?" he finally said, looking at me with genuine interest.

"What money?" I said.

He smiled. "It cuts pretty close to home, after all."

"Well, certainly not Fornes," I said.

"Then who?"

"I honestly don't know. That's your job."

"Good, I'm glad you understand that. So do me a favor: I can't prevent you from talking to people in your bar, but you're in over your head. Stay out of this and let us do our work. But pass along anything you think we ought to know about, anything you hear at the bar or from your wife or from your friend Teukes. This is a high-profile case. Way too much publicity. Too many theories and insufficient evidence, at least for the moment. I don't know, maybe it's too much evidence. Boot prints, tire tracks, rubber gloves—a winery's a messy place for a murder. Anyway, we're close. We haven't found a print that didn't belong there. You have to have motive, and you have to have opportunity."

Ciofreddi stood and handed me his card. "Stay in touch," he said.

"No problem," I said, standing, grateful that he hadn't scolded or ridiculed me.

"And call me if you stumble on something you think I should know."

"I promise. Really."

He nodded and escorted me out.

"Brenneke tells me you used to be a pretty famous wine guy," Ciofreddi said as we entered the main room. Two uniformed cops and another detective were talking and threw me supercilious looks as we passed. In one of their cubicles I saw signed photographs of Jerry Orbach, Dennis Franz, and William Petersen. *We're all play-acting*, I thought to myself.

"Yeah, very famous. Once upon a time," I said to the lieutenant and waved good-bye to Joan.

As I opened the door to leave, I heard Ciofreddi say, "He's harmless. He has no idea what he's doing. There's nothing to worry about."

Unable to quibble with that assessment, I decided to wander down to the water for a peek before driving home. The slime-green current of the Napa River moved sluggishly, an objective correlative to the way I felt. Just as I was about to turn away, an osprey fluttered momentarily, then dove precipitously and plucked a glinting, silver-spangled fish from the murky surface of the river.

11

decided to call Janie from the parking lot. Her secretary told me she was hoping she'd hear from me.

"How are you?" she said, slightly breathless.

"I'm all right."

"Where are you?"

"The Napa sheriff's department."

"My God, Babe," she said. "Danny said they questioned you in St. Helena, too. What's going on?"

"Nothing. It's fine. It just looked a little suspicious when I started searching for Richard."

"Well, stop, will you? It's over."

Her concern for my safety touched me.

"How's Danny?" I asked.

"He's pretty scared. I wish you hadn't involved him in this. I set him up in one of the labs. He's got his own little lab coat and a microscope. You should see him. I just want to take his mind off all of this if I can."

"That's good. Thank you." We were walking the thin line of caring about each other, and neither of us knew what to say. "Have you made plans for the funeral?" I asked.

"I need to wait for them to finish the autopsy. I'm not sure. Lieutenant Ciofreddi said he'd call and let me know when they're ready to release the body." Janie paused. "There's something you probably should know, something they're not telling the public." I waited patiently. "One of Richard's hands was cut off," she said.

"What do you mean, 'cut off'?"

"Cut off. Amputated."

So that's what Brenneke had nearly told me and then decided not to divulge.

"Where is it?" I said.

"They haven't found it yet. They're looking."

I pictured the hand adrift in the *foudre.* Would it have floated or sunk to the bottom? It was probably resting on the lees.

"Tell Danny I love him," I finally said, the only thing I could think to say.

"Okay." She paused. "Babe, take care of yourself, will you?"

"I'll try," I said. "You too."

I was going to have to confront Biddy—I had no choice—but I doubted that he'd unburden himself with a full confession. Clearly, he'd removed the issues of the *Maven* that might have implicated him so I wouldn't see them. He probably didn't want me spending an evening with Jordan Meyer either, dredging up old stories. That explained the look on his face when I told him I might call Meyer. I chided myself that I'd never asked him about his own résumé. He felt betrayed that I hadn't told him about my relationship to Wilson. *Okay*, I said to myself: *We're even.*

It was a little before noon, but during crush, there's no such thing as a lunch break. As I ran down 29 to Rutherford, I pieced together what I *did* know of my friend's career. I had always assumed that Biddy's having been named winemaker at Tanner had been a feather in his cap—a certain amount of prestige, certainly, but, especially, more money. It had never occurred to me that his position at Tanner, a large commercial winery, represented a step back, a demotion. Both Tucker and Clos du Carneros were small boutique operations known for their obsessive attention to detail. They were aiming for the top tier, and though they probably couldn't hope to fly with Screaming Eagle, to hit the level of Colgin or Bryant Family, they might find themselves in the esteemed company of Staglin and Sir

Peter Michael. That is, if the wines had been any good. Biddy's botching successive vintages at two quality wineries had forced him out of the heady precincts of the "handcrafted" and consigned him to the bottom soil of mass production.

I found him on the sprawling floor of Tanner, directing a crew of Mexican workers who were cleaning the facility after a long morning of crushing and pumping Cab into giant, temperature-controlled, stainless fermenting tanks. As I stepped into the winery, they were finishing up. They had rinsed the gondolas, hosed down the cylinders of the crusher and destemmer, and flushed the press and were heading out. Biddy was making the rounds of the tanks, checking that their temperatures were right.

I stepped over a hose snaking its way across the slab. Biddy saw me from a distance and waved me to his side.

"An early day," he said. "Gimme just a minute," he added, examining the controls on a tank and making notes on a clipboard. "So, *que pasa?*"

"I just had a conversation with the sheriff," I said. "Very interesting."

"Yeah? Have they arrested anybody yet?"

"Not yet, but they're getting closer." It wasn't true, but I had a sudden urge to make him sweat. He looked up from the clipboard. "Why didn't you ever tell me about your history with Wilson?" I said.

"Why didn't you tell me he was your brother-in-law?" His voice had an edge to it.

"You left out a few very important issues from the saddlebag you gave me."

"What issues would those be?" he asked with mock innocence as he scribbled up the chart, not bothering to look at me. Then he handed the clipboard to one of the crew and told him to hang it in the office. I followed him across the vast expanse of the winery floor to a door labeled HOMBRES.

He towered over the urinal and sighed deeply as he pissed. "Jesus, I needed that."

"That he slammed you twice, nailed you at Tucker and Carneros," I said.

"Ancient history, Babe." His tone was genially dismissive as he rinsed his hands at the sink.

"Bear any grudges?" I said.

"Hey, man, life goes on. 'Keep on truckin'.'"

"Thanks. That's just what I came for. A little philosophy from Mr. Natural to allay my suspicions."

He pushed the door open, and we emerged into the quietly humming, refrigerated universe of wine.

"You ever threaten Richard?" I asked. "Charlie Ciofreddi at the sheriff's department says Wilson received a death threat a few years ago. Seems to think you might know something about it."

At last he turned to face me. "I refuse to testify."

"You're incriminating yourself."

"A youthful prank."

"It's a fucking crime," I said, my voice echoing in the cavernous space.

He dropped his voice and knelt to retie a bootlace. "I just thought I'd shake him up a bit. He needed to understand that people's livelihoods are at stake."

"Ciofreddi's gonna call you."

"Whaddya go and tell him for?" He looked up in disgust and walked toward the hangar door.

"I didn't tell him anything. He told me."

"So, now what do we do?" I could feel him cutting distance, waiting for my next move, but the assumption of a *we* who were in this together presumed a complicity I couldn't share. He rolled one of the two enormous doors shut. I followed him to the other side.

"Look, Bid, I'm not suggesting I think you did this. There are other people with motives."

"That's reassuring," he said disgustedly.

He pulled the second door closed and locked up, walked to his motorcycle, hoisted it off its kickstand, and with one stroke set its engine aroar.

"What do you take me for, man? You think I'm a fucking criminal?" He glared at me from the saddle, revving the bike ferociously.

"You trying to scare me with that thing?" I asked.

"I'm beat, dude. Got one afternoon to crash. I need to be back before dawn."

He roared off, the engine's growl fading to a purr in the distance.

I decided to take the long route home. I wanted to soak in the air, the light. With harvest nearing completion, the vineyards looked skeletal, their leaves golden and browned. I took the Rutherford Cross past the Silverado Trail and followed Sage Canyon Road around Lake Hennessey. The wind had picked up. The willows lining its banks shook, and waves broke in tiny whitecaps across its face. The sun played on the hills as I cut through to Pope Valley. The farms were peaceful here, and its tranquility seemed a world away from the monstrous egos and petty vendettas that gripped Napa.

I got back to the trailer and lay down. My head was spinning. I wasn't sure where I stood with Janie. We seemed to be dancing around each other, not certain whether we were in this together. I was worried about her, and about Danny, and my fears for them kept fighting with my affection for Gio. I couldn't make up my mind whether to drop the whole thing and declare my undying love for my girlfriend, or if I should tell Gio that I still loved my wife and hoped to return to her, or at least try to. The only thing not in doubt was that I adored my son and regretted having involved him at all. That I had been shortsighted and self-serving. I seemed to be more interested in proving to him that his old man could step up to the plate and hit it out of the park. Who was I kidding? Fat chance, as Fornes had said. Try to make peace with your ghosts and see how far you get.

Teukes was another matter altogether. We had assumed there was a friendship, a shared set of interests and passions, but it ran only skin-deep. I hadn't really told him much about myself, and he hadn't opened up to me about the setbacks he'd suffered in his peripatetic career. More than that, the story Ciofreddi had told me suggested that Biddy had a violent streak I didn't know was there, something bottled up just beneath the surface that threatened to erupt if you crossed him or rubbed him the wrong way. I had felt it on the floor at Tanner.

I thought about canceling the dinner with Jordan Meyer. What was the point? Wilson was dead. Both Ciofreddi and Brenneke had warned me to back off. I was out of my depth, as Ciofreddi put it. But there was something gnawing at me that wouldn't let me drop it.

It was time for a nap. I put on a Bill Evans CD. *At least I'd get a decent meal out of it*, I said to myself as I drifted into an uneasy sleep.

12

Jordan Meyer was seated on the edge of the dining room at a deuce on the banquette. I'd remembered the man as tastefully put together, but the image collapsed as I neared the table. He was now huge, his shirt straining across his gut and his jacket tight on his swollen limbs.

"Babe, how nice to see you" he said with exaggerated warmth, looking me up and down, visibly disappointed. Time had worked its sorry magic on us both.

"Nice to see you again, too, Mr. Meyer."

"Let's pick something to drink, shall we?" he said hurriedly, hiding behind Bouchon's oversize *carte des vins* with relief. "Any suggestions?" he queried. How would I know? I couldn't see a thing. "So," he said, settling back and rather too obviously feeling the lurid pleasure of the topic at hand. "The estimable Richard Wilson crushed and fermented. That must have been some barrel!"

"An oak *foudre*," I said. He'd obviously already made inquiries and knew at least a few of the details of Wilson's murder.

"Excuse me!" Meyer called out to a passing waiter. "Get us the *grand plateau de fruits de mer*! And an order of the caviar. You do like caviar, don't you? Oh," he looked up at the waiter he had waylaid, "and a large bottle of Vittel and a bubbly Badoit. I never know what

I'm going to want, flat or sparkling, so we'll have them both. And find the wine steward, pronto. We want to order some wine." As soon as the waiter was certain Meyer had finished with him, he evaporated.

My companion turned back to me.

"The curious thing about our dear and departed Mr. Wilson is that he thought of himself as the great crusader, the champion of the consumer. Yet, by setting himself up as an arbiter of fine wine, he opened the Pandora's box of wine scores. Now people cower in fear at ordering any bottle with less than ninety points. I think it's safe to say that Richard Wilson might be held personally responsible for inflating the market value of wine by at least four hundred percent in the past decade, don't you?"

His look was challenging, and he expected an answer.

"Your magazine followed suit, didn't it? You use the hundred-point system."

"What is one to do? You have to keep up with the Joneses," he said.

"I can't say I follow it all that closely anymore. I used to. Back when I first met you."

"Yes, when was that? I'm sorry I couldn't place you immediately, but then, I meet so many people."

"Seattle. At Diva."

"Ah, yes, of course, of course." It was obvious he had no recollection of it at all. He sent his eyes to the menu. "So, what do you think? I'm contemplating the *gigot*. Have the *steak frites,* and we'll order a nice bottle of red."

"I was thinking about the roast chicken. You know what Julia says."

"Seems a bit pedestrian, but have it your way. And I think we should have a little intermezzo. The salmon *rillettes*, perhaps. But you're from salmon country, so that would be silly, wouldn't it?"

"I left Seattle a while ago. I'm living here now."

A pert brunette approached the table, radiant in her crisp white apron and black vest.

"Ah, our sommelier! Or should I say *sommelieuse?*" he offered coyly.

"Good evening, Mr. Meyer. What shall it be this evening?"

"Let's start with the Nuits-Saint-Georges *blanc* from Gouges. Fascinating wine," he said, turning to me. "A mutant strain of Pinot Noir that flowered and fruited as white wine. Quite exotic. And slip in a couple flutes of Clicquot for the caviar. That's a good girl." He lowered his voice as she left the table to locate the bottle. "Women sommeliers, all the rage right now," and raised his eyebrows in disapproval. "*Garçon!*" he bellowed, expecting the waiter to materialize at his beck and call. Which he did. There, just like that. "*Eh bien*, we'll have a fish course of the *rillettes de saumon*. And then I will have the *gigot d'agneau*, and my colleague, Mr. Stern, will try your *poulet rôti*. And find the mistress of wine again, would you? We need to have a little chat about Burgundy. Save room for cheese," he admonished me, leaving the waiter hanging. "Where were we?"

We were nowhere, as far as I could tell.

"Tell me about the crime! Describe it like you would a fine wine: bouquet, color, texture. First impressions, midpalate, finish." He rubbed his hands together and leaned into the table as the Champagne appeared as if by magic.

I told him as little as I could, just enough of the crime scene to whet his appetite, the forlorn figure of Francisco Fornes, the motives of Matson and Feldman. I was interrupted midtale by the wine ritual and the serving of the first course. He smeared crème fraîche on a slice of brioche and spooned half the caviar in a single heap, stuffing the whole thing into his mouth. I slurped a dollop and was reminded of how long it had been since I had tasted a woman. He ate greedily, wiping a few errant fish eggs from his moustache with his thumb. Then he started in on the oysters. Even so, I couldn't tell which he was devouring more avidly, the story or the food. One frenzy seemed to feed the other.

"Well, we'll get to Feldman. That's a story worth savoring!" Spoken like a tried and tested gourmand, saving the best for last. "You know, Matson's not the only poor soul Wilson pilloried," he continued. "There are others. Indeed, there are."

The waiter cleared the caviar and repositioned the enormous platter of shellfish.

"Slip in a little foie gras before the *rillettes*. Don't you think?"

he asked me. "You'll take some foie gras, won't you? Of course you will. And have our young lady bring us a glass of Sauternes, something simple. We'll save the last of the Gouges for the salmon." He stopped momentarily, to catch his breath. "Did you see his reviews of Tucker? Scalding! 'Thin, dry, putrid, amateur.' I've never read such vitriol. And then there was his treatment of Clos de Carneros! Unimaginable! The lowest scores I've ever seen awarded to a winery in successive vintages. I don't think either ever recovered."

As he replayed the reviews, his pleasure at seeing a winery taken out at the knees was palpable. The foie gras arrived, and, slathering a chunk on a wedge of toast, Meyer seemed to inhale it in one gulp. Then he dispatched the salmon *rillettes*, mopping it up with bread and then, when the basket was empty, with his finger, every act of ingestion infused with his innate lasciviousness.

At last he came up for air to order the red wine. The steward stood patiently at the table's edge as if she had all the time in the world. I felt for her and looked around the dining room. I wanted her to know that I was on her side.

"I'm thinking the Nuits from Arlot. What do you think?" Meyer asked distractedly.

"It's beautiful," she said approvingly. "Gorgeous, supple fruit. Elegant but nicely structured, very complex."

"What else?" he said, scanning down the list. "We could go California. We're here, after all. Sonoma Coast is hot. The Flowers, maybe," he proposed, waiting to see if she would endorse his selection.

"You could do that. It's a wonderful wine," the sommelier concurred, glancing across the dining room at a man I'd noticed trying to catch her attention, her tone salted with impatience, hoping Meyer would just pick something. I knew the game and felt sorry for her.

"No!" Meyer exclaimed. "Let's stick with France. Two Nuits. That's more intriguing."

He handed her back the list with finality, lapsing into a momentary and uncharacteristic silence. She fled and, after dealing with the guest across the room, returned with the bottle and two enormous goblets. She presented it to Meyer.

"Excellent!" he bellowed. "You're in for a treat, my boy."

She carved the lead, expertly pulled the cork, and sniffed it. She poured a splash in Meyer's balloon and stood at attention.

"Ah!" he moaned, rolling his eyes. "Blood of the gods!"

"Would you like me to decant it?" she asked.

"Oh, let's dispense with formalities. We're professionals, after all."

She carefully poured a few ounces in our glasses, set the bottle on a silver coaster, readjusted our stemware—we each had four wineglasses in front of us, cluttering the table—and disappeared.

We twirled and sniffed and sipped.

"Delicious," I said. It had been a while since I had tasted this caliber of French juice. The scent of violets rose to my nostrils. The flavors unfurled on my tongue. All the pretentious vocabulary came flooding back and suddenly seemed perfectly appropriate: sweetly roasted game laced with black cherries and chocolate.

"So, what do you know of the desiccated Mr. Feldman?" he probed.

I shared my dossier, which wasn't much. I told him about the wife's affair with Wilson—of which Meyer, of course, was already aware—and recounted the story of Wilson's and Feldman's tasting in France, which he told back to me in an even nastier version.

"He's a dry one, Feldman. A great intellect, certainly. Possesses a rare palate. But my God, what a lifeless fellow! As shriveled as a raisin. Where's the *joie de vivre*? I don't think the man likes food! I mean it. I've been at table with him. Don't tell my bosses," Meyer said, dropping his voice. "We're not supposed to fraternize with the enemy. He picks at his plate like an anorexic girl. For me, half the pleasure of wine is having it with fine cuisine. Wine and food. Of course, that's why I do what I do. Why drink the stuff if you can't enjoy it with a superlative meal? What's the point? To taste it and score it and think about it? Wine is a passion of the body as well as the mind. The pleasure is physical. Sensual."

I could feel his excitement mounting as he spoke. The entire ritual surrounding the wine seemed a kind of foreplay. But, obnoxious as he was, you had to admire his fervor, even if gluttony characterized everything he fixed upon.

"Do you think he hated Wilson enough to have killed him? Would he have the stomach for that?" I asked.

"Well, he's always seemed utterly spineless to me. But you have to admit, to lose your wife, your job. And you know these murderers. Have you ever noticed that the most notorious ones are these quiet, mousy little characters always lurking in the shadows? No one suspects anything, and then . . . *poof*! Somebody's dead. But if I were you," he said and dropped his voice to a whisper, leaning over the table, "I'd look at Tucker and Carneros. The winemaker at Tucker lost his job after Wilson reviewed them, then proceeded to Clos de Carneros, and *boom*, same thing." He glanced furtively around the room. "You know, Wilson got a death threat once. Right here, while he was in Napa. Fled in horror, but then, who wouldn't?"

"And you suspect that winemaker who went from Tucker to Carneros?" I asked.

"I have no idea," he said, his nose disappearing into the wineglass. "What *was* his name?"

"Teukes," I said.

"That's it! So, you know about it? Quite a giant of a fellow, with a firebrand's disposition. Benjamin Teukes. Got thrown out of Berkeley in the early seventies. The man has a huge ego and an indubitably shady past. Wholly unpredictable, in my opinion."

Just as I suspected, Meyer knew everything. He had it all—a pig with his nose in the dirt, rooting around for truffles.

"You know that Wilson's mother died recently?" he said.

I shook my head. I thought I'd hear Meyer's version.

"Robert Wilson, Richard's father, is reportedly hugely wealthy. But I understand he's quite ill. Probably not very much time left. The estate must be worth a fortune. Your employer . . ." He paused, his eyes teasing, provocative, the hint of a smile creeping over his lips. "I don't mean to suggest," he stuttered.

Sure you do, I thought.

"But families are, as we know, extremely tricky. Ah!" he exclaimed as the entrées arrived. "How marvelous!"

Conversation ground to a halt as Meyer devoured his lamb. Now his comments were reduced to a series of grunts and wheezing sighs of satisfaction. I remained firm in my conviction that Julia Child was right: Roast chicken is the test of a kitchen, and Bouchon's passed with flying colors.

When the table had been cleared, he opened another avenue. "I'm sure you know that Wilson infuriated our French friends a few years ago when he insinuated that they were showing him wine that never made it to the bottle. Mind you, they've never hesitated to fiddle with their wine when it suited the tune *du jour.* They chaptalize, they blend, fudge their appellations, water down with lesser stuff. But this was something of an entirely different order. He basically accused them—well, one *négociant* in particular—of arranging scores for the tastings and then bottling and selling a completely different wine for export. *Un vrai scandale!*"

"There's a young Frenchman working at Norton." I was hoping that Meyer might, finally, know something I didn't.

"Really?" He looked interested. "What's his name?"

"Pitot, Jean Pitot."

He shook his head. "Never heard of him. I doubt there's any connection. The French are sending their sons over all the time. Teach them the ways of the world, international-style, that sort of thing." He paused. "Have you met him?"

"Yes."

"Well, you might want to find out who his relations are."

After the waiter had cleared the table, Meyer ordered a sampler of cheese. There was just enough wine left in the bottle to pour us each a sip. Meyer made certain that I got the sediment.

"This is all very interesting, Babe. But if I were you, I would look more closely at the sister—no offense, but she did jump on this with suspicious avidity—and Teukes. There's a bona fide vendetta lurking somewhere in his oversize brainpan."

He lapsed into silence as he examined the plate of cheese, then said, "How about a Cognac? A glass of port?"

"I don't think I can." I was stuffed.

"Are you sure? *Wine Watcher's World* is paying."

"I can't. But thank you."

"All for the best, I'm sure. I have to get back to the city myself. The dreaded deadline."

We seemed to have exhausted the subject, and I watched as Meyer polished off the cheese plate one hunk at a time.

After he'd signed the bill, Meyer pushed the table out with dramatic finality, momentarily blocking the aisle. Then, as we made our way to the front of the restaurant, he received the bows, curtsies, and gestures of homage offered by everyone from the busboys to the hostess as if he were a prince.

Standing on the patio in front of the restaurant, Meyer gazed at the sky, a beatific smile spreading across his countenance.

"I will follow your progress with great curiosity," he said, fumbling for a business card from an elegant leather case. "I wish I could write about it myself, but Wilson and *WWW* . . . well, you understand. For our purposes, he mustn't exist. And now he doesn't." Laughing at his bon mot, he snapped his fingers like a magician.

13

Fog had seeped into the valley during dinner, and a light mist slickened the road. I took the Yountville Cross to the east side. The Silverado Trail glistened in the moonlight, wending its way north like a luminous ribbon. I was lit myself, the glasses of Champagne and Sauternes and two bottles of wine dulling my senses. The truck's headlights bounced off swaths of fog drifting across the road, and the regular click and swish of the windshield wipers lulled me into a trance as I took the curves up the mountain.

I turned onto the dirt road leading to the trailer. My eyelids fluttered heavily. All I wanted to do was sleep. And then my world exploded. The rear window of the cab shattered, the noise deafening in the confined space, and shards of glass showered across my neck and head. I slammed on the brakes, my heart pounding, pumping through my chest. I frantically searched the rearview mirror. Nothing. No light, no movement. I scrambled out of the truck and scanned the darkness. It was impossible to see anything through the fog. I shook bits of glass out of my hair and off my jacket, and peered through the open door on the driver's side, and then I saw it, incongruous and impossible: an arrow sticking out of the dashboard.

For a few moments, I was afraid to get back in the truck and just stood there, frozen with fear. Then I wiped the glass off the seat. I told myself to calm down, but all I could hear was my pulse throbbing in my head. I took a couple of deep breaths and gradually regained my composure, wondering what might happen next. Slowly, I pulled back onto the road, and the headlights picked out the gleaming shape of the Airstream. As I cut the engine, I thought I could make out the faint sound of a motorcycle through the shattered window disintegrating into silence but told myself I was hearing things, that it was only the rush of wind through the trees that swayed and shook against the moonlit sky.

The trailer squatted in a pocket of dead air beneath the towering pines. I staggered up the steps. I didn't see its rear window until I stepped inside. Glass lay splintered across the dining table and on the benches to either side.

"Fuck," I said. "What the fuck is going on?"

I just stood there, looking at the floor of the trailer, the fragments of glass at my feet like the pieces of a life I no longer knew how to put back together.

I went to the utility closet and got a broom and dustpan.

I'd stepped across a line I hadn't even seen and been declared fair game. Fear cramped my stomach as I bent to sweep the pieces into the dustpan. My hands were shaking as I dumped the glass into the waste basket.

It had never occurred to me that I might fail, that I might be afraid, that I might be next.

Calm down, focus, I told myself. But then an older, more destructive command crept into my consciousness, one I couldn't quite formulate.

Escape, it whispered.

In the medicine cabinet, I found an expired prescription of Xanax that dated to my breakup with Janie, and popped two, then a third just in case the pills had lost their potency. Even so, it took more than an hour to fall asleep, to escape.

I didn't surface from my drug-induced oblivion until late morning. I thought I'd better call Brenneke. I wasn't sure what else to do.

When you're in trouble, call the cops. Maybe Jensen had given him a Sunday off to play catch with his boys, though, under the circumstances, I doubted it.

Megan Brenneke, Russ's impossibly perfect wife, answered the phone.

"Hey, Megan. Babe Stern. Is the old man around?"

"Right here. Feet on the coffee table. But I should warn you: It's second quarter, and the 49ers are down by ten. Honey!" she hollered over the TV set. "Babe Stern's on the line."

I heard Brenneke moan. "Tell him I'm taking a nap."

"Honey!" Megan said, knowing that I'd heard him.

"Fine, fine, fuck it," he said, taking the phone. "Yeah? Whadda *you* want? I've got half a day with my family."

"Then turn off the game, cocksucker, and play with your kids."

"Fuck yourself. Sorry, honey. Turn down the tube, will you? Okay, what's so important?"

"Someone tried to kill me last night," I said.

"Sure they did," he said after a moment.

"I'd like to swing by, if you don't mind."

"Okay, but the game stays on. And pick up a pizza and a six-pack. I need to eat something before I go back to work."

The Brennekes lived in a small, tidy house on Tainter Street two minutes from the police station. The front yard was taken over by a jungle gym and swing set, and soccer balls, baseballs, and footballs lay strewn across the lawn as if a referee had just called time-out in some bizarre, mixed-genre sport. Megan answered the door in a jogging suit, her hair pulled back tightly from her face in a ponytail.

"I sent the boys off to play with friends. He's in a foul mood, just so you know."

Brenneke moved his feet a foot to his right on the coffee table to make room for the pizza. I pulled two bottles of Fat Tire from the carrier, cracked one, and handed it to Russ, who hadn't moved his eyes from the game.

"Argh!" he cried. "I can't believe it! How can you miss a pass like that? Where's the line? What have you got?" he asked, lifting the lid of the box.

"Italian sausage, pine nuts, and black olives."

"The case, shithead. What the hell happened last night?"

"Somebody shot an arrow through the back window of my truck. And broke a window of the trailer."

"An arrow?" Brenneke looked at me with disbelief.

"No shit," I said. "I have it outside, if you'd like to see the evidence."

"Weird," he said.

"That's it? That's all you've got to say?"

"I'll tell Jensen. And Ciofreddi, too. He needs to know." He turned back to the game. "You okay?" he said after a minute.

"I'm fine. A little freaked out."

"Where were you last night?" he asked.

"Having dinner with a source, a big mouth in more ways than one. These wine writers, there's little love lost."

"I thought you told Ciofreddi you were leaving this to us," he said through a mouthful of pizza.

"I'd already set it up." Brenneke just shook his head. "Look, neither of us thinks Fornes could have done this," I said.

"I never said that."

"And Norton has no motive. But Eric Feldman, his main competition, had a serious axe to grind. His answering machine says he's gone to Europe."

"And?"

"Wilson fired Feldman a few years ago. They got into an argument at some winery in France. It was bitter. But what made it worse is that Wilson was shtuping his wife on the side. She ended up leaving Feldman and went to work for Wilson in New York."

"All very interesting, very elaborate." Brenneke sat up just as the 49ers' quarterback got dumped for a ten-yard loss. "No protection," he said, taking a bite of pizza. "Anything else?"

"You need to talk with the French kid."

"Pitot."

"Wilson got into some big squabble with the French a few years ago. He thought they were giving him different wine in France than they were shipping to the States—first-rate juice over there, plonk for export. And pocketing the difference."

"How would you know?" Brenneke asked, looking at me.

"Well, you open a bottle here labeled as the wine you tasted in France, and you can tell the difference."

"No, idiot, I understand that. How would you know if Pitot had a motive?"

"You need to check his background, that's all. See if his family is the same one Wilson accused of defrauding the wine-drinking public. It shouldn't be hard."

"Who has time for this shit?" he said.

We watched the game together in silence until the clock ran out on the third quarter. The 49ers were still behind. Brenneke muted the set to spare us the beer commercials.

"So, what about the autopsy?" I asked finally.

"They found marks. He was hoisted with a forklift."

"That should narrow it down."

"You're really a fuckin' genius," Brenneke said. "Fornes just makes the most sense," he continued. "It has to be someone with access to the winery, for one thing."

"What's his motive?"

"Hatred and jealousy, pure and simple. Needed to vent his rage at the injustice of life. Happens all the time."

"The guy's legal," I protested. "He's got a green card."

"Could be a forgery. INS has it. They're giving it the once-over. And we found blood and hair on his rubber boots. And it was his knife—you know, the kind they use to harvest grapes—that was used to cut Wilson's hand off. It'll be a few days until the DNA results come back, but Jensen thinks it's a slam dunk."

I said nothing. It still made no sense to me.

Brenneke sat wrapped in a funk. His team was losing. *Both teams*, I thought. I rose to go.

"Go get me the arrow," he said. "We'll look into it. I'll show it to Ciofreddi. We'll follow up, I promise."

He went back to his game. As I reached for the doorknob, I heard Brenneke shout, "Hit 'im, you cocksucker!"

When I got back to the trailer, I called Janie.

"There's something I need to tell you. You have to promise not to get upset." She said nothing. "Someone tried to take me out last night."

"You had a *date*? It's about time! Why would that upset me?" She sounded relieved, even amused.

"No, not that kind of 'take me out.' Somebody tried to kill me. They shot an arrow through the window of my truck. And smashed a window at the trailer."

"Jesus, Babe! This is crazy." She was silent, then said, "I'm sorry I ever dragged you into this."

"Tell me about the estate," I said after a moment.

"What are you talking about?"

"A guy I had dinner with last night suggested that you were fighting with Richard over money."

"How about some sympathy for the loss of my mother and brother?"

"Relax. I'm not suggesting you killed him for the inheritance."

"There is no inheritance. Not yet. My father's still alive, if you don't mind."

"So, what was it over? Real estate?"

"Do you have any idea how much Richard makes, made, a year?"

"Not a clue."

"A couple million. Licensing, appearances, royalties. The newsletter's the least of it."

"You sound jealous."

"Oh, please."

I decided to change the subject yet again.

"My friend Biddy Teukes would appear to have made a death threat against your brother years ago."

"You're kidding," she said.

"Richard never told you about it?"

"Never."

"Well, he destroyed Biddy in print. Twice."

"Do you think he's the one who shot at you? What are you going to do?"

"I'm not going to do anything. The police know about it. I'm sure they're going to haul him in for questioning."

"Look," Janie said, "Forget it. This is ridiculous and really terrifying. Let the police do their work."

"I am. Is Danny around? I'd love to speak with him. By the way, would you mind if I pick him up later today? I'd like to get a visit in before he starts school. I sort of blew the last one."

"'Sort of'?" she said. "And do you really think that's a good idea, under the circumstances? I mean, if someone *is* trying to hurt you."

"It'll be fine, Janie. I'm fine. Nothing's going to happen. I'll protect him with my life."

And what if you lose your life, asshole? I thought. *Then what?*

She relented, and I drove into the city to pick him up. It was tough to get a conversation going with him on the way back to Napa.

"Dad, did you find out what happened to Uncle Rich?" Danny finally said.

"I haven't, sorry to say."

"It would be really awesome if you could solve it."

Leave it to your kid to cut to the bone.

"I thought we might fly some kites," I said, unwilling to own up to my failure as a detective. "Do something different. I picked up some stuff on my way to get you." I didn't want him worrying about Richard or his mother or his ailing grandfather. He needed a break. For that matter, so did I.

"Hunh," he said. "Okay. That sounds neat."

We spent that night cutting ripstop nylon, painting dragons' faces, and fastening sticks to the fabric. We cooked together, and after dinner I picked up where we'd left off reading *The Sword in the Stone.* At the rate we were going, we might finish *The Once and Future King* by the time he turned twenty-one.

The next morning I took him to a field not far from the trailer. The kites were less than perfect, but they flew, and we ran and laughed and launched each other's until mine got strung up in a pine tree at the edge of the field, its face gazing down at us fiendishly. In the afternoon I drove him back to the city. We parked, and Danny led me down a flight of steps to their bungalow. Janie answered the door, threw me a cool look, and hugged our son.

"You want to come in?" she said. Her invitation lacked conviction. I took my cue and embraced Danny, enfolding him for a little too long.

I drove home, feeling more bereft than I could ever have imagined. I was like a kite myself, cut loose from its string, sailing out of sight, as if no one were holding on.

14

By Labor Day the harvest was pretty much done. Families relaxed and picnicked, the wine was laid down in wood, and life went on. Kids started school; the tourist season let up but not too much. The valley took on its autumnal robe, the leaves yellowing to mustard and deep scarlet. The well-heeled clientele that could afford to wait until the masses had taken off thronged the verandas of Meadowood and Domaine Chandon and the Auberge du Soleil. By early October the evenings had grown as chill as the case.

Occasionally Russ Brenneke would wander into Pancho's, but he never took a stool. He and Yablonski, the Asian-looking corporal, would hunker down in a booth and keep to themselves. The Wilson case was, technically speaking, an "open investigation," and they continued to try to pin it on Fornes. He suffered for the unhappy coincidence of proximity and a string of damning physical evidence. They had his blood-spattered boots, but anybody could have slipped them on. All the workers' boots stood in a neat row in the employee changing room. Likewise, his gloves. But the fact of his pruning knife could not so easily be swept away. No one else's prints were on it.

But I knew, and was waiting for Ciofreddi to concede, that the Mexican's sole possible motive was flimsy at best. It simply made no sense. It turned out that his green card was bona fide even though it looked counterfeit, having been put through a washing machine inadvertently, and that the night of the murder he had left early to celebrate his daughter's birthday. A veritable village of Chicanos testified that he never left her side, though fewer cared to risk deportation by agreeing to testify on his behalf.

In any event, Francisco Fornes had resumed his responsibilities at Norton and could afford, with the fruit in, to keep a low profile until the pruning began. Our fall was his summer.

They'd questioned Matson repeatedly, but his alibi remained tight. He bounced back and forth between the two wineries that time of year and had spent the night at Chateau Hauberg, too exhausted to go home, just as Daniel Hauberg had said.

Ciofreddi remained unconvinced that Biddy hadn't finally resolved to pay Wilson back for the reviews, but that could hardly be proved in the face of Biddy's own alibi. Even Mulligan said that he'd come to Pancho's after getting off work and hadn't left until late.

And, just as Ciofreddi had told me, Jean Pitot had a sister married to an American winemaker. They lived in Sonoma County, and Jean had ridden his motorcycle over for a visit, his sister and brother-in-law confirming his story.

That left only Colin Norton. Though no one had seen him leave the winery, he'd arrived at Tra Vigne to meet his father for dinner. A maître d', waiter, and busboy all stated that he appeared to be in an ebullient mood, pleased by how the harvest was going. He was even overheard telling his old man that Wilson was certain to give the wines stunning reviews and astronomical scores. He had given a sworn statement that he'd left Wilson to write a few final notes and had raced to join his father. He'd been seated by seven o'clock, and they had lingered over port till nearly ten. While his departure from the winery presented a complication that couldn't be corroborated, there was no motive. In fact, he had every reason to want Wilson alive. No Wilson, no reviews.

There was still the arrow and the shattered window of the trailer to explain, but it turned out I hadn't been the only target. There'd been a series of late-night incidents and random acts of vandalism that the cops traced to the very troubled teenage son of one of the dysfunctional Holy Roller families that scratched out a living up near Angwin. They'd confiscated his crossbow and gotten a court order that put him into counseling for the foreseeable future. An unlucky coincidence was the official conclusion.

The press that had been hanging around disappeared as suddenly as it had materialized. On to the next inflated scoop, playing to a public with the attention span of a three-year-old. I returned to work, the petty tasks and details of managing the bar drowning me with their pointlessness. I had failed to crack the case and had let Janie and our son down. Too many permutations. I'd never been good at math.

One good thing had come out of all of it, though: I started calling Danny every few days. He hated his new school. Change is always rough on kids, but I wondered whether the death of his uncle, the deteriorating condition of his grandfather, and Janie's growing anxiety over both weren't equally the problem. She was worried, too, I knew, about both of us.

Gio and I picked back up, but the relationship had cooled. She couldn't understand why I'd never told her that Richard Wilson and I were related. Worse than that, she suspected I hadn't really cut myself off from Janie and that I harbored some deep longing to put the marriage back together. She wasn't wrong.

When I wasn't at the bar, I was home, listening to Monk or Chet Baker or Coltrane, reading Rilke and Machado, and making my way one recipe at a time through Richard Olney's *Simple French Food*. Thing was, there was nothing simple about Olney or his food, nor was there anything simple about the gnawing sensation that Richard's death constituted unfinished business for me personally.

As I trod my well-worn routine at Pancho's in the following weeks, I kept going back over the case. Danny was right, of course: I would have felt great had I figured out who'd killed his uncle. I was convinced that the cops had it wrong, but that's all I was convinced of. A migrant worker, especially one with a green card, doesn't kill a wine critic. Winemakers would love to kill wine critics—I'd heard them say so plenty of times, though their threats were all bluster and braggadocio fueled by alcohol—but winemakers are farmers, and farmers, as a rule, aren't really lunatics, even the ones who bury cow horns stuffed with manure in their vineyards.

I knew that Biddy Teukes was a little crazy—aren't we all?—and maybe he had fried a brain cell or two with too many hits of acid, but I was sure that, despite his perverse sense of humor, he wasn't a murderer. A rival writer seemed a more likely possibility, but neither Eric Feldman nor Jacques Goldoni had been anywhere near Napa the night Wilson had his hand amputated, his head stomped on, and his body forklifted into a cask of Cabernet Sauvignon. Even so, it was strange that both had decamped to Europe right after the murder.

No, this had to be a wack job, and I kept returning to the figure of Jean Pitot as if he were a weevil boring into the heart of a vine. Why didn't *he* figure higher on the cops' roster of suspects?

The last week of October, on a crystal-clear morning, I lit up a Cohiba a customer had laid on me as a tip and called Brenneke.

"Well, well," he said. "What's up?"

"I know you've been up shit creek for almost two months."

"Yeah, well, it seems to me your paddle's missing, too," he retorted.

"After the murder, Goldoni disappeared."

"He's been interviewed. We've got his statement."

"What about Feldman?" I asked.

"Ditto."

"Doesn't he get he's a suspect?" I said.

"He's not a suspect if he wasn't here, Sherlock. There's absolutely nothing to tie him to the scene."

"Doesn't it strike you as a little odd that they both left the country right after Wilson's body turned up?"

"You're the wine pro—you tell me. I thought that's what they did."

Brenneke was right.

"You guys follow up with Pitot?" I asked.

"Went home right after harvest. Norton said he had to help his own family make wine."

"He's the key to the whole thing," I said.

"Says who? What do you want us to do, extradite him?"

I paused a moment.

"I want to go over there," I said. "To follow them, follow the scent."

"You're nuts, Stern."

"I'd like you to talk to Ciofreddi, see if he can arrange a contact for me. A cop or something."

"What makes you think you can figure this out?" He sounded exasperated.

"Because I'm the only one who can."

He hung up on me, but two days later the phone rang. It was Ciofreddi.

"You know, I thought about sending someone over myself," he said, "but there's no budget, and I can't spare the manpower. We're understaffed as it is."

"Why don't you go yourself?" I suggested.

"Sure, take my vacation in the French wine country like I do every year." He paused. "I contacted the embassy in Paris. They contacted the consulate in Lyon. The bureaucracy is positively . . ."

"Byzantine," I offered.

"Exactly. Anyway, I asked if they could just keep an eye on these guys. They're over there every fall, as I guess you know."

"Not to mention Pitot," I said.

"Problem is, the Frogs don't have homicide detectives. Not in Burgundy, where Pitot lives. And no crime's been committed on French soil, so there's nothing they can do anyway."

I waited.

"If you go, it's got to be on your own dime and strictly ex officio, but I think I can set up the contact. There's a guy I've been in touch with, a colonel. All I ask is that you call me if something crops up."

"How are you on hunches?" I said.

"I get one every once in a while. Like you, I have an odd feeling about Pitot. Norton says he went home to help his family, but . . . I don't know. I figure you can blend in," he concluded.

"I know my way around," I said.

"So I hear. Let me think about this a little more." He paused, then said, "I'll get back to you in a day or two when I have it all set up."

I thanked him and looked at my cookie jar. I had a little over a grand saved in tips, plus Janie's fee, which she graciously refused when I offered her a refund. I'd need to travel simply and put my ticket on a credit card, but more than the money to pay for the trip, I'd need to make sure that it went smoothly, if I went at all. I decided to make another phone call.

"Biddy, I need to ask a favor of you."

"Oh, really? In exchange for what? Ciofreddi hauling me in for questioning?"

I ignored the gibe. "I'm going to France," I said. "I need a contact in the wine trade, to help me move in the same circles as Eric Feldman and Jacques Goldoni."

"And I should do this for you why?"

"Because you're well connected, and because it's important."

I could feel him mulling it over.

"You had nothing to do with Wilson's death," I said. "We both know that. It was just Ciofreddi, dredging up—what did you call it?—'ancient history.'"

"I don't know. It's not easy this time of year. There's one possibility: Frederick Rosen, an importer. Everybody calls him Freddie. He's in New York, but he usually goes to France after harvest to check on his growers. Occasionally he'll take two or three people with him. Let me make a call and see what I can do." He paused. "No promises," he said and hung up before I could say thanks.

I put Olney, Rilke, and Machado back in the bookcase and spent the next few days reading, reviewing maps, and making notes. From my old files I pulled the notebooks I'd kept years before. I made a list of the domaines I'd visited, their proprietors and phone numbers, and each night after I returned home from Pancho's, I made a few calls to France. On my last trip I'd stayed at a sweet little hotel in Aloxe-Corton, Le Chemin de Vigne, owned by a winemaker I'd once entertained in Seattle. The place had changed hands, as it turned out, but the woman who answered took the reservation. Les Trois Glorieuses, a weekend of debauched wine consumption, and its main event, the Hospices de Beaune, the gala auction of new wine held each year to benefit the local hospital, were scheduled midway through my visit. In normal circumstances, all hotels would be fully booked, but the woman at Le Chemin de Vigne had had a cancellation and told me that I was lucky to get a room.

I needed to call Janie to let her know what I was up to.

"I'm going to France," I announced. "I leave next week."

"If you think I'm going to pay for this . . ."

"You already have," I said. "I booked my ticket yesterday."

"What do you know that I don't?"

"Call it a hunch." I decided not to reveal anything else. It was better that way.

"What are you up to? It's over." Underneath the flippancy, I could hear the tension in her voice.

"Call it a hunger for real information. I'm following my nose and something stinks. Anyway, you asked me to find your brother's killer."

"I asked you to find my brother," she corrected me. "And you did."

I couldn't tell her I wanted to prove to her that she'd made a mistake ever leaving me.

"I promise to be home by Thanksgiving. Tell Danny," I said.

"What makes you think I'm going to give him up for Thanksgiving?"

"I just thought . . ."

"Just promise me something: that you'll be careful," she said quietly. "I don't think I could bear losing someone else."

That got me.

"I didn't know you cared," I said.

"I do."

It was only the second time I remembered ever hearing her utter those words.

I asked Frank if he could handle the bar for a couple of weeks, give or take a few days, and he agreed. In fact, given my recent state of distraction, he seemed relieved to get rid of me. He even offered to look in on the Chairman and make sure his bowls were filled.

I got a SIM card for international calls installed in my cell. I didn't want to pay a hotel's tariffs every time I needed to hear Danny's voice. And Ciofreddi asked me to let him know if and when I came across anything interesting. When I looked at it in the cold, hard light of day, the whole thing seemed a fool's errand, but who could say?

I wasn't sure what was coming, but just as I knew I'd had to walk out on my life in Seattle, I knew that something had changed, that I'd reached a turning point, and that there was no going back.

As the plane banked over the bay, I was blinded momentarily by the sun, then picked out the Golden Gate Bridge as it extended from the city in a sagging blood-red arch across the water, its far span disappearing in fog.

15

had a window seat on the plane, and as we descended into Paris, I could just make out the spire of the Eiffel Tower in the distance. It felt as if I'd traded one landmark for another, as if the arc of the case had simply been translated into another language.

I had a couple hours before I needed to catch my train to Dijon and decided to pay a visit to Jonathan Jasper, a Brit who owned a sweet little wine bar on Cherche-Midi. I'd met him years before, but he was still at it—I'd seen the shop mentioned in an issue of *Wine Watcher's World* devoted to Paris—and I knew that English-speaking denizens of the wine world passed through the place.

My heart sank when I spotted the FERMÉ sign on the door. I peered through the window. It was tiny, with a classic zinc-topped bar at one end and wine stacked neatly in crates from floor to ceiling. The hours posted said the shop was about to open, and as I turned, wondering if I should wait, I saw a man roughly my age bounding across the street. He dodged a motorbike and leapt to the curb, out of breath.

"*Veuillez excuser mon retard, Monsieur,*" he panted, as he unlocked the door.

"No problem," I said. "I'm glad I caught you."

"*Pain de mie* from Poilâne. Can't make a sandwich without it. Come in, please. I'll just be a minute."

A brass bell tinkled as he pushed his way in. He stepped behind a curtain and emerged wiping flour all over his jeans.

"May I help you find something?" he asked, his British accent pure and high-pitched.

"Babe Stern," I said, extending my hand.

"Babe! Of course. I thought I recognized you. So sorry. What are you doing in Paris?"

"On my way down to Burgundy," I said.

"For the Hospices? Lovely!"

"No, I'm here to track down Eric Feldman and Jacques Goldoni." Jasper lifted his head and examined me with an air of trepidation. "I'm working for Richard Wilson's sister." I figured I'd skip the association with the Napa sheriff's department.

"Dreadful business," Jasper said. "Positively awful."

"You ever see Feldman or Goldoni in the store?"

"Oh, absolutely. They both passed through just last week."

"Together?"

"No, never. Impossible," he laughed.

"How'd they seem to you?"

"Well, Feldman was a bit dour. Rather standoffish, if you know what I mean."

"The subject of Wilson's murder didn't come up, by any chance?"

"Unavoidable," he said. "I couldn't help but get the impression that Eric thought Wilson had gotten his just deserts, but he seemed reluctant to discuss it."

"What about Goldoni?"

"He was different, more as if he needed to talk about it with someone."

"What did he say?"

"He appeared genuinely distraught. He's not convinced that he can pull it off, taking on the newsletter, I mean. He knows full well that Richard's was the reputation. Nor is he sure he can cover the ground. It's a grueling schedule."

"He say anything about the murder itself?"

"Only that it's left him in a state of shock and disbelief."

"Wilson's sister suggested he's actually pretty competitive. You ever get the feeling he resented working in Wilson's shadow?"

"Not really. But he's certainly aware of the power accruing to him now."

"He didn't trot out any theories as to who he thinks killed his boss, did he?"

"I suppose I should confess that I asked. He seemed quite keen on the state of the investigation. He mentioned somebody named Matson, whose wines he acknowledged they'd thoroughly trounced. And a vineyard manager, a Mexican chap. I don't remember his name."

It was obvious Jasper had learned less than I had hoped. We shook hands.

"Take care," I said.

"You, too. *Bonne chance.* And drop by on your way home. I'd love to hear how it comes out. Cheers."

I grabbed a taxi and made my jet-lagged way to the Gare de Lyon, where the great board of arrivals and departures clicked and clicked and clicked, the syncopated codes charting the grand metamorphoses of track and gate and train. I bought my ticket, hurried to find my place in a second-class car, and slumped between the window and a businessman working furiously on a spreadsheet on his laptop.

Lulled by the track rattle as the train picked up speed, I dozed, every now and then opening my eyes to the evanescent landscape—the outskirts of the city, the terra–cotta–tiled suburbs, the telephone poles and water towers—and finally slept. When at last I opened my eyes, I took in the rolling hills, the windbreaks, the houses of once-upon-a-time burghers lodged beneath giant oak trees. I closed my eyes again, and when they reopened, I was in the midst of vineyards.

I'd spent my last days in Napa poring over Feldman's newsletters, correlating the names of winemakers with places on the map, and tried to imagine how he might set his itinerary. I'd done the same with Goldoni. It seemed that the writers could do the Côte d'Or in four or five days, tasting intensively in three or four daily appointments, with another two spent working south from Beaune, the first devoted to the Chalonnaise and the second in Beaujolais. I knew these guys were brisk. I'd organized the domaines by village, but it was obvious that the writers' affections, and thus their schedules, favored the north.

I stood at the curb of the train station in Dijon, searching for a police car. Ciofreddi had arranged for his contact to meet me, a man named Sackheim who was a *gendarme* in Beaune, but all I saw were ordinary Renaults, Peugeots, and Fords as people bustled in and out of the station. Across the street a bum swayed, his bottle hoisted in a mad toast, but it was empty, and he smashed it against the pavement. He turned to the shopping cart that held all his worldly possessions, digging furiously through plastic bags, cursing existence. Whatever it was he was looking for, he couldn't find it.

I hoped this wasn't a portent. At the same moment, a dark brown Citroën pulled up in front of me, the window slid down, and a man stuck his head, silver haired and flat cut like a marine's, out the window.

"Stern?" He pronounced it *Shtayrn*. He was older than I'd expected, sixtyish, and elegantly if simply dressed in a dark gray wool suit, matching V-neck sweater, pale blue shirt, and burgundy-colored tie.

"*Oui,*" I said.

"Émile Sackheim. Get in. There's work to do."

I tossed my bag in the back and settled into the comfortable leather seat. He examined me with ice-blue eyes.

"But first," he smiled, "we must have lunch." He spun out of the station and headed into the old quartier of Dijon.

I like a cop who's got his priorities straight, I thought to myself. *He should give Ciofreddi and Brenneke lessons.*

The restaurant was fancier than I'd expected. We were seated at a corner table discreetly isolated from the other diners, and it was clear my companion was a habitué. The maître d' handed me a menu and Sackheim a menu and wine list. Sackheim donned a pair of reading glasses, looking more like a professor than a *flic.*

"They have an excellent cellar," he remarked and then, swiftly to our waiter, "A bottle of the '91 Lafarge Volnay, Clos des Chênes."

A cop ordering a bottle of Volnay. *No, Toto*, I said to myself, *we're definitely not in Kansas anymore.*

Over a ripe fig stuffed with foie gras and a perfectly roasted partridge carved tableside and served in a *verjus* sauce with white grapes, he asked me to lay out the case as I saw it. I told him what had occurred; the several theories I had developed; that I thought Francisco Fornes had too quickly been tagged as the logical, and easiest, suspect.

"Yet Lieutenant Ciofreddi contacted me, pleased to put us at lunch together, and asking me to offer you what assistance I can during your stay."

"What does he expect you to do?" I said. I was genuinely curious. I wasn't sure what was supposed to happen.

"Feldman, Goldoni, they are well known here. They tour the region almost continually, it seems, as I suppose they must. The Napa sheriffs, they want us to watch them. This is, of course, impossible."

"I don't get it," I said. "Forgive my naïveté, but why is it impossible?"

"First of all, we have no such thing as a 'detective' in the *gendarmerie* on the Côte d'Or. Paris, certainly, but not here. And who has time? There's work to do. Stolen cars, a burglary, the endless stream of drunks driving up and down the *nationale.* Secondly, no crime has been committed in France. You cannot follow people around waiting for them to do something." He shrugged and held up his hands as if this were obvious.

"But how do you think I should work this? I thought maybe you could tag along—you know, come with me."

"'Tag along,' *c'est drôle. Non, comme j'ai dit, c'est impossible.*"

He explained that locating Feldman and Goldoni would be straightforward. Both men had their predictable routines. Appointments were set. A few inquiries would quickly establish their starting points on any given day. I told him what I knew, that Feldman tended to follow the same winemakers vintage to vintage. The names were all in the newsletter.

"Yes, I've read a few issues. And Goldoni?"

I said that, though I'd focused my attention on Feldman, their paths appeared to intersect all over Burgundy. I wondered how they managed to avoid bumping into each other.

"Ah, you have Feldman in your sights?" He smiled and took a sip of the Volnay.

"It's just that, in terms of motive, Feldman had more reasons to want Wilson dead."

"Are you sure?" Sackheim said. "Subordinates can be vindictive, too, *non*? Goldoni may have resented Wilson."

"Maybe. The problem is, there's no evidence that either of them was in Napa."

Sackheim shrugged. Clearly, it was going to be my problem to sort out their itineraries. Then I told him about Pitot.

"Piteau?" he asked, spelling it out.

"No, *P-i-t-o-t*. Jean."

Sackheim frowned. "I don't know. But you will find him, I'm sure."

He pulled a card from the breast pocket of his jacket. "If you see something you think I should know, if something serious should happen, you call me," he said, scribbling a number on the bottom of the card. "My cell phone."

My curiosity was piqued.

"Do you mind if I ask you why you agreed to this? Why you're helping me out?"

"I am not helping you, I'm buying lunch." He smiled. "But I am intrigued by this case, not to mention that we received a call from the American consulate in Lyon. If I could accompany you legally, I would, but I can't. Besides, you, you will get near to them, whereas I, I am a little obvious, *non*?" He cleared his throat. "There is something else."

He straightened the tablecloth, brushing the bread crumbs off before the waiter had the chance. "You have heard the name Gaston Laurent?" I nodded that I had heard of the three-star chef. Laurent's death had made news even in the States the year after I left Seattle. "I was assigned to that case. It was a suicide, obviously. He put a gun to his head. There was no question as to what transpired. He was in debt; he had done too much too quickly. The restaurant outside of Beaune, the bistro in Paris, his plans to conquer New York. But when they took away his third star, it killed him." He surveyed the dining room. "I was a regular at his place. I knew him well. We shared many Cognacs late at night. He was a madman, *fou.* He spent too much, was obsessed with his *produits: petites courgettes*, the perfect *loup de mer*, everything. He could talk for hours about linen and wineglasses. The smallest details." He paused. "These critics—it doesn't matter if they're French or American—they hold a person's fate in their hands as if it were nothing. Their arrogance is . . . too much." He shook his head in disgust.

"No, I understand," I said. And I did. I'd felt the same way for years.

"They destroy people *très cavalièrement.* How do you say?"

"'Very cavalierly,' it's the same."

"So, this case. It is interesting, *non?* Somebody kills a critic. Who? Why? This interests me. And Richard Wilson . . . *en France* . . ." Sackheim curled his lower lip and nodded gravely. He clearly understood the power Wilson had come to wield, how revered he was, and how despised. "Now, this drama, it moves to France. Lieutenant Ciofreddi believes so, and I, too, fear that this is so. I wish that I am not constrained by the law. But you, you have more freedom. You must do this, Monsieur Stern. But you must find the killer before he finds you." He smiled again, though there was nothing gentle or friendly or humorous in his expression.

"I am serious. There are people here who hate, *hated*, your Richard Wilson. They count themselves as his enemies, but, of course, he has made some *vignerons* very rich. For every winemaker he ruined, there is another he made a wealthy man. Here, I have to tell you, we can be quite ruthless. You will need to keep your wits about you and to tread carefully."

I pondered the warning, and our conversation lagged. We ordered coffee.

"I know it probably seems a very American thing to do, but would you mind telling me a little about yourself? Your English is incredibly good," I said.

"No, my friend, my English is proficient. This partridge paired with the Volnay was incredibly good."

His story transfixed me.

He was, he admitted himself, a curiosity: There weren't many Jews in the *gendarmerie*. Studious and scholarly in his youth, he found himself almost rabbinical in the fastidious way he tackled criminal cases. He credited this, ironically, to a Jesuit education and the fact that his father had been a lawyer and had trained him to ask questions and split hairs, and had always adopted an adversarial posture to get to the heart of whatever they talked about when Émile was a boy.

"The Talmudic school of criminal investigation," he smiled.

His father held small interests in a number of domaines, miniscule and insignificant shares, really, given as payment for legal work he had performed on behalf of the *propriétaires*. But these had entitled him to help in the harvest—a yearly event Sackheim *père* had looked forward to as a welcome distraction from the staid practice of law—and to small amounts of wine annually that he greatly enjoyed.

Banned from practicing law under the Statut des Juifs in 1940, Émile's father had been cheated out of his vineyard holdings a year later. A gentile *négociant* and friend had convinced him to sign over his shares, "until all of this is over, to keep them safe." His parents barely eluded deportation to the death camps and managed to survive, eking out a living in a series of ever more menial jobs, moving from place to place. Young Émile was born in the aftermath of the war, and though the conditions of their family life remained precarious, his memories were reasonably happy. Still suffering from a residual paranoia, they even found a parochial school that had agreed to accept the young Jewish student as a gesture of atonement for the Church's complicity in Vichy. Offered conversion by a particularly assiduous priest, Sackheim had graciously declined.

"I know where I come from. Now I am nothing—neither Jew nor Catholic. I am a true child of the Republic, a practicing member of the Church of Justice. But you see, when I describe the French as vindictive and vengeful, I know what I'm talking about."

The waiter served coffee, and Sackheim waited for him to leave the table before continuing.

His father, nonetheless, despite his family's survival, died a bitter man. To honor his memory, his mother insisted Émile go to law school, but Sackheim was restless and quit after his first year.

"Why practice law if they can pass laws that make it illegal?" he asked sardonically. I had no answer. His mother died when she heard the news. "That's a joke," he said. "A Jewish mother dying when her son, how do you say, 'drops out' of law school. In fact, she had all along been ill, never completely recovering from her ordeal."

Instead he joined the *gendarmerie*, and his natural abilities and ready intelligence made for swift advancement. Growing up under such circumstances, he felt himself to be an outsider; now he turned it to his advantage.

I didn't know what to say.

"Never mind. It was a long time ago. Anyway, I received an excellent Catholic education. *Alors!*" he called to our waiter, "*l'addition, s'il vous plaît.*" He regarded me again with startling blue eyes. "I am an old man, nearing retirement. They are reorganizing the *Police Judiciaire* and have been trying to get rid of me for several years, but I am holding out until the end. This will probably be my last case. So what if I break a rule or two? What can they say? 'You're fired'? *Eh, bien.* Who cares?"

Once we were in the car I said, "Forgive me. I know it's an impertinent question, but your name, Sackheim, it sounds so . . ."

"German?" he laughed. "My father was from Alsace. My mother was Lyonnaise. But my hair—it was red when I was a boy—and my blue eyes, they provided, how do you say, 'protective coloration' at the *lycée*. But you, Shtayrn, you're a Jew, *non?*"

I nodded.

"I thought so. Your name. And, unlike me, you, my friend, look Jewish." We both smiled. "So, do you need to check into your hotel? No? Excellent. First you need a geography lesson. This place, Bourgogne, is maddening."

We drove south down the N74, turned off the highway at Fixin, and found ourselves on a narrow road.

"This is La Route des Grands Crus. It goes through Gevrey-Chambertin, Morey-Saint-Denis, Chambolle-Musigny." We passed through one legendary village after another, and I remembered back to when I'd first attached these real places to the names I'd memorized as a young sommelier.

On the far side of Chambolle, we switchbacked by the Clos de Vougeot, and Sackheim pulled over to take in the legendary vineyard and domaine. The place floated on a sea of mist broken by the tips of vines that fanned out in unending rows, the château's volumes of gray stone massed and fractured as if they had split and multiplied over centuries. He gazed at the place in awe.

"These wines, they are . . . *incroyable, extraordinaire.*" English was insufficient, obviously, and the wines, a few of which I had tasted in my glory days, were a luxury I could no longer afford on a bartender's tips.

In Nuits-Saint-Georges, Sackheim pulled into a parking space across from a *tabac*, took the map I had in my hands, and ordered me out. He spread the map on the hood of the Citroën, overlooking a stream that passed through the south side of the town.

"In two months this river, le Meuzin, will be full, rushing . . ." He extended his arm to the west.

In broad strokes he explained the Côte d'Or, a patchwork of vineyards forming an irregular and inscrutable checkerboard of names— *communes, premiers crus, grands crus*—so complex in their array that I wondered how a worker found his way through the maze of plots and parcels and rows.

"But you know all this, *non?* Lieutenant Ciofreddi told me that you are a distinguished sommelier." I thought I detected a touch of irony. No American could be the real thing in a Frenchman's eyes. "Come, I will take you to your hotel."

We turned off at the sign for Aloxe-Corton. The road passed through a corridor of ancient acacias and narrowed, winding its way through two small squares. Sackheim dropped me in front of the hotel. I stood at the curb, my bag at my feet. He rolled his window down.

"Tell me, is there a restaurant in town where guys like Feldman and Goldoni might tend to go?" I asked. "Somewhere people talk about?"

"Perhaps you should try La Bourguignonne. She is a very good cook. *C'est branché.*

"Thanks."

"Happy hunting," Sackheim said. "And pay attention," he added. "You must watch your back, eh?"

16

Le Chemin de Vigne stood off the street, set back from a low stone wall, the vestibule framed by trellised roses, its façade awash in a crimson scrim of ivy. I entered the hallway and, finding it empty, walked into the common room. A woman was bent at the fireplace, sweeping ashes into a dustpan. Hearing my steps on the flagstone, she craned her neck.

"Ah, *pardon, Monsieur,*" she said, standing and wiping her hands on an apron. She was young, her black hair in a wild tangle, and she wore black jeans and flip-flops and a loose sweater beneath her apron. She led me to the front desk, where I handed her my passport and a credit card. Then she took me upstairs.

"*Voilà, votre chambre,*" she said. "It is okay?"

"Better than okay. It's perfect, lovely."

"Enjoy your visit, *Monsieur.*"

I looked around. The room had a rustic elegance, its off-center lines framed by rough-hewn beams, the walls washed with pale mustard-colored plaster. I splashed my face at the marble sink to shock myself awake and did a circuit of the room, wondering if I'd have a chance to enjoy it. The windows faced a vineyard to one side and a small park to the other, a towering linden and an ancient, stunted holly set amidst a table and chairs that had been covered for the season.

Downstairs, I asked if she had a phone book.

"*Oui, bien sûr.*" She returned a moment later with a thin Pages Jaunes in her outstretched hand.

"Is this just for Aloxe-Corton?" I asked.

"*Mais non*, it has all the communes surrounding Beaune," she said, then disappeared through a door at the far end of the room.

I sat at a table and leafed through the book until I arrived at *P*. There were two listings for Pitot in Nuits-Saint-Georges: Gilbert and Henri. I copied the addresses in my notebook and walked to the door through which the woman had gone.

"*Excusez-moi, Madame,*" I called. I thanked her and asked if she could call me a taxi.

I had the cab drop me at the Hertz office in Beaune, where a prim attendant handed me the keys to a sporty Rover sedan, fittingly painted a rich burgundy red. I went over the map with her and figured I'd start at the Novotel, the place Eric Feldman said he'd be staying.

The Novotel, the local representative of a national chain that catered to the business traveler—in France, an exclusively male club—occupied a square block on the edge of town not far from the Hertz office. I'd stayed in one of these places on my first trip to France, organized by a distributor in Seattle. Made a Day's Inn feel like the Plaza Athénée. I remembered how I'd felt in the morning. The coffee alone had made me homicidal, not to mention the day-old croissants, foil-wrapped butter, and recycled *confiture*. Personally, I'd want to punch my first client in the nose. Given the range of accommodation available, it seemed an unlikely choice for a wine writer, but Feldman was doubtless on a budget, and his pick fit Jordan Meyer's description of him: dry, lifeless, keeping himself ascetically aloof from the sybaritic pleasures of his métier.

Management had seemingly abandoned ship, leaving the operation on autopilot. I rang twice, and a man peered out from the office behind the front desk.

"*Oui, Monsieur?* May I help you? Checking in?"

"*Non, merci.* I am looking for Eric Feldman. He arrived . . ."

"On Sunday," the man answered efficiently.

"He is not here?"

"*Non, Monsieur.* Mr. Feldman has his appointments. Would you like to leave a message?" He placed his hand on the lip of Feldman's room box. It was empty. When I said nothing, he busied himself with paperwork and fiddled with the computer.

"If you would like to leave your card, *Monsieur*, I will make certain that Monsieur Feldman gets it," he said, staring at the computer screen.

A card. That was good. What would mine say? That I was a retired sommelier and unsuccessful sleuth?

"*Non, merci, Monsieur,*" I said.

I stood in front of the desk, contemplating my next move. The man stared distractedly at me from the tops of his eyes and then, when I didn't budge, retreated to the excitement of his office. I dawdled at the desk, checking out the lobby. He peeked out a few minutes later and, seeing me still standing there, disappeared back inside.

Come on, I thought, *be a Frenchman. Stand firm and be rude to me. I'm an American, damn it*. But he refused to cooperate.

I found my way to the center of town and parked off the Place Carnot. It was too early for dinner, even for an American. I wandered into Athenaeum, a famous bookstore specializing in the subject of wine, and browsed the shelves. I wasn't sure what I was looking for. *Why French Winemakers Hate American Critics? How to Kill a Wine Writer?* I was out of luck.

By the time I left the store, dusk had fallen. The sky was a flat gray mirroring the expanse of gravel that swept across the square. I asked a woman rushing home for directions to La Bourguignonne. She shrugged and shook her head, but, after wandering around for thirty minutes, I found the alley that led to the little bistro.

The place was virtually empty. I explained to the young man who greeted me that I'd just arrived, and apologized for not having a reservation. He seated me at a table tucked in a corner of the dining room, by the door to the kitchen. The menu, written in chalk on a blackboard, hung on the wall. I asked for a wine list. It read like a who's who of the *côte*, the big names cheek by jowl with the up-and-coming stars of the younger generation I'd seen featured in the wine mags.

I ordered a plate of *petit-gris* snails and a bottle of Pommard and sat back. A few minutes later, just as the maître d' poured me a taste of the Pommard, two unmistakable Americans entered the restaurant. I immediately recognized the shorter of the two—I'd seen a photograph of him in *Wine Watcher's World*. It was Frederick Rosen, Biddy's contact, for whom I'd left a message. He hadn't returned my call. He had bushy eyebrows that drooped over sweet, dark eyes ringed by sallow folds. A thick moustache followed the sagging line of his lips, which immediately broke into a huge, phony smile revealing a mouth full of nicotine-stained teeth as he greeted the young man who'd suddenly abandoned me—obviously, the chef's husband and co-owner—and introduced his companion.

"Gérard, I want you to meet Smithson Bayne, *un avocat.*"

The lawyer must have stood six-four and wore ostrich-skin Luccheses, jeans, and a Hawaiian shirt, its tails loose beneath a buckskin jacket. His sandy hair was pulled back in a short ponytail. He stretched out a hand that could have palmed Gérard's skull and winked.

"Hey, Jirard, how ya doin', buddy? Pleasure," he said, his voice bellowing in the tiny dining room.

"There'll be four of us," his companion reminded the host.

"*D'accord*, Freddy. *S'il vous plaît.*" They were seated at a table in the middle of the room.

As I waited for the escargots, I watched the two men pass the wine list back and forth. Just then, a young woman entered the restaurant. Her hair, straw streaked, was pinned up in a tight chignon, revealing strikingly beautiful eyes, slightly sunken, that were heavily lined with kohl. Taken separately, her features were a little off: her forehead too broad, the chin too weak, her mouth too wide. She was like a young wine whose elements had not yet come together, but as an assemblage, their effect was startling, an immature first-growth claret wrapped in a brown paper bag for a blind tasting. You had to work hard not to look, and I gave up without a fight.

"Monique," Rosen said, rising from his chair to kiss her. "This is Smithson Bayne," he continued. "This is the young woman I was telling you about, Monique Azzine."

"Bone swah, Mamwazell," Bayne boomed, rising to his full height to shake her hand.

At the same instant, a new arrival came through the door.

"Freddy!" he said, heading for their table.

I watched, fascinated.

"Jacques Goldoni, Smithson Bayne. And this is Monique."

It seemed too good to be true: I was getting a look at Goldoni on my first night in Burgundy, but, as I knew too well, the wine world was small and all too predictable. Eric Feldman was the only one missing. I thought about going over and introducing myself but decided to stay put and watch the evening unfold.

"Hi, Monique," Goldoni said, offering an unattractive grin that he undoubtedly fancied seductive.

"Hello, Jack," she said, looking at him with barely disguised distaste and making a point of pronouncing his first name *Jack*. He seemed unfazed and seated himself.

Goldoni was around my height but had to weigh at least half again as much. He had an immature face, open and clean-shaven, but his eyes darted with a calculating energy as he looked from Rosen to the girl to Bayne. His tweed sport coat, rumpled and devoid of shape, stretched across his back as he sat down. Gérard fussed over them, describing the evening's specials in detail.

"So, tell us, how goes the *stage?*" Rosen inquired.

"I arrived just in time for the harvest," Monique said, fiddling with her napkin. Her accent was nearly imperceptible.

"But Richard said he saw you in Barsac," Rosen said.

"Yes," she said, glancing at Goldoni. "I started there. A second growth, third-rate château. Terrible *propriétaires.* So arrogant. I was very alone. They treated me like a servant. I left before the harvest."

"Am I missing something? You two know each other?" Bayne said, showing more perceptiveness than I'd have credited him with.

"Last spring Jack was with Richard in Barsac" was all she offered by way of explanation.

"They treatin' you any better here?" Bayne asked.

"Well, you know, the Bordelais, they make jokes about Burgundy. 'They are so primitive. Monkeys. You will hate it.' But I don't mind. Anything is better than *la fausse noblesse Sauternoise. La hauteur, vous comprenez?*"

"You're at Domaine Beauchamp, right?" Rosen said.

"In Pommard," she nodded.

"But you're just about done now, aren't you?" Rosen asked.

"*Oui*. We are finishing up. Another week, maybe."

"And what then?" Rosen said.

"I don't know. André wants me to stay. I'm going to stick around for the Hospices. Work the tasting. Party." She said *party* like a true Valley Girl. "But the wine is laid down. I need to figure out what I'm going to do next. Maybe I should come to America." She batted her eyes at Rosen. "So, you have to find me my next position."

"I'm so hungry, I could eat the ass out of a leather duck," Bayne interrupted them.

"*Quel délice!*" Monique said. "Leather duck ass. One of my favorites."

Gérard returned to take their order, then stopped by my table. I decided to insert a course of *jambon persillé* to prolong the meal.

When I looked back, Rosen had leaned into the table, and I could hear him counseling Monique about how to further her career. Why not let him try to find her a job as an assistant winemaker in Oregon? He had connections.

Now excluded from their conversation, Bayne had begun holding forth to Goldoni, obviously enjoying himself as he described how he'd relieved one poor bastard of a client of his entire cellar.

"I cleaned up on that baby!" the lawyer boasted, stealing looks at Monique to see if she was listening. "Two cases of Gaja, couple o' mags of Petrus, some ole BV Georges de Latour. Must a been ten, twenty cases in all. Man, he never knew what hit 'im!" he chuckled. Clearly, he'd come up with a creative way of collecting his fees.

Rosen had ordered their first bottle of wine, and Bayne followed with a request for a Chambertin. I could tell Goldoni, now examining the *carte*, intended to up the ante with an even more extravagant choice.

"I'm really sorry about Richard," Bayne now said to Goldoni. Goldoni nodded without interrupting his appraisal of the wine list. "What do you think happened?" the lawyer said.

"I don't know," Goldoni replied curtly. "They thought they had a Mexican guy, the vineyard manager, but it didn't hold up."

"It's really unbelievable," Rosen said. "A wine critic drowned in a vat—it's like something out of a made-for-TV movie. And Richard? Someone we knew."

"Someone I worked closely with," Goldoni amended, glancing up.

"But who?" Bayne asked. He sounded like a lawyer, zeroing in on the question they were probably all asking themselves.

"Well, it's not like everybody loves us," Goldoni admitted.

"I know, but, come on . . ." Rosen pleaded.

"We've murdered a few wines between us. Of course, they deserved it," Goldoni joked.

They laughed uncomfortably.

"So, Smithson. Is that what people call you, 'Smithson'?" Monique said.

"Call me anything you like, sweetheart," Bayne said in his deepest Southern baritone, looking down at her.

"Smithson, what are you into?" she asked.

"Me, kid? I'm into new oak and fuckin' goats!" he howled. "I'm into girls on Harleys and takin' the cellars off unsuspectin' clients. Have some more wine, darlin'," he said, emptying their first bottle into Monique's glass, pumping its neck in blatant sexual allusion, delighted by his own puerile obscenity.

"He's a lawyer. And a collector," Rosen said.

"Wine?" asked Goldoni.

"Wine, women, Harleys," Bayne said.

"He can't drink a fraction of what he buys," Rosen said. "What do you have, fifty thousand bottles in your cellar?" he asked, turning to Bayne. "Last year he dropped a hundred grand on wine," he added.

"An expensive hobby," Goldoni remarked.

"You rich guys are like that," Monique said. "You just like to have it around. It's a prestige thing, isn't it? Like a pretty girl," she added. "But why do *you* like to have him around?" she asked Rosen.

"Well, as you can see, he's funny and smart," Rosen said. "He makes me laugh. Not to mention, he buys a lot of my wine."

As their entrées were served, the wine list made the rounds again. Bayne aced out Goldoni, ordering a pricey bottle of Charmes-Chambertin before the other man even had a crack at the list.

"Ya know," he said, raising his glass of Chambertin as the *patron* returned with the next bottle, "Charlopin, in Gevrey, was asked once, 'What's the difference between Chambertin and Charmes-Chambertin?' An' he said, 'You put one finger in your wife's pussy and another in her bunghole. You take your fingers out and sniff 'em. They're the same, but they're a little different. *C'est comme ça.*'"

The men exploded in laughter. Monique rolled her eyes.

"Par-done-ay mwah, Ma'am-wah-zell," Bayne drawled in apology. Monique stood up.

"Yes, I can see," she said tartly. "Very funny, very smart. Would you excuse me, please, gentlemen."

She tossed her napkin on her plate and walked out. That shut them up. They had no way of knowing I spoke English and didn't even look up when I stood and slipped out to find her. She was standing outside, kicking the dirt aimlessly. She glanced at me as I pulled out my cigarettes.

"Want a smoke?" I said.

"Shit, another American," was all she said.

"A little different from them, hopefully," I protested, lighting her cigarette.

"You are here for Les Trois Glorieuses?" she asked after a moment, blowing smoke in my direction.

"No, not really." I studied her, trying to make up my mind how much to say. "It sounds like you knew Richard Wilson." Monique didn't say anything. "You know he was killed? That's what your friends were talking about," I said.

"They are not my friends," she said. "Yes, of course, I know that he is dead. Everybody knows this. And you? Did you know him?"

I told myself to keep my mouth shut. I told myself not to reveal anything, to keep the purpose of my trip a secret. And then she took a step toward me, looking me straight in the eye, and her lips parted. She merely tilted her head, and my resolution dissolved.

"I'm in France to find out who killed him."

She shifted her head, and I couldn't read her eyes.

"You're lying," she said.

"I wish I were. Look, Goldoni's one of the people I came here to talk to. Maybe you could help me."

She inhaled, examining me. Then she exhaled. "I don't even know your name."

I introduced myself as a friend of Wilson's.

"How? How do you want me to help you?" Her directness was arresting.

"Ask him what he knows about Richard's death. He's key to understanding what happened. So is Eric Feldman—I'm looking for him, too." Her expression changed again; now she seemed alarmed. There was no mistaking it. "I've upset you," I said.

"I can't . . ." she started but wasn't able to finish. Rosen appeared at the front door.

I turned to go back inside, and she started to follow.

"Hang on, have another with me," Rosen urged Monique. "Do I know you?" he said to me.

"Babe Stern," I said. "I'm a friend of Biddy Teukes. I left you a message a week ago. I was going to try and find you."

"Huh, what a coincidence. I was going to call you tomorrow. Where are you staying?"

"Le Chemin de Vigne, in Aloxe," I told him.

"Well, you seem to have met Monique already. Maybe you'd like to meet us in the morning. There's a tasting at Collet-Favreau. Eric's going to be there, too."

"I know Claudine Collet," I said. *The wine world isn't just small*, I thought; *we're all connected by one degree of separation.* "In fact, I called her from the States," I added.

I returned to the restaurant, resumed my seat, and settled the bill. Rosen and Monique came back a few minutes later. I stopped by their table on my way out. Rosen introduced me to Goldoni and Bayne, not alluding to the purpose of my trip, which he, if course, was aware of, thanks to Biddy. I was silently grateful for his tact. We agreed to meet at Domaine Collet-Favreau the next morning and to have lunch with Goldoni later on the Place Carnot.

As I drove back to Aloxe-Corton, I played back everything I'd witnessed. I hadn't learned much. Rosen wasn't tough to read. He was patently happy to play the concerned mentor to a beautiful young French girl, clearly relished being a cosseted regular at Gérard's restaurant, and enjoyed serving as power broker between

Goldoni and Bayne. And then there was Monique. Who was she? How had she met Wilson? And what had so upset her before Rosen interrupted us?

Impulsively, I decided to call Gio when I got to my room. It was, after all, lunchtime in California.

"I'm here," I said.

"In France?"

"In Burgundy. You wouldn't believe it. I met the friend of Biddy's I told you about. And Jacques Goldoni, Richard's sidekick."

"Really? What's he like?" She sounded disinterested. I couldn't be sure—it may have been the connection—but she didn't seem all that thrilled by the call.

"Just the way Janie described him: overweight and underwhelming."

She was even less pleased that I cited Janie's authority on the subject, and said nothing.

"Where are you?" I asked.

"At the winery. I have to get going. My father's waiting for me."

"Sorry."

"It's okay. I hope you find what you're looking for."

"Thanks," I said.

I lay down in bed. What *was* I looking for? Why did I continue to believe I was the only one who could figure this out?

I fell asleep, the questions spinning into oblivion.

17

The next morning I went downstairs. The dining room was empty. I took a seat at a table set for breakfast and stared at the ashes in the fireplace. An ember released a wisp of smoke. The woman I'd met the day before came bustling into the room.

"*Ah, pardon, Monsieur,*" she apologized. "You have been waiting long?"

"No, not at all. Just got here."

"*Ah, bon. Du café?*"

"*S'il vous plaît.*"

A minute later she emerged with a platter. She set down a cup and saucer, a ceramic pot of coffee, and a creamer of steamed milk.

"*Vous voulez le petit déjeuner?*"

"Please."

She returned with a basket of croissants, brioches, and bread, ramekins of butter and plum *confiture*, a plate of prosciutto and melon. I sat and made mental notes on my plan of attack. I'd met Claudine Collet-Joubert, as she now was known, on my first trip to Burgundy. Her family had been *vignerons* for generations, with extensive holdings. I knew she'd married since I'd last seen her, at the International Pinot Noir Conference in Oregon years before. When I'd called her from the States, she'd told me that her father had died and that she was living with her mother and husband in

Nuits-Saint-Georges. I'd begin there with Rosen, then start looking for Jean Pitot at one of the two addresses I'd found.

As the woman reappeared with a small dish that held a perfectly baked apple, a young man in a jogging suit staggered in, gasping for breath, sweat dripping off his forehead.

"*Pardon, Monsieur*," he heaved. He stood momentarily, his hands resting on his knees, facing the floor to catch his breath. "I'm sorry. Seven Ks around the Bois. I'm really out of shape. Lucas Kiers," he introduced himself, extending his hand.

It was a name I recognized. I'd read several of his pieces in *Wine Watcher's World*, and it struck me that, beyond the reviews of any given vintage, he seemed to specialize in human interest stories, features that delved into families feuding over their property— father against son, brother against brother. There was an off chance he might have stumbled across the Pitot family in researching an article.

"Aaron Stern," I said, shaking hands. "Babe."

"*The* Babe Stern?" Kiers said.

"The same."

"I haven't seen your name in ages. Still in the game?"

"I dropped out. I own a little bar in St. Helena."

"You're here for the Hospices?" he asked, uncomprehending. It made no sense for the owner of a bar to attend so prestigious an event.

Having blown my cover the night before with Monique, I figured I had nothing to lose. "I'm interested in the murder of Richard Wilson. He used to be my brother-in-law."

That got his attention.

"I don't quite get it. It happened thousands of miles away." He reached over to an adjoining table, took a napkin, and wiped his face. "So, I'm assuming that you have a theory that caused you to hop a plane."

"I have too many theories."

"So, what do you hope to find out? Assemble the suspects like an Agatha Christie mystery and expect one to confess?"

"Eric Feldman called Richard the week he was murdered. I want to know why, what he wanted. And of course, there's Goldoni, whom I saw last night."

Kiers laughed. "I'll be surprised if Eric's willing to talk about it," he said.

"So I hear." I thought I'd plumb his area of expertise. "You ever come across a family named Pitot? Winemakers in Nuits?"

"Pitot, Pitot . . ." he pondered. "No. Definitely not. Why?"

"There's a kid by that name who was working at Norton when Richard was murdered. I want to track him down, if I can."

"Well, everybody makes wine here. And lots of families send their kids to America," Kiers said.

"How long are you here for?" I asked.

"Just a week. Do the rounds. And you?"

"Not sure. I need to be back by Thanksgiving."

Kiers glanced at the clock that hung over the mantelpiece.

"Look at the time! I need to get going. Already late for my first appointment. Good luck and good tasting!" He stopped at the doorway. "Keep me abreast of what you find out. I'd love a scoop."

As I headed north on the *nationale*, I could see the cemetery in Corgoloin in the middle distance, a patch of earth carved out of the vineyards and walled in for the dead, and, a little farther, the limestone quarries above Comblanchien, the flesh of the hillside scraped clean to reveal the bare stone beneath. *Graves and headstones*, I said to myself. It all seemed so close, but I wondered if I'd get that far, close enough to carve an epitaph for my murdered friend.

Once in Nuits-Saint-Georges, I took a right off the highway and drove down a narrow lane to a house, pulling into an open driveway. As I got out, Claudine came through the front door.

"*Bonjour*, Claudine!" I kissed her on both cheeks.

"*Bonjour*, Babe," she said with a warm smile. She'd put on some weight since I'd seen her last and had dyed her hair, a shock of henna flaming her head. Her eyes, though, were the same, playful and penetrating.

"Has Rosen arrived?" I asked.

"Not yet."

"And Eric Feldman?"

She shook her head.

"So, you are a detective now?" she said, grinning impishly.

"Just call me Sam Spade. I'm digging around." I could see she failed to get either the reference or the pun. "Tell me, have you ever heard of a family named Pitot?"

"Gilbert and Henri Pitot?" she asked.

"Yeah, exactly."

"Yes, they both live not far from here."

She was on the verge of telling me just how to find *les* Pitots when a mud-spattered Peugeot pulled into the drive. Rosen leapt from the car and greeted her, air-kissing both cheeks.

"Where's Bayne?" I asked.

"Lost in the time difference on his BlackBerry. Lawyers! So?" he said, turning to Claudine.

"*Alors*," she said, "Roland is expecting you."

"I'll see you in a little while," I said to her.

Rosen and I passed through the winery, a concrete fermenter taking up one side. A conveyor belt, dormant after the harvest, rose to a pneumatic press. In the barrel room, a man was stooped in a far corner. Our footsteps echoed in the cavernous space.

"*Allô*, Freddy," he called. "*Venez.*"

Rosen introduced us as he handed me a stem, and we shook hands. Roland Joubert was thin, too thin for a winemaker, I thought. He was dressed in jeans and a sweatshirt and wore a sour expression, as if he knew what was coming and dreaded it.

As we stood there, Eric Feldman entered. He had an intelligent face, but his manner was aloof, just as Jordan Meyer and Jonathan Jasper had described him. He stood slightly too erect in a vain attempt to hit six feet and wore a tan shirt and navy blue sweater, green corduroy slacks, and a pair of ankle-high Timberlands. He eyed me suspiciously through surprisingly hip plastic-rimmed glasses that seemed out of place, given what seemed his more low-key sartorial style.

"A friend from California, Babe Stern," Rosen said.

We shook hands. I pulled out a notebook and pen, ready to play my part. I knew the ropes.

"Can we get started?" Feldman asked. "I have another appointment at eleven." He was all business, not a smile in sight.

We set to it immediately, the drill repeating itself with each wine. Roland would dip his thief, a long glass tube like a baster, into a barrel, pull a *voleur* of bright purple juice, and dribble a few ounces in each glass. We held our stems up to examine the wine for color, smelled it, swirled it, sipped it, swished it around as if it were mouthwash, and spat it into the gravel.

"Domaine Collet-Favreau, Nuits-Saint-Georges, Les Maladières," Rosen prompted for my benefit.

"Les Perrières."

"Aux Boudots."

I pretended to take notes and studied Feldman. If he were enjoying himself, you'd never know it. He looked like a cub reporter covering a lousy story—dutiful but reluctant. His questions were formulaic. He gave no sign of what he was thinking, which I guessed was the whole idea. Keep 'em guessing. Joubert appeared tentative around him and stepped from one foot to the other. The whole thing was an exercise to which Roland was forced to subject himself if his wines were to gain any notoriety, but you couldn't say he relished the experience any more than Feldman.

"Chambolle-Musigny," Freddy whispered, as we changed villages.

"Les Amoureuses."

"Chambolle, Les Cras. *Premier cru.*"

I nodded, playing along as if I actually did this every six months. I inched forward and tried to steal a look at Feldman's notebook. The handwriting was crabbed, his notes dense with scribbling up and down the side of the page: arrows, squiggles, and cross-hatchings from margin to margin, making it all comprehensible only to him.

His questions were terse. They talked clonal selection, yields, cold maceration, pH, that sort of thing—the techno-geek side of the wine game.

When we'd completed the round, we started all over again, tasting through the exact same sequence from the previous vintage. Then we turned to another eight bottles that stood on a separate table, representing four vineyards from two vintages.

"Roland took over when Claudine's father died," Rosen explained, "but he makes wine under his own label, Domaine Joubert. Now he's going to show Eric his work."

The bottles in the second group didn't possess the depth or breeding of the Collet-Favreau wines but were well made: properly structured but lacking flesh.

"They're coming along," Feldman remarked. "How old are the vines now?"

"Nine years," Joubert said.

"You'll get there," Feldman reassured him coolly.

By the twentieth wine, my gums ached. I could feel the acids etching my teeth and thought I felt blisters breaking out on my tongue. I was already flagging, and Feldman, hearing me sigh, looked at me contemptuously. But it was time to stop anyway.

Offering a cursory *merci*, he shook hands and excused himself.

Rosen turned to me. "I have a little business to discuss. Wait for me outside. I'll be a minute. See if you can open him up," he said, his tone suggesting he didn't think I stood a chance.

The morning cloud cover had broken, and I followed Feldman out into an exquisite November morning. I lit a cigarette and offered him one.

"No thanks," he said. "Who are you with?"

"I'm between jobs," I lied. "I recently moved to Napa from Seattle, where I ran a wine program." He nodded. "Terrible news about Richard Wilson," I said.

"Yeah, unbelievable," he agreed, but without a trace of emotion.

"You knew him. You worked together." He stared out the gate to a vineyard that had been picked over, the cordons stretched like emaciated limbs along a wire trellis. "So how do you figure it? The whole thing's pretty weird," I said.

He thought a moment. "If it had happened in Bordeaux, that would narrow it down some. I can think of a dozen winemakers who might have done it gladly," he said. "But Napa? I don't know."

"You phoned him right before he died," I stated bluntly.

"How'd you know that?" He glared at me. "What'd you say your name was? Stern?"

I knew I wouldn't get anywhere unless I let him know that I'd heard the phone message he left on the voice mail.

"Janie, Richard's sister, my ex-wife, took me to his apartment in San Francisco. I listened to his messages. One was from you. So, why?"

"You were Richard's brother-in-law?"

I nodded. "That's right."

"As a favor to someone. I'd never have been in touch with him otherwise. But you're not here to taste wine at all, are you? You used to be a sommelier, right? Seattle. I remember your name. You won that competition. What was it?" His tone was withering. "You fall off the flat side of the earth? What are you now, some kind of investigator?"

"Not really. It just seems like family business. And we were good friends." I studied him. He seemed unmoved. "I don't get it," I went on. "Janie said that you and Richard weren't on speaking terms. The whole world seems to know what happened between the two of you. Why would you do someone a favor if it meant you had to call him?"

"I wanted to hurt him as much as he hurt me," Feldman said. Now it was his turn to study me. He waited a few moments before continuing. "If you're his brother-in-law, then you probably know that Richard has a child he refused to acknowledge. A French child, in fact."

There was no mistaking the look of disbelief on my face.

"No, I didn't think so. One more in Richard's long list of ex-relationships," he said. "I'm sorry I can't help you." He turned to go.

My head was buzzing. I wanted to keep him there another minute until I figured out where to take the conversation. After what he'd just told me, I was too flummoxed to know what to say.

"What about Michael Matson? Any chance he could have done it?" I asked, buying time as I followed him to his car.

"Matson paid dearly," Feldman said, opening the door. "Those were very unfair reviews. But he's a reasonable person, a decent human being. I don't see it."

"What about Biddy Teukes?" I asked.

"Teukes is a poseur, a minimally talented winemaker with a flair for self-promotion. But murder? I doubt it. Maybe." He paused. "Well, look," he said, glancing at his watch, "I don't know what's keeping Freddy, but I have another tasting now."

"Oh, where?" I tried to be casual.

"Trenet," he offered reluctantly.

"Maybe we'll see you down the road." I was still reeling.

He started to pull out of the driveway, stopped, and rolled his window down.

"Did it ever occur to you that Richard was murdered not because of what he did but because of who he was?" Feldman said.

Before I had a chance to respond, the window slid noiselessly shut and Feldman drove off.

Jesus. I didn't know what to make of Feldman. He'd played his hand tight to his chest, then trumped me with a single card. Richard had never said anything, and I was certain Janie knew nothing about it. And then it occurred to me this was probably what Wilson had wanted to tell me the day he showed up at Pancho's. The day he was murdered.

Freddy appeared suddenly, fuming. He had a cigarette in his hand and stabbed at his lighter until it ignited.

"That arrogant son of a bitch!" He was furious.

"What happened?"

"You know, I made Joubert what he is. He was nothing until I picked him up. Nobody knew these wines. I purchased barrels for him, elevated his program, spent time in the vineyard. Presented his wines at IPNC last year. Both domaines. Got him some great press with Wilson. And Eric. Now he thinks he's a superstar. Wants to double his prices. I mean, his wines are fine. You tasted them. But double? I don't think so. What happens if he has a lousy vintage? Even this year. The wines are half what they were last year. Then what?"

"You tell me."

"He'll price himself out of the market. I stand by my producers year in, year out. Fine if you make great wine vintage after vintage, but it never happens in Burgundy. You hit one year, you miss the next. He's sabotaging himself."

"How'd you leave it?"

"I walked out."

He dropped his butt to the ground and stubbed it violently with the sole of his sneaker.

"Come on!" he commanded.

"Where are you headed?" I asked.

"I told Bayne I'd pick him up. I have another tasting."

"Love to come, but I think I'll just meet you in town. What time will Goldoni be there?"

"We said one o'clock."

"*À tout à l'heure.*"

Rosen wasn't pleased I was bailing on him. I waited until he had taken off, then knocked on the office door.

"*Entrez,*" Claudine said.

"Boy, Freddy doesn't seem very happy with your husband," I said.

A moment later, Joubert walked into the office. Claudine looked at her husband, and he launched into a rapid-fire description of his conversation with their importer that I couldn't follow. When he'd finished, she turned to me.

"You know, it is impossible," she explained. "Everything is expensive: the equipment, the barrels, the way we work in the vineyard. Freddy asked us to do all this, and then, when we ask for more money, he goes crazy."

"I'll see if I can calm him down," I said.

18

I followed Claudine's directions to the eastern edge of town. The vineyards there were planted on bottom soil, and the houses appeared run-down, their owners' stoic efforts to maintain appearances in the face of ill fortune and poverty visible in every meter.

I located Henri Pitot's place first. If its neighbors were humble, chez Pitot itself was a wreck. Weeds choked the rusted cyclone fence that surrounded a barren patch of ground. The courtyard was a shambles: barrels, split and grayed by weather, stood or lay on their sides in front of an open shed. One of its doors, ripped from its hinges, had been propped against the weathered barn board, and I could see an ancient wine press standing dormant in the dark. In the center of the yard, a well had been covered with a wooden disk, the metal armature above it broken and its length of rope thrown in a heap at its foot. A bucket lay on its side in the dirt. A vine, its leaves turned brown, twined above the front door, little clusters of moldy grapes unpicked on its few, wizened cordons.

I knocked on the door and waited. Crows cawed from a neighboring field, fluttering and flapping and fighting over the rotten dregs of the harvest. I knocked a second time. The woman who opened the door was gaunt. She wore a faded housedress, a moth-eaten sweater, and slippers. She stood, one hand on her hip, the other still on the doorknob as if she were about to slam it in my face. She stared at me, her expression suffused by suspicion.

"Is this the Pitot household?" I asked in careful French.

"*Oui*," she said.

"Does Jean live here? Jean Pitot?"

She nodded curtly.

"He is your son?" I asked. She said nothing. "Is he home? We know each other. I met him in Napa a few months ago," I said.

She turned and disappeared toward the back of the house.

"Jean!" she barked. "Get up! There's someone here to see you."

The door creaked open. I could hear them whispering furiously but couldn't make out what they were saying. The woman wouldn't stop. She seemed to be lashing him with a string of curses. A moment later she reappeared, opened the front door, and reluctantly beckoned me in. Then she walked to the far corner of the hallway and stood in front of its entrance as if to block any passage to the private portion of the house.

Jean emerged, his hair a mess, in jeans and a T-shirt. He stood in the doorway, hiding behind the indomitable figure of his mother, stupefied. She turned and slapped his head with the back of her hand.

"He says he knows you from California." His expression was blank. "You're late for work," she added without looking at him and walked across the front hall to the kitchen.

"I'll be right out," Jean said in English, and disappeared.

The foyer was barren, a simple hall tree sporting some jackets and caps, its mirror pocked and cloudy. An old woman, her hunched shoulders draped with a crocheted shawl, sat in the cluttered living room just off the hallway, staring blankly at a television set. The rugs, the furniture, the walls—all seemed worn and tawdry.

Pitot reemerged after a few minutes, his hair hastily combed, in a sweatshirt and jacket. He walked past me into the front yard. I followed him outside. He stopped at the well.

"You! What are you doing here?" he demanded.

"I'm trying to find out what happened to Richard Wilson," I said simply. "You were there."

"I had to come home. To help my family with the harvest."

I looked out to a field of scrappy vines. There was nothing to suggest that extra assistance was necessary to bring in whatever nonde-
script fruit the vines had yielded.

"You work here?" I asked.

"I'm late," he said. "I have to go."

He walked to a carport on the side of the house and lifted a motor
scooter off its kickstand.

"What happened the evening Richard was murdered?" I said.

He ran alongside the scooter and jump-started it. The bike
lurched and sputtered.

"I wasn't there," he called.

"Eric Feldman just told me that Wilson has a kid, a child who's
French. Know anything about that?" I shouted.

"I have nothing to do with it!" He turned out of the drive and
onto the road and sped off without looking back.

As I crossed the square in Beaune, I saw Rosen and Bayne coming
from the opposite side. Workers were unwrapping a small carousel
as if it were a giant present the town had given itself to celebrate the
Hospices de Beaune. The public tastings and auction always drew
thousands.

On the far side of the *place*, I could see Goldoni pacing in front of
a hamburger joint that seemed grotesquely out of place.

"Where the fuck have you been? I've been here twenty minutes!"
he reproached us.

We ordered from a small outdoor window and took a table
inside, sipping beer. Rosen and Goldoni tested each other on
where they'd been and what they'd tasted. When the burgers
finally came, Goldoni ate with tasteless and unseemly abandon
and, not even through one sandwich, hobbled outside to order
another and to demand the whereabouts of the *pommes frites* he'd
requested the first time around.

"Where are you off to next?" Goldoni inquired, his mouth stuffed
with a mixture of ground beef, cheese, and potatoes.

"We have an appointment at Chabosson. And then Thibaut,"
Rosen told him.

"You really have to taste Gauthier," Goldoni insisted. "His wines are incredible this year."

"He's not my grower," Rosen said. "But you're still on for the tasting Friday?"

"*Bien sûr.* Who's coming?"

"Everybody. The total lineup."

"What time do we get started?"

"Ten. We'll break for lunch around noon, one o'clock, then finish up."

The girl dropped Goldoni's second burger on the table.

"*Une autre pression, s'il vous plaît,*" he called after her, needing another beer to wash it all down. As Goldoni scarfed the sandwich, Rosen and I lit up. The light flooding in from the *place* filtered through the smoky haze.

"You were close to Richard," I said to Goldoni. "Maybe closer than anyone. Who do you think killed him?"

He looked at me, then at Rosen.

"What's going on?" Goldoni said.

Bayne, who had been uncharacteristically subdued throughout the meal, stared at both of us in turn, suddenly in his element.

"I'll tell you what's going on," I said. "You don't seem terribly concerned about it. You're sitting pretty right about now, aren't you? The newsletter all to yourself, winemakers kissing your ass. You're a big, powerful critic."

"I don't like your tone. Or your insinuations," Goldoni responded, setting the half-eaten burger on the paper plate.

"Why aren't you scared?" I said.

"Scared of what?" Goldoni said.

"I don't know. Of being a suspect. Of being next."

"If he's afraid of anything, it's probably the power he has now," Rosen broke in.

Goldoni took an enormous bite of the sandwich. I took a different tack.

"Did you know that Richard has a child?"

"Bullshit," he said. At this, Bayne let out a guffaw. Rosen remained silent but intent on the exchange.

"He never mentioned it?" I said.

"Complete, total bullshit. Who told you that?"

"Eric Feldman. An hour ago." Rosen now stared at me.

"And you believe him?" Goldoni rolled his eyes. "Eric would say anything to get back at Richard. He keeps it up, I'll sue his ass." He dropped his napkin on the plate, got up, and trundled outside.

Bayne rose from the table, casting a critical eye in my direction. Rosen stood and crushed his cigarette out.

"Very delicate touch," Bayne said. "This your idea of extracting information?" He towered over me. "A word of advice, Stern: You're supposed to make 'em think you're their best buddy in the world, be a good ole boy. Get 'em to trust you. Tell 'em a story, and then, when they start correctin' you, you let 'em spin it out till they trip themselves up. That's when you go for the jug'lur. They'll hang themselves, if you let 'em." His expression changed: the cold, ruthless attorney. "Cross–examination one oh one," he said and turned. "Count yourself lucky you never went into the law," he added over his shoulder.

Rosen scowled and followed him, leaving me to take care of the check.

By the time I got outside, they'd taken off. My eyes fell on the unwrapped carousel, the horses frozen midgallop in the frigid air, as if time had stopped.

I had no choice but to pick up the trail where I'd last seen Feldman. I found my way back to the highway and headed toward Nuits. *Did it ever occur to you that Richard was murdered not because of what he did but because of who he was?* What was that supposed to mean? Aren't we what we do? And what did Wilson do? He traveled and tasted and judged and wrote about it. He made and destroyed reputations. That's what he did. And what *was* he? A wine critic. A preternaturally talented palate. What had Feldman meant? What was he hinting at? What did he know, beyond the astounding fact of Wilson's having an illegitimate child?

Something, that much was obvious. That's why he'd made the call to Wilson, whom he otherwise despised and avoided like the plague. Then again, maybe Goldoni was right. Maybe Feldman wanted to get back at Wilson for everything Richard had done to him when he was alive.

But the revelation that Richard had fathered a child had stunned me. I was sure Janie knew nothing about it, or else she certainly would have told me. I needed to find Feldman, and this time, I promised myself, I wouldn't let him off so easily. Not until he'd told me everything he knew.

I drove back to Collet-Favreau. Claudine sat at her computer in the office. She was surprised to see me.

"*Salut*, Babe. What do you need? You are not with Freddy?" she said.

"No, they went on to another tasting. I'm trying to find Eric Feldman."

"But I have not seen him. He did not come back today."

"No, I realize that. He said from here he was going to see Trenet."

"Ah, *oui*, Domaine Trenet."

"It wouldn't, by any chance, be near here, would it?"

"Yes, it is very close." We walked outside. "You go down this road about two hundred meters, turn left and then right. The domaine is on your right. You will see the sign."

"*Merci, Madame.*"

"*Je vous en prie*, Babe." She seemed slightly mystified by the whole thing.

I followed her directions and parked on the side of the road in front of a low wall. A bronze plaque read DOMAINE G. TRENET ET FILS. A wrought-iron gate stood open, framing a graveled court-yard that contained a tractor, one ancient and one modern wagon, a rusted wheel, and a child's bike. The place seemed poised to break into motion at a moment's notice. A black Labrador bitch dutifully rose to her feet, barked once, then circled and flopped in the shade of the archaic wagon, her sagging teats splayed in the dust. At the sound of the dog's warning, a man emerged from a shed.

He was an elderly, elfin fellow dressed in the traditional blue work clothes of the countryside, a small beret perched on the crown of his head. His face had been baked by the sun, and his hands seemed carved of wood, as if they were some mysterious human extension of the vines they had pruned for seventy years.

"I am looking for Monsieur Trenet."

"*Je suis Trenet.*"

I explained that I'd been with Freddy Rosen and Eric Feldman earlier in the day at Domaine Collet-Favreau and that I was looking for Feldman, who'd mentioned that he was on his way here.

"*Oui*" was all he said.

Did he know where Feldman was going after their tasting?

He shook his head.

What about an educated guess?

He thought for a moment. "Feldman arrived here from Collet-Favreau. It was before lunch. He tasted quickly, took notes."

"What did you talk about?" I said. "Did he mention anything about his other appointments? Did you ask where he was going next?"

Trenet shrugged. "We discussed the usual. And then he left."

"But where did he go? Who was he going to meet?" I repeated irritably.

"He didn't say. I think he was having lunch."

"At a restaurant?"

"I'm not sure. He was late. He left in a hurry. *C'est tout.*"

It was pointless. I was wasting my time, thanked him, and shook hands. He disappeared into the shed.

Restaurants were probably a dead end. You go to one from your last appointment in order to continue the conversation. If you're met by another grower, it's because he *is* the next appointment, the liaison between the morning and afternoon tastings. No one has the time to waste on lunch unless it's going to result in *commerce*, and, anyway, it wasn't possible to stop by every restaurant in the area to try to pick up Feldman's trail.

I turned around and drove back to Collet-Favreau. In the courtyard where Rosen had railed against Joubert's impudence, the *vigneron* and his wife were standing sharing a cigarette, talking. They looked startled as I came through the gate.

"I'm sorry to bother you again. You're quite certain that you don't know where Monsieur Feldman was having lunch?"

Claudine looked to her husband.

"No, I do not know," he said.

"Did Eric mention, by any chance, where he was going later?"

They both hesitated, and she was the one who finally answered, "No, I don't think so." She gave me the names of several domaines in the immediate vicinity, all of which I'd seen in his newsletter, then said, "And perhaps you should try Domaine Carrière in Chambolle-Musigny. It would make sense. I know he visits every year."

"Do you mind if I call you again? I hate to keep bothering you," I said.

"As you wish," she said. "*Au revoir.*"

I could see them in the rearview mirror as I executed a three-point turn. They gazed at me, baffled as to what I was up to. I wasn't sure I knew, myself.

I dropped by the domaines Claudine had suggested, only one of which I knew from my former incarnation. Each conversation was a version of the useless exchange I'd had with Monsieur Trenet; none of the *vignerons* dared to ask Feldman where he was headed next.

I thought about packing it in, then figured I might as well swing by Domaine Carrière before driving back to the hotel. I had nothing to lose.

19

I drove through the twisting, narrow streets of Chambolle. Domaine Carrière was located on the back side of the village set beneath an outcropping of rock. I pulled into the shadow of a brick wall topped with wrought iron. The domaine was beautifully kept, its stone buildings like rustic barns covered in ivy, a willow and lacy pine enclosed in a brick-lined, fenced garden. I crossed the court-yard where a man was stacking cases of bottles sheathed in plastic and asked for the *patron*. He pointed toward the buildings.

I crossed the *cuverie*, its floor and walls concrete, the room outfit-ted with a row of *foudres*, a double concrete fermenting tank, and a pair of stainless steel fermenters, and descended to the *cave*. A small anteroom led to the first cellar, where a man crouched over a barrel with his back to me, topping it off with wine from an unmarked bottle.

"I am looking for the *patron*, Monsieur Carrière. Is he here?"

"*Oui*," he said, not looking up from his work. I did a double take. It was Jean.

"Pitot?" I said. He glanced up from the barrel. "What are you doing here?" I asked. "Is this where you work?"

Panic crept into his eyes. The bottle in his hands shifted and wine spilled across the barrel.

"*Merde!*" he muttered. He set the bottle on the ground and stood up. He didn't move, nor did I. Neither of us knew what to do.

"I'm not afraid of you," he said, his chin raised defiantly.

Nor was I afraid of him. I simply hadn't expected to run into him there. In my mind, I was on the trail of Feldman and, wanting to exhaust the possibilities of where I might find him, needed to get the conversation with Carrière out of the way.

"*Le patron?*" I said.

He jerked his head to indicate that the winemaker was somewhere farther inside the *cave*.

"You and I have to talk," I said. "Don't go anywhere." I turned away and then looked back. Pitot was visibly squirming where he stood, his body language suggesting he couldn't make up his mind whether to follow me or run for his life.

Off the first cellar was a second, twenty by forty feet, with two aisles running between three rows of double-stacked barrels. As I entered it, I looked back over my shoulder. Pitot was watching me.

Cave gave onto *cave*, each portal linteled by an I-beam set into the stone so low that I had to stoop as I passed from room to room, each chamber smaller than the next but all vaulted, the individual blocks of their construction indiscernible beneath a darkened slick of mold. Electrical conduit ringed each room at regular intervals, and from the zenith of its belt, a white porcelain shade hung like a corona around an oversize bulb that cast a dim light into the gloomy atmosphere. The *marcs* and *sous marcs*, wooden struts like train ties that anchored the oak barrels, ran the length of each chamber above pea gravel. The *barriques*, held in place by wooden chocks wedged beneath them, were topped off so completely that the base of the bungs oozed, the juice leaching across the oak staves like wounds that wouldn't stop bleeding. My boots crunched on the broken stone.

I turned a corner into the fourth chamber and found Carrière standing alone. He turned suddenly, startled by the sound of footsteps.

"Monsieur Carrière?" I asked.

"*Oui, c'est moi.*" He was built like a prizefighter, dressed in jeans and a heavy charcoal-gray sweater.

"Forgive me, but do you speak English?"

"*Un peu.*"

"I'm looking for Eric Feldman, the wine writer."

"Yes, I know who he is." He furrowed a thick brow that ran unbroken across his face beneath a crown of dark, curly hair.

"I was led to believe that he may have come by here this afternoon for a tasting."

"Feldman, no, I do not see him," he said tersely.

"Absolutely not? You're sure? He couldn't have tasted with someone else?"

"*J'en suis certain.* He is not here." His tone was insistent.

"I know he isn't here now. I mean earlier today."

"I tell you, he is not here. Not now, not before." He stood up straight and squared his shoulders. "You think I do not know who comes to taste?"

"No, of course not. I'm sorry to disturb you. *Merci, Monsieur.*"

At the entrance to the second cellar, I stopped and turned around. He was following me out, and I thought he was going to say something. Unexpectedly, there came a creaking noise, a groan of wood, and, suddenly, an explosion as first one, then two barrels broke loose from their struts, rolling furiously and crashing toward me. I leapt just as one of them careened to the floor, knocking me off my feet.

"*Merde!*" Carrière shouted.

Workers, hearing the deafening clatter, appeared out of nowhere and scrambled to stop the barrels' frenzied rolling. Miraculously, only one had been compromised by the impact. It lay there, its staves cracked, leaking its contents into the gravel.

"*Vite!*" Carrière screamed at the men. "*Une autre pièce!* And some hose!"

When they had gotten the situation under control, he turned to me.

"*Ça va?*" he said, regarding me suspiciously, as if the accident had been my fault.

"Yeah. I'm fine. It's okay."

I was standing in a puddle of red wine, the barrels squatting at odd angles at the entrance to the room.

"*Nom de Dieu*, what a mess," Carrière said, shaking his head in disbelief. "Well, I think you are lucky, *non?*"

"I guess so," I said, taking in the scene and feeling my knee. "It could have been much worse."

"Worse for you," the winemaker said.

"I'm fine. Do you need any help here?" I offered.

"No, my men will clean up."

I walked out to the car. Pitot was nowhere to be seen. I may have been mistaken before about the incident with the arrow near my trailer, but this time it really did look like he had tried to take me out. But with a wine barrel? It was like a bad joke. Or a cruel joke, clumsily delivered.

The light had turned. Low clouds broke off the Golden Slope, swirling overhead and skimming the vineyards. I crawled through the village, ran down through Vougeot, and turned out to the highway. After a few kilometers, I saw a pair of headlights in the rearview mirror scream up behind me at maniacal speed. They were blinding me—I couldn't tear my eyes away from the mirror—and I panicked. I hit the gas, but within a second my pursuer was again climbing up my ass. I thought whoever it was was going to ram me. And then I saw a familiar sight: a police car and motorcycle parked on the shoulder, a team of *gendarmes*, their white belts and shoulder straps reflecting the light of the cars' headlamps, flagging down drivers and demanding that they pull over to perform a sobriety test.

On an impulse, I pulled in behind the police car. As one of the officers approached the driver's side window, I saw the car tailing me shift to the center lane and speed past. It was a dark Mercedes. Probably a businessman impatient to get home in time for dinner. I knew I'd been driving too slowly, thrown by what had just happened at Carrière. *You really need to get a grip*, I told myself.

"Sorry, it's a rental," I said in English to the *gendarme*. They hadn't signaled me to pull over, and by the time I produced the contract and my driver's license, the cop waved me on irritably.

"*Merci, Monsieur*," I said. He'd never understand what I was thanking him for, and it didn't matter.

Back at Le Chemin de Vigne, I stole upstairs to my bedroom before I could bump into anyone. I was shaking.

Sackheim had said that the French cops couldn't trail anyone because Wilson hadn't been murdered on French soil. Was it possible that the barrels had broken loose in Carrière's *cave* by accident? Would there be any evidence tying Jean Pitot to the incident? The only time I'd ever heard of barrels clattering to the floor of a cellar was when an earthquake had hit Santa Cruz and several dozen had shattered at David Bruce Winery. But now the earth seemed to be shifting under my feet. My knees felt weak, and my nerves were rattled as if I'd just come through an earthquake myself. The car's lights blinding me in my rearview mirror had completely unnerved me.

I needed to lie down and, not bothering to undress, crawled under the covers. Wired and exhausted, I quickly fell into a deep and disturbed sleep.

I dreamt I was searching for something, wandering through a series of cellars, their walls slick with mold, the air clammy. On my first trip to Burgundy years before, I'd visited a domaine that had a glass panel on one end of a barrel so that you could watch the wine fermenting. The image had come back to me in sleep, only this time its contents were bloody and frothing, a trickle of bubbles rising to the surface.

Jet lag had caught up with me, and by the time I woke up, it was past ten o'clock in the morning. I opened the door of my room, startling a maid who apologized on behalf of the *patronne*, who had driven into Beaune to buy supplies. She set a pile of towels on a table in the hallway and pulled a slip of paper from her apron pocket. It was a phone message; Rosen had called, asking me to meet them. I decided to pass. I had prepared my own list of domaines, places Feldman and Goldoni visited regularly.

I showered, needing to rinse away the stale sweat from sleeping fully clothed and the fear that had congealed on my skin. Downstairs, I tried calling several of the *vignerons* from the front desk, but no one was picking up. The maid offered to make me coffee, but I declined. Out on the highway, I pulled over at a café, ordered a café au lait, and pocketed two croissants for the road.

I made my way north, retracing La Route des Grands Crus that Sackheim and I had taken south from Dijon, stopping by two or three domaines in each village. It was slow going: spotting the names of winemakers on the small signs that dotted the squares and narrow streets of each town; parking and walking and knocking on doors. I just missed Goldoni in Morey-Saint-Denis, but no one had seen Eric Feldman. Two *vignerons*—one in Chambolle-Musigny and a second in Gevrey-Chambertin—seemed particularly miffed that Feldman had blown off his appointments with them.

Around three o'clock, I gave up and took the N74 back to Aloxe. As I entered the common room of Le Chemin de Vigne, the *patronne* knelt at the fireplace, poking the logs that quickly flared into a crackling blaze.

"*Bonjour, Madame.*"

"*Bonjour, Monsieur.*"

"Would you care for an apéritif?" she asked. "*Un morceau* of fruit and cheese?"

"That sounds lovely, but what I need is to find someone, a young woman who is working at a domaine in Pommard. Beauchamp," I said.

"Yes, Domaine Beauchamp. A very fine domaine, but it is difficult to find. I will draw you a map."

She returned with pen and paper and placed a *kir* on the coffee table. I thanked her and drank the apéritif as she drew the map and described how to find Beauchamp. I'd lost Feldman's trail in a pool of wine. I wasn't sure where to pick it up. I thought I might have better luck locating Goldoni, and Monique seemed the best place to start.

Monique Azzine had met Richard Wilson and Jacques Goldoni a few months before Richard was murdered. She'd obviously been upset by Goldoni's appearance at the restaurant two nights before, a response that made no sense unless something had happened when they'd met in Barsac. Since Goldoni seemed attracted to her, and since I'd blown any chance of getting him to open up myself, I thought it was worth it to see if I could enlist her help. When we'd shared a smoke at the bistro in Beaune, we hadn't been able to finish our conversation.

Still, I knew that I'd aroused her curiosity and that, if only for a moment, we'd connected.

The narrow streets of Pommard were a labyrinth, and by the time I pulled into the gated drive, twilight had deepened, tinting the sky a dirty purple. The shuttered mansion stood to one side, a neat garden planted at its edge. Pallets of boxes wrapped in plastic were stacked in a perfect square in the graveled yard, composing a post-modern sculpture. A tractor was parked beside the *cuverie.* A giant wooden door stood open, a faint light spilling from within.

The first room, an office, sported a desk, a darkened computer, and some lovely antiques hanging on the wall, old winery tools: a pitchfork; an auger for boring holes in barrels; a scythe; and a broad-handled, double-bladed axe.

I stood still momentarily to get my bearings. I entered a second room. Barrels set two-high lined the walls and ran neatly front to back. I could hear voices from the third cellar. A group of four men stood, glasses in hand, and turned to face me as I came through the door.

I introduced myself. One of them, André Guignard, was the winemaker. He was young—maybe in his late twenties—and casually dressed in jeans, a fleece jacket, and sneakers. The second, a Frenchman, was an exporter, and the two others were American, an importer and a distributor who were in town for the auction and the week's festivities.

"I apologize for the interruption," I said. "I'm looking for Monique Azzine."

"I am sorry, I don't know where she is," Guignard said in heavily accented English, but at that instant she came through the door, wiping her hands on the faded overalls that draped her body. Beneath the floppy bib she wore a tight, long-sleeved, white V-neck T-shirt. As she entered she loosened her hair, which had been pulled back in a ponytail, and shook it like a mane.

"So, here she is," Guignard said.

She was astonished to find me there.

"I've finished for the day." She smiled at Guignard.

"Then join us," he said, pulling a stem from an upended barrel and holding it out to her.

"I can't. I'm sorry. I have a dinner engagement," she explained.

"Ah. With whom?" Guignard asked.

"Freddy Rosen," Monique said.

The Americans exchanged smiles.

"Okay. Good-bye. Go!" Guignard said, turning his back on her.

Monique rolled her eyes. "I can only give you a few minutes," she told me as she led me back through the cellars.

Seeing the computer in the foyer, I said, "Do you mind if I check my e-mail?"

She walked to the desk, shifted the mouse, and stepped back.

"Help yourself. My room is down the hall on the right."

I sat down and navigated the search engine. An utterly compelling and predictable mix: two ads for cut-rate Viagra; an offer of First and Second Growth Bordeaux I'd never be able to afford; and a not-to-be-missed franchise opportunity that would have had me frying chicken and slinging burgers for the rest of my life.

I passed down a short hallway. Her room was sparsely furnished: a bed, a desk, an armoire. A few books stood on a nightstand. A faded hooked rug covered most of the floor. She was showering, the door of the bathroom left slightly ajar. As she stepped out of the shower, I caught a strip of her body from behind: a shoulder, the length of her torso, one leg. She was built like an athlete. She glanced up and, realizing I was in the room, shut the door.

"I have to get ready," she said.

"I was hoping you'd join *me* for dinner," I said.

"I'm sorry. But it's true that I'm meeting Freddy."

"Where are they staying?"

"He and the lawyer have a *gîte*, a small house, that Philippe Frossard owns. Do you know him?"

"Only by reputation," I said. Frossard owned the finest *tonnellerie* in Burgundy. His barrels cost a small fortune.

"You must meet him. He's fantastic."

She emerged wrapped in a towel. She really was something.

"Have you ever been to America?" I said, looking away.

"No, but I'd like to come. Someday. Freddy says he can find a job for me," she said, crossing to the closet and closing the door behind her.

"How'd you meet Richard? You said it was in Barsac?"

"So, you were listening to me?" She craned her head out the door and smiled. Her neck was exquisite.

"It was a small restaurant." I looked contrite, and she laughed. "You met him by accident?" I said.

"Yes. By accident," she said, ducking back into the closet. "They came to taste."

"'They,' meaning Richard and Jacques?" I said.

"Of course."

"So, you didn't know Richard that well?"

She was shuffling through hangers and suddenly stopped.

"No, I didn't. Why?"

"I told you, I came here looking for some kind of solution to his murder. You seemed very upset to find Goldoni at that restaurant. I'm interested in the reason."

She didn't say anything. I could hear her slip on some clothes. She emerged from the closet wearing black jeans and a sweater. She held a pair of boots in her hand, dropped them in front of the bed, and walked back to the bathroom.

"Did Richard ever make a pass at you?" I asked.

"I thought we were talking about Jacques . . ."

"Did *either* of them hit on you?"

"Unh!" she grunted, exasperated by my impertinence. She turned on a hair dryer, then shut it off.

"Do you wish to find Richard's killer, or do you just want to know about my personal life?" she said loudly. She flicked the dryer on again.

"I saw Eric Feldman this morning," I said over the noise of the hair dryer. "He told me Richard has a child."

She turned the dryer off again and looked at me from the mirror.

"What did you say?"

"Apparently Richard has a child."

"A child? *Vraiment?*" she said, her voice low. She flicked the hair dryer back on and brushed her hair out roughly.

"You ever meet a guy named Jean Pitot?" I asked loudly.

She took a moment before saying, "Jean Pitot? Yes, I think so." She turned the dryer off and emerged from the bathroom, sitting on the edge of the bed. "But one meets lots of people," she said, leaning down and pulling her boots on.

"I could really use your help," I said. "You don't seem to have much use for Goldoni, but I'd like you to try and help me find out what he knows."

She stood. "It isn't any of your business. Or mine. Why are you doing this?" It was more plea than question. *Please don't force me to talk about it, to talk to him,* her expression said.

"I was asked to. By Richard's sister."

She searched my face, then said, "I'm late. I told Freddy that I would be there by now."

"Is Jacques going to be there?" I asked.

"I hope not," she said, grabbing a jacket and purse.

I followed her into the hallway. As we passed through the foyer, I looked up at the antique implements suspended on the wall above the desk.

"I guess they didn't fuck around in the olden days, huh?" I said.

"They've always fucked around," she said and walked out to the courtyard.

A slight drizzle glazed the crushed earth. The cube of wine sheathed in plastic looked as if it had been cast in polished steel.

"You haven't answered a single question," I said.

She stopped and faced me.

"How should I know any of it?" she said. Then, in a low voice she added, "I didn't know Richard. He didn't talk to me."

She walked to her car, an old beat-up Fiat, and opened the door. The same panic I'd seen in Pitot's face suddenly took hold of her features, a mute fear.

"I have to go," she said.

20

I didn't know what to make of Monique Azzine. On the one hand, she was like many young professionals I'd met in wine circles, moving from job to job, working her way up the ladder, seeking the next opportunity wherever it presented itself. On the other, given her looks and the powerful attraction she exerted over men, she might sleep her way to the top. I hadn't seen enough of her to pass judgment on her competence as a winemaker.

But I was convinced something had occurred in Barsac, between her and Wilson or between her and Goldoni, something she wasn't letting on about. Like everyone I'd come across so far, she was keeping what she knew to herself. She'd definitely reacted when I mentioned Eric Feldman and his stupefying revelation, not to mention her awkward response to my question about Jean Pitot.

Could Pitot possibly be Richard's illegitimate son? Was the phone call Feldman had made to Wilson in San Francisco the favor he'd been asked to do? Maybe that was the reason Pitot had gone to Napa.

More than ever, I needed to talk to Feldman.

As I passed through Beaune, I decided to drop by the Novotel to see if I could find him. A different and more congenial attendant stood behind the reception desk. She tried Feldman's room, but there was no answer. Several messages were folded in his mailbox, and she seemed surprised he hadn't gotten them.

"I am sorry. I think he must be at dinner. Would you like to leave him a message?" she said.

"*Non*," I said. "*Merci.*"

As I drove north toward Aloxe, I realized I was famished. Passing a little roadside bistrot that seemed charming enough, I pulled over.

Its walls were artlessly painted with cartoons of the Folies Bergère, preposterous and misshapen figures that resembled toreadors and señoritas enthralled by the tangos of courtship, seduction, and submission, and I pictured the scene unfolding now at Rosen's farmhouse, with the importer and his sidekick posturing for Monique's benefit.

A plump and jovial woman came out of the kitchen to seat me and handed me a menu. There was only one other party in the place, a couple of impossibly large Brits, and, as I examined the menu, I was subjected to their rambling, pompous rehashing of what they'd tasted that day. A carrying case lay at the foot of their table, and as the *patronne* left me, one of the men asked her to bring a dozen wineglasses so that they could continue to range through the samples they'd been given. I caught her attention and asked her to bring a bottle of Chambolle-Musigny made by Jean-Luc Carrière that was on the list.

I took my time over the wine. It was supple, luscious, the fruit opulent and fragrant. Black fruits and bacon fat, as muscular as the man who made it.

The meal was simple but sumptuous: a platter of sautéed frog's legs and *côte de boeuf*, cooked *à point* with a cream sauce that floated a small forest of morels. I concentrated on my food and wine, intent on ignoring the two men, but they were too loud and offensive, so I ate quickly.

I wasn't ready to head back to my hotel. Staying on the *nationale*, I drove instead to Nuits, took the turnoff to the east, and found rue Cussigny, where the Pitots lived. I killed my headlights just before I reached the house, and parked at the dead end by the railroad tracks.

The night air gripped me. A slight wind rustled the crown of a line of poplars. The street felt abandoned. The lights of a TV flickered through the Pitots' lace curtains. I moved as quietly as I could, tiptoeing to the back of the house. Jean's motorbike was still gone. I walked into a field that bordered the property and crouched in a furrow between two rows of vines.

I could see into the kitchen. A man was sitting with his back to me, his shoulders hunched, as Madame Pitot moved around the kitchen, preparing dinner. From my vantage point, I could hear her screaming at him, and he seemed to be cowering under the onslaught. Finally, she set a plate down and stood there, glowering. He ate his dinner in silence, shoveling the food. I watched him refill his wineglass three or four times. And then a sudden beam of light arced across the front of the house and cast a yellow glow through the cluttered confines of the carport into the field, just missing me. An engine died, and a minute later Jean entered the kitchen. The woman exploded again.

I could hear nothing of what she was saying, but the rage that impelled it was clear enough. Her anger seemed uncontrollable, and after venting at her son for several minutes without pausing for breath, she stormed out of the kitchen. Jean sat down at the table to join his father, and at last the two men were able to eat in peace.

I inched my way back along the edge of the vineyard. There was now a worker's vehicle—a three-wheeled scooter with a little pickup bed—in the carport. It was too dark, and I was too anxious to get out of there to be able to see very clearly. The only other thing I could make out was a wheelbarrow, like the ones workers used to burn vine cuttings, that stood propped against the tailgate.

As I drove past the house, I saw Pitot and his father enter the carport. Henri held a flashlight as his son opened the back of the diminutive vehicle. Hearing my car, the elder Pitot fanned the flashlight across the street. I hit the accelerator, the crisp, bright odors of earth and rotting fruit still clinging to my nostrils.

I was somber the next morning at breakfast and decided to limit myself to a café au lait. If Jean Pitot was Richard Wilson's child and

Wilson had rejected him, mightn't Pitot have wanted him dead? It seemed a perfectly serviceable motive to me.

I played back the scene at the Pitots' in my mind. The mother had been ferocious, a tyrant. The men were terrified of her, husband and son both. Jean had left that morning on a motorbike and returned in a work vehicle—not all that strange, since everyone, with the harvest completed, had begun to cut and burn. But the vineyard I'd knelt in was so ill tended that it seemed impossible Jean and his father would have set to pruning it so promptly. Perhaps he'd been pruning Carrière's vineyards. But if that were the case, why had they needed to go out to the truck right after dinner?

My musings were interrupted by two nearly simultaneous events: First, a telephone was placed before me on the table, and, a few seconds later, Lucas Kiers, back from his morning jog, made his puffing entrance into the dining room.

The call was from Rosen. "Where'd you disappear to yesterday? You should meet us this morning," he said. "I have a big tasting at Domaine Gauffroy in Gevrey at ten. Jacques will be with us. Smithson thinks you ought to give it another crack after your performance the other day. Anyway, it will be interesting. All my growers will be there."

Since I was getting nowhere on my own, the invitation was hard to refuse.

"Sure," I told him. "*À tout à l'heure.*"

"So, where are you off to?" Kiers asked as I set the phone down.

"Domaine Gauffroy. Freddy Rosen has some major tasting he's put together. He said that all of his guys would be there."

"Gauffroy? Jesus, I wish I could go. I've been wanting to revisit them. I didn't treat them very well when they were first released. You think you could get me in?" he said.

"I don't know. Jacques Goldoni's going to be there. If you know him, you could give him a call."

"Goldoni? Well, that settles it. Can't do it. And I wouldn't want to, even if I could."

"Tough luck," I said.

"Well, *bonne dégustation*!"

He left me to the last swallow of my coffee. Returning to my room, I called Colonel Sackheim. He picked up on the first ring.

"*Oui*, Sackheim."

"Colonel, this is Babe Stern."

"*Ah, Monsieur.* How goes the investigation?"

"I can't seem to find Eric Feldman. Not since Freddy Rosen, an American importer, and I met him Wednesday morning at a domaine in Nuits-Saint-Georges. I swung by his hotel last night— the Novotel, just outside the walls of Beaune—but he hadn't picked up his messages. I have no idea where he is."

"Well, he is a busy person. He races from one domaine to another."

"That's true, but I saw a couple *vignerons* yesterday who seemed pretty upset that he hadn't arrived for appointments he had scheduled with them."

"Curious," Sackheim said.

"Yes, but there's more. After a tasting with Rosen the day before yesterday, I went to find Jean Pitot. I had two addresses, one for an Henri and a second for Gilbert Pitot. But Henri is Jean's father. They live on the edge of Nuits-Saint-Georges. Rue Cussigny, by the railroad tracks."

"Yes, I know where this is," Sackheim said.

"Pitot was there, still asleep. I met his mother."

"And? What did you learn from him?"

"Not much. He said he had to come back home to help with the harvest."

"Naturally," Sackheim said with a certain impatience.

"But he doesn't work with his father. After lunch Wednesday, I picked up where I'd last seen Feldman, at Collet-Favreau, and then went on to Domaine Trenet, where he'd said he was going next. But he was long gone, and I couldn't get a thing out of Trenet, so I went back to question Claudine Collet-Joubert. She suggested that I drop by Domaine Carrière, in Chambolle. It was just a hunch she had, knowing Feldman."

"Yes. And?" the colonel said testily.

"I ran into Jean Pitot at Carrière. He was topping off barrels."

"So, Pitot, he works there?"

"Yeah, absolutely."

"*Et alors?*" was all Sackheim said.

"That's not all. As I was leaving, some barrels broke loose."

"The barrels, they fell, in the *cave?*" he said.

"They must have come loose. One almost took me out at the knees." There was a silence. "Colonel, are you there?"

"*Oui,* I am here. I am thinking." He paused. "You suspect Pitot?"

"Sure, don't you? I mean, it's possible that they just broke loose, that it was just a coincidence," I said.

"Possible? *Oui, c'est possible, mais*—you are correct, the probability . . ." Sackheim was quiet again.

"Feldman told me that Richard Wilson has a child here, an illegitimate child. A French child." Silence again. "Colonel?" I said.

"And you think . . ."

"If Pitot is Wilson's son, and Wilson refused to acknowledge him, a lot of things begin to make sense."

"What are you doing today?" he asked.

"Attending *une grande dégustation* at Domaine Gauffroy."

"And you are going to this tasting why?" he said.

"Jacques Goldoni's going to be there. I still haven't had a chance to find out what he knows."

"So, you are out of commission today, *non?*"

"*Je le regrette.* You could do a favor for me."

"And what is that?"

"See if you can find Feldman. If that isn't a problem."

"No, it is no problem. I think we have enough to make an inquiry, at least."

"I'll call you after I get back," I said.

"*Bon. À bientôt.*"

"Thanks," I told him.

Talking to Sackheim made me want to call Ciofreddi to tell him that I'd found Pitot, about what had happened at Carrière, and that I suspected he was Wilson's son—a vengeful bastard driven to kill the father who refused to accept him—but it was one in the morning in Napa. It would have to wait.

21

Domaine Gauffroy was housed in a thirteenth-century Cistercian abbey opposite a church. The setting, improbably grand and beautiful, finally obscured the boundary between wine and religion. If Pinot Noir was worshipped anywhere, this was it.

Cars were lined up side by side in a parking area, and I saw Rosen's Peugeot. I proceeded through a small courtyard and entered a massive, heavily timbered door. In the anteroom, pieces of plywood had been laid out on trestles, the table running some fifty feet in length and draped with pink damask cloths. I surveyed the room, all stone and timber. Stained-glass windows, recessed in oblique niches and depicting scenes of the harvest, lined the wall behind the tables. Opposite the wine, a woman I assumed was Gauffroy's wife, assisted by the wives of the other *vignerons*, busied herself setting out platters of fruit and cheese and *charcuterie*, baskets of bread, paper plates, and napkins. The place was bustling. Smithson Bayne was randomly opening cases of wine across the enormous flagstones, and I saw Rosen talking with his producers about the arrangement of the bottles in an appropriate order.

Roland Joubert was the only *vigneron* I recognized. The winemakers—some twenty in all—comprised a bizarre and opaque pecking order, and, predictably, most of them appeared put out by their placement on the table. Another two dozen people—assistants, children, friends—were circulating around the periphery of the room, where giant spittoons had been strategically placed.

I wandered, looking at the pictorial windows. In one a woman stooped over a vine, harvesting bunches of grapes. In another a *vigneron* stood at an antique wine press. In a third two laborers were bent over barren vines, pruning shears in their outstretched hands. *So little has changed*, I thought. *Here I am, standing where peasants delivered their tithes eight centuries ago, and here they are again, offering up the fruits of their labor to that great, implacable deity, Commerce.*

Goldoni now arrived, full of bluster, slapping the winemakers on the back, kissing their wives, prattling on in his enviably idiomatic French. The throng seemed to distance itself from him, the members' expressions ranging from the intimidated to the merely wary. Maybe it wasn't a god at all they were hoping to appease, but the self-appointed priest who would pass judgment, consigning them to their annual heaven or hell, an arbiter of taste who pretended to a convivial commonness but, in fact, lorded it over all of them.

Goldoni dawdled, stuffing himself with morsels of *jambon persillé*, *baguette*, and *fromage*, while the winemakers milled about, supplicants awaiting their appointed turns. Finally he assumed his position at a small table in an interior cellar. I was hoping to join them there, but Rosen waved me off. Too bad. I wasn't sure how or when I'd get a chance to confront Goldoni—undoubtedly, the opportunity would present itself later in the day—but I'd wanted to observe him up close, not from a neutral distance.

The tasting commenced unceremoniously. Rosen ascended the three steps from the lower *cave*—impeccably laid out with oak barrels lined along the walls and down its center—and asked the first winemaker to step down.

This was the cue for the tasting to begin, and the winemakers, their guests, and hangers-on slowly made their way to the long table in the common room, randomly or systematically as they chose, pouring an ounce or two of wine, and drifting back to sip, spit, and gossip. The older *vignerons* stood singly or in pairs, shuffling their feet, isolated and silent, while the young winemakers clustered together and were generous with their opinions and toward each other, joking and talking. Bayne stood in a corner, isolated by his lack of fluency in French, and would occasionally saunter up to the table to pour himself a sip of the wines in which he was interested.

I nonchalantly approached the entrance to the cellar where Goldoni and Rosen stood, making my way down the length of the table as I counted the bottles. One hundred six wines. I'd been to my fair share of trade tastings set up in the ballroom of some fancy hotel or spread across the concrete slab of a distributor's warehouse, the banquet tables chockablock with bottles, spit buckets, and loose-leaf wine labels fanned like calling cards, but this, I told myself, was a preposterous exercise.

It wouldn't result in a handful of restaurant or retail orders but rather would determine the fate of the domaine internationally for the next year, maybe two. *Village* wine, *premier* and *grand cru* red Burg from every imaginable appellation: Givry and Mercurey from the Chalonnaise; Volnay, Pommard, Ladoix, and Savigny from the Côte de Beaune; Nuits-Saint-Georges, Vosne-Romanée, Vougeot, Chambolle-Musigny, Morey-Saint-Denis, and Gevrey-Chambertin from the Côte de Nuits. Each *vigneron* was represented by four, five, or six bottles from their chosen appellations, three of each on display to cover the crowd, nearly twenty-plus winemakers in all. Who could possibly taste so much exquisite juice and keep track of what he was doing?

It was clear by the sequence of bottles that the lush, opulent wines from the northern villages were favored. Their placement on the table conveyed an implicit message by which the importer was already signaling the critic, pointing him toward a final verdict.

It was exactly the sort of exercise I'd begun to loathe in my last years as a sommelier. I'd realized well before his death that I'd come to resent my brother-in-law's arrogance and power far more than I could ever admit. Now Goldoni had stepped into Richard's shoes— he was, in fact, wearing a pair of Mephistos that looked just like the ones I'd seen in the closet at the apartment they shared.

The tasting quickly fell into a pattern, no winemaker spending more than ten or fifteen minutes within the inner sanctum. *"Comment allez-vous?"* Goldoni could be heard bellowing from the lower

room. "How did you do this year? Have you overcome your faults
with the last vintage? I would like to treat you well, but . . ." and
he would pause dramatically, taking his first sip, self-importantly
swishing the wine. Each winemaker was on the hot seat, forced to
launch into excuses, attempting to defend his decisions and trying
to justify what, it had to be admitted, was a less than perfect expression of what he'd hoped to attain.

"The flowering went well. The summer was hot. The grapes ripened in good form. The crop was generous. I dropped fruit in July
and all was going well. Then, of course, it rained. The first week of
September . . ." Every explanation sounded like an admission that
the *vigneron* himself had sinned, that owing to his *own* faults or fail-
ures, the weather had acted to punish him. How else could it have
happened that the wine had failed to achieve its full potential?

"*Eh bien*, you did the best you could, under the circumstances."
Goldoni sounded merciful, as if he had the power to forgive the
misdeeds of the poor sinner and explain away the mightier and irre-
vocable actions of an unforgiving and merciless deity. My stomach
churned at this ritual groveling—or was it the acid in the infantile
juice that gurgled in my belly?—and I drifted off.

As the morning wore on, sunlight filtered through the cut pieces
of aquamarine, gold, and garnet glass, refracted across the pitted
stone floor in distorted and illegible splashes, and splintered against
the pink tablecloths, each fragment tinted a light rosé. Corks littered
the trestle tables. The bottles stood in silent ranks, shedding their
blood for a higher cause drop by drop. The tasters sipped, slurped,
sucked, swished, slowly drifted to the spittoons that sat on upended
barrels, and expertly shot thin streams of wine past each other's ears
to the center of plastic funnels.

When his name was called by Rosen, the *vigneron* would break
into a sweat like a kid called to the principal's office, exchange
sympathetic looks with his comrades, and proceed to the fate that
awaited him.

I walked outside. In the brilliant light, finches flitted from the
eaves of the abbey, and mourning doves cooed plaintively in the
towering cedars. The church bell chimed again. A dog barked at the

arrival of each intruder, real or imagined. One real one was Monique, who pulled up in her battered Fiat. We kissed on both cheeks—the usual, insignificant greeting—verveine scenting the air.

"What happened last night?" I asked.

"We need to talk," she said, "but I must go in. I'm already late."

"I'll catch up with you in a little while," I told her. She smiled as she disappeared inside. Was she being suggestive, provocative, mysterious? I couldn't tell.

In the distance, trucks could be heard running north and south between Paris and Lyon. High overhead, twin Mirages drew vapor trails crisscrossing heaven.

I went back in and lingered by the door, eavesdropping as best I could. Monique had joined them in the lower cellar, and I watched her flirt with Goldoni and Rosen, turning first to one, then the other, listening, sipping, taking issue with their running commentary. Both men quickly strove to impress her. "*Bon nez!*" "*La fraîcheur!*" "*Quelle couleur!*" The standard banalities I'd been accustomed to hearing in my former life.

Goldoni sensed me at the doorway. His nonchalance seemed forced. Business as usual, but with an edge. It bugged me. I pretended not to see him, at the same time wondering if he could have had anything to do with Feldman's disappearance. His mentor had been murdered, and his main competitor was nowhere to be found. Why wasn't he scared? I was.

Everyone, including Bayne, had started in on the food. I assembled a plate of ham and cheese and a bunch of grapes and headed outside for another break. I sat in the courtyard on a stone ledge in the shade. A light breeze rustled a flowering plum that stood at the center of the courtyard. Swallows swooped, gulping insects in violent arcs, and a butterfly careened against invisible barriers above a patch of grass—*the manic pattern language of the natural world against which man plays out his own sordid little dramas*, I thought to myself.

The tasting wore on into the afternoon. I wandered up and down the table, sampling randomly. Even though I spat religiously, the wine began to seep into my bloodstream. I felt sodden and slug-

gish. Sometime after two, Pitot's mother showed up. She was poorly
dressed and carried a terrine wrapped in tin foil. From what I could
see, the other wives shunned her, whispering and smirking behind
her back. I couldn't tell if they resented the late hour of her arrival
or the fact that she'd shown up at all. Her presence struck even me
as odd. Rosen had nothing to do with Domaine Pitot. Nonetheless,
Gauffroy's wife dutifully made a place for her contribution. Still, no
one touched the food she'd brought.

I decided to take another break, and as I passed her, Madame
Pitot beckoned me, encouraging me to sample her dish.

"*Bonjour, Monsieur*," she said. "Please try my *pâté de campagne*. It's
an old family recipe." Her knife was poised and ready.

"No, thank you, I've eaten. Maybe later," I said politely. Then
I wandered outside, crossing the yard to examine the church and
have a cigarette. I could see a young man in the parking area at the
far corner of the abbey who was waving his arm and arguing vehe-
mently. I walked a little farther, merely to see to whom he was talking. The scene was dreamlike, weird: No one was there. As I crossed
back to return to the tasting, the figure I'd been watching heard my
footsteps on the gravel and turned suddenly. It was Jean Pitot. He
held a bottle of wine in his other hand and had a peculiar look on his
face. I did a lousy job of disguising my shock.

"What are you doing here?" was all I could get out. "I just saw
your mother."

"*Il fait beau aujourd'hui*," he said. "A beautiful day." His smile
was offset by the light in his twitching eyes, which were focused on
nothing. The effect disturbed me.

"You following me?" I said.

"Why would I?" he said. "*C'est bizarre, ça.*"

"You tell me. Why did you try to crush me in the cellar the
other day? Was that you behind me in the car? What the fuck is
going on?"

Pitot backed up, slowly at first, then turned and ran toward the
abbey. People were mingling in the courtyard, eating and visiting
and smoking. They ignored him as he entered the doors, which had
been thrown open. I followed him inside.

He stopped at the food table, and the women stopped what they were doing, watching him. He and his mother were staring at each other. They seemed engaged in intense conversation without saying a word. The tension was palpable. No one knew what to do.

Pitot broke off from his mother, and as he walked the length of the tasting room, the *vignerons* all stopped talking, glancing at each other nervously. He hesitated at the threshold of the lower cellar, Bayne following some ten feet behind him as if sensing trouble. Rosen, suddenly aware of the hush that had fallen on the adjoining room, looked up, and Goldoni stopped midsentence. Monique appeared panic-stricken. Then Pitot bounded down the steps.

"You have to taste my wine," he shouted at Goldoni.

"I . . ." Goldoni stammered and turned to Rosen.

"Who the hell are you, barging in here like this? I don't even know who you are," Rosen said.

"*Je m'appelle* Jean Pitot. I am a *vigneron,* too," Pitot said, gesturing to the winemaker standing between Rosen and Goldoni who just stared, slack-jawed.

"I'm sorry. Everybody here works with me. I'm their importer," Rosen said. "It's not an open tasting. You can't just walk in here and make a demand like that."

Smithson Bayne stepped down into the cellar, positioning himself between Pitot and Rosen, looking to Freddy for a signal to eject the young interloper.

"But I want him to taste it," Pitot said, pointing to Goldoni. "I brought it especially."

"I couldn't care less," Rosen said in English. Then, dropping back into French, he added, "It's not possible. I won't allow it."

Pitot took a few steps up from the floor of the *cave* and turned back. "*Trou du cul*!" he shouted.

"Fuck off!" Rosen retorted.

Pitot raced the length of the room, set the bottle of wine he'd brought in front of his mother, and hurried back outside. Everybody broke into frenzied conversation. I followed Pitot. The first thing I saw was that he'd waylaid Monique, whispering to her in suppressed fury. He reached out and grabbed her, but she tore herself away. I ran up behind them and took Pitot by the arm.

"Hey! Let go of her!" He turned at the sound of my voice, and I thought he was going to take a swing at me. Just as suddenly, he turned again and ran toward the parking lot.

I reached for Monique, but she jerked her arm away.

"Are you all right?" I said. "Did he hurt you? You *do* know him, don't you?"

"Don't touch me!" she barked. "Leave me alone." I raised my hands and just stood there as she strode back into the tasting. I was at a loss and ran after Pitot, but he was already on his motorbike, skidding across the gravel.

I walked back to the abbey. The scene with Pitot had effectively ended the tasting. Everybody was talking about it, and I had no doubt that Pitot's intrusion would provide enough fodder for a week's worth of gossip, at least. I looked around for Monique, didn't see her at first, and walked to the lower cellar. She was standing between Rosen and Bayne.

"Are you sure?" she was saying, her tone transformed, coy and teasing, as if the whole thing had never happened.

"You've got to come," Rosen said. "Roast chicken, some leftover wine. It'll be perfect. We just have to wait for Kiers. He should be here any minute, though."

So, Lucas Kiers had finessed an invitation after all.

"Tell me, Jack," Monique said, turning to Goldoni. "Should I spend the evening with *les* boys?"

I could see the blood rise from his neck to his cheeks.

"Please," Rosen was putting on the pressure. "I insist." Then he changed tack. "Come on, help me with the wine."

"I can't now. I have to go," she said, looking at me. "But I'll be there later. I promise."

"Okay, I'll see you then," Rosen said, kissing her on both cheeks.

He and Bayne went over to the long table, now covered with empty bottles. Monique hurried outside, and I followed, catching up with her in the parking area.

"What was all that about?" I said.

"Give me a cigarette," she said. She took one from the pack I offered, and I lit it. She repaid me by blowing smoke in my face.

"Who are you?" she demanded. "What are you doing here? You're fucking up everything."

"I'm just trying to protect you," I said. "Not piss you off."

"Well, you are. You're really pissing me off," she said and got in the Fiat, slamming the door.

"I think Jean is Richard's son," I called. "That's why he killed him."

She stared at me and started the car. As she pulled out of the parking lot, I could have sworn she was looking at me in the rearview mirror.

It was nearly four o'clock. The *vignerons* gathered one last time to talk about Pitot and compare their impressions of the tasting and how they thought their wines had fared. Most seemed unsure, if their shrugs were any indication, both of what had prompted Pitot's outrageous incursion and of how Goldoni had scored them.

Bayne and I helped Rosen marry the remnants of the wine, pouring what was left in the bottles into others of the same appellation that were half or a quarter full, and by the time we'd finished we'd put together a case of spectacular juice.

"You should join us tonight," Rosen said to me. "Monique's coming, you heard. In fact, you should spend the night. There's plenty of room. The Chemin's too expensive, anyway. Save yourself a few bucks. And I got a ticket for you to the public tasting tomorrow."

"That's awfully nice of you," I said, "but would you mind explaining what the hell happened just now?"

Rosen bit his lip and shrugged. "I have no idea. I've never seen him before. I have no idea who he is. But people get crazy around these guys," he said, meaning the wine critics. "Crazy," he repeated.

He left Bayne and me standing there and walked over to chat with his growers as they packed up, trying to reassure them that their wines had shown well and that he was pleased with how it had gone. Goldoni, meanwhile, was grazing through the remains of the buffet. Madame Pitot approached him and presented him with a generous slab of pâté.

Goldoni took a chunk in his fingers and popped it in his mouth.

"It tastes like shit," he pronounced, rudely spitting the pâté onto the plate as if it were wine and setting it down.

I looked at Madame Pitot. It hadn't been a very good day for her. She took her coat from the back of a chair and walked out, abandoning her terrine and her son's bottle of wine on the table. The women watched her go, obviously glad to be rid of her.

I calmed myself down by assisting Madame Gauffroy as she gathered up the tablecloths; then Bayne and I broke down the boards and trestles. By the time Lucas Kiers arrived, we were the only ones left.

"Sorry I'm late," Kiers offered as he entered the room.

"You're fine," Rosen assured him.

"You're sure it's okay?" he asked, directing the question at Lucien Gauffroy, who stood calmly behind Rosen.

"*Absolument*," Gauffroy reassured him. He looked as fresh and attentive as if it were his first appointment of the day. "*On y va.*"

We followed him down a steep staircase I'd seen earlier. It descended from the room where the tables had been set out to a basement cellar, a narrow room that ran the length of the abbey, a single file of barrels on each side, to a small chamber at the very back that housed older, rarer bottles caked with dust and cobwebs behind a wrought-iron grate. A small table stood in the center of the tiny cell.

Gauffroy offered us each a glass, and we started in on the least of his wines, a *village* Gevrey-Chambertin, proceeding to his two *premiers crus* and finally to a *grand cru* Charmes. We ended sampling his *pièce de résistance,* a *grand cru* Griottes.

Having assumed that my attenuated palate couldn't endure another sip, I was astonished as we ascended from one level of complexity to the next, the lush brilliance of Gauffroy's Pinot eliciting a string of exclamations from Kiers. "*Incroyable! Superbe! Magnifique!*" His boyish enthusiasm bubbled over. Gauffroy stood politely, his arms folded in mute repose, a smile etched on his face. Clearly, he was not surprised. Supremely confident and completely unassuming, he awaited the verdict.

"I'm really going to have to completely revise what I said a year ago," Kiers finally pronounced. "I had no idea that this vintage could come around like this."

"That's because of the way you write, the way you taste," Rosen said testily. "You don't taste wines, you taste a vintage." Kiers looked startled, but Rosen was on a roll. "You tell people what they should drink instead of letting them discover it for themselves. 'Drink the '01s. Forget '04; '02 and '03 look good. Mortgage your home to buy '05.' What kind of advice is that? Each one of Lucien's wines is unique." He uttered the last statement as if daring anyone to contradict him.

"Freddy . . ." I interjected.

Kiers, promising to recant his earlier opinion, was already clearly poised to highlight Rosen's producer, and yet Rosen was intent on riding his hobbyhorse into the dust. I pulled him aside and led him to the rear of the cellar, suggesting a more diplomatic approach. But, fueled by five hours of tasting, the disturbance caused by Jean Pitot, and what he anticipated would be only a qualified endorsement of the wines by Goldoni, he was unable to contain his irritation, which soon erupted again.

"You generalize every vintage!" he said, now raising his voice for emphasis. "Do you have any idea how hard someone like Lucien works to bring this in? Any of my growers, for that matter? They give all their attention to their work. Do you know how much fruit they drop in a year like this one? Thirty percent! Maybe forty!" By now he was practically shouting. "And then they have to deal with the weather, the harvest . . ." He looked at Lucas Kiers, glowering.

"Look, Freddy, we're writing for the consumer, not the insider," Kiers remonstrated. "The average person isn't going to travel to France each year. He needs guidance, and we're here to help him. It's a public service."

"But what kind of service is it when you write off an entire vintage?" Rosen simply wasn't to be appeased. Finally Gauffroy, who'd obviously been able to follow the twists in the argument, grunting so inscrutably that it was impossible to know what he was really thinking, decided to weigh in.

"*Écoutez*," he said, getting both's attention. "If I screw up, I pay," he said to Rosen. "But if *you* screw up," he added, turning to Kiers, "*I* pay!" His argument seemed unassailable, yet his contribution imposed only a fragile peace.

It was left to Kiers, his face flushed, to thank Gauffroy and excuse himself.

"Great work," I said to Rosen. "That ought to produce some positive press."

"Fuck you," he said. "What do *you* know?"

He had a point. The only thing I knew for sure was that the Pitots had made their unsettling presence felt at the tasting and that I needed to report my impressions to a certain colonel in the *gendarmerie.* Given the hour, I thought I might check in with Sackheim's California counterpart as well. I doubted that Ciofreddi was stationed by the phone, waiting to hear from me, but that hardly damped my eagerness to report in.

Bayne and I helped Rosen haul the leftover wine to his car.

"Look," he now said by way of apology, "I let myself get too into trying to psych Jacques out. I don't think he's going to score the wines very well. But you tasted them. How did you find them?"

"Well, it's not the kind of tasting I prefer—a hundred wines in a single go—but I thought they were pretty impressive."

"Hey, I'm sorry I told you to fuck yourself. I really wanted to tell Kiers to go fuck himself."

"I know. Don't worry about it. But he was on your side. I was just trying to save you from yourself."

Ignoring my nobler intentions, he said, "So, you'll join us?"

"I need to make a couple of phone calls first. Just give me the address, and I'll find my way there. A phone number, too, if you have one. I'll catch up with you."

22

Dusk had settled, a light rain beating against the windows of my hotel room. The moon, one night from full, blinked on and off through swiftly racing clouds. I found Ciofreddi's card. I'd try to keep it short.

I lucked out: The good lieutenant's day was only just starting.

"I was wondering if I'd hear from you," he said. "What's going on?"

"I just finished a five-hour tasting with Jacques Goldoni. You'd never know his boss had been murdered. 'The king is dead; long live the king.'"

"Meaning?"

"The whole thing stinks. And Eric Feldman's missing."

At first he didn't respond. Then he said, "Does Sackheim know?"

"I called him this morning."

"You might suggest he establish Goldoni's whereabouts."

"Yeah, but the problem is, where *isn't* he?"

"What about Pitot?"

"He lives with his mother and father. Though he claims to have left Napa to return here to help his family with the harvest, he actually doesn't work with them but has a job at a domaine in Chambolle-Musigny, a village not far north of here. He's a nutcase, if you ask me. In fact, the whole family seems fairly unhinged."

"You talk to him?"

"I keep trying, but every time I get close, he bolts. He's a creepy kid. And I think he tried to kill me."

"Let's not start that again," Ciofreddi said.

"I mean it."

"You do, huh? And what did he try this time?"

"Some barrels in the cellar where he works. They broke loose and nearly crushed me."

"Well, I guess you'd better tell Sackheim," he offered grudgingly, though I could tell he didn't take it seriously.

"I already did."

"Good move. Anything else?"

"I think Pitot is Wilson's son. Feldman dropped the bombshell that there's an illegitimate kid somewhere over here. It could explain everything. Well, nearly everything," I amended.

"You're shitting me," Ciofreddi said. He gave my news a moment to settle in, then said, "You're almost his uncle."

"Jesus, I hadn't thought of that."

He paused. "What next?" he asked.

"I'm moving in with some people I've met. They're staying in a house, a little rental place."

"But you're still going to be keeping your eyes and ears open?"

"I'll call you if I see or hear anything I think you ought to know. I'll be in an even better position."

"Well, I'm going to be here in the office all day. And tell Sackheim for me I think it's time the French cops got to work."

"I'm pretty certain he opened the investigation in earnest today. But I'll tell him. *Eh bien, au revoir.*"

"Yeah, *ciao* to you, too."

I fished Sackheim's card out of my wallet and dialed the number.

"*Oui,* Sackheim." Prompt as ever.

"*Bonjour, Colonel. C'est Babe.*"

"Ah, Babe. So, you have finished *la grande dégustation?*"

"On all fours and somehow still kicking," I said.

"*D'accord.* But is everybody else kicking, as you say, as well?"

"Everyone with the exception of Eric Feldman. He still seems to be missing in action."

"We will talk about that in a minute. What else?"

"Jean Pitot was there at the tasting, too. He showed up with his *maman.*"

"And?"

"She doesn't appear to be very popular. That much is clear. And her cooking wasn't winning her any awards, either."

"*Pardon?*" I described Goldoni's response to her pâté. "What about the boy?" Sackheim said.

"Weirdly carrying on in the parking lot, having some sort of one-sided conversation."

"Did he taste wine?"

"I don't think so, but he brought a bottle he wanted Goldoni to sample. It didn't happen. And he made contact with a woman there."

"What woman?"

"Monique Azzine, a young winemaker. She and Pitot got into a fight."

"And what was it about?" He was naturally curious but couldn't disguise his impatience.

"I don't know. But she knows all the players. She met them in Bordeaux last summer. I have to assume that Wilson asked Rosen to check up on her before he was killed."

"*Intéressant.*" Sackheim was silent for a moment. "Do you think this woman suspects that young Jean is someone other than he appears to be? Perhaps Wilson himself said something?"

"Hard to tell," I said.

"You are now at the hotel?"

"Yes, but I'll be changing my base of operations. I need to get out to Saint-Romain. The house I'm moving to is owned by Frossard. In the morning we're in Beaune for the Hospices."

"Ah, Frossard. The barrel maker. Very famous, very rich people. They sell their *barriques* all over the world. Perhaps your friends will take you."

"Maybe." Barrels now, for me, had become personal. "What did you find out about Feldman?" I asked.

"He did not return to his hotel Wednesday night. He had been scheduled to meet some colleagues for dinner. And as you said, he missed his meetings yesterday. His schedule, it was written on a notepad by the telephone."

"You were in his room?"

"*Bien sûr.* After all, I am a colonel in the *gendarmerie.* On the same pad, Feldman wrote down his appointment at Domaine Carrière."

"But Carrière claimed he hadn't seen Feldman, that Feldman hadn't been there."

"Hnh!" Sackheim snorted. "It is written down." He paused. "Was there anyone else with you at Carrière when you had your accident?" he asked.

"No, he and I were alone. I mean, there were other workers in the winery. And Pitot, whom I saw when I arrived. But, no, not back in the *cave* with us when the barrels fell. A bunch of men ran into the cellar when they heard everything crash."

I sensed wheels spinning on the other end of the line.

"So, Monsieur Feldman went out two days ago and never came back," Sackheim muttered.

"Lieutenant Ciofreddi," I said. "I called him."

"Ah, Charlie!" Sackheim exclaimed. "How is he? He does not trust us to do the job!"

"I wouldn't say that!"

"Oh, come, you know it is true. Repeat to me what he said. Spare me nothing."

"He suggested I keep an eye on you and said it was about time you guys got to work," I admitted.

"Ha, you see!" he chuckled. "I told you so."

"I said you were doing a great job."

"Perhaps. It is too soon to say, *non*? We will see, we will see," he said. "It is the Americans who are best at crime—both the committing of them and the solving. But it would be unwise to write off our French police too hastily."

"You could do another favor for me," I now said tentatively.

"And what is that?"

"I'd like to see a genealogy of the Pitot family. I'm sure you have civil records—births, deaths, marriages. That's a good place to start." I wanted to see for myself how Pitot's paternity was explained in their local records.

"Hmm," Sackheim said. "I will ask for this. *Et puis*, you will be moving where? You have the address and a phone number?"

I gave him both.

"Perhaps we have enough to warrant a real investigation by the *gendarmerie*. I will call you. And, Babe," he said after a moment, "be careful now." Then he clicked off.

I gathered up my stuff—there wasn't much to pack—and took stock of my situation. I had been attacked—maybe or maybe not for the second time—but still, it'd been an unsettling experience. I'd offended Rosen, had insulted Goldoni, and had upset Monique. Pitot may have fled, but I was the one who felt like a hunted animal. The odd angles of the room appeared like the fractured planes of the case: Richard's body awash in wine, his hand missing; Eric Feldman now nowhere to be found; and Jean Pitot, who seemed to embody the awful secret at the heart of Richard's murder. I missed Danny suddenly, wanted to hold him and read to him, and thought about calling Janie, but I had so little to tell her—a series of questions with no real answers—that I thought better of it and went downstairs.

I had to wander back to the kitchen to find anyone. The woman who greeted me each morning was at work in the kitchen, making an omelet for dinner. She was so pretty, so delicate in her movements, that I considered for a moment asking her to make two. Instead, I asked to settle my bill.

"You are checking out?" she said. "Is there a problem?"

I explained the situation—that I had friends who'd offered me a place to stay, told her that I would pay for the night—and apologized. She turned off the stove.

"It will just take me a moment."

I drove through the gathering gloom, the high beams bouncing off tree trunks, shattering and multiplying shadows through the vineyards lining the road that twisted and turned as it followed the landscape. Everything was dank, as if the earth had the cold sweats. I slowed as I passed through Auxey-Duresses. There were

walls everywhere, and it gave the town a closed-in, nearly suffocating feel, as if the homes, as well as their inhabitants, had turned
their backs to me.

As I reached Saint-Romain, I pulled over and took out the scrap
of paper on which Rosen had scrawled the directions. I negotiated
the narrow streets at a crawl. The house, well lit from the street, had
been done up in fake farmhouse style, stuccoed concrete and new
black tile.

Monique was sitting on the center island, vamping it up, as I
entered. Rosen stood with his back to her, pulling the roasted birds
from the oven. Smithson Bayne, meanwhile, was surveying the
booty plundered from the tasting, naming each wine at the top of
his lungs as he hoisted the bottles from a cardboard case. I said hi,
dropped my bag, and set to work building a fire in the enormous
fireplace that dominated one corner of the living room.

After we'd finished dinner, Monique threw herself onto the sofa
next to me. I could feel her thigh against mine.

"What's wrong?" she said. "You are sad."

"I'm fine," I said.

"Bullshit. Anyway, I accept your apology."

"What apology?"

"I am not angry. I know you only wanted to protect me. Thank
you." She kissed me on the cheek. "I have a present for you." She
hopped up, ran to the kitchen island, and rummaged through her
purse, returning with a tin *tastevin.* "This is for you. You must come
to the tasting tomorrow. It will be fantastic."

"The tickets are by the front door," Rosen announced, "on the
table. You're all set."

"Thanks," I said to them.

"Promise me you'll be there." She waited.

"Yeah, sure. What time are you going?" I said to Rosen.

"I have an appointment first thing in the morning. You're welcome to come with us. Then we'll head into town. I like to get there
as early as possible. It's a mob scene."

We sat there several hours. Rosen railed against Goldoni and his
response to the wines. Then he launched into an attack on Kiers and
the penchant of critics to lump whole vintages together. I fed the

fire two or three times, just to have something to do—the last thing I wanted was to listen to Rosen bitch. Bayne pulled out a bottle of *fine de Bourgogne* he'd bought at one of the domaines they'd visited, and they started in on that. With some serious juice under his belt, Rosen then went off on the impertinence of Jean Pitot's showing up at the tasting, demanding they sample a bottle of his wine.

"Who the fuck does he think he is?" Rosen said.

"Richard Wilson's son," I said. "Probably thought he had a right."

Monique fixed me with her eyes and twisted her mouth in reproach, but she seemed reluctant to wade into the incident in Rosen's presence.

"I wouldn't believe everything Eric Feldman tells you," Rosen said.

"Well, if I could just find him, I might be able to figure out what he meant," I said.

"He's around," Rosen said. "He's just too busy to waste his time on you."

We regarded each other uneasily.

"*Bonne nuit,*" I finally said, pulling myself off the sofa and taking my bag.

I was spent. Bayne had dozed off in an easy chair next to the fireplace and was snoring loudly. I excused myself, headed upstairs, and found a loft overlooking the living room with a mattress on the floor. After fifteen or twenty minutes, I could just make out Rosen's whispered entreaties through the crackling of the fire. He was begging Monique to stay, promising she would love it, swearing he would do anything she wanted.

"I don't know. I have to be up at dawn to work at the tasting," she said.

"No, come on. Come downstairs. Stay with me." I heard him pour another two glasses of the *fine de Bourgogne.* A moment later, the lights were turned off, and they tiptoed down the carpeted staircase.

23

The next morning I heard the front door close and wandered down-stairs. No one else was up. I assumed Monique had taken off to work the public tasting. The kitchen was a disaster: bottles and glasses, bits of chicken carcass, greasy napkins. I did the best I could to tidy up without waking anyone. Just as the coffee I was making sputtered and was done, I heard a knock on the door. It was a little before eight.

Sackheim was standing at the door, backlit by a blinding sun.

"*Bonjour.*" His uniform was crisply starched. "Ready to get to work? First, you come with me, then I leave you at the tasting."

I trotted to the bathroom and looked at myself in the mirror. Not a pretty picture. I pulled myself together as quickly as I could, grabbed one of the tickets and programs Rosen had set out and the *tastevin* Monique had given me, and joined Sackheim.

"If you have time, you must discover the little park. It's just down the street," he said as we got in the police car.

He parked in front of a small café on the road that ran through Saint-Romain. "*Deux crèmes, s'il vous plaît,*" he said to the old guy standing behind the bar. "*Et un seul croissant,*" he added, pushing a ring of hard-boiled eggs and a saltshaker in front of me. "You look the worse for wear, my friend. Eat something."

He explained that he'd set his lieutenant to finding out what he could about Jean Pitot, but that our time together now would be spent tracking down Jacques Goldoni.

"It is strange, *non?* Perhaps Goldoni was in Napa when Wilson was there. Yes, yes, I know about the phone message Feldman left for Wilson. And the calendar with Wilson's and Goldoni's itineraries. Lieutenant Ciofreddi told me. But, it is possible, *non?*"

"But I thought that . . ."

"Yes, I know, you think that Feldman had a motive for killing Wilson. And maybe he did, but he was not in Napa, either, as far as we know. As for Goldoni, *je ne sais pas.* Maybe he simply wants to, how do you say, 'clear the field,' eliminate the competition. First, Monsieur Wilson, and now, Monsieur Feldman."

"But he's an oaf."

"An 'oaf'?"

"*Un crétin.*"

"Hah. You should see some of the *imbéciles* who commit murder. The human heart is a dark mystery, my friend. It is our job to provide . . . illumination." He swallowed his coffee, plunked three euros on the counter, and led me outside.

We passed through Auxey-Duresses and Pommard, but on the ring road that circled Beaune, he turned off before entering the town. He parked in the lot of the Novotel and smiled.

"But I thought we were . . ."

"Yes, very curious, *non?* Feldman and Goldoni, they are staying at the same hotel. But did Feldman know this?"

We entered the Novotel lobby, jammed with tourists in town for the Hospices. Sackheim approached the front desk and patiently waited while the same guy who'd hidden from me that first day drew an itinerary for an older British woman on a map of the town. He grew increasingly testy as she asked him to clarify his directions yet one more time.

He rolled his eyes, looking for sympathy as Sackheim approached, but didn't acknowledge me.

"*Oui, Monsieur,*" he said, deferentially.

"*Je cherche* Monsieur Jacques Goldoni," Sackheim said.

"*Oui, Monsieur.* I think Monsieur Goldoni is in the *salle à manger.*

I saw him just a little while ago." A bit more forthcoming this time around.

"Stay here, if you don't mind," Sackheim instructed me. "Hide behind a newspaper. I don't want him to know you are here."

I found a copy of the *Herald Tribune* on a table and positioned myself behind a column. From where I sat, I had a perfect view of Goldoni's table in a floor-to-ceiling mirror.

The dining room stood off the main lobby. A group clustered at the buffet and turned to stare at the entrance of a *gendarme*. Goldoni was seated in the corner with a copy of *Wine Watcher's World*. Sackheim approached him and waited a moment—Goldoni was lost in the pages of his magazine—before introducing himself. It was impossible at my distance to tell what they were saying. Sackheim appeared to ask a question, Goldoni would answer, Sackheim would pose another. None of Goldoni's responses seemed very expansive. The interview lasted no more than ten minutes.

Exiting the lobby, Sackheim walked straight past me. I folded the *Trib* and followed him out.

We sat in the car, our eyes trained on the entrance to the hotel. Sackheim pulled out a small black book and jotted a few notes.

"He says that he had dinner Wednesday evening with Monsieur Rosen. On Thursday he dined with two British importers, and last night he met a winemaker who is trying to get his name before the American public. After dinner he returned to his room. He agreed to provide his schedule so his appointments can be verified. We shall see."

We drove in silence. As we approached the highway, I could make out the Gothic spire of Saint-Nicolas in the distance rising from the center of Meursault. Flocks of sparrows landed and rose again in the vineyards in unpredictable and ever-changing clouds while crows picked at clusters of shriveled fruit that had been left on the ground to rot. Minivans were parked on the dirt tracks, and workers crouched in the vineyards, paring the vines down to stumps and burning the cuttings in rusted-out wheelbarrows. Fumaroles wafted from the barren rows in the morning light and settled into a low, pungent haze that hugged the hills. I lowered the window. The sweet, acrid smoke scented the air, burning my nostrils and stinging my eyes.

As we headed north from Beaune, I gazed out at the lichen green wash of the ground cover glistening between the rows of vines, the pearlescent skies of Burgundy, the neat hedgerows like sutures on the land, the white of Charolais cattle an absence of color in abstract against the sienna of pruned vines and the dazzling emerald of pastures. The last leaves of the chestnuts feathered the air. Autumn had arrived, and the sere slopes of the *côte* composed a kaleidoscope of earth tones: umber, ochre, burnt sienna, the blood red burgundy of ivy trained across the raw stone of châteaux, and the gold and carmine spangles of grape leaves, desiccated and frozen in the still light.

Entering the village of Nuits-Saint-Georges, Sackheim parked in front of the *gendarmerie.*

"*Bonjour, Colonel,*" the officer on duty greeted him as we entered.

Sackheim was on his own turf, all business. He led me through a door and down a hallway to a small office. A uniformed man sat at a desk, reading what looked like a thick ledger. Sackheim introduced us.

"Lieutenant, our American friend, Monsieur Stern. Lieutenant Georges Ponsard."

The man nodded, unimpressed, and returned to his work.

"We are digging around, doing a little excavation among the stones of *la famille Pitot*, searching through the buried foundations." Sackheim paused, then said, "*On y va.*"

"I came out here the night before last," I said as we crossed the highway to the east side of Nuits.

"Chez Pitot? *Vraiment?*" Sackheim said, glancing at me. "With what purpose?"

"I'm not sure. I wanted to go back after seeing it the day before. I walked around to the back of the house."

"You trespassed?"

"Yeah, I guess I did," I said.

Sackheim smiled. "Do not be concerned. I am not going to arrest you, but it was not wise." He paused. "What did you learn?"

"Wait till you see the place. It's a real dump. Anyway, Jean's mother was in the kitchen, making dinner for her husband. She was just going off on him."

"What does this mean, 'going off'?"

"Screaming, shouting. She was out of control."

"Screaming about what?"

"Sorry, my French isn't that good. And I wasn't that close, anyway. He just sat there, taking it."

"It is too bad. It would be interesting to know what she said."

"This is it," I said as we pulled astride of the house.

Sackheim parked in front of the fence.

"In English we say, 'Born on the wrong side of the tracks,'" I remarked.

"*Précisement*," he said.

We crossed the near ground, and I glanced over to the carport. The diminutive work vehicle was gone.

Sackheim knocked on the door, and we stood there. A moment later Jean's mother opened the door. When she saw me, her jaw tightened, then she looked back to the policeman, a trace of fear playing across her features.

"Madame Françoise Pitot?" Sackheim said.

"*Oui*," she said, looking past him, her eyes fixed on mine.

"I am Émile Sackheim, colonel in the *gendarmerie*, Compagnie de Beaune. I am looking for your son, I believe: Jean Pitot."

"He is not here."

"Do you know where we can find him?"

"He is working. He is at the public tasting today."

"*Ah, oui*. And where does he work, *Madame*?"

"Domaine Carrière," she said, returning her attention to Sackheim. He and I exchanged looks.

"But he lives here?" the colonel asked.

"*Oui*."

"May we come in?"

She opened the door.

"Jean worked at a winery in Napa Valley this last summer?" Sackheim said.

"Yes."

"An American wine writer, Richard Wilson, was murdered while he was there," he said.

"Yes, he told me," she said.

"Did he tell you anything else about what happened during his stay there? Or about the crime itself?"

"Of the crime, nothing. He wasn't there. He had gone to visit my daughter—his sister—when it happened."

"Has Monsieur Wilson ever visited your domaine, *Madame*? Did he ever review your wines?"

She snorted, an explosion of air that dismissed the question as absurd.

"Is your husband at home?" Sackheim inquired.

"He is downstairs, I think. Would you like me to find him?"

"If you don't mind."

She walked slowly back to the kitchen and opened a door, calling into the depths below, "Henri!" She turned to face us. "Go on. He's downstairs."

We passed through the kitchen, which I had seen only from the distance of the vineyard out back. It matched the state of neglect and decrepitude prevalent throughout the house. Frayed rugs inadequately masked the cracked linoleum floor. The pots and pans hanging from iron pegs on the walls looked as if they hadn't been scrubbed in years. A stack of dishes tipped precariously in the diminutive stone sink, the spigot marking time in a regular drip that ticked off the seconds that had added up to years of slow but ineluctable despair.

I steadied myself against the wall as I followed Sackheim down the rickety steps to the basement. The subterranean portion of the house was, if possible, even more depressing than the living quarters, which at least saw some sunlight each day. Metal racks held makeshift shelves of dusty bottles obscured by cobwebs, an off-white mold sprouting from their corks and spreading down their necks. Three rooms snaked irregularly one to another, their gloomy confines illuminated by a single bare lightbulb that dangled from an exposed wire in the central space. We picked our way, stepping precariously on raw planks that protected us from the floor, part dirt, part rotting wood. The place stank of filth and yeast, musty wine and decay.

A man straightened himself from his stooped position. He was large, ponderous, his face etched with stubble. He wore tall rubber work boots over a pair of faded, muddy blue jeans and a thick, poorly patched sweater. He peered at us from a pair of watery, bloodshot eyes.

"*Bonjour, Messieurs,*" he said in a surprisingly hearty voice, its edges scratched by years of cigarette smoke and what I suspected was a predilection for *marc de Bourgogne.* "You are here to taste?" His eyes lightened perceptibly.

"We are looking for your son," Sackheim said.

"Ach!" he muttered, flicking his hand in disgust. "That fucking idiot. He's useless. Works at Carrière, when he could have his own property. Kids nowadays. They don't know what it means to work, really work, like we did in the old days. What does he think? That I'm just going to give it to him? No fucking way. He's got to pay."

"So, I presume that it was Monsieur Carrière who arranged his *stage* in Napa, and not you yourself?"

"Fucking Carrière," the man cursed.

"Do you know where Jean is now?" Sackheim asked.

"I never see him. He's out till all hours, leaves at the crack of dawn. Sometimes he sleeps till noon. I can't keep track of him. He's a waste. He should have taken after his sister. At least she made something of herself."

"Domaine Carrière? Do you think he's there now? Your wife said that he's to be pouring wine at *la dégustation publique.*"

"How should I know?" Pitot suddenly shouted. "Go ask Carrière! Why waste your questions on me?"

"Well, thank you for your time," Sackheim said, not rising to the bait.

Pitot calmed down. "Are you sure you don't want to sample? I have a very fine Nuits-Saint-Georges, Les Maladières," he said placatingly.

"No, thank you," Sackheim said.

"How about a little sip of *marc*? I make my own. We have an old still out back, a real antique," he entreated.

"I regret," Sackheim apologized. "We have important business."

"Fine, fine, as you wish," the man muttered, waving his hands in the air. He turned back to his labors.

Sackheim and I looked at each other, shrugged, and made our way carefully back as we had come.

Upstairs, Françoise Pitot stood in the kitchen, staring into the sink.

"*Excusez-moi, Madame, mais,*" Sackheim cleared his throat, "I must ask you again: The American wine writers, Messieurs Feldman and Goldoni, have they ever been here to taste?"

"You have met my husband, *Monsieur*? You have been downstairs, to the *cave*?" She enunciated the word as if it had an acrid taste. "And you ask if Americans come here to taste our wine?" She gazed out the kitchen window to the field where I had crouched two nights before, its furrows converging at the train tracks just visible in the distance.

"*Pardonnez-moi, Madame.* Thank you for your time."

In the car I asked, "Where to now?"

"Domaine Carrière, of course."

It was a drive of no more than ten minutes. Sackheim pulled into the gates and parked in the courtyard.

"Stay here," he ordered in a voice I hadn't heard before.

He approached one of the men in the first building, who directed him to the residential wing of the property. A woman answered the door, and they stood conversing for two or three minutes. When he returned to the car, he sat in the driver's seat, his hands on the steering wheel, staring straight ahead, as if he couldn't decide which way to turn.

"Do you ever get the feeling that you are chasing your own tail?" he asked the rearview mirror.

"Often," I said.

He turned the key and pulled out into the street.

"You want to tell me what's going on?" I asked.

"Not yet," he replied. "So. We will move on now to the public tasting."

We drove most of the way in silence, until he said, "*Alors*, I found

Madame Carrière in the house and told her that I was investigating the incident that occurred in their *cave*. I made reference to your 'accident,' without implying that any complaint had been filed. She said it was unfortunate, a coincidence. Her husband couldn't explain it. I asked her about Jean Pitot, and she said that he works at the domaine but that she would not see him today because he is pouring wine at the tasting, that he is unreliable, and that his situation at home is *'compliqué.'* Then I asked about Feldman. She, of course, has not seen Feldman and knows nothing about this."

He paused. "Her husband said that he failed to arrive for an appointment that they had, but 'these wine writers, they run from meeting to meeting, tasting to tasting, what can one do? They arrive late, they cancel.' She is not wrong, you know." He looked at me pointedly. "You Americans are *fou, non?* You work incessantly. You don't know how to rest, how to enjoy life. Have dinner, have a glass of wine, relax a little." It was a lecture, and he glanced at me to see how I was taking it. "Now you are making us in Europe live the same way. It is a slow death, *mon cher.* A slow death from too much speed." He made a little explosion of air through his lips.

I didn't mind. I understood his frustration, and, frankly, I agreed with him.

We entered the walls of Beaune and were immediately stuck in traffic.

"Okay," he said, "You will be better walking. You have your ticket, yes? And your *tastevin? Bon.*" He gave me directions to the Hôtel-Dieu and rolled the window down as I got out of the car. "Remember to spit."

24

An endless sea of people milled through the streets. As I entered the plaza in front of the magnificent edifice of the Hôtel-Dieu, I confronted an unbelievable scene. It was as if the entire town had shown up for the grand event: old and young, couples and families, mothers and fathers and children—a public infatuated with wine. The mood was festive, the air electric.

There was no way I was going to find Rosen. People were pushing and shoving, trying to make their way through the doors into the tasting. I stepped into the crowd, clutching my ticket and program.

Tables lined the perimeter of the stone-walled, low-ceilinged room, and the crush before the tables was frenzied, people hoisting their *tastevins* and calling out for a sip of wine. I was sandwiched on all sides, pushed to and fro by the mass of humanity. I tried to scan the room for Rosen, but it was hopeless. I spotted Jean Pitot, who averted his eyes when he caught sight of me, and just caught a glimpse of Monique before the crowd blocked my view.

By the time I reached her table, she was gone. André Guignard had taken over. He was laughing, rosy cheeked and jolly, but he dropped the façade when he recognized me. He dutifully poured a dram of raspberry-hued Pinot Noir in my *tastevin* and diverted his attention to the next customer.

I decided to approach Carrière's table. Lucas Kiers was standing there next to a short, humorous-looking fellow dressed nattily in an unseasonal seersucker suit and bow tie, his small, birdlike eyes peering out through perfectly round, clear-rimmed glasses.

"Stern!" Kiers greeted me. "Do you know Tad Peck? The most influential barrel broker in Burgundy."

"I've not had the pleasure."

Peck and I shook hands. Carrière reluctantly poured me a little wine. When I looked up, Jean Pitot had reappeared behind the table.

"My assistant, Jean Pitot," Carrière said to Peck.

"So, this is the young man I arranged the *stage* for at Norton?" Peck said. "Nice to meet you, finally. Sorry I missed you in Napa. How'd everything work out? I can't believe you were there when Richard Wilson was murdered. I'd love to hear about it."

Pitot didn't respond. Peck hardly seemed to notice and turned to me without losing a beat.

"Who are you with?" he inquired. "Do you purchase barrels from Frossard? I don't think I've ever heard your name."

"I'm here with Freddy Rosen. I own a bar in Calistoga."

"He's being modest," Kiers said. "Babe was considered one of the finest sommeliers in America before he dropped out. But he's not here for the Hospices. He's investigating Wilson's murder."

Peck pushed his way forward to get closer to me. I was incensed that Kiers had revealed the purpose of my trip so casually, and I turned my back on both of them.

"I'd love to have a chat," I said to Jean. "If you can take a break."

He looked at Carrière, who wasn't about to agree to anything, least of all a conversation with me. It was obvious that Carrière, not Pitot's father, had arranged the gig at Norton through Peck.

"*Pardon*, Monsieur Carrière," I said, "I just wanted to make sure that everything was fine at your *cave*. I'm sorry for what happened. That was terrible."

"What happened?" Peck asked, insinuating himself into the conversation.

"We had an accident in the *cave*. Some barrels fell. He was almost injured," Carrière said, never taking his eyes off mine, his voice all but lost in the din.

Unsure what Carrière had just said, Peck suggested that we have a drink after the tasting. "You've got to tell me all about this." Then he picked up where he'd left off with Kiers.

Carrière leaned across the table. "You should be more careful," he said.

I could tell from where I was standing that Kiers and Peck, were, in fact, following my exchange with Carrière, who looked as if he wanted to murder me on the spot. I could see him working his clenched jaw. An artery was throbbing on the side of his neck.

"What did you say? The barrels just came loose?" Peck suddenly said, turning to face us. Carrière grunted, then shrugged.

"Were you hurt?" Kiers asked.

"My knee's a little sore, but nothing serious," I said. Peck and Kiers resumed their conversation, but I could see Kiers glancing at me out of the corner of his eye.

"You will feel worse if you don't stop," Carrière whispered, leaning across the table again.

"Stop what?" I asked.

"You know what I am saying," he said. He stood up and, putting on a smile, poured an old woman a taste of his wine.

Kiers watched me as I turned to go, and called, "I'll see you later at the hotel."

"I moved," I said. "I'm staying with Freddy Rosen in Saint-Romain," but I wasn't sure if he could hear me in the crush of people clamoring for wine.

I wandered aimlessly through the tasting. It was an exercise in futility. No matter how much I might once have enjoyed it, sampling another thirty or forty wines now held no interest. I searched the crowd for the unmistakable figure of Smithson Bayne, but if he and Rosen had made it to the event, they were long gone. Probably on to another appointment. Jean Pitot refused to leave Carrière's side and seemed to be hiding behind his threatening presence. And Monique hadn't returned by the time I made my way back to Domaine Beauchamp's table. There was no reason to stick around.

I caught a taxi back to the house in Saint-Romain. I was exhausted, but it was impossible to sleep. I walked down the street, past an old house framed by walls that lay in ruins, to the *parc* Sackheim had mentioned. The sun lay obscured by the lacy branches of a willow. Vineyards stretched below me, glazed with ice, the fields silvered by mist. On the drive to Nuits, Sackheim had said that the villagers deconstructed an old Roman town to build their own. As I descended a narrow path through the broken walls, a mourning dove cooed from an elder, "Who, who, who?" and I remembered the owl I'd heard that evening on Howell Mountain. It seemed so long ago now, but I seemed no closer to being able to answer the question.

Off the path I read a sign that had been mounted for tourists, explaining that in ancient times, wolves came down from the hills to hunt men. The villagers had to fight them off, but the wolves always took a few people each winter. The path bottomed out at a well. LEGEND HAS IT THAT IF YOU THROW A STONE DOWN THE WELL AND WAIT FOR IT TO HIT THE POOLS OF THE UNDERWORLD, YOU'LL HEAR THE VOICES OF THE DEAD, another sign read.

I picked up a pebble and tossed it into the gaping blackness. I put my ear to the lip of rock. The stone seemed to descend forever.

Not a ricochet, not a plop. Either the dead hadn't yet made it to Hades, or they were tongue-tied.

I walked back to the *gîte*. Rosen and Bayne hadn't returned. I built a fire, found some pâté in the refrigerator, pulled a hunk from a stale *baguette*, and ate a simple dinner by myself in front of the fireplace.

I felt as though the trip to France had been a great and expensive mistake. I was barking up the wrong tree. Maybe Pitot wasn't a murderer, just a troubled young man whose family was a disaster. No wonder he'd gone to work somewhere else. Who would have wanted to slave away in that dungeon I'd seen chez Pitot? Feldman might not have been missing at all. He was, as Rosen said, too busy to spend time with the likes of me. He had two dozen growers to see in Burgundy alone, wines to review, and a newsletter to get out. And being in Beaune during the Hospices, he probably had receptions and events he was obligated to attend as well. Just because he'd missed an appointment at Domaine Carrière or hadn't picked up messages at his hotel didn't mean he'd disappeared. I didn't much care for Jacques Goldoni, but that was neither here nor there. He'd have to figure out how to manage without Richard. I gave him a year, at most. I felt terrible for imposing on Sackheim, who had more important things to do.

I thought I'd call Gio. I needed to hear a tender voice. It was nine o'clock in the morning in Napa, and November. *No problem*, I said to myself, and it wasn't.

"How are you?" she asked sweetly.

"Fine, I suppose. I had an accident in a cellar, but other than that, it's been a nonevent. I should probably never have left. It's a waste of time. I think I'll call it quits and come home."

"Babe, there's something I need to tell you. I almost called you yesterday, but the time difference . . ."

"Is something wrong?" I said.

"No, nothing's wrong. In fact, it's great. My father's opening a new winery with an old friend of his. He wants me to run it, or at least be his representative."

"That's fantastic, Gio. Is it anybody I know?"

"You've never met him. It's not here."

"Where is it? Down south? Paso Robles? Santa Ynez? I've always wanted to see it down there."

"Much farther south." She paused. "It's in Chile."

"Chile?"

"The Colchagua Valley. It's gorgeous. The operation's incredible. I don't think I can afford to pass it up."

"No, of course not. You should do it," I said, my heart sinking. "When do you start?"

"That's the thing. My father wants me to leave right away. He wants me to see the entire growing cycle. I already missed bud-break." She hesitated. "I'm leaving the day after tomorrow."

"I don't think I can get home that fast," I said, but my attempt at irony fell flat.

"I'm sorry, Babe. I really wanted to see you before I left."

"When do you think you'll be back?"

"They usually harvest in March. I should be home by Easter."

We told each other how much we missed each other. She asked again how it was going, and I repeated that it was going nowhere. Our good-byes were stilted.

Rosen and Bayne got back late. They'd visited a couple more

domaines after zipping through the public tasting and had attended a party that Frossard had thrown at his *tonnellerie*. I asked Rosen why they hadn't waited for me before going on to the party, but he chided me for taking off without saying anything and didn't seem to care when I explained I'd searched for them at the tasting. I decided not to make any wisecracks about his having slept with Monique and left the two of them sitting in front of the fireplace, discussing where they were going to go once they left Burgundy.

It was barely light out when the phone exploded through my dreams. I hoped that Rosen would pick it up, but no one answered, and it kept ringing. I pulled myself out of bed and staggered downstairs.

"*Oui?*" I said, yawning.

"Babe, *c'est toi?*"

"Yes. Colonel?"

"Get up!" Sackheim ordered. "Get dressed! Hurry! Meet me in the little square of Aloxe, just before you get to Le Chemin de Vigne. *Vite!*"

The roads had iced over. I drove slowly, slower than I wanted. The fields looked as if they'd been carved out of crystal, and the sky glowed in the morning light, a dome of polished mother-of-pearl.

Sackheim was waiting impatiently in the car, drumming his fingers on the steering wheel, the motor idling.

"What took you so long?" he asked irritably as he turned out of the tiny square.

"I drove as fast as I could. What's going on?"

He didn't answer me.

The road ran up through vineyards and paralleled a paved irrigation ditch and past a cistern set into the earth that looked like a subterranean bomb shelter, a series of narrow chimneys giving vent to the gray, fog-laden atmosphere. Low walls, constructed of tightly set, perfectly cut stone, girdled the terraced vineyards.

"His dog found the body. Carrière. He was hunting" was all he finally said. Then, after a moment's silence: "He called the station on *son portable*, and Ponsard called me."

"Who?" I asked, unsure what had happened, who had found what body.

"Kiers."

I turned in the seat to stare at him. "What? What are you talking about? Lucas Kiers is dead?"

He looked at me for an instant and kept driving.

The road turned over a culvert and switchbacked past a *cabotte*, a hut built into the slope where workers would huddle for warmth in the old days. The vineyards, stepped into the hillside, curved gracefully, rising progressively to the edge of a forest, all but the tips of its woods sheathed in fog.

"Le Bois de Corton," Sackheim announced.

The paving ended abruptly, the track continuing on, deeply scarred, its ruts puddled with muddy water. The car bumped and scraped as Sackheim hopelessly swerved to dodge the potholes. He came to a stop as we reached the border of the wood. Two police cars had pulled in at the end of the track, parked beside a dark blue Mercedes-Benz. I did a double take. It looked like the same car that had chased me down the *nationale* after my first visit to Domaine Carrière. Sackheim flung his door open and hurried up the path. The air was fragrant with the perfume of rot.

In the middle distance Carrière stood surrounded by policemen, a dog standing at his side, alert. I followed Sackheim up the path.

The leaves had turned, dirty spangles cut loose in the morning breeze, fluttering to earth. Carrière would have been walking slowly, his shotgun cradled in the crook of his arm. I could almost hear the quick whistle he would have used to roust his Brittany spaniel, who wouldn't have budged, her tail extended and her nose turned to the wind. She would have known something was terribly wrong.

As we approached the scene, I could see Ponsard taking a statement from the *vigneron*. Kiers's body lay face up in his jogging suit, one arm extended, reaching and catching nothing at all. A film of dead leaves exposed portions of his torso. The blast had gone completely through him.

Carrière explained that he'd poked the body with the barrel of his gun. He'd knelt down and peeled a layer of leaves from the face, stood, and set the muzzle where the man's cheek met the ground to wedge it up. He had recognized Kiers immediately and promptly summoned the *gendarme*s, who had arrived within minutes.

Sackheim instructed his men to comb the brake, though it would be a hopeless undertaking. Hunters walked these tracks every weekend. The leaf rot had been tamped down and glistened, a mirror without reflection.

I walked over and looked down at Kiers, and Sackheim ordered me to step back. He was describing the angle of the pattern with his hand—a single shotgun blast from the front—which clearly revealed that Kiers had been confronted by his assailant, and the extended reach of his left arm suggested that he had pleaded for his life, attempting to fend off the imminent fact of his death.

They cordoned off the crime scene with plastic tape. A photographer made the rounds. Sackheim instructed Ponsard to call in the Brigade de Recherche from Lyon and the K-9 unit from Dijon. Then one of the cops crouched beside the body, a look of studious and systematic detachment on his face, the way a freshman biology student would hesitate before dissecting his first splayed frog.

"Leave him alone!" Sackheim commanded. "Wait for the team." The man, chastened, rose and rejoined the others.

Sackheim was talking with two of his officers. The younger of the two had closely cropped light brown hair, and he was muscularly built and handsome—until you saw the right side of his face and head. The ear was sheared off at the top, and his hair revealed a weirdly angled part that ran from the top of his head to a spot just over his right eye. Another scar traced his jaw from cheek to chin, each cicatrix livid in the morning light. You couldn't help but wonder what had happened to him.

On Sackheim's instructions, his men took Carrière's shotgun, asking him to follow them back to the station in Beaune. An ambulance arrived, and its attendants waited, smoking, letting the cops finish their work.

When it was time for Sackheim, finally, to summon me to the car, we sat for a moment in silence before proceeding slowly back through the placid landscape of vineyards and stone walls.

"Can you confirm the identity of the victim?" Sackheim asked.

"Lucas Kiers. He writes for an American wine magazine, *Wine Watcher's World.* He covers Burgundy."

"You have met him on this trip?"

"He was staying at my hotel. I'd see him every morning. He'd jog, you know, run, for exercise. He mentioned that he'd do a circuit of the Bois. I didn't know what that meant until we came up here."

"He was at the Hospices yesterday?"

"Yes, and at Domaine Gauffroy the other day. He arrived late in the afternoon."

"Ah, *oui*, you told me. I remember now. And did he have any, how shall I say, any disagreement with the *vignerons*?"

"No, not really. Just with Freddy Rosen."

Sackheim glanced at me. "Describe this."

I told him about Rosen's argument with Kiers.

"And Rosen, he is where?" Sackheim asked.

"At the *gîte*," I said. "Asleep."

"*C'est très bizarre*," he muttered to himself. "I had hoped you would know more. Something that might have happened between Kiers and one of the *vignerons*. Now, I do not know."

He was silent as we descended the road that ran past the cisterns.

"Who is the man you were speaking with? The one with the scars," I asked.

"A corporal. Marcellin. A good man." Sackheim satisfied my curiosity even before I ventured to ask. An Algerian grape picker had been suspected of stealing some money. They had found him in an *allée* in Beaune. It seemed a routine cuff until Corporal Marcellin reached down to hoist the poor fellow to his feet. But the guy still had his pruning knife and got a few slashes in before they subdued him.

"Not such a nice story, eh?" Sackheim asked. I shook my head.

He dropped me at my car. "*Eh bien*," he said. "Meet me at the station in Beaune at *onze heures*." He spun around in the square and returned to deal with the murder of Lucas Kiers.

I decided not to go back to the house. I didn't need the third degree from Rosen or Bayne. I wandered the streets of Beaune, which were oblivious to tragedy and full of life on a damp Sunday morning, the air reverberant with the chiming of church bells.

"Incroyable," Sackheim said, sitting at a desk in the *gendarmerie* in Beaune. I sat in a chair and Ponsard paced the room. The walls were

the color of the veins running through fine Roquefort. The tables
and blackboard made me think I was back in the fifth grade. "First,
Wilson in California," Sackheim continued. "Then the disappearance of Eric Feldman. Now, Lucas Kiers. It seems impossible."

"That's just what I was thinking," I said. "It's unreal."

"These guys make enemies," Lieutenant Ponsard pointed out.

"*Bien sûr*, they have enemies," Sackheim snorted. "But who?
Why?"

"Think of all the shitty reviews," Ponsard said. "These American
bastards are arrogant sons of bitches. Imagine, telling us how to
make wine!" He looked indignant.

"Kiers was not American. Dutch," Sackheim corrected him.

"But he wrote for the American press. Same thing."

"*Peut-être. Ou peut-être pas.*"

"Fine. His blood is Dutch. But the effect, pure American," Ponsard insisted. His neatly trimmed moustache twitched. "At any rate,
the murderer has to be a hunter."

"Ponsard, you are a fucking genius," Sackheim said.

Ponsard brightened for an instant, then realized his boss was
being sarcastic. "I know, but . . . Maybe it was Carrière himself. He
claims he found the body, but he is a hunter, too, *non?*"

"Every second *vigneron* is a hunter," Sackheim said dismissively.
"This time of year, they go out in packs, like wolves. The woods
are full of them. It's a miracle they don't kill each other every
weekend."

"An accident, perhaps," Ponsard ventured.

"Impossible. Someone would have called for help. Anyway,"
Sackheim countinued, "he was shot at close range. Face to face. No,
my friends, Lucas Kiers was murdered. By a hunter, perhaps . . . or
someone pretending to be a hunter."

Their conjectures seemed to go nowhere. I knew cops everywhere
speculated much the same way, but my companions were engaged in
what I thought of as a quintessentially French exercise: exhausting
all possibilities until they at last arrived at the obvious.

"Why Kiers?" I said.

They ignored me. I wasn't even sure I'd said it out loud.

I gazed out the window. The beautiful tiled roofs of Beaune were nowhere to be seen, only the gray wash of clouds and the filigree of drizzle like a beaded curtain obscuring the view.

"You cannot stay here," Sackheim said, finally acknowledging my presence. "We must interrogate Carrière."

"No, of course, I understand completely."

He'd summoned me here, and now I was being dismissed. I had to wonder what the point had been. Sackheim appeared unsure himself. As bustling as Beaune was, especially during an event like the Hospices, the police station was a fairly provincial outpost. Whether Kiers was Dutch or, as I suspected, a naturalized American citizen, his murder would certainly draw more sophisticated authorities from Lyon, if not Paris. And if Feldman was indeed missing—Sackheim had said there were no detectives on the Côte d'Or—his disappearance would prompt attention at the highest levels. Wilson's death had been splashed across the French press. The police would want to contain any scandal or damage, if they could.

"What will you do?" Sackheim asked, but he said it as if he were posing the question to himself, confirming my suspicions.

"I don't know," I confessed. "I'd like to stick around, but . . ."

"No, I don't mean in the future. I mean right now. I must deal with Kiers. First things first. And we must find Jean Pitot," he said pointedly to his lieutenant. "You should rejoin your friends now," he said, turning back to me. "But I will need a statement from you."

No one was at the house when I returned. I stretched out on the sofa, my mind awash with images and theories. I closed my eyes and saw the body of Lucas Kiers, his hand reaching out to the void. Then I opened them and stared at the ceiling, thinking about Pitot and Carrière, Jean's parents, Marcellin with his scarred face. At some point I fell asleep. I was awakened with a start by Rosen and Bayne coming through the front door. They had sandwiched in one last appointment before hitting the road. I told them to take a seat.

"Lucas Kiers is dead," I said. "Shot."

"What?" Rosen exclaimed. Bayne, who hadn't bothered to sit, turned, training his full attention on me.

"In the Bois de Corton. It happened this morning. He was out jogging. It looks like a hunting accident, but . . ."

"I can't believe it," Rosen said. "This is nuts, insane."

"You actually saw it?" Bayne asked.

"Not the murder, but the crime scene, yes. I was up there with the *gendarmes*. That was Colonel Sackheim who was calling this morning when the phone rang."

"Christ," Rosen muttered, collapsing on the sofa. Bayne walked to the French doors that led onto a terrace. The weather had broken. The sun was out, and steam rose from the fields.

They were quiet, visibly shocked, and didn't know what to say.

"We're supposed to take off," Rosen finally said. "I have appointments in Côte-Rôtie and Hermitage on Monday. I'm supposed to make a quick stop in Beaujolais tonight." He paused. "Maybe we should stick around," he said to Bayne.

"This doesn't concern us," the lawyer said. "There's nothing for us to do. What about you?" he asked me.

"I don't know. I'm in way over my head. I thought I was looking for Richard's killer, but now . . ." I shook my head. "The situation's out of control."

"You're welcome to come with us," Rosen offered.

"Thanks. That's generous. But I need to wrap things up here. I'm supposed to get back in time for Thanksgiving."

Each of us was lost in thought.

"I'm sure your intentions were of the best," Bayne finally said. "But if you're willing to take my advice, I'd suggest you leave this to the authorities. You don't want to get involved. This is gonna get very complicated. You keep sticking your nose in this shit, they may not *let* you go."

I hadn't thought of that. It was the last thing I needed.

"Let me call Philippe Frossard," Rosen said, lifting himself from the sofa. "I'll see if I can arrange for you to stay here a few more days until you decide what you want to do." He went downstairs.

They packed up their stuff. The silence that had descended on the house was unnerving. When they'd finished, they set their bags by the front door.

"I spoke to Philippe," Rosen said. "The place is yours for the moment, but you might want to call him." He handed me a piece of paper with Frossard's phone number.

"I appreciate it."

I walked them out to the car.

"Have you spoken to Goldoni today?" I asked.

"We said good-bye last night at the party," Rosen said.

"How about Monique?"

"I called her this morning to see if she wanted to join us on the road, but she didn't answer. I'm not sure where she is." He and Bayne exchanged looks, Bayne's suggesting he thought her absence would simplify their trip considerably.

We shook hands.

"Thanks for everything," I said. Rosen just shook his head.

"Take my advice," Bayne said, "and get your ass home just as fast as you can."

25

I was sure Ponsard had it all wrong. The notion that Kiers had been murdered in a hunting accident, or that he had been shot by a winemaker he'd savaged in print, seemed too pat. My thoughts kept returning to Monique and Goldoni. They shared a secret. Something had happened in Barsac, something that involved Wilson and Monique, something that may have involved Jean Pitot. Were she and Goldoni conspiring together? Or had Goldoni threatened her?

I spent a restless night tossing and turning, and woke up with my T-shirt soaking wet. I pulled myself out of bed and shaved and showered. I found a CD player in a cabinet in the living room and sat at the table, drinking coffee and smoking, enjoying the solitude and listening to Michel Petrucciani. Every time I listened to Petrucciani, I couldn't help but picture his diminutive frame carried onstage and set down awkwardly on the piano stool. And then he would take off, like a figure out of a fairy tale, the tortured body with perfect hands producing lyric sweetness of virtuosic purity and power. His music nearly made the whole sordid mess fade away, but it was no use. I still wasn't done. I drove into Beaune. Sackheim wouldn't welcome my intrusion, but I had little choice.

I parked on the gravel in front of the police station on rue des Blanches Fleurs. An officer directed me to an office at the rear of the second floor where Sackheim stood at a bulletin board. Just as I expected, he wasn't pleased to see me but waved me in and gestured for me to take a seat.

"Feldman is the key," he was saying to Ponsard. "And, of course, there's Wilson. But Napa has the body, so this won't help us."

"*Sans sa main,*" Ponsard pointed out.

"*D'accord,*" Sackheim admitted. "Yes, they must find the hand. But Kiers, Kiers . . . is interesting."

Ponsard dutifully awaited his further edification, as did I.

"You recall what Carrière said. He called the body '*dur,*'" Sackheim continued. "But if Kiers was shot just that morning, rigor mortis had barely set in. And it was covered with leaves. Did you notice that?"

Ponsard and I looked at each other.

"How can the body be covered with leaves if he is shot the same morning?" Sackheim asked.

I ventured the obvious: "Whoever killed him put leaves around the body to make it look as if he'd been there a while."

"*Bien sûr, précisement.* And who would do such a thing? Kiers was seen at the public tasting Saturday by many people. And Ponsard confirmed that he was at the *fête* chez Frossard that night. Only someone who hadn't seen him would try to disguise the time of death."

"Or someone who'd been there but wanted to hide the fact," I said.

"*D'ac,*" Sackheim nodded appreciatively. "Tell us, my friend, you are experienced, a sommelier, someone who's been around these writers, and now you have met some of the *vignerons.* You have read the journalism of Wilson and Kiers. Is there anyone who seems to have a motive for wishing these men dead?"

They trained their eyes on me. I took a moment to reflect.

"Wilson certainly made a lot of enemies, but not in Burgundy. Not in a long time, anyway. He gave it up several years ago. It's too complicated to explain, but that's why he hired Jacques Goldoni to cover this area."

"But if that's the case—and you are here to find Wilson's murderer—why come to Burgundy at all?" Sackheim expected an answer.

"Because I wanted to talk to Feldman and Goldoni, and I knew they'd be here. And because Jean Pitot was at Norton when Wilson was killed."

He thought about this for a moment, then said, "And Kiers?"

"Kiers specialized in Burgundy. I haven't read all that much, but he certainly might have written some reviews that could have angered a *vigneron* or two. He also wrote human interest stories— you know, about families, conflicts, that sort of thing."

Even I realized how little help that was. But, then, Kiers hadn't really been on my radar. How was I to know that he'd get himself killed?

"This Jean-Luc Carrière, I don't trust him," Ponsard interjected.

"*Oui*, there are inconsistencies," Sackheim said. "We have to continue our interrogation of him, and we must locate Jean Pitot. He is Carrière's protégé. He was in Napa when Wilson was murdered, as you say. We must unravel the mystery of *le jeune* Pitot and find him before another wine writer turns up dead."

"Are there any left?" I asked. "Other than Goldoni?"

Sackheim smiled ruefully, then nodded, a signal that sent Ponsard to the blackboard on the wall.

"*La généalogie*, as you requested," Sackheim said.

There Ponsard copied a simple diagram from a page he held in his hand.

"*Alors*," he began, "you have Henri Pitot." He wrote the name in the uniform longhand French schoolchildren learn and never seem to lose. Next to the name he wrote 1945. "His brother, Gilbert," and wrote the second name out beside the first, "born 1949." He drew a little looping line. "Henri marries Françoise Ginestet and," he paused to draw a descending line, "in 1975 they give birth to a daughter, Eugénie."

"A disastrous vintage," Sackheim remarked.

"And, in 1978, Jean is born," Ponsard continued, writing his name and connecting it to Eugénie with a horizontal line. Ponsard returned to the top of his chart. "The father, Etienne, is born in 1919 and is killed in an automobile accident in 1974." He paused, then said softly, "*Une famille qui est dans le malheur.*"

"The family has such bad luck," Sackheim translated for me. He needn't have. "You see, Babe," he went on, "we have the birth records. Your theory about Jean's paternity, I think it is mistaken."

I gazed at the diagram.

"Anything else?" Sackheim said.

"*Oui.* I inquired of some men in the village," Ponsard said. "For reasons that we cannot understand, Etienne favored his younger son, Gilbert."

"Nonsense," Sackheim interrupted. "It is perfectly clear: '49 is a legendary vintage, while 1945 was a disaster. Although tradition would favor the older son, the father associates his offspring with the material conditions of the year in which he was born. It is guilt by association. Henri can never escape the stigma that attaches to him from the quality of the wine made in the year of his birth."

"An interesting theory," I interjected, "but you're off by a year. It was '46 that was the disaster; '45 was spectacular."

"Ah," Sackheim sighed, crestfallen. "Too bad. Forgive my interruption, Ponsard. Go on."

"*De toute façon*," the lieutenant said, "the management of the domaine goes to the older son as his patrimony. But he is no good at it. Etienne gives all his instruction, pays all the attention, to Gilbert. All the men said the same thing last night. 'The old man loved Gilbert and despised Henri.' The rivalry between the brothers is bitter. The domaine falls into ruin, and after the father's death the family must sell off some property to pay the estate taxes."

"They lost the farm," I said.

"*Exactement*," Sackheim said. "Now Henri has nothing. A few poor pieces of land and a son who hates him."

"And maybe hates Americans even more. But why would he blame the Americans?" I asked, feeling a little defensive.

"We are French," Sackheim said. "We blame the Americans for everything. Nothing is our fault."

The three of us stared at the blackboard.

"What a tortuous path," I said.

"*Mais oui*, and it leads to Jean Pitot," Sackheim concluded. "One can only imagine the resentments he heard at his father's kitchen table."

"*C'est tragique*," I said.

"*Oui, c'est ça*," Ponsard agreed.

"Ah, well, let us end this tale," Sackheim said, rising. "It is time for the *dénouement*. You will drive with us," he said to me.

As we passed through the outer office, Sackheim instructed two of the officers who'd been at the Bois de Corton the day before to follow us.

We drove north. The day was lovely: cold and crystalline, the colors in the vineyards brilliant, the air fresh and cleansing. The crows were out again, cackling and fighting for the leftovers from the harvest, and a few workers straggled over their wheelbarrows, completing their pruning and burning. Traffic was light, a few trucks racing up and down the highway. The officers followed Sackheim's car in their matching Renault Laguna, their lights spinning in silence.

"You are very quiet, Babe," Sackheim now said to me.

"I still think Jean could be Richard Wilson's son," I said. Ponsard turned in his seat, and Sackheim glanced at me in the rearview mirror. "I think Goldoni knows this. And maybe Monique, too. On the other hand, maybe he's just a screwed-up kid trying to make a life for himself."

"*Ça suffit*," Sackheim said, sorry he had prompted me to say anything that might distract him, and I kept my mouth shut.

"When we arrive," he finally said, "follow us but stand back. You never know."

At Nuits we turned off to the east and followed the road to the edge of the village. We parked outside the fence chez Pitot, and Sackheim gathered his team.

"Let us be swift, professional, correct," he said. "*Allons-y!*"

An eerie hush hovered over the property. Even the crows seemed to have abandoned their endless haggling. Sackheim pushed open the gate; it creaked on its rusted hinges. He and his men walked single file across the dirt and dead grass that covered the yard. I followed at a discreet distance. The wooden lid had been pulled from the top of the well, and as Sackheim stooped, picked it up, and reached to put it back in place, he looked down. He was suddenly frozen. We all stopped.

"*Mon Dieu*," he whispered hoarsely, shaking his head. Then, very calmly he said, "Ponsard, call for help." He searched out my face. "We are too late. *Quel dommage.*"

I walked up and peered over the lip of the well. Twenty feet below, the figure of Jean Pitot lay facedown, bobbing on the surface of the murky water, his limbs twisted and broken by the fall.

I looked at the house. Françoise Pitot stood at the window, staring at us from behind the faded lace curtain. She screamed then, her cry rending the silence. A flock of crows took off from a vineyard, cawing madly.

"Why did Jean kill himself?" Sackheim mused. "*Did* he kill himself?"

He looked toward the house. Françoise Pitot dropped the curtain and disappeared.

For the second day in a row, they brought the K-9 unit from Dijon. The handler worked his dog systematically over every inch of the courtyard, and when he failed to turn anything up, Sackheim instructed him to go down to the cellar. There the animal's nose went crazy, his senses confounded by the overlapping scents—the rot and mold and fermentive stink sending him off on fits of barking that we could just hear from the yard—but when the officer ascended, he approached the colonel and said, "*Rien.*"

It was only when the man walked the dog outside the property to the edge of the field behind the house to let the poor creature relieve himself that the German shepherd produced a definitive yelp, three barks in quick succession, and the cops raced around back. Sackheim put a team to excavate a low mound of earth, its surface darker than the soil that lined the plowed field of stubble, not twenty feet from where I had hidden the night I had gone to snoop around. Even in the cold they sweated, their shovels appearing over the piles of dirt as they dug deeper.

Sackheim joined me by the well.

"Did you not notice that Françoise Pitot screamed when she saw us standing here?" he said. "She already knew. But how?"

Sackheim lit a tiny cigarillo and offered me his lighter. We smoked in silence.

An hour into it, one of the men called out and Sackheim went to look. I watched from a distance as one of the cops turned around and vomited into a furrow. A forensics team that had arrived disappeared into the hole. After half an hour they carefully pulled a decomposing body up and laid it onto a stretcher.

Before they pulled the plastic sheet over him, I got a good look. My own stomach gave a severe turn. Pieces of skin and flesh had been cut and peeled off the torso, bits of muscle and bone left exposed, worms crawling and twisting over and into the tissue. His skin had been notched dozens of times as if with the tip of a knife, the cuts tiny slashes of black clotted with blood and bits of earth. His left hand had been severed at the wrist. I had to look away. Two hay bales were stacked at the far edge of the field. The shaft of an arrow stuck out of the upper bale, its stiff red feathers like a blood-soaked, trifoliate coxcomb, and I wondered whether Jean Pitot had, in fact, tried to kill me that night near the trailer. Maybe there had been more than one deranged young man in the neighborhood.

No one asked me this time to make a positive identification, but had they done so, I'd have told them it was Eric Feldman.

I walked back to the entrance to the house. Standing at the gate, I looked out at the train tracks and lit another cigarette. Sackheim materialized at my elbow.

"Do you know, was Monsieur Feldman left-handed?"

I tried to picture the morning we had tasted together, recollecting the crabbed handwriting, and closed my eyes to reconstruct the scene.

"Yes, I think he was. No, definitely. I remember now." I paused. "It's very strange," I said.

"*Qu'est-ce qu'il y a?*" Sackheim said.

"It sounds bizarre, I know, but I'm fairly certain Pitot did this to make wine. He tried to peel Feldman, like a grape, though from what I could see, he didn't do a very pretty job of it."

Sackheim squinted. "And then?" he said.

"Pressed the skin and flesh. But why didn't the dog find anything in the house?" I continued. "Nothing in the shed, at that old wine press? Where did he make the wine?" I paused again, but Sackheim didn't respond. "Well, I'm sure you'll figure it out, though he probably washed down the equipment," I said.

He turned away and ordered Ponsard to call for a truck to have the ancient press taken in as evidence.

I lingered at the car, then walked the edge of the field as the police completed their horrific job. Sackheim spent some time questioning Madame Pitot. Her husband, informed of their son's death, promptly descended to the cellar, cursing at the top of his lungs, no doubt intent on drowning his sorrows. He'd be soused by the time Sackheim got to him.

The work took a couple hours. Other cops arrived, and I saw Sackheim speaking to one in particular at length. After twenty minutes or so, he came up behind me and placed his hand on my shoulder.

"So, what do you know now that you did not know before?" Sackheim said.

"I can't think. It's impossible to take it all in. I feel like a walk-on in some Grand Guignol."

"I agree, my friend, but you must force yourself, *s'il vous plaît.*"

I sighed. "We know they were killed because they were writers, wine critics. That's why you asked me whether Feldman was left-handed. His writing hand."

"Good."

"Pitot took a trophy from each victim."

"*Oui.*"

"But you'll need to find the wine. '*Le cépage critique.*'"

"Very amusing," Sackheim said, without cracking a smile.

"When you find it—if you find it—you'll need to subject it to chemical analysis to check for traces of Wilson's and Feldman's blood," I continued.

"*C'est extraordinaire,*" he murmured, shaking his head.

"But then there's Kiers . . ."

"*D'accord.* Who shot Lucas Kiers?"

"There's something fishy about Carrière. You know, at the Hospices, he threatened me." Sackheim glanced at me sharply. "I know— why didn't I tell you? But he only implied it, that I had to stop snooping around or something would happen to me. I don't know. I think you guys need to look more closely at the family tree."

"What is this, a 'family tree'?"

"You know, the genealogy that Ponsard drew."

"*Ah, la généalogie, oui*," Sackheim nodded. "I could not agree more. No, the investigation must continue. Nothing is as simple as it seems."

He paused, then spoke slowly, thoughtfully: "We French are less sanguine in our pursuit of the truth. We love to talk, to argue the fine points, to labor over *toutes les nuances*. We do not presume innocence. *Au contraire*, we presume guilt. And it is this system that charges the *juge d'enquête* to conduct his inquiry, to pursue all the crucial bits of evidence in his search for the truth. Something is wrong here. He will take his time. He will make an exhaustive inquiry into the facts of the case until he feels that he has achieved an accurate understanding of what has taken place."

"I'm afraid I won't be able to help you. I've got to get home. I promised my son we'd be together on Thanksgiving. If I screw this up . . . I have to be there, that's all."

"Of course, I understand," he said.

For the moment, there was nothing else to say.

Sackheim called me a taxi, and I picked up my car at the *gendarmerie*. I stopped at a café in Auxey-Duresses on the way to the *gîte* and ordered a ham and cheese sandwich and a glass of red wine. Then I had a second glass. After lunch I walked out behind the restaurant to a stream that ran through woods. I watched the water for a while, hoping it would wash everything away. It didn't. Back at the car, I called Air France and booked my flight home. I couldn't take any more.

26

Monique was in the house waiting for me when I got back. I was
surprised to see her and even more startled to learn that she
was worried about me.

"How'd you get in?" I asked.

"The door was unlocked. Anyway, I spoke to Philippe Frossard.
He said it was okay." She looked directly at me. "I didn't know
where you were, and no one was here."

I hesitated. I wasn't sure if I should tell her anything about where
I'd been or what I'd seen, but I didn't see any way around it.

"How well do you know Jean?" I began.

"Jean?"

"You know, the guy you were arguing with at Gauffroy," I said,
too sarcastically, given what I was about to tell her.

She sat down on the sofa. "He wants to be with me. I told him to
leave me alone."

"That's it? That's all?"

"Yes," she said.

"You ever meet his parents?" I asked, sitting next to her.

"Once," she said. "He hates them."

"Why?"

"Have you seen them? His father?" I nodded. "He's a bastard, a
drunk. A dreadful person."

"What about his mother?"

"She scares me." She peered into the dead embers of the fireplace.

"The only one who scares me is Carrière," I said. "What's the deal with him?"

"What do you mean, 'the deal'?"

"Jean works there. But why would Carrière send him to Napa?" She eyed me warily. "You knew he was there, working at Norton, when Richard was killed, right?"

"He didn't talk about it," she said, her voice suddenly distant.

"I know what you mean. And I think there's a reason."

She picked at a loose thread on her sleeve, pulling it until there was a visible rent in the fabric.

"I tried asking him, but he wouldn't talk to me," I added.

"Ask him what?"

"About Richard. Why he really was in California and why he left."

She bent over and cut the thread with her teeth, then rolled it between her fingers into a ball and set it on the coffee table.

"But his *stage* was over," she said.

"Just like yours here," I said.

"*D'ac.*" She said nothing, only stared at me. "So, what have you learned? You have figured it all out, right?" she finally said.

"Absolutely nothing. Every person I've wanted to talk to is dead. With the exception of Goldoni, that is."

Her eyes searched mine for an explanation.

"Jean is dead," I said. "Drowned. We found him in the well at the Pitots' house." She put her hand to her lips as the color drained from her face.

"Who are you?" she asked. "All these terrible things happen around you." Her eyes were accusing, her voice tense and shrill.

It was time to tell her what I knew, what Ponsard had learned about the Pitots, about my search for Feldman and the incident at Domaine Carrière, about Lucas Kiers. When I got to the part about finding Feldman's body, I left out the grisly details. She sat with her legs tucked underneath her, her expression uncomprehending.

"But why you?" she said. "What is happening?"

I described my relationship to Janie, my history with Richard.

"So, you are his . . . how do you say, *beau-frère?*"

"His brother-in-law. Ex–brother-in-law."

Her expression was pained. She touched my hand.

"So, you are here because you love your wife still and you thought maybe, if you solve this crime, she will come back to you."

"Something like that," I said, though I knew it was far from that simple.

"You think you figured out who killed him?" she asked.

"It seems pretty obvious."

"Jean?" she said.

"Jean."

"And why did you think you could do it, solve the crime?" she said softly.

"Richard and I were very similar. I think people misunderstood him."

"But you're better than him."

"Not better," I said. "Different, maybe, but not better."

"Well, I think so. And maybe more sensitive."

"Listen, all I know is that we experienced wine in a similar way. But then he succumbed to the myth of his own power."

"And you?" she asked gravely.

"I keep running away from myself."

"I will think about that. Because when you do, you seem to run into dead bodies."

"I know it seems that way, but none of this has anything to do with me," I said.

"Are you so sure?"

"Believe me, I'm sure."

We sat there, at a loss for words.

"*Écoute*, do you want something to eat?" Monique finally asked.

"What I'd like is a stiff drink. Something that wasn't bottled around here."

"I know just the place—Pickwick's." She pronounced it *Peekweek's*. She grinned at me.

Her mood was celebratory, giddy. It made no sense. Four men were dead, and not of natural causes.

Pickwick's was as unlikely a place as you could hope to find in the French wine country: an ersatz Irish pub on a darkened street corner. We walked in, and the bar stink hit our nostrils. Aretha, Springsteen, the Beach Boys on the jukebox. Photographs, posters, and plaques cluttered every wall, every shelf. Firelight and TV shadows flickered against the timbered ceiling, while the horse racing and golf paraphernalia appeared ludicrously out of place. A rail lined with empty boxes for *eaux de vie* and single malts ran the perimeter of the tables. I felt oddly at home seeing Coors and Guinness on tap, Murphy's, Baileys, and Graham's tilted bottoms-up at the dispensers. Drinks on the menu sported names like Pappagallo, Cuba Libre, Exotique, and Acapulco. Where did they think they were, Mazatlán? Two drunks lurched at the dartboard, hitting the floor, the wall, everywhere but the bull's-eye.

We grabbed a booth and I ordered a Johnnie Black and a Coors back. Monique asked for a beer, then walked up to the jukebox and selected Otis Redding to serenade us out of our misery. I might as well have been sitting at Pancho's. I kept looking at her, pretending we had a future. In the booth behind us I overheard two guys talking in French.

"*C'est vrai?*"

"Is what true?"

"What they're saying, that they put him through a crusher-destemmer."

"Well, the rumor is that he was bottled." His friend laughed. "It's terrible, but . . . it's funny, no? The joke is that the skin-to-juice ratio wasn't very good. And that given his natural *acidité*, he probably isn't worth drinking. A good writer but a shitty wine." He cracked up uncontrollably.

Even we had to laugh. But how the hell did they know about Feldman? It seemed impossible.

"It's true," I said, leaning over the back of the booth, breaking into English. "How did you hear about it?"

"A friend of mine is a *flic*," one of them replied, looking startled for only an instant. "He was out at Nuits this morning. Everybody's talking about it." His English was fluent.

"Who do you think did it?" I asked. Why not ask? I had nothing to lose.

"Well, one thing's for sure: Pitot was too stupid and Jean-Luc is too arrogant to have screwed up his own wine."

"Yeah, right. So, who?"

"Who knows? Unlike Wilson, Feldman made more reputations than he wrecked. He could be hard, but he was fair. Very careful. Meticulous. He did his own work. Every year, the same domaines. *Boomp, boomp, boomp.* His memory was excellent."

"I guess he was making up for the national deficit," his friend chimed in. "With exceptions, of course," he said, nodding in apology. *"Pardon."*

I scrunched down in the booth. "Unbelievable," I whispered. "This place is as bad as Napa."

"Worse," Monique said.

"Well, then, how about another *pression?*" She nodded.

"How are you feeling?" I said when I returned with our second round. I didn't know why I asked it, except that she appeared too relaxed.

"About what?" Monique said. She seemed strangely unsurprised by the question.

"I don't know. About life. You seem relieved, almost happy."

"I feel cleansed." It was an odd thing to say under the circumstances.

I asked her what she was going to do.

"I have to get out of here. Home first. Then I'll see."

"I'm leaving Wednesday morning," I said. "Colonel Sackheim will have to solve this insanity without me. One night in Paris, and then . . ." I imitated a plane with the flat of my hand.

She looked down at her hands.

"Come with me. To Paris. One night," I said. I hadn't planned on asking her. I wasn't even sure why I said it, except that Gio would be gone by the time I got home, and the prospect of explaining to Janie everything that had happened suddenly loomed as an impossible task that I wanted to put off as long as possible.

She smiled and looked down again and then up at me, her eyes pleading and sad. Abruptly, she stood up. I paid our tab at the bar and followed her out.

We strolled down the street to a little park, and I pissed against a stunted tree. My urine smoked in the cold, and the stink scented the air. I zipped my fly and stepped back, barely dodging a pile of dog shit.

We walked slowly, and she held on to my arm, but two rounds without any food in my stomach left me unsteady, and I realized I was leaning on her. The scudding clouds opened and closed across the moon's face, and the stones of a belfry glowed and darkened in and out of the light. We took a circuitous path. In the center of a square, a statue of a monk stood in repose, a Mona Lisa smirk frozen on its mouth, his hand furled in an odd way.

"You know," I said, "in Greece that gesture—the funny way he has his hand—means, 'Come here.' But in Italy it means, 'Eat shit.'"

"How in God's name will we ever make ourselves understood?" she asked in faux protest.

I hugged her to keep her warm, to warm myself, and groped her ass. She slapped my hand and I stumbled a step, and as we zigzagged down the street, I brushed against a man.

"*Pardon,*" I mumbled. He grunted but said nothing, and I looked back at him. He was burly and held himself tightly. From the back, his silhouette reminded me of Carrière, and I shivered uncontrollably.

"Take me home," I said.

I lay down on the sofa in the living room in front of the fireplace. It was filled with ashes and half-consumed logs and smoldered, hissing and crackling quietly. I was drunk, I knew, but beyond the physical condition of inebriation, I was drunk on death.

Monique leaned down and kissed me—long and deep—and I felt myself falling into her, falling forever, and fell asleep.

I slept late. When I awoke, I could hear the shower running downstairs. She had left the door to the bathroom open and had failed to pull the shower curtain. It was an invitation, and I gazed unabashedly at her body as she soaped her limbs and washed her hair. Breathless, I tore myself away from the vision of her and went upstairs to brew a pot of coffee. When she emerged she had her hair swathed in a towel. I looked at her, shaking my head in disbelief, and she laughed at me like a little girl.

"I need to see Sackheim one more time. You should come with me."

"Do I have to?" she protested.

"Yes, you have to."

When we arrived at the *gendarmerie*, we learned that Sackheim had been designated DE, *directeur d'enquête*. The *gendarme* on duty directed us to Ponsard's office, and as we headed up the staircase, we could see Sackheim's foot soldiers racing up and down the halls, sheaves of paper in hand. Ponsard, seizing the excuse of our arrival, was visibly relieved to abandon the computer keyboard he was punching with two fingers. When it turned out that Sackheim was too busy to see us, Ponsard escorted us back downstairs and told us to wait.

Monique and I sat there flipping through dog-eared copies of *Paris Match*, and I was starting to think that we should come back later. Just as we were about to head outside for a smoke, Lieutenant Ponsard appeared.

"*S'il vous plaît, venez avec moi.*" He led the way. "Here is not the place to talk. Meet the colonel at Le Gourmandin. *Une heure et demie.*"

"*Merci*, Ponsard," I said as he opened a door at the end of the hallway.

It was drizzling outside.

"I love Sackheim," I said as we walked to the car. "Here he is, in the middle of a triple-murder investigation, and he makes a lunch reservation. Unbelievable."

"He may be a cop," Monique said, "but first he's French. Nothing gets between a Frenchman and *un bon repas.*"

We drove to the center of town and parked.

"Let's walk. We have half an hour," I said.

We strolled down the street and soon came into a small square, a church at one end.

"Come on," I said.

"Church?" she asked in disbelief.

"We need all the help we can get," I said, taking her by the hand up the steps. We entered the quiet sanctity of l'Église de Notre Dame, our footsteps echoing, the drone of confession and contrition noticeably absent on a Tuesday, and stood gazing up to the figure of Christ. In the sacristy I dropped a two-euro coin in a box and took three candles, lighting them from one that had nearly sputtered out.

"One for each victim," I explained.

"And I shall light one," she said, taking another candle, "for Jean."

We walked outside. The rain had quickened, driving in a fine sheet and shattering against the cobblestone.

Sackheim had already arrived. A waiter directed us to a staircase at the back of the restaurant, and we picked our way toward it between tables and through the parties that were midway through their meals.

Our host stood as we approached the table. There was no one else in the room.

"I know the owner. They keep this *salle* closed at lunch, but I thought it would be more private," Sackheim said.

But he never broached the subject of death, murder, or suicide. He asked instead about Monique's family.

"Your parents, they live where?"

"Bordeaux," she said. "But they are divorced now."

"I see," Sackheim said. I could tell that he was curious about her name, and so could Monique.

"My father, stepfather, is Moroccan. He adopted me when I was very young."

"This explains it," he said. "And your English, it is impeccable."

"My mother insisted, when I was a young girl. She found a tutor for me."

Having learned these facts, Sackheim didn't pursue the subject of her family any further. He wanted to talk politics. He was obviously relieved that Obama had won the election.

"We French did not like your President Bush and his cowboy mentality," he said to me. "'You are with us or against us.' 'Bring it on.' 'Dead or alive.' At this stage of human evolution, it is, how does one say, primitive, *non*? Now, perhaps, one can love America again."

Feeling the press of time, Sackheim had taken the liberty of ordering for us and apologized for his presumption. He needn't have. The food was simple and nicely done. He seemed particularly pleased with the wine, an utterly remarkable Givry from a young man whose name sounded surprisingly like Joe Blow.

"If every Joe Blow made wine like this," I couldn't resist commenting, "the world would be a better place," but the play on his name was lost on my companions.

The owner sat with us a minute over coffee as we savored three portions of crème caramel.

"You know, these scores for wine, *c'est criminel*," he said. *"Pardon, Colonel, mais* I care nothing of scores. Ninety-two, seventy-two, what's the difference? The purpose of wine is to give pleasure. You sit here. You have a good meal, nothing fancy. A little fish, a morsel of duck, some good bread, a wine that satisfies you. What more do you need?"

"Absolutely nothing," I said. "And thank you. It was delicious."

"We are content," Sackheim said. "Bring me the check, please. I regret that I must get back to work."

The *patron* shook hands and went downstairs.

Outside the weather had broken, patches of blue breaking through the racing cloud cover. Sackheim turned to face me.

"And you, my friend." He took my hand. "We do not say goodbye. We say *au revoir.* 'Until I see you again.'" And he embraced me, kissed me on both cheeks, and walked away.

"An amazing individual," I said, watching him disappear around a corner. "Come on. Let's do a little shopping. Tonight I'm going to cook for you."

I put a mattress in front of the fire and we lingered, eating slowly, savoring the quail I'd roasted over the coals. Curious about Jean-Luc Carrière, I'd picked out a bottle of his domaine's Les Amoureuses. The wine was intense: silky and seductive, lovely and luscious, the fat contours of its fruit as full and ripe as the curves of Monique's body. When we had finished, we lay our plates on the floor.

"I'm not going to Paris with you," she said. "This is our last night together. I need to be alone, to think. I can't stand saying good-bye twice." She straddled me. "I've got you," she whispered. She locked her legs around me and tightened them, squeezing harder and harder until I thought she might crush me, and then released them and laughed.

"You could have killed me," I said, only half joking.

She smiled. "But I am not a killer," she said, her hair wash-ing against my face. She buried her lips in my neck. "*Mon pauvre Babe.*"

I could smell her, and it came to me, a shock of recognition that made me sit up suddenly, sending her to the mattress.

"Jesus," I said. "You were there." She crouched on all fours, uncomprehending. "Your perfume. I've smelled it before. At Rich-ard's apartment in San Francisco."

"What are you saying?" she demanded angrily.

"You were in California. It was you who asked Feldman to call Richard. He never said that Richard had a son, just that he had a child. I assumed it was Pitot. But it wasn't, was it? It's you."

"You're crazy! You don't know anything!" Her eyes flashed as her voice rose.

"He refused you. So you called him. I listened to the goddamned messages. I can't believe I never placed your voice. 'You have to talk to me.' That's what you said. But he wouldn't. So you followed him to Napa."

She picked up the bottle of wine and flung it at me. It shattered against the fireplace, the wine hissing in the flames.

"Were you and Jean in on it together?"

"You sick son of a bitch!" She ran to the door and turned to face me. "You think I killed my own father?" she screamed. "Go home!" she yelled, grabbing her purse and jacket and slamming the door behind her.

For a while, I just sat there, stunned. Eventually I roused myself and cleaned up. I felt like I'd come full circle—sweeping broken glass into a dustpan, just as I'd done at the trailer—and yet the circle seemed less than complete, as if one critical section were missing. I fed the fire one last time and called Janie.

"I've been dying to hear from you," she said. "Why haven't you called? Is everything okay?"

"Nothing's okay," I said. "You simply wouldn't believe it, if I told you."

"Tell me. I want to know everything."

I wasn't about to tell her everything. I certainly wasn't going to tell her about Monique—neither that I had nearly slept with her nor that she was Janie's niece. I limited myself to the murder of Lucas Kiers, the suicide of Jean Pitot, and the discovery of Eric Feldman's mutilated corpse. That was enough.

"This is the most insane thing I've ever heard," Janie said. "I can't believe it." She was practically frantic. "What about you? How are *you*?"

"I feel like I'm standing in the center of a hurricane. I'm surprisingly calm, but I think the shock's going to set in any moment. It's totally out of control."

"What are the police doing? They should arrest someone."

"There's no one to arrest. The French kid is dead. It's a mess, but it's one they're going to have to clean up."

We were quiet for a while, and then she said, "When are you coming home? I told Danny he could spend Thanksgiving with you, and he's really looking forward to it."

"I've got a few loose ends to tie up. I'm going to try to get out of here tomorrow. I'll call you from Paris."

"Babe, please take of yourself. Be safe, okay?" Her voice started to work on me, and I had to choke down a sob as I realized how close I'd come to being in real danger myself and how much I missed her and Danny.

I couldn't sleep that night. I sat in front of the fireplace until it died. I didn't know what to do. I wanted to get home for Thanksgiving, but I also needed to call Sackheim. I decided that I'd call him from the airport, relay what had happened, and leave it to the French cops to arrest Monique Azzine. *Let Sackheim work it all out with Ciofreddi*, I said to myself. *I just want to get back to my own kid.*

In the morning I drove into Beaune. I turned in my car and had the attendant call me a taxi. The cab arrived and I settled into the backseat, then sat up and said, "Never mind. Sorry," and grabbed my bag. He cursed me as I got out of the car.

"Hey! I changed my mind, okay? Fuck yourself," I said in English, tossed him ten euros, and went back into the Hertz office.

27

I **apologized to the** agent and explained that something had suddenly come up and that I'd need the car for another day or two. She was aggravated at having to print out another contract. As she prepared the paperwork, I stepped outside to call Janie.

"There's one more thing I need to do before I take off. It's too complicated to explain. I'm not sure how long it's going to take." Her silence was damning. "I might not make it back tomorrow."

"Christ, Babe. I can't believe you."

"Tell Danny I'll make it up to him. I promise."

"Do you have any idea how much he was counting on this?" she said and hung up.

Then I called Air France and changed my reservation to the following day. I'd need to wake up at dawn to catch a train back to Paris, but I had little choice. The ticket cost a fortune, and I was suddenly grateful that Janie had refused my refund of her check.

I drove to the *gendarmerie*. Sackheim hadn't arrived, and I waited in the car. I couldn't get Monique out of my mind. She had implicitly conceded the salient fact that Richard was her father but had failed to answer the only question to which I wanted an answer: Had she killed him?

Sackheim arrived in his Citroën. I caught up with him on the gravel. He was astonished.

"This isn't over yet," I said. "I couldn't leave. I need you to come with me."

He pondered this for a moment, examining me skeptically.

"No, you come with me," he said.

I followed him into the station, where he greeted the officer on duty with a cursory *bonjour* and led us up the staircase and down a hallway. The place was virtually empty. Other than a few computers at which several officers were tapping away and what sounded like a whirring fax machine, the station was strangely quiet. Sackheim escorted me to the room where he, Ponsard, and I had met two days before. Ponsard's geneaology was still on the blackboard, but now the bulletin boards lining the walls were covered with photographs, reports, and handwritten notes.

"Wait here," Sackheim ordered me. "I have a few things to attend to. Then we will talk."

He disappeared, and I walked around the room. There were photographs of Lucas Kiers from a dozen different angles interspersed with photographs of the Bois de Corton and photographs of the Pitots' house—the front yard, the well, the antique wine press, and, of course, the grave from which they had disinterred Feldman's body. The photos of Feldman were particularly gruesome. It was hard to say, but it looked to me as if Pitot had tried to flay him, had found the task too difficult, had given up, and then had furiously sliced chunks of the writer's arms and legs off. I was no expert, but the nicks that dotted his corpse appeared to have been made in an outburst of frustration, completely random and violent slashes inflicted by a mad young man overwhelmed by the horror of the act he was committing. I stopped in front of the photograph of Feldman's left wrist. It was a clean cut, probably done with a pruning saw.

Sackheim returned to the room, came up beside me, and gazed at the photo.

"I'm sorry to barge in on you like this," I apologized. "I know your hands are full, but where is everybody? I thought this place would be a madhouse."

"Yes, well, we have three deaths to deal with, but two of them are Americans. Paris has taken charge of the investigation. It is out of my hands." Sackheim seemed at a loss. "But you, I thought you were leaving today, *non?*"

"Yeah, well, I thought so, too. But there's something I have to tell you, something that happened last night."

He walked to the table and took a seat, gesturing for me to do the same. He folded his hands and nodded for me to proceed.

I described the scene at the *gîte* the night before. I left out the part about my rolling around with Monique on the mattress and cut to the part of her confessing that Richard Wilson was her father.

"And how did you . . . ?" Sackheim's face was knotted.

"I smelled her. Her perfume . . . I smelled the same perfume at Wilson's apartment in San Francisco. When I told her, she went crazy. She basically admitted it was true."

"That what was true—that she was in San Francisco? That she is Wilson's daughter?" He hesitated before saying, "Or that she killed him?"

"Only that Wilson's her father. But she didn't deny that she'd been there."

"And the murder?" he said.

"We didn't get that far. She ran away."

Sackheim sat there, working through everything I'd told him. He rose, walked to a corner of the room, and hit an intercom.

"Marcellin, *venez ici*," he said.

Corporal Marcellin entered a moment later.

"*Oui, mon colonel?*" his corporal said.

"Marcellin, I want you to locate Mademoiselle Azzine." Sackheim turned to me. "Do you have any reason to believe that she's in Saint-Romain, at the *gîte*?"

"I doubt it. I think you should try Domaine Beauchamp. That's where all her stuff is, where she's been working."

"*Bien.* Domaine Beauchamp, *à* Pommard," Sackheim said to Marcellin.

"*Oui, Chef*," Marcellin said and raced out of the room.

"Thank you, Babe," Sackheim said, and rose. "I appreciate your coming here to tell me this before you left."

"There's something else," I said.

"And what is this?" He looked at me warily.

"The wine," I said.

"What wine?"

"The wine Pitot made from Eric Feldman."

"Paris has the press," he said. "They are analyzing it in their *laboratoire*. If he did as you suggest, they will know."

"But we have to find it," I said. "The wine, I mean."

"And where do you propose . . . ?"

"Domaine Carrière," I said. "I'll find it, I promise," I added, hoping this one wouldn't be as empty as the string of broken promises I'd made my son.

"Give me just a minute," Sackheim said.

We took my car and parked outside the gates. Sackheim followed me into the courtyard. No one was around. I led the way into the *cuverie* and walked straight to the wine press. I circled it twice.

"Make sure the guys from Paris check this one out, too," I said. He nodded.

Sackheim trailed me as I entered the first cellar, passed through the second and third, and finally arrived in the fourth and smallest room. I hadn't really noticed on the day I'd been here to question Carrière about Eric Feldman that this *cave* had no barrels. Metal racks held tightly stacked, unlabeled bottles. Small pieces of framed slate hung on chains and were scrawled in chalk with the provenance of each wine laid to rest in its shelves: CHAMBOLLE-MUSIGNY, CHAMBOLLE 1ER CRU, LES CHARMES, LES AMOUREUSES, BONNES-MARES, MUSIGNY.

I examined the last few nooks and pulled a couple of bottles to see if anything was amiss. The wine looked fine. Short of opening several hundred bottles, it would be impossible to know if Jean Pitot had hidden anything in the cellars of Jean-Luc Carrière.

"This is crazy," I said, suddenly unsure of myself. "We're never going to find it. Forget it."

I could see the chagrin on Sackheim's face. I'd let him down again. Disappointment and failure seemed to be dogging me everywhere I turned.

In the courtyard he told me to wait by the car. He crossed to the house and knocked on the front door. I peered through the wrought-iron fence. The door opened and Sackheim stood there, speaking to whomever had answered, a moment later gesturing for me to join him. A young woman stood at the door and led us inside.

"*Après vous,*" Sackheim said. The woman disappeared through a door at the end of the hallway and emerged a minute later with an older woman. I had seen Carrière's wife only from a distance, the day Sackheim had returned with me to ask about the incident in their *cave.* She was an attractive middle-aged woman with an open, inquisitive face.

"Yes, Colonel? May I help you?" she said.

"If you have the time, I would like to ask you a few questions," he said.

She led us into the kitchen. "I hope you don't mind, I was just making coffee." She busied herself measuring out the coffee and filling the coffeemaker with water. She switched it on, pulled four cups and saucers from a cabinet, and turned to face us.

"*Asseyez-vous, s'il vous plait.*"

We arranged ourselves around the square kitchen table. It was awkward and uncomfortable, and no one knew what to say.

"Forgive me, *Mademoiselle,*" Sackheim opened, turning to the young woman, "I don't believe we have met. I am Colonel Émile Sackheim. And you are . . . ?"

"Jenny Christensen," she said. "That's my California name. Here I am Eugénie Pitot, Jean's sister. I just arrived from California to be with my family. For his funeral."

Sackheim and I exchanged looks. She was slender and pretty, dressed in woolen slacks and a bulky sweater. Her hair was like her brother's, fluffy brown curls. She looked at us through doelike brown eyes.

"Please accept my condolences, *Madame.* It is terrible, what happened," Sackheim said. "Ah, forgive me, this is a neighbor of yours, my colleague from California, Monsieur Stern."

"I'm sorry about your brother," I said, trying to smile sympathetically. She eyed me suspiciously, said nothing, and turned to my companion.

He responded by saying, "I am pleased you are here. It will be helpful, I think. Let me start with you, then," he began, and we all

settled uneasily into our chairs. "Do you mind if we speak English?
I would like my friend to follow what we say."

"As you wish," she said quietly, her accent barely detectible.

"It is all right, *Madame?*" he said, looking at the woman of the
house. "You understand English?"

"Yes, some. It is fine," Madame Carrière answered him.

"Your brother," Sackheim started in, "did you see him often when
he was in California last summer?"

"Occasionally. He would come to visit. But he was very busy at
the winery."

"Your husband, he is a *vigneron* too?"

"Yes."

"You own your vineyards?" His tone suggested astonished appre-
ciation of the good fortune of owning land in America.

"Yes, but we lease them. Paul works at Agostino. It's a big place.
Industrial."

"And you met him . . . ?"

"Here, in 1994."

"You were twenty?"

"Nineteen."

"Love at first sight, eh?" Sackheim prompted.

"You might say that." The sun filtered through the kitchen window, washing Eugénie's face with a fine grid of mottled light.

"Your brother, did he seem disturbed when you saw him? Was he
angry or troubled by anything?"

"Oh, you know, the usual."

"I am afraid I do not, *Madame.* What do you mean, 'the usual'?"

"He wasn't a very happy person. But I guess you know that."

"Was there something in particular that made him unhappy?"

"He didn't like American wine very much."

"Well, in this he is joined by many of his countrymen," Sackheim
said with a shrug. He wasn't winning her over, and her features
seemed frozen. "You have children?"

"No. We're trying, but not yet." Her voice faded.

"Well, you will, I'm sure. You are young," Sackheim reassured her.
"If I might ask you a few questions about your family." She waited.
"Your father . . ." he started, and she looked down at her hands, then

gazed out the window. "He is an unfortunate man. I am sorry. It must have been quite painful growing up. But your uncle, Gilbert? What can you tell me about him?"

"He is going blind, drinking himself to death," Eugénie said, her voice stony. "It is from breathing the *sulfatage*. They don't protect themselves. You can taste it, you know. I would help my grandmother sometimes. It is sharp, metallic. It stings your tongue. My uncle, he gets cramps, diarrhea. His skin is turning yellow. Not as yellow as Grandma's, but . . . The year I left, I saw him in the vineyard. He hid behind a row of vines so that no one would see him vomiting."

"He has seen a doctor?" Sackheim asked.

It was an obvious question but one that, I guessed, masked his ignorance of what she was talking about. I wanted to interject that the *vignerons* used copper sulfate to prevent oidium, a fungus that appears on grape leaves, but decided to hold my tongue.

"Yes, of course," Eugénie went on. "But he only accused him of drinking too much, warned him that if he kept it up, he would develop cirrhosis. Well, maybe he will now. He's so depressed. But he never drank more than a glass or two at dinner. Holidays, maybe, but no, he is not like most Frenchmen. My grandmother, though, my grandmother's condition is worse."

"We saw her at your home, I think. She was watching TV."

"Hnh!" she snorted dismissively, a little explosion of air through her nose. "She always mixed the *sulfate de cuivre*. In the kitchen, like she was baking. At first she thought it was conjunctivitis. Her eyes would get irritated, the lids all swollen by harvest. By the time she was sixty, the tissue in her cornea was so ulcerous, it started to break down, like rotting grape skin. Now she sits there all day on the sofa staring at the television set. Did you see her eyes? No, of course not. They're like . . . they're like clouds. She sees nothing."

Neither Sackheim nor I said anything.

"My mother has anemia," Eugénie continued. "She took over when my grandmother couldn't see. She's wasting away. She eats like a sparrow. For a long time I thought it was from despair: a bad marriage, no grandchildren, no money. But I think it's probably from the *sulfatage*, too."

The coffeemaker made a gurgling sound as it sucked the last of the water.

"*Mon Dieu*, it's a calamity." Sackheim looked at me, raising an eyebrow.

"Yes, my father is miserable, he's crazy. He suffers from delusions. You know, he used to threaten to kill these wine critics. No, really, he did. His life was a mess. He had no one to blame but himself, but, of course, he couldn't accept it. So he blamed the American wine writers. He would sit at the dinner table like a madman. 'They infect each other, these Americans! They are like a blight, a scab on my *feuilles de vigne, mon bon fruit!*' He saw what was happening to his mother and his brother, and he wanted to take revenge, but it was all in his mind. He was never capable of doing anything about it. He would talk about inviting one of them to the house to taste wine. As if anybody would ever come to Domaine Pitot! What a joke. He said he'd fix something with a strong flavor—a *terrine de foies de volailles* or *pâté de campagne*—that would hide the taste of copper sulfate. And then he'd offer the man a plate, *une petite tranche*, that the unsuspecting idiot would welcome after a long day of tasting, and . . ." Her voice trailed off.

I saw again, in my mind's eye, Françoise Pitot appearing at Domaine Gauffroy with her terrine. Goldoni had spat it out. Had she wanted to poison him? Had she wanted to poison me?

"Ah. I am sorry to bring these memories back. Please forgive me," Sackheim said. Eugénie placed her chin on her hand and seemed to carry the whole weight of the world there. "And you wished to escape this," he said. "Is that why you left? Why you married an American?"

"Would you have stayed?" Eugénie asked. "To listen to my father, drunk, complaining, blaming everybody but himself? To hear my mother screaming at him, angry that he had lost everything? Do you know what it was like? Night after night?" She was trembling.

"No, my dear, I do not censure you. You have no fault. I understand completely." His tone was patient. "And you met your husband?" he asked, to change the subject.

"Yes."

"How?"

"I was working at the public tasting in Beaune, pouring wine. He came to the table. And then he came back. And then . . ."

"*Vraiment. La famille en France*, it is impossible to escape."

"Everyone knows everything about you. My father, my uncle, my grandfather." She and Madame Carrière looked at each other, then she turned back to Sackheim. "Who was going to marry me in France? What kind of future do you think I had?"

"No, you are right. You were right to leave. In America, anything is possible. And, of course, the taxes are less punishing," he smiled, attempting a note of levity, but no one laughed. "I have one more question. I know this is difficult, but I am trying to understand. I want to understand your brother. May I continue?" She nodded, but her face was haggard, and suddenly I could see her mother in her exhausted features. "I am trying to understand Jean's relationship with your husband, *Madame*," he said, acknowledging Carrière's wife, who stiffened visibly.

Eugénie now seemed to take on her mother's expression the day we had come to her door, suspicion and hostility twisting her eyes and mouth. I could see her tense in anticipation of Sackheim's next barrage of questions.

"I do not understand why Jean would choose to work here, rather than for his own father," Sackheim said, looking from one woman to the other.

"My father wouldn't give him anything," Eugénie said. "He made him pay. Rent. For everything! *Vouz comprenez?* He wanted him to pay for the barrels, for the vineyard, for his parking. To rent his own inheritance. He incorporated the domaine. Maybe, maybe by the time Jean died, he would have paid off the mortgage." She stopped. "If he wasn't already dead," she added, her voice breaking.

"It is insupportable, for a father," Sackheim said, shaking his head. He looked at her, his gaze unwavering, and she returned the look, her eyes seething.

Madame Carrière sighed, then stood up.

"So he chose to work here, for his uncle," she said, her hands gripping the back of the chair.

Sackheim glanced at me with a look of suppressed confusion, as if I could answer the riddle.

"I do not understand. Monsieur Carrière is your mother's brother?" he said to Eugénie.

"Her *beau-frère*," she corrected him.

"Françoise is my sister," Madame Carrière said, placing the coffee pot and a tray of cups on the table.

Sackheim sat there in silence, his eyes closed. I could see him trying to reconstruct Ponsard's diagram in his mind, but his lieutenant had described only one-half of the family.

"I apologize, *Madame*," Sackheim said to Madame Carrière. "I am quite confused. *Votre nom de jeune fille?*"

"Ginestet. Sylvie Ginestet."

She was standing at the kitchen counter, her back turned to us.

"You think you understand now," she said in a whisper. "But you understand nothing. Nothing at all."

She put a creamer and a bowl of sugar in the center of the table and poured us each a cup of coffee. "*Comme vous voulez,*" she said, sitting down. She added a cube of sugar and a little milk to her coffee and stirred, her teaspoon tinkling against the porcelain.

"It was hard after the war," she began. "No one had any money. You had to sell your wine to the *négoce*. My father was unhappy. No matter what he did, it was never enough. Once he even tried to get an American wine writer to come to our house to taste his wine. He was here for Les Trois Glorieuses. It was a long time ago—I don't remember the year. But of course the man never came." She paused and took a sip of coffee. "My father made good wine, nothing special. And the house was simple, not *un grand domaine*. Papa continued to make wine, but he never recovered. He would tell the story over and over again. He drove my mother, my sister, and me mad with his talk. Every night the same thing. He would complain, *Maman* would cry, we would run to our room." She stared down at the table.

"And then?" Sackheim asked.

"Nothing. He drank himself to death," Sylvie Carrière said. "*Maman* did not weep. In fact, it was almost a relief. She sold one small parcel to pay off the estate taxes. It was not much—we were not a wealthy family—and she took what was left and swore on his grave that neither of her daughters would marry a *vigneron*. But of course, what the parent wants, the child refuses. I married Jean-Luc. He was handsome, and he was a hard worker. At least my mother told herself that he might succeed where her own husband had failed. Jean-Luc builds up our domaine slowly, buys more vineyards, each time elevating the property. He bought this house. But he is a cold man, and I was very unhappy." For a moment she seemed overwhelmed by the memories, then went on. "Françoise married Henri. You know this. What you do not know is that my sister and I competed with each other," she said, looking at her niece. "She envied me. I had the better property, the richer husband. There was only one problem." She paused. "I could not have children. I was, how do you say, *stérile.*"

Eugénie was staring at her, her eyes beginning to well up. "You do not have to . . ." she said.

"No, I do, *ma chérie.* I have lived with this, this shame, long enough. I cannot hold it inside anymore. It is killing me."

A tense silence enveloped the kitchen. Eugénie looked out the window, the tears now streaming down her cheeks. "Don't, please," she whispered.

"Françoise hated me and her husband. I do not know whom she hated more, me or him. She wanted her revenge." Sylvie Carrière paused. "So she seduced my husband."

"Why are you doing this?" Eugénie protested. "Why are you telling them?"

Sackheim folded his hands on the table. "Tell me," he said. "I need to know. I want to know." His tone was even, insistent.

Sylvie Carrière sat mutely, staring into her coffee.

"Yes," Eugénie said dully. "Jean-Luc is Jean's father. He fucked my mother." She seemed to spit the words out. "Or she fucked him. She hated my father, she despised him. He disgusted her. So she fucked her brother-in-law and tortured my father. They fought. All the time. And she would scream at him, 'What kind of a man are you? You can't even give yourself a son! It took my brother-in-law to give you an heir!'"

Eugénie buried her head in her arms, sobbing. Her aunt stared across the table, looking at nothing, her eyes blank, her expression lifeless. I turned to look out the window, embarrassed by what

Sackheim had unknowingly brought me to witness. I could see nothing but the shadow of the house cast against the cliff face.

"*Vous comprenez maintenant?*" Sylvie Carrière whispered.

Sackheim leaned over to place his hand on Eugénie's shoulder and said, "I am sorry, *Mesdames*. I deeply regret the pain I have caused you both. I am grateful, however, that you chose to share with me this very difficult history."

Rising, he signaled me to stand as well.

"I'm sorry," I said, turning back as we neared the door. "There's just one more thing." Sackheim looked at me in surprise. "Have you seen your family since getting back?" I asked Eugénie. "Your mother and father?" I added, needing to clarify what had become terribly murky.

"Yes, last night," she said, her face still buried, her voice muffled.

"Did you bring any presents for your family?"

She lifted her head. "Yes, how did you know this?"

"A package that your brother asked you to carry?"

"How did you know?" Her eyes locked on mine.

Instead of answering her question, I asked another one: "Didn't it seem strange that Jean would ask you to bring something back when he'd already left in September?"

"He left it at my house on his last visit. He told me he had forgotten it. Is it a crime to bring your mother a gift, a gift your brother is no longer alive to deliver?" Her tone now was sharp.

"No, *Madame*, it is not a crime," Sackheim replied for me, casting a look my way that said we were done. "*Merci, Mesdames.*" He nudged my shoulder, and we walked down the hallway and left the house.

28

We sat for some time in the car in the shadow of the brick wall.

"What are you thinking?" Sackheim said.

"Well, for one thing, this condition Eugénie described in her grandmother and uncle: It comes from excessive exposure to copper sulfate. Winegrowers dust the leaves with it to prevent powdery mildew, a fungus. You can take it in through your eyes and skin, and they breathe it when they mix it up, like her grandmother did."

"I still do not quite understand. All *vignerons* do not suffer from this, or am I mistaken?"

"No, of course not. And copper sulfate doesn't kill you. I mean, it can, in sufficient doses, but they probably used too much of the stuff. I don't think they knew as much about it back then as we do today. But that's not the point."

"And the point is?" Sackheim asked.

"This family, they possess a genetic disorder that absorbs and stores the copper in the body." I paused as Sackheim took in the awful nature of the malady. "I don't know about her grandmother's blindness. I never heard of that. But it makes you tired, and in really extreme cases, it can lead to seizures, Parkinson's, a whole host of neurological and psychiatric problems. In their case, I'd say it's made them crazy."

"Very interesting. And hideous, *non?*"

"In English it's called Wilson's disease."

He just stared at me. "Wilson's disease? *Vraiment?*"

"Can you believe that?" I said and shook my head.

"This irony, it is too cruel."

"And so sad," I said.

"Sad, yes. In fact, it's tragic. Unfortunately, it doesn't help us at all. None of this explains why Jean killed Richard Wilson. Or Feldman."

We sat silently a moment. It was all too much.

"Explain to me, *s'il vous plaît*, your question about the package," he then asked.

"Richard Wilson's hand," I said. "Jean didn't forget it. He left it at his sister's on purpose. He needed to put some distance between himself and the crime."

Sackheim looked at me with attenuated exhaustion. "And where is this hand?" he said.

"Chez Pitot," I said. "But we have one stop to make first. I'd like to drop by Domaine Gauffroy in Gevrey, if that's all right."

The abbey was sheathed in silence. I knocked—there was an iron ring on the timbered double doors—and we waited in the courtyard where Jean had accosted Monique. Gauffroy's wife opened the door. She and Sackheim both looked to me for an explanation.

"*Pardonez-moi, Madame.* The day of the tasting a young man, the son of Madame Pitot, who brought the terrine late in the day, left a bottle of wine on your table. Do you remember?"

"*Oui,*" she said tentatively.

"Do you have it? Is it here?"

She thought a moment, then shook her head. "I am sorry." She started to close the enormous door.

"Perhaps your husband knows?" I suggested.

"*Un moment, s'il vous plaît, Messieurs.*"

She excused herself and reappeared a few minutes later with her husband. I repeated the question.

He had to think for only a second before saying, "*Suivez moi.*"

We descended to the tiny cellar where Kiers and Rosen had had their argument. He pulled open the wrought-iron gate at the very back of the cellar, leaned down to a niche, and pulled out a bottle of wine—the only one not displaying a skin of dust.

"I don't know why I saved it," he told us. But it didn't surprise me. He might not have admitted it, but he'd been curious and probably intended to taste it. I'd never met a Frenchman who simply poured a bottle of wine down the drain. They weren't that profligate.

A half dozen glasses sat on an upturned barrel surrounding a corkscrew that had been fashioned from a gnarled grapevine, the screw embedded in its shellacked knuckle.

"May I?" I said.

Gauffroy nodded. I put the bottle between my knees and pulled. Sackheim was studying me. I poured a couple ounces. I held it to the light, twirling it until it sloshed up the side of the glass, then concentrated on the wine, smelling it, twirling it, then smelling it again. Over and over. I held it up one last time and finally took a sip. I let it swirl around my tongue and paint the sides of my mouth. Then I aerated it and let it sit on my palate a long time before spitting it onto the ground.

Sackheim watched me, his impatience mounting.

"The color is too evolved for a wine this young. See this?" I said, indicating a bricky tint that rimmed the wine. The slightest tinge. "Here you call this *pelure d'oignon.*" Lucien Gauffroy nodded. "But you should never see this in a new wine. And the nose isn't fresh. Not just tight, but off," I added.

"And the taste?" Sackheim said anxiously. "How does it taste to you?"

Gauffroy, curious to understand my commentary, poured himself some wine.

"It's not as ripe or as generous as it should be," I said. "Even wrapped up—which you'd expect—it should possess a lushness, a concentrated fatness and depth, an undercurrent of fresh fruit held in check by the tannins, that it just doesn't have."

Gauffroy sipped and nodded but remained silent. He followed my English, but I wasn't sure how much he had understood.

"And you explain this how?" Sackheim said.

"Do you understand the term *fining*, Colonel?" I said. I racked my brain for the French translation.

"*Collage*," Gauffroy said, just as the word came to me.

"Exactly: *collage*," I said.

"Gluing?" Sackheim said, confused. "This is what an artist does, gluing things to paper," he said to the *vigneron*.

"Yes, but it's also a stage in the winemaking process," I said, acknowledging Gauffroy.

"*Expliquez, s'il vous plaît*," Sackheim said.

"Fining—*collage*—is the process of clarifying wine," I explained.

"*Et puis . . . ?*"

"You add an agent to the wine."

"*La colle*," Gauffroy interjected.

"Egg whites, milk, bentonite," I went on, "that coagulates and absorbs the colloids in the wine, pulls out the particulates so the wine won't be cloudy."

"It helps to stabilize the wine, too," Gauffroy added.

"*D'accord*," Sackheim said, following along.

"But historically, in the olden days, the French used to use dried blood powder, ox blood, to fine their wines. *N'est-ce pas?*" I said to Gauffroy.

"*Oui, c'est vrai*," he said.

Sackheim looked at us, an expression of bafflement slowly giving way to one of triumph.

"You see," he said proudly, turning to Gauffroy, "our American friend is truly a scholar of wine. But how did you . . ."

"Last night I drank a bottle of Carrière's Chambolle I bought in town. It was incredible. Gorgeous, opulent fruit. This," I said, holding the glass to the lamp hanging from the stone ceiling, "is the same wine. And not the same wine."

Lucien Gauffroy seemed utterly confused.

"It is the addition of the blood that makes it so?" Sackheim said.

"If I say the word *saignée*, what does it mean to you?"

"'Bled'? Do I understand correctly?"

"Yeah, literally, sure. But it's another winemaking term. You say, 'to perform a *saignée*' or, 'a *saignée* of Pinot Noir.'"

Back on familiar territory, Gauffroy nodded authoritatively.

"Typically, *saignée* refers to a rosé," I continued. "But in Burgundy, they sometimes bleed the skins to get rid of extra juice, to concentrate the wine."

"*D'accord*," Gauffroy said.

Then they looked at me and fell quiet.

"Jean, maybe Carrière as well, bled the skin of Eric Feldman," I said. The *vigneron* set his glass on the barrel, staring at it, realizing what he had just tasted. "And then used it as a fining agent. Instead of purifying and stabilizing the wine, the blood spoiled it."

"*C'est ça*," Sackheim said. "*C'est brilliant, et c'est diabolique, n'est-ce pas?*"

"*Non, mais c'est horrible, c'est affreux*," Gauffroy muttered, a look of total revulsion contorting his face.

"Yes, you're right. It is. Horrifying and evil, both," I said. "And very hard to detect."

"Come, take the wine," Sackheim said.

"Chez Pitot," Sackheim commanded. "*Allons-y.*"

At his instruction, I threaded my way back through Gevrey-Chambertin and headed toward Nuits. We were silent on the drive south. On the east side of town, Sackheim ordered me to pull over at the public swimming pool. He called Ponsard and told him to bring two cars and some men, and to meet us chez Pitot.

We parked on the street in front of Jean's house behind Monique's Fiat and a dark blue Mercedes that appeared distinctly out of place in the run-down *quartier*.

"Carrière," Sackheim said. "And . . ."

"Mademoiselle Azzine," I whispered.

The house was even shabbier than I remembered it. Sackheim seemed uncharacteristically nervous. He pushed open the gate—the crime-scene tape that ribboned the house was already torn—and we passed the shed and the well, both of which had also been cordoned off with tape, and approached the house. We stepped up to the front door. The TV was on. A game show. Sackheim motioned for me to keep quiet. He led the way around the side of the house. We passed through the carport, and as we reached the far corner of the house, we could hear voices from a shed. It stood just outside the fence of the property. I'd noticed it two days before when we found Jean in the well and Eric Feldman buried in his shallow grave but hadn't given it a second thought. Smoke seeped through chinks in its walls and roof.

Sackheim crouched down and I followed suit. The first voice I heard was Françoise Pitot's.

"*Idiot*! *Con*! He dumps the body in a *foudre* and cuts off his hand. What am I supposed to do with a hand?"

"That should teach you!" It was the voice of Henri Pitot. "Fuck this asshole and that's what you get! *Un arriéré*!"

"You should know!" she screamed.

"Leave this to me," Henri said.

"This is ridiculous!" Now we heard Jean-Luc Carrière. "They will find this. You are crazy."

"My God, I can't believe this!" a woman said in English, and I realized it was Monique. "What are you doing? It's disgusting!" she exclaimed, again in English, as if by the mere fact of language she might separate herself from whatever it was she was seeing.

We heard a car, two cars, in the street.

"Stay here," Sackheim whispered, pointing to his ear, and backed up to intercept his lieutenant.

Though I hadn't noticed it, the wind must have shifted. An odor reached me, foul and noxious.

Sackheim, in a running crouch, hurried to my side. I followed his eyes to the near edge of the field and saw Ponsard take up a position behind the hay bales I'd seen the day Feldman had been found. The arrow was still there, its feathers glinting in the sunlight.

"Don't move!" he said and rose, gesturing for Ponsard to follow, and hurried to the entrance of the shed. I couldn't resist running after him.

The scene we met was bizarre. Henri Pitot stood bent over an antique still. It looked like an hourglass fashioned from hammered copper, the upper chamber smaller than the lower, the whole thing no taller than a couple of feet. The contraption sat on a cast-iron wood stove. As I reached the entrance, Henri Pitot fed the fire and slammed the door shut. A pipe emerged from the top of the still and twisted its way to a rusted copper bucket that sat on a wooden stool.

I inched my way forward and gagged. An overpowering stench filled the tiny room.

"*Arrêtez!*" Sackheim shouted. "You, all of you, I am putting under arrest!"

Jean-Luc Carrière stood there, his arms akimbo, paralyzed. Françoise Pitot glowered at us. Her husband wore a hunted, terrified expression. Monique simply stared at me.

"You see!" Carrière screamed. "Just as I said!"

"I have nothing to do with this," Monique pleaded. "They're crazy, all of them."

"Liar!" Françoise said. "She helped Jean. You don't really think he could have killed Wilson by himself, do you? He was nothing, a weakling. Your father rejected you," she said, turning back to Monique. "You wanted revenge, too."

"It's not true!" Monique cried.

"Quiet! All of you!" Sackheim shouted. "Come with us," he ordered.

At that moment, Henri Pitot somehow shoved his way past Sackheim and fled in the direction of the house. Ponsard took Carrière by the arm to make sure he, too, didn't escape. Monique came up to me and took my hands in hers.

"You have to save me," she said, her eyes desperate. "I don't belong here. It's a mistake. You have to believe me."

"Bastards!" Françoise Pitot said. "You're all bastards!"

"Be that as it may, *Madame*, it is over," Sackheim said. "Lieutenant," he added, indicating that Ponsard should take Carrière and lead the way. We ducked under the low door and walked in single file toward the house, Ponsard in front, followed by Jean-Luc Carrière, Monique, Françoise and me. Sackheim took up the rear.

As we entered the back gate of the property, I could hear Françoise Pitot muttering under her breath, "This is all your fault. I told Jean to get rid of you." I glanced back, and Sackheim took her by the shoulder.

We entered through the kitchen and gathered in the foyer and living room. The old woman sitting before the television screen stirred at the commotion.

"*Qu'est-ce qu'il se passe?*" she said. "Is that you, Françoise?" She turned, and I looked into the milky whites of her eyes, spectral against her jaundiced skin.

No one knew what to say, and nobody moved. Finally Sackheim ordered Ponsard to take Carrière to one of the police cars and to have another officer join us.

Ponsard was back within two or three minutes, accompanied by another *flic.* Sackheim told them to keep an eye on everybody and disappeared to search the cellar for Henri Pitot. He returned empty-handed and turned to the old woman, who hadn't budged from the sofa.

"*Pardon, Madame,*" he said. "I apologize for the disturbance. And permit me to express my sympathies. It is horrible, what the *sulfatage* does to your family. I had not realized . . ."

Françoise snorted. "What do *you* know?"

"Your daughter, Eugénie, she explained this terrible condition."

"This is what you think? That she is blind from the *sulfatage?*" she asked contemptuously.

"*C'est vrai, n'est-ce pas?*" Sackheim said.

"True? You want the truth, *Monsieur? Monsieur le gendarme? Le grand détective?* Do you think you can stand the truth?"

"Is it not so?" Sackheim appeared confused.

"That she is poisoned? *Oui, bien sûr.* But not as you think. It is not the poison of sulfur that kills her, though truly her insides have been eaten away. Tell him, tell him what you think," she said to her mother-in-law.

"Forgive me, *Madame*, but I do not understand," Sackheim said.

Françoise moved to the sofa and sat down heavily next to the old woman. I stood by the half wall that separated the foyer from the living room and could see the line of the elder Madame Pitot's coarse stockings rolled above her knees. She slouched, her chin resting on her chest, her breath coming heavily.

"Two years ago, she thought she was dying," Françoise Pitot said. "She finally confessed. She had never told anyone."

I could barely hear her. Sackheim lifted his head as if he had picked up a scent. The old woman appeared disoriented, baffled by the commotion and cacophony of voices.

"Are you going to tell them, or should I?" Françoise asked. The old woman turned to face her, but without her eyes, it was impossible to tell what she was feeling.

"Henri's mother was a young girl during the war," Françoise started, nodding at the diminished figure.

"I was pretty then," Madame Pitot suddenly said. Her voice was thin, frail. "There is a photograph somewhere," she said and waved her hand distractedly, then lapsed into silence.

"When the Americans came that September," Françoise continued, "she told her father she wanted to go to Dijon to welcome them. He said no, but she went anyway. You always did whatever you wanted."

"Many people went. It was like a holiday, everybody in the streets waving American flags," the old woman said, reliving the scene in her mind.

"That night—one night—she spent with an American, a soldier," Françoise said.

"He was with the army of Patton," her mother-in-law whispered. "He took me to a warehouse. We drank wine. He was so handsome, so gentle." Her voice trailed off, swept away by the undertow of memory.

"And then, the next morning, he was gone," Françoise said.

Sackheim stared from one to the other. Monique, who had gone to the window, turned back into the room.

"You know about Henri's father," Françoise said.

"The car accident," Sackheim responded. "Yes, I have seen the records."

"Hnh," she snorted. "There was no accident. He killed himself, hung himself in the shed," and she gestured with her chin through the window to the little outbuilding that teetered in near collapse toward the well. "It is the shame that killed him, the disgrace."

The old woman's face crumpled.

"And this . . . child," Sackheim said tentatively.

"This bastard?" Françoise said. "He is my husband, *Monsieur.*"

"*Mon Dieu,*" Sackheim muttered.

"Yes, God, that's what she says," Françoise Pitot went on. "She believes that her blindness is God's punishment for her sin."

"It is true," the old woman insisted, her head pivoting vacantly.

"And this explains, perhaps, your husband's feelings for Gilbert?" Sackheim asked the old woman. She did not reply.

"What do you think?" Françoise answered for her. "They were married that October. Henri was born in June. By then, Etienne was trapped. He knew the child was not his, but he could tell no one. For thirty years, this disgrace, it gnawed at him. So, yes, of course, he adored Gilbert."

"And you never heard from the American again?" Sackheim asked the old woman.

"He said he would return after the war. He promised. Bob, that was his name. Bob." She pronounced it *Bawb*.

Sackheim's eyes bored into her as if the sheer intensity of his gaze would unlock the secrets buried in the walls and floorboards and cellar of the house.

"That was his *prénom*," Sackheim said.

Françoise Pitot turned to him with a look that disfigured her face.

"But, of course, you saw the patch on his uniform," Sackheim said.

A silence enveloped the room. I could sense Sackheim holding his breath.

"Oh, yes, Colonel," Françoise said. "It was Wilson. Robert Wilson."

"But what makes you think . . ." Sackheim started.

"You do not see it?" she said.

Sackheim didn't answer. He didn't have to. It was obvious to all of us. You had only to look beneath the stubble and shabby clothing. Henri Pitot's resemblance to his half-brother was unmistakable, even to Sackheim, who had only seen photographs and had never met the great Richard Wilson in person.

Monique raised her hands to her lips, her eyes widening, dawning comprehension suffusing her face with horror. Old Madame Pitot seemed to collapse in on herself, a blind and broken old woman.

"I deeply regret . . ." Sackheim said but stopped. He seemed at a loss for words. What could he possibly say that might staunch the overwhelming tragedy that had engulfed their family?

"I am sorry," he said. Then he faced Françoise. The tension between them unnerved me. I couldn't look. I let my eyes survey the living room, moving over it inch by inch, an exercise in concentrated distraction. Françoise Pitot labored to rise from the sofa, and I could see her following my gaze.

My eyes stopped at a hutch that stood against the wall. Behind one of its doors, an oddly shaped bottle was tucked between a Bas-Armagnac and a bottle labeled VIN CUIT. It was small, no larger than a split of Champagne, its lip curled back to reveal a tiny cork.

I walked up to the hutch, opened the brass-knobbed door, and took it in my hand. A wan smile flitted across her lips, and a strange light, a look half fascinated, half demented, shone in her eyes.

As I held it to the light, I could see that its contents—the bottle was only half full—were deep gold in color. On a thin label, like one you would find on a medicine bottle or a home canning jar, a fine, formal, old-fashioned hand had written MARC PITOT— RÉSERVE DE LA FAMILLE. I pulled the cork, held the bottle to my nose, and winced.

"You're sick," I said to her. She clamped her jaw. I could see the veins working in her neck. "You'll need this," I said to Sackheim.

"Don't you dare!" Françoise Pitot yelled. She rushed at me, one hand grabbing me around the throat, the other trying to wrest the bottle out of my hand. I struggled to break free, to keep it out of her reach, but her grip was ferocious. She grabbed my arm, caught me at the elbow, and wrenched it violently. The bottle flew out of my hand and shattered against the wooden floor.

Sackheim and Ponsard ran toward us and pulled her off me. They held her by the arms. She struggled momentarily and suddenly gave up. We stood there, looking into each other's eyes. Hers were dark with malice. They terrified me.

Slowly, imperceptibly at first, and then with increasing pungency, a stench filtered through the air that made me want to vomit. It was putrid, a mix of powerfully distilled spirits and rotten meat.

"I told Jean to stop you, but you wouldn't stop," she hissed. "And then you arrived here, and he tried again, at Carrière. But he's an *imbécile.*"

"*Madame!*" Sackheim commanded. "You must come with us."

"*Oui,*" she said in an exhausted voice, her breast heaving. "I will get my overcoat."

They released her, and she backed away, turned, and disappeared through the doorway.

"Keep an eye on her," Sackheim instructed Ponsard. "What is this, this disgusting odor?" he asked, looking down at the pieces of broken glass and the puddle of liquid splashed across the floor.

"I'll explain it to you later. Let's just get out of here. Before we die of asphyxiation," I said.

We heard a door slam, and Ponsard, hapless, stuck his head out of the hallway a moment later.

"Get back there!" Sackheim commanded. "You must come with us, too, *Mademoiselle,*" Sackheim said, turning to Monique. "*Je regrette.*"

"But I have nothing to do with this," she protested. "It was all her idea," she said, flinging her arm at the hallway through which Françoise had disappeared.

"Even so," Sackheim said. "We must do what we can to untangle this . . . this mess."

At that instant we heard an explosion from one of the bedrooms.

Racing down the hall, we found poor Ponsard standing outside a bedroom.

"It's locked," he said. It was a limp excuse. I didn't envy him Sackheim's fury as the colonel pushed him aside and heaved himself against the door, which instantly gave way. They burst into the room.

Françoise lay on the floor. Half her head was gone, the bed linens and faded wallpaper spattered with brains and blood, fragments of skull and strands of hair. In the corner, Henri Pitot cowered, his eyes bloodshot and crazed. He held the shotgun in both hands, staring at what remained of his wife.

"She promised that she would tell no one," he said.

Sackheim nodded to Ponsard, who took the gun.

"*C'est fini*," Sackheim said. "*L'histoire est terminée.* Come, we have much to do." He looked at Ponsard and sighed, shaking his head. "*Mademoiselle, s'il vous plaît*," he said, placing his hand on Monique's shoulder, "do not look. Come. And you, *Monsieur*," he said to Henri Pitot, taking him by the arm. He led them down the hall, and I followed them outside.

I could see Marcellin standing by one of the police cars. Jean-Luc Carrière stared out the window from the backseat.

We walked through the yard. Halfway across it, Monique loosened herself from Sackheim's grasp and grabbed the shotgun out of Ponsard's hand. She ran to the edge of the well and turned to face us.

"It's all your fault!" she screamed at me. "Why didn't you stop? Why?"

She lifted the muzzle of the shotgun to a point beneath her head and pulled the trigger with her thumb. Nothing happened. Henri had emptied the thing into his wife. She flung the gun at Sackheim, who was racing to stop her, and as he dodged it, she clambered onto the edge of the well. Sackheim took her around the waist and pulled her to the ground. She raised herself on all fours and stared at me through a mass of tangled hair, tears streaking her face.

"I hate you!" she cried

"My God, my God!" Sackheim said. "*Quel désastre!*" he stammered and put his hands to his head as if to blot out the string of calamities that had engulfed him. Ponsard, who had been paralyzed up till that moment, ran toward them and, after stooping momentarily to check on Sackheim, lifted Monique off the ground.

"It's too much, too terrible," Sackheim said, gazing down into the darkness of the well, then collected himself and walked to the police cars. He took the radio and called for help.

29

I walked to where Monique had fallen, bent down, picked up a pebble, and pitched it into the well. I heard a faint *plop* as it hit the water.

It took only a few minutes for the first police car to show up. Others followed over the course of the next hour. The *flics* from out of town were immediately recognizable, some in plainclothes, most in uniform, their authority acknowledged deferentially by the locals. Sackheim had been cornered by one of them—a detective, from what I could tell—who was vexed that Sackheim appeared to have continued the investigation on his own in contravention of his orders, as if the tragedy that had unfolded before our eyes had been the predictable result of provincial incompetence.

The Brigade de Recherche stood in a cluster at first, whispering and smoking, unsure who was in charge or where they should start. The man to whom Sackheim had spoken finally issued various instructions, while Sackheim himself picked up the shotgun from where it leaned against his car, handed it to Marcellin, and told him to get Carrière to the *gendarmerie*. Ponsard drove Monique, and a third car ferried Henri Pitot.

Sackheim came up to where I stood in the opposite corner of the yard, looking through the chain-link fence.

"Henri must have been hiding in the bedroom after he ran from the shed," he said. "He heard everything. I am an idiot."

It was as if the situation had taken on such enormous dimensions that Sackheim needed to anchor himself to one detail, an explanation of a single element to which he could attach his own culpability.

"I am going home now. And you should, too," he said.

"If only I knew where that was," I said.

For an instant, he looked puzzled, then he nodded. "Come," he said.

"Where are we going?" I asked.

"Where would you like to go?" he said.

"I'd like a drink, to be perfectly honest."

"*Quelle bonne idée. À Beaune,*" he said.

Neither of us spoke after that. We entered the old part of town, parking across from Athenaeum. I doubted I would find any narrative as tortured as the one I had just witnessed anywhere on its shelves. We walked across the square, our shoes crunching the gravel, and entered a garishly lit brasserie a few doors down from the burger joint where I'd botched my own interrogation of Jacques Goldoni. Sackheim stopped at the bar and ordered for us.

"Come this way. It's quieter," he said, directing me up a staircase to an empty dining room on the mezzanine.

"*Alors,*" he said, as we sat down. "It is a sad day. Let's have a Calva to soothe our souls." Sackheim pulled a brown leather cigar case from his inside pocket and offered it to me.

"*Merci,*" I said, pulling one out and handing the case back to him. He took my cigar, carefully clipped it, and set a box of matches on the table between us. We slowly turned the cigars, the flames flaring and dying in quick succession. The barman set our drinks down and disappeared. Sackheim took a puff to ensure his was properly lit.

"So, why did you suspect the gift Eugénie brought for her mother was Wilson's hand? I still don't understand."

"Just a hunch."

"What is this, 'a hunch'?"

"You know, a guess, a feeling."

"*Un pressentiment, oui.*"

"What's a hand, Colonel?" I said.

"A hand?" he repeated. *"Je ne comprends pas."*

"Skin and bones. And what's the oenological corollary of skin and bones? We know that Jean killed Richard. But he screws it up. He places the body in a cask where, naturally, they find it the next day. It's the middle of *vendange*, after all. What did he expect?" Neither of us could suppress a smile. "But before he drops the body into the vat, he cuts off the hand, the writing hand, the symbol of everything he believes has ruined his family. He brings it to his sister, who, thinking that he had forgotten a package at her house, brings it with her. For his funeral, as it turns out."

"Continue," Sackheim said.

"The day we met Henri Pitot in the cellar, he mentioned the old still he had out behind the house." Sackheim nodded. "Skin and bones. Skin, seeds, and stems. What's left over: pomace," I said. My companion, swirling the snifter of Calvados in a lazy circle, stopped. "Henri, sick bastard that he is, gets it into his head to distill the hands—Wilson's and Eric Feldman's writing hands—with pomace and blended what you saw, smelled, in the shed."

"Henri was distilling . . ." he said.

"Richard's hand that Eugénie brought home. The gift for her mother."

"And the little bottle you discovered?"

"Le Marc Pitot, Réserve de la Famille? Feldman's hand, of course. Henri had left room in the bottle for the second batch."

"Mon Dieu," he muttered.

"Do you drink *marc*, Colonel?"

"Too harsh. I prefer this," he said, lifting the Calvados and taking a sip.

"Yeah, it's an acquired taste," I said. "Not that one could ever acquire a taste for *marc* blended with a dead person's hand," I added. "I doubt I'll ever be able to drink the stuff again."

"But how did you solve this puzzle?" He looked at me, genuinely curious.

"I kept asking myself, *Where are the hands? What the hell can you do with hands?* And then, when we were at Pitot's, it came to me. It's the same method I applied to the mystery of *le collage*: to employ *les techniques de vinification* to the elements of the case. The hands had to be somewhere."

Sackheim thought for a moment. "You know, this piece of furniture in which you found the bottle today, in French we call this *un buffet deux corps.*" He paused. "But it contained only one body. It awaited the arrival of the second."

He stared down at the table. His cigar had gone out. Slowly, meticulously, he relit it, sucked it with relish, blew a long, precise stream of smoke into the thick atmosphere of the café, and looked at me. Then he sipped the Calva and stared at the ceiling.

"They have taken me off the case," he said.

Smoke swirled in heavy waves around the globe of light ensconced on the wall.

"Jesus, Colonel. It's my fault, isn't it?" I felt wretched.

He didn't answer me directly. "My men will need me, but there is nothing I can do for them." He signaled for the check. "Give me just one minute," he said. He pulled out his cell phone and walked away.

"I have made a reservation for you in your old hotel," he said, returning to the table. "One requires the comfort of the familiar after such a day."

He had me drop him at the *gendarmerie.*

"There is no need for one to go back to see the carnage," he said. "In fact, they will not let me go back. I think perhaps, in the end, I broke a few too many rules." I started to say something, but he put his hand up. "Get some rest. Tonight I will cook. I need something to keep my mind off this . . . *catastrophe.* I'll pick you up at seven o'clock."

Le Chemin de Vigne was nearly empty after the frenzy of the Hospices, and the owner gave me the same room I'd used the week before. I wanted to sleep, but my mind was whirling and I decided to take a walk.

I stepped out the front door and wandered down the street, passed through the tiny plaza, and skirted the vineyard I could see from the window of my room. I stuck to the road that fronted a walled mansion and passed the hillock that contained the cisterns that fed

Aloxe-Corton. They really did look like bomb shelters, their vented chimneys rising out of the earth like ventilation pipes.

The road paralleled the irrigation ditch, a channel I now realized fed the wells from the hills and vineyards of the Bois de Corton. I walked uphill against its current, the water descending the channel in a trickle. At the end of the road, I turned left and crossed a concrete bridge. Brush and weeds all but obscured a modern *cabotte* dug into the hillside like a pillbox.

As I ascended to the wooded crown of the hill, I passed the ancient stone hut I had seen that morning when Sackheim had driven us to the body of Lucas Kiers. A small van was parked on the side of the road, and workers stood in a vineyard watching me. We nodded from a distance. Mist hugged the hollows of the land that rose and fell in gentle waves across the imperceptible microclimates of Aloxe. At the end of the track where Sackheim had parked, I turned and looked back toward the village, turned again, and headed up the path.

Just beyond where we'd found Lucas Kiers lying on the ground, I saw a sapling with a hand-carved sign set into the earth. It was a beech tree, the plaque marking the convergence of the four communes of Aloxe-Corton, Ladoix, Magny-lès-Villers, and Pernand-Vergelesses. I did a circuit of the Bois, following the same path I was sure Kiers had jogged on the mornings he'd staggered into the Chemin's dining room, breathless and drenched in sweat.

As I came down the hill and descended toward the village, the sky unleashed a rain shower and I ducked into the concrete hut to sit it out. My mind was numb, empty, and I sat on the ground, listening to the endless *pit pit pit* of water hitting the earth.

When the rain had passed, I returned to the hotel and slept for a couple hours, undisturbed by dreams. I was empty. There was nothing left.

Twilight came on early, the sky darkened by a storm front moving in from the north. The *patronne* served me an apéritif unbidden as I lingered in front of the fireplace in the dining room. I smelled the *kir* but couldn't get the odor of the *marc* out of my nose.

At seven I heard a horn honk twice. Sackheim's Citroën sat idling on the street. We drove to the western edge of Beaune.

"I must extend to you Burgundian hospitality," he said, pulling into a driveway beside a modest house that was beautifully situated at the base of the Montagne de Beaune. "No restaurants tonight," he said and winked.

As we got out of the car, he pointed to vineyards that might as well have been his backyard—Les Grèves, Les Toussaints, Les Mariages—indicating their boundaries. Before us stretched a cemetery, and in the middle distance, a half mile from where we stood, I could see the radio tower that rose from the *gendarmerie* on rue des Blanches Fleurs.

He had set the table formally: white linen, china, sterling silver that had seen daily use, its surfaces tarnished with age.

"A simple meal," he said, his blue eyes refracting the shiny crystal stemware. "I did not have much time."

"I can't believe you had any time at all. What happened? Did they really pull you off the case?"

"They have taken it out of my hands. Even Lyon's hands. Paris has taken charge. It is now a triple-murder investigation: Feldman, Kiers, Françoise. Not to mention Jean's suicide. And two of the victims are Americans. It is too, how do you say, 'high profile.' We are unaccustomed to this."

"I hope my being here . . ." I started, but he didn't let me finish.

"Well, they are not pleased that I permitted you to accompany me to the scene of Kiers's murder, that you were present chez Pitot, that I involved you at all. But these, these are technicalities. I told you, they have been trying to get me to retire. For the moment, I'm on temporary leave. But they have sent me out to pasture." He paused. "It is fine. I am ready," he added, and walked to the kitchen.

I felt awful. To avoid thinking about it, I examined the photographs on the mantel. I could hear Sackheim at work. He came out bearing two plates.

"Meursault, Les Charmes. Comtes Lafon, 1989," he announced as he took his seat and lifted a bottle from a silver coaster. He poured the wine and raised his glass.

"*À votre santé*," he said, and we clinked. "*Et à votre santé mentale*," he added. "Forgive my buying a *boudin de mer* at the *charcuterie*, but

I'm sure you understand." He took a bite. *"Coquilles Saint-Jacques, brochet, et écrevisses.* How do you say?"

"Scallops, pike, and crayfish." He had finished the dish with a simple *beurre blanc.*

"Pas mal," he shrugged.

"What happened this afternoon?" I asked.

"We were overwhelmed. The team from Lyon took control chez Pitot. Another from Dijon started at Domaine Carrière. And then Paris arrived. My men? It is quite beyond their capabilities. They stand around and look at each other in shock. *C'est incroyable."*

"What about Feldman? I'm still trying to figure out what happened, exactly."

"I am convinced that Feldman discovered the real father and son. He overheard them at Domaine Carrière arguing the day he arrived for his appointment. But Jean, Jean is crazy, *non?* It is like a disease."

"And you think this explains Kiers?" I said.

"Not exactly. I believe that Carrière shot Kiers."

"Why?"

"You know this yourself, do you not?" he said. I put my fork down. He regarded me with studied restraint. "You said that Carrière threatened you at the *dégustation publique,"* Sackheim went on. "And you said that Kiers was there. And you have said that Kiers's specialty was, how did you say, 'human interest stories,' stories about families." He paused. I sat back in my chair. I could see it coming, but that didn't make it any easier. "Carrière knew all about you, about your investigations in Napa, about the purpose of your trip to Bourgogne. He realized that he had threatened you in public, and he was afraid—apparently Kiers said something about your staying at the same hotel—that you would tell Kiers everything. And then, of course, Kiers, being a journalist, would write this story."

"Jesus," I muttered. "I got him killed."

"Please, do not blame yourself. This family, they are mad, all of them. And they hate all wine writers, it would seem. Besides, what did we learn about Madame Pitot today?"

I didn't respond. I was shaken and just sat there, guilt stricken.

"That she hates men, all men. I think that she goaded Carrière, insulted him, told him that he was not a man. He had to prove himself. He, too, had to be an accomplice. But, of course, he could not permit this story to be published."

Sackheim rose from the table, cleared our plates, and served a salad of butter lettuce. He ate his in silence. I picked at mine.

"You saw the photographs?" he asked as he cleared the salad plates, not bothering to chastise me for not finishing mine. "My wife and daughter. My wife, Mireille, died in 1985. Breast cancer."

"And your daughter?" I said, shaking myself out of it.

"She works for Microsoft. In Paris." He shrugged, walked to the kitchen, and set to work on the next course. I could hear him opening and closing the oven door, and then the light sizzle of a sauté pan on the stove.

"There are two great French contributors to the investigative arts from the last century," he called from the kitchen. "Who are they?"

I got up from the table and walked around the dining room, racking my brain to think of the French equivalent of Sherlock Holmes.

"No idea," I said.

"Marie Curie and Louis Pasteur."

"She invented X-rays, and he invented fermentation," I said, standing at the door to the kitchen, wanting to reassure him that I wasn't a complete moron.

"The X-ray, *oui*. To unlock the mysteries of energy and see into the heart of matter. Not to be fooled by surfaces. Measure the constant of energy and follow it into the realm of the invisible," he said as he pulled a roast from the oven. "*Sanglier*," he said. "How do you say?"

"Wild boar."

"But Pasteur," he continued, "no, my naïve and ignorant American friend, Pasteur did not discover fermentation. Man has been fermenting things for thousands of years: honey, grain, grapes."

"I knew that," I said, leaning against the doorjamb and shaking my head. "I meant, he discovered how to control fermentation."

"How to *stop* fermentation, to isolate the microbe from the ferment itself. Pasteur said, '*La génération spontanée est une chimère*': 'spontaneous generation is,' how does one say in English, 'an illusion.'" He tossed the sauté pan like a pro. "*Trompettes des morts*," he said. "I adore them. And appropriate for the occasion. 'Only products originating under the influence of life are asymmetrical because the cosmic forces that preside over their formation are themselves asymmetrical.' That's a quote. One of the most perceptive things ever said of the criminal personality."

He carved the pork into two portions and spooned a little pile of mushrooms on the side of each plate.

"Pasteur said that since every active substance originates from life, then fermentation itself must be the work of life, not the work of death. Yeast, microbes, germs come from life! Not from death! But . . ." and he paused, it seemed, for dramatic effect: "The conditions under which fermentation takes place, this corruption and putrescence of a living thing, is anaerobic, without air, stifling, suffocating!"

His eyes gleamed. He gazed at me imperiously, astounded by the brilliance of it, as he carried our plates to the table. He moved slowly, like an elderly waiter in a one-star restaurant, then brought an open bottle of wine I hadn't noticed from the sideboard. It was an old-vine Musigny from Comte de Vogüé.

"A '59?" I remarked, examining the label as he held it before me.

"The year of your birth, *non?*" he said, delighted with himself. "An auspicious year *en* Bourgogne."

"No, sorry, I'm younger than that. But thank you for the thought," I said.

I twirled the wine and smelled it. I was on the point of describing it, but he put his index finger to his lips.

"Do not speak. It requires no words. Drink it. Enjoy it. Trust me, it is . . ." and then, putting the tips of his fingers to his lips, he kissed them into a petite explosion signifying nothing, signifying perfection. We tasted the wine. "Just remember it," he said. "*Ça suffit.*"

The meal was impossibly delicious. I hadn't realized how ravenously hungry I was, and as I ate, I felt completely restored.

We ate in silence. When we had finished I said, "So, who is guilty? Other than me, I mean," and winced.

He placed his knife and fork on his plate and pushed it back.

"*À la fin*, we arrive at an understanding of *la famille Pitot*. And truly, it is an unhappy story. Remember what I said of Pasteur. His insight was that the process by which wine is degraded is biological. The hatred of Françoise, it is like a bacterium, a germ, and it feeds on her, devours her, and through her, the entire family. Does it derive from her father? Her mother? Is this defect biological, genetic? Perhaps, but I am not a scientist, *mon ami*, I am a detective, a cop. What we know is that first she poisons her mother-in-law with her spitefulness, a woman who already lives secretly in disgrace; then she poisons her sister with her *cupidité*, how do you say, her greed. Then she infects her husband, who, too, is ashamed, though she does not yet know the secret of Henri's birth. All she knows is that he's a failure, so she uses her lover, her own sister's husband, to inflict the ultimate injury on her husband, and then doubles back, as you say in your Westerns, and corrupts Carrière with her hatred, itself an infection passed from father to child. Even so, she is not finished. No, she has a son, and she will not be finished until she turns him to acid, too."

He paused. "Would you like a little *fromage*? Some dessert? I have a *petite tarte aux pommes* from the *patisserie*."

"I don't want to appear ungrateful, but, to mangle the words of Brillat-Savarin when he stood on the verge of death and was peering into the void, life is short. Let's dispense with the cheese course—and in this case, dessert, too—and have a cigar with the last of the wine."

"*Formidable*," Sackheim said and fetched his humidor.

We took our time over the ritual.

"So, who is guilty?" I repeated.

"Who is guilty? Who committed the crime?" Sackheim asked. "It begins with Etienne Pitot, who is ashamed of the bastard he must call his son, and Pascal Ginestet, who is, in his own eyes, a failure. But how can you say they are guilty when one had taken his own life and the other . . . Well, I think he took his own life, too. One by the rope and one by the bottle. And of course, there is Robert Wilson and his son."

He took a long drag on the cigar and blew two perfect smoke rings, the second passing through the first and blowing it apart.

"*Magnifique*!" I remarked at the feat. "But what about Françoise? I don't get it."

"She is the most important. The mother." He nodded gravely.

"I get *that*," I said defensively.

"No, I mean, she is the mother of the crime. Remember what Monique said today—maybe the one true thing she has said: 'It was all her idea.' It is Françoise who gives birth to the plan. She uses her son, her husband, her lover, everyone around her as if they are weapons." Sackheim took a deep sip of wine. "Françoise wanted her revenge. By the time she met Monique, she knew the truth of her husband's paternity. These things came together in her mind—and yet, she has killed no one. In fact, she is a victim herself."

"What do you mean, by the time she met Monique?" I said.

"Ah, forgive me." He got up from the table and reached into a briefcase that sat by the front door. "Monique asked me to give this to you."

He handed me a letter. It had already been opened. On the envelope, in a feminine hand, was written BABE.

"Please, go ahead," Sackheim said. "I have already read it."

My hands were shaking as I opened the letter.

30

Dear Babe,

I am sitting alone in my cell. It is quiet and dark. I have never been so lonely in my life.

I know the case is coming to an end. I'm not sure how it will finish. No one tells me anything, not even you. I just sit here, lost in my thoughts, wondering what will happen to me.

There are so many things I want to say to you. I'm sorry I ran away last night. Now I wish you were here so we could talk.

The thing I need to tell you is that you were right. Richard was my father. My mother told me this last year. I don't know why she told me this now, after so many years. She met Richard when she was very young. Richard was young, too. Too young, maybe, to understand what he was doing. I thought a long time about what I should do, and I finally wrote him a letter telling him who I was. Last spring when he came to Bordeaux, I found him. It wasn't hard. Everybody knows where he goes.

He wasn't nice about it at all. I think he thought I was trying to get money from him, which isn't true. Do you know what it's like, suddenly finding out that you're not who you thought you were? That you've never known your real father? That your mother lied to you her whole life until the moment when she felt so much guilt that she had to tell her secret?

I went to his hotel in Bordeaux early in the morning. He didn't believe me.

He asked me what proof I had, other than the word of my mother. I never felt so humiliated in my life.

I told him the only thing I wanted was the chance to love my father and to have him love me. I hugged him. At that moment Jacques came into the room, saying that they were late and that he had been waiting for Richard downstairs. Then he saw me with my arms around my father. I know that Jacques thought we had slept together and that I was saying good-bye to the great and powerful wine writer.

After that, no matter what I did, Richard never responded to me. I tried calling his hotel, I sent notes to him at his office, but he never called or wrote back. Nothing. He must have said something to Jacques, but I'm not sure what he told him. Not the truth. Just something about a young woman who was bothering him.

Jacques knew where I was in Barsac. He would call late at night and send me postcards. Everyone in the office at the château read them. It was awful. They accused me of harassing the great Richard Wilson, of trying to seduce him and his assistant, and fired me. That's when I went to California to find my father.

I didn't see Jacques again until that night at the restaurant in Beaune. He wouldn't leave me alone. After the dinner he said that he was sure I had something to do with Richard's murder and unless I slept with him, he would go to the police. I didn't know what to do. If my own father wouldn't believe me, why would anyone else? And then, at the tasting at Gauffroy, he said it was my last chance, that unless I screwed him, he would destroy me. Well, it doesn't matter now. I am destroyed anyway.

What am I supposed to do?

I don't think Jacques ever said anything to the police. What could he say? All he wanted to do was screw me. But I think that Sackheim believes I had something to do with it. That I killed my own father.

I don't know what I'm going to do. You have to save me.

Monique

"It is true," Sackheim began, "I did believe that she was involved in Wilson's death, but I could not see why. This letter, it explains so much. And it confirms everything you told me this afternoon." He paused. "What do you know of Mademoiselle Azzine?"

It was a strange question. I wasn't sure what he was driving at.

"She's gorgeous, smart, ambitious," I said. "I think she could have been a star."

Sackheim sipped his wine and then puffed the cigar till it flared.

"Monique is not telling the whole truth. I am not saying that she is a liar, but she is playing with the truth." He set the cigar in the ashtray. "Today I had the opportunity to talk with her. And Jean-Luc Carrière. I had nothing else to do, and they are the only ones left."

"There's Henri," I said.

"Yes, well, you can imagine. Anyway, a year ago, before the events of these past few weeks and months, Mademoiselle Azzine made another *stage* in Burgundy."

"I didn't know that." I tried to brace myself for what was coming.

"But she did. She worked at the domaine of Jean-Luc Carrière. At Carrière she met Jean Pitot, and he, like so many others, was taken by her. He was a lonely boy, vulnerable. She got to know him quite well. He even invited her home for dinner several times, and there she met Françoise. It was only a matter of time until the bitterness of this family was communicated to her. But Monique Azzine had her own, how do you say, agenda, which only now we understand. Her father had rejected her. She was humiliated and angry."

I regarded the length of ash that extended from the tip of my cigar.

"When she left Bordeaux in the summer," Sackheim went on, "she did not come directly to Burgundy, as you know. Lieutenant Ciofreddi has established that she was, in fact, in San Francisco on the day Wilson was last seen. But by then, it was too late. The plan, it was already made. Perhaps if Wilson had accepted her, she might have stopped it. He could have saved himself."

I was dumbfounded. "You think she had a hand in *killing* him?"

"You suspect this yourself, but we do not know, do we?"

"Maybe she tried to stop Pitot," I said. Sackheim regarded me across the table. "It's possible, isn't it?" I asked.

"I am not certain," he said. "But we will learn the truth of this. Of that I am quite sure."

I wasn't sure of anything. I was reeling.

"*Enfin*, one thing we are beginning to understand is the strange relationship this young woman had with *la famille Pitot*. You know, the day you visited Domaine Carrière, the day the barrels fell, Monique had been there."

"You're kidding!" Jesus, was I a patsy or what? She had played me for a chump.

"I am sorry," Sackheim apologized. "Carrière has told us."

"What about Feldman, then?"

He regarded me sympathetically, then gave a slight nod. "You know the phone message Feldman left at Wilson's apartment in San Francisco. He said that he made this call as a favor for someone. We know from her cell phone records that Monique contacted Feldman. He, too, had been hurt by Wilson—everyone in Burgundy, it turns out, knows this story—and she thought that he would be sympathetic, that he would help her. But he did not. Just a phone call. I think maybe she arranged to meet Feldman at Domaine Carrière. We do not know yet. But this, too, we shall learn."

"Did she murder Richard?" I asked again after a minute. "Kill her own father?"

"We don't know." He was quiet, then said, "We know so little."

"Fine. What do you think?" I asked.

"Well, she had the opportunity. She rented a car at the airport in San Francisco. Ciofreddi discovered this, and we have confirmed it from the records of her credit card. The odometer, it suggests that she followed Wilson to Napa. There is no other explanation. You do not put three hundred kilometers on the car by driving around San Francisco, eh? But personally—it is just my *pressentiment*, my 'hunch'—that the killing itself was the work of Jean. The violence, the sloppiness, the hand. She had her own reasons for wanting Wilson dead, but I suspect you are right, that she may have tried to stop Pitot. After all, she desires a living father, not a dead one. Even if he was, in a manner of speaking, dead to her."

My mind folded in on itself.

"On the other hand," Sackheim went on, "maybe after Wilson rejected her for the last time, she decided to help Jean. The evidence at Norton, it is still not conclusive." He paused. "And then you arrive in Burgundy," he continued, "asking questions—as you say, sticking your nose into everything. I am sure that Jean had already told her about you. The American. I do not wish to imply that Mademoiselle Azzine was not attracted to you, Babe, but, you must admit, she needed to find out what you suspected, what you knew. It was Jean, of course, who tried to stop you in Napa after you started to inquire about Wilson's death." I thought about correcting him, telling him that it was just some crazy kid from Angwin, but held back. For all I knew, it *had* been Pitot. Maybe it was Brenneke, too eager for an easy mark, who had it all wrong. "And then you discovered him at Domaine Carrière," Sackheim went on. "It had to have been Jean who pushed the barrels. But you were not hurt. And you were not scared away. In fact, you were getting very close."

We sat for a few minutes in silence, puffing our cigars and sipping wine.

"Who is guilty, you ask," he finally said. "The family." He looked, suddenly, terribly sad. "The whole family is guilty."

We grew quiet again, pondering the mysteries of crime and retribution, of passion and hatred, of blood and wine.

"It is late. I should take you to your hotel," Sackheim said.

He hoisted himself out of his chair and walked slowly to get his overcoat. He was not a young man. He was tired, and I realized this would be his last case.

As we turned off the highway toward Aloxe-Corton, Sackheim said, "It is dangerous."

"Yes, at night especially. No streetlights," I said.

"Not the driving, Babe. The search for truth."

I didn't respond at first, then said, "You did what you had to do. It's your job."

"You think that is all? That I am just doing my job?" He was irate.

"I don't know. Anyway, I owe you an apology for costing you yours."

"It is not your fault. It was only a matter of time. The fact is, I am looking forward to retirement. And I'm happy that you came. I don't think we would have solved this without your help." With that one statement, Émile Sackheim had redeemed me. After a moment he added, "I regret that Eugénie's husband is not with her."

"Why?" I asked.

"I believe that I would have been able to discern if she is happy."

"Does that really matter?"

Sackheim blew air through his lips. "Ey! Please. I am not a beast.

It would give me satisfaction to know. Now it will trouble me. Did she merely escape, or did she fall in love?"

We passed through the little squares of the town, abandoned at that late hour.

"Don't worry about tomorrow," I said when we pulled up in front of the Chemin de Vigne. "I'll call a taxi to take me to the station."

"Yes, it is better. Good-bye, Babe. It seems we say good-bye too often." He seemed wistful.

"*À la prochaine*, then," I said, patting his arm, and then, "You take care of yourself. And retire, for chrissakes. Neither of us has the strength to go through this again."

I called Janie from the hotel room.

"It's over," I said.

"You figured out who murdered my brother?"

"Yeah, sort of. It's pretty crazy. I'll explain it all to you when I see you."

"And when is that?" she asked, her voice tinged with censure.

"I'm leaving first thing in the morning. I'll call you from Paris."

"You're actually going to make it back for Thanksgiving?"

"I told you I would. And tell Danny. I'll pick him up on my way from the airport."

I lay in bed, unable to sleep. I walked onto the balcony off my room and gazed out over the vineyards. In the courtyard, the giant linden stood silhouetted against the dim shape of the Bois de Corton. I heard an owl hoot softly, and then it lifted—I could hear the *whoosh* of its wings—and it struck, some small creature squealing from its talons. I shook my head at the profound, murderous mysteries of nature and went to bed.

I slept like a baby.

31

called Janie from the airport. I would never have been able to pull it off had it not been for the nine-hour time difference.

Given that I'd kept my word, she didn't seem all that happy when I knocked on her door. The important thing right now was Danny, though—we both understood this—but the look she kept throwing me over his head told me that she expected a full account.

"As I said, it's complicated. Give me some time. I'll call you when I'm ready."

"At least you made it home in one piece," she said.

On the drive, Danny expressed skepticism about cooking a turkey at the trailer. "Your oven's too small," he said.

We stopped at the Safeway in Napa—the only store open on the actual holiday—and stocked up on canned cranberry sauce and wild-rice salad. He picked out a sweet-potato pie with whipped cream. The only things we had to cook were the bird and stuffing. He insisted on cutting up the celery and chopping an onion. I had to take over when he started to cry. He sat at the table watching me, tears streaming down his face. He looked unutterably sad, and the whole event tottered on the verge of disaster until my eyes began running.

"Don't cry, Dad," he said.

"You don't cry," I said.

"No, *you* don't cry," he said, and we erupted in laughter. Then we dressed the bird. Danny sewed up the cavity with the agility of a surgeon.

He was right about the turkey. Though I had bought the smallest bird we could find—there were only a few left in the case—it barely fit in the oven, and I had to turn the temperature down to keep it from burning. We didn't sit down until sometime after ten.

We ate in silence. I apologized for the lack of merriment. The only stories I could think of seemed too gruesome to tell. The next morning he asked if he could go home, so I drove him back into the city.

"Tell your mother I'll call her next week," I said. But I couldn't wait that long. I wanted to get my conversation with Janie out of the way. I phoned, suggesting we have dinner on Saturday in the city.

It was an awkward date. The story I had to relate was not a pretty one, and the fact that Richard's death was woven inextricably into a larger and more complex tragedy, involving a family she'd never heard of, was hard to take in. Not to mention that she now possessed a niece whose existence to this moment she knew nothing about.

"A daughter?" She shook her head in disbelief. "What's she like?"

"Beautiful. Very lovely, really. Smart. Tortured." I bit my lip. I needed to get this part right. "She tried to get Richard to accept her. It would appear that he refused."

I then explained the history of Monique's finding Richard, her repeated attempts to get him to acknowledge her, her trip to California.

"We don't know," I finally said, anticipating what she was thinking. "She was there, in Napa, when he was killed. She was probably involved. An accomplice, at least, technically speaking. But I think she may have tried to stop it."

"Is she all right?" Janie's expression now was unreadable.

"She's being held as an accessory," I said.

"Jesus" was all she could say. I didn't blame her for being at a loss for words.

I allowed for a reasonable interval, giving her a chance to digest everything I'd told her.

"There's more," I said.

"Come on!" she scoffed, not believing there could be any more.

"Your father. At the end of the war. He had a one-night fling with a young French girl. She gave birth to a son."

I watched it sink in.

"I have a brother in France?" she whispered.

"A half brother," I said.

"Why didn't you tell me?"

"I'm telling you now."

"I want to meet him."

"You don't. Trust me."

I poured us both another glass of Turley Zin, and we picked at our food. Jardinière had always been one of our favorite places, but neither of us had much of an appetite, and after what I'd revealed, it was difficult even to pretend we were savoring the meal.

"It's a terribly cruel irony," I said at last.

"What is?"

"The bad joke life plays: the father, the son, each had a child by a French woman. The son, ignorant of his father's sin, commits the same one." My hand brushed against hers on the table. "I've been trying to figure this out, and I can't wrap my mind around it."

She turned her head and pulled her hand away. I knew it was a lot to assimilate and accept, and she would never be able to discuss any of it with either her father or her brother. She refused to look at me. It didn't matter. I understood. But at least I had done what I said I would do. I'd found out what had happened to Richard; in fact, I had probably found out too much.

Our good-bye on the street felt excruciating. It was plain to me, at least, that we didn't stand a prayer, that we were going nowhere, nowhere but home to our separate and inextricably connected lives.

One thing was certain: I was in no condition to drive, and Janie noticed.

"You're coming with me," she said, taking the keys to the truck out of my hand. "I'll bring you back in the morning."

I sobered up a bit in the passenger seat, the scent of her sitting next to me in the car focusing my mind. At her house, much to my surprise, she led me upstairs, past Danny's room. The door was ajar. We both looked in on him, a ritual we'd performed so many times that I choked on the emotion. Then, facing me, she led me to her bedroom.

She undressed me, sat me on the bed, and then undressed herself. There was no reason to speak, nothing to say, and as we found ourselves holding each other, all the tension, the years' separation, the bitterness and recrimination, dissolved as if we had never been apart. The sweetness and tenderness of our lovemaking seemed the most natural thing in the world.

I kissed the tears out of her eyes, off her cheeks, and she fell asleep in my arms, and as I fell into my deepest sleep in months, I thought I might be dreaming.

Danny was flabbergasted and giddy when he found us in bed together the next morning, and though an awkward silence hovered over the breakfast table, it felt more like a silent prayer that somehow we might find our way back as a family.

A week or so later, I arose early one morning. It was still dark. The moon, past full, was just setting. Roosters acknowledged an imperceptible dawn. I decided to walk. I'd seen Chateau Hauberg many times on my excursions through the hills beyond Angwin. It presided amongst sloped vineyards on the east side of Howell Mountain, a massive stone building—more European farmhouse than winery—constructed in the late 1800s and built to last for centuries, nestled into the hillside beside a small man-made lake. I'd admired it from a distance, its stolid permanence and old-world charm so different from the mock palazzi built as monuments to the egos that had invaded the valley. Daniel Hauberg had arrived in the late seventies with his wife and daughter after selling off his property in Bordeaux—an unlikely trade, it seemed to me.

As I walked along the side of the road, the sun gained in the east, casting a pink glow on the underbelly of the cloud bank lacing its way from the Pacific. Fog lay like a thin blanket in the hollows of the hills, and as I descended the road, I could make out the massive stone volume of Chateau Hauberg rising above it. The road dipped and rose to the winery. Across from it I could see its proprietor walking in a vineyard, accompanied by his dog in the early light of dawn. I watched as he bent to examine and caress his vines. He walked slowly down a row, the ivory-colored German shepherd limping behind him. It was a touching scene, the profound paternal attention he brought to the land.

"Hello!" I called from the road. Daniel Hauberg stood and squinted at me.

"*Bonjour*," he said, surprised to see a visitor at that hour of the morning. He walked toward me. "Ah, Monsieur Stern," he added when he got close enough to recognize me. "I heard you were in France."

"I got home just before the holiday. I wanted to get back in time to share Thanksgiving with my son," I said. He nodded.

"If you're looking for Michael," he said, sweeping his hand across the vista of vineyard and lifting it as if to suggest that Matson had disappeared only a moment before.

"I'm not sure what I'm looking for anymore," I confessed.

Hauberg nodded, scratched his chin, and said, "Come, I'll make us coffee." He whistled for his dog. As we approached the house, he pointed to the pond. "I put that in around '82, to water the vines. *Vas-y!*" he commanded the shepherd, who gazed up at him through sad, limpid, nearly human eyes. The animal flopped under a massive oak tree that towered before the château and laid his head on his outstretched forepaws.

"King Lear, he loves that tree," Hauberg said tenderly.

We passed under an arbor and into the bottom floor of the stone winery, the barrels wrapped in the cool, damp air. He stood at a hot plate and brewed a pot of espresso. I wandered across the floor of the *cave*. The ceiling rose twenty feet above me, the stone held in place by beams milled in another century.

"We bring the grapes in up above, on the top floor. The *cuverie* is just above us on the second floor. And down here is the *cave*. The whole operation is gravity fed. I never have to pump the wine. *Doucement, doucement*," he smiled, gesturing with his hand to show how gently he handled his fruit. "Come," he said. "It is not too cold for you outside?"

"Not at all. *Merci*," I said, taking the steaming cup.

"You see this," Hauberg said as we crossed the threshold, pointing to a brass unicorn nailed to the giant wooden door of the *chais*, a ring looped through its flared nostrils. "This is the only thing I brought from my home in France. It was used to tie up horses in the old days."

He led us outside to a picnic table under the arbor.

"So," he asked, "what did you learn on your trip? I heard that you solved the crime."

I conveyed in broad strokes what had happened: the shooting of Lucas Kiers, Jean Pitot's suicide following the murder of Eric Feldman, and the violent death of Françoise Pitot at the hands of her husband. He already knew most of it from following the story in the French press on the Internet and shook his head at the litany of disasters.

"Here's what you probably haven't read," I said and told him about Robert Wilson's fathering a child at the tail end of World War II. I described the shame and hatred that had come to afflict the Pitot family. I left out Richard Wilson's replication of his father's indiscretion, thinking that I would do what I could to preserve what was left of Wilson's reputation.

He gazed out to his vineyards and took a sip of the scalding coffee.

"*Je comprends*," he said. "You see, the only way in France is to have one child. Under the Napoleonic Code, if I die—when I die—the property must be divided between my children. It creates bitter fights. I refused to subject my family to this . . ." His voice failed, imagining the feuds that would have ensued following his death. He took another sip of coffee. "Of course, if you have only one child and he is killed in a car accident . . . *pfoof*. Your life is over. You have lost everything. At least this family has a daughter who survives and is safe."

We sipped slowly and contemplated the cruelty of life.

"I don't know. Maybe, either way, you lose everything," he added. "So, now, I start over." He smiled wistfully.

"It's beautiful here," I said, "a beautiful place."

"*Oui, c'est beau ici*," he said and disappeared into himself.

We sat for a few minutes, looking out at the land. The sun was up, and the earth was steaming.

"Well, thank you for the coffee," I said, rising.

"Not at all. It was my pleasure." I turned to go. "I think you did a fine thing, going to France to solve this," Hauberg said.

"Thank you," I said. "*Au revoir.*"

"Good-bye," Daniel Hauberg said and stood, taking our coffee cups.

It was a glorious morning for a drive. I headed north from Calistoga. Fog drifted through the breaks in the hills and crested in ragged and dissolving waves over the peak of Storybook Mountain.

I'd called Ciofreddi upon my return and given him a stripped-down account of events as they'd unfolded on the *côte*. He said that Sackheim had told him my help had been invaluable.

"Well, at least I didn't fuck it up too badly," I said. "The whole thing got a little out of control." Then I asked him if he'd give me the Christensens' address. He said Eugénie's husband's name was Paul and that they were listed in the phone book. I thanked him, and that was that. As Jenny, she had moved thousands of miles away— starting a new life very different from the one she'd left behind— but I knew that she'd never really escape, that the past would follow her forever.

I was sure that whoever had taken over after Sackheim's dismissal and retirement would close out the case successfully, that Jean-Luc Carrière and Henri Pitot would go to jail, that the French would do their jobs, just as Russ Brenneke and Ciofreddi had done theirs. Spring was right around the corner. The nights would soften, the days lengthen, the eucalyptus grow fragrant. The bottle may have been empty, but I had savored it right down to the dregs.

I knew it was time, now, to end my exile. I needed to remain close to my son; he needed me, maybe as much as I needed him.

I finally felt freed from Janie, free to leave for good or free to go back. I didn't know why she'd turned to me, whether she wanted me back herself or regretted ever having left. But she had left, and though our last meal together had made me think that we were finished, that last night had left me thinking that maybe we had a chance after all.

She had been right about one thing, though: She couldn't have trusted just anyone. I'd wanted to prove something, and I had. Helping in some small way to solve Richard's murder, I had at last tumbled out from under his shadow, even if that shadow had existed only in my own mind. Perception is everything.

When I passed the Jimtown Store, I dropped down on Alexander Valley Road into Healdsburg. I drove slowly along Kinley Drive to West North Street and pulled over opposite Jenny's home. She and her husband were working side by side in the garden, weeding and raking, bent, silent. I watched as Paul stopped suddenly and went over to his wife. He took the trowel out of her hand, set it on the ground, and lifted her. He held her at the waist and looked into her eyes. He smiled and took her face and kissed her. They embraced in a long, deep hug and released each other. He walked back and picked up the rake, and she knelt down, sticking her hand into the soil. Only then did they seem to notice the sound of the truck and turned to look at me at the same instant. I felt sure she didn't recognize me as I drove off.

I slowly headed back to town. At a shop, I bought a postcard and wrote a brief note to Émile Sackheim to let him know that, as far as I could tell, Eugénie Pitot and Paul Christensen were in love. The only address I had for him was the *gendarmerie* on rue des Blanches Fleurs in Beaune. At the bottom of the card I would have to write PLEASE FORWARD.

ACKNOWLEDGMENTS

Robert Kacher, Sophie Confuron-Meunier, and Christine Jacob, who opened more than doors in Burgundy; and Michel Alexandre, for clues only you will recognize;

Franck Marescal, Chef d'Escadron, Région de Gendarmerie Est, Groupement de la Côte d'Or, and Lieutenant Colonel Gilbert Frossard, Gendarmerie de Lyon; Chief Brian Banducci of the American Canyon Police Department and Jane Watahovich of the Napa County Sheriff's Department; and Sergeant Matt Talbott and Sergeant John Wachowski of the St. Helena Police Department, for giving so generously of your time and knowledge;

Jim Fergus and Jim Harrison, without whose help I would have found neither agent nor publisher;

Eric Overmyer, Richard Rosen, James Crumley (*in memoriam*), Guy de la Valdène, Jamie Potenberg, Sue Mowrer, and Cyril Frechier, a readers' circle of a writer's dreams;

Lannan Foundation, for the delicious space of L3 and the profound silence of Marfa, where, in the course of a six-week writing residency, this story found its most fertile soil; and Chuck Bowden, for the coffee, the conversation, and the example you set across the backyard;

Judy Hottensen, Rick Simonson, and Patrick McNierney, for encouragement all along the way; and the gentlemen of *Invisible*

Cities who heard the first inklings of this story what now seems like so long ago;

Al Zuckerman, for your tutelage and abiding sagacity; and Michele Slung, for your insight, your expertise, and for keeping me on *le chemin de vigne* right down to the bedrock;

Ben and George Nikfard of Swifty Printing—the only two who really know how many rewrites this story has been through—for your shared faith and conviction that this novel would find its way into print;

Charlie Winton, for seeing the story-within-the-story, and for sticking with it—with me—to the end; and the marvelous women who compose the staff at Counterpoint—Julie Pinkerton, first amongst them—who served as mid-wives to this book;

And Johnna Turiano, for your patience, love, and support, without which nothing would be possible.

The wisdom and wine are all yours, the faults and *faux pas* all mine.

Merci mille fois,
PL

©Kathleen King

ABOUT THE AUTHOR

Peter Lewis is a successful restaurateur and restaurant industry consultant. He was a contributing editor for *Virtuoso Travel & Life*, for which he wrote the column "Wine Country Notebook." His work has also appeared in *Pacific Northwest* and *Arcade*. *Dead in the Dregs* is his first novel. He lives in Seattle.